# DOMINO ISLAND

# DESMOND BAGLEY

# *Domino Island*

*Curated by Michael Davies*

HarperCollins*Publishers*

HarperCollins*Publishers*
1 London Bridge Street,
London SE1 9GF
www.harpercollins.co.uk

Published by HarperCollins*Publishers* 2019

1

A catalogue record for this book is available from the British Library

ISBN: 978-0-00-833301-0 HB
978-0-00-833464-2 TPB

Typeset in Meridien by Palimpsest Book Production Limited,
Falkirk, Stirlingshire

Printed and bound in the UK by CPI Group (UK) Ltd, Croydon CR0 4YY

**MIX**
Paper from
responsible sources
**FSC™ C007454**

This book is produced from independently certified FSC™
paper to ensure responsible forest management.

For more information visit: www.harpercollins.co.uk/green

# CURATOR'S NOTE

Desmond Bagley's novel *Running Blind* has a brilliantly gripping opening sentence: *To be encumbered with a corpse is to be in a difficult position, especially when the corpse is without benefit of death certificate.* As a teenager introduced to this master thriller writer by my older brothers, I was hooked. *The Golden Keel*, Bagley's debut novel, came next on my reading list, quickly followed by *The Enemy*, *Landslide* and the rest of his exhilarating output. My hunger for more was only stopped by the untimely death of the author in 1983.

Ever since, Desmond Bagley – or Simon, as he was known to family and friends – has been woven into my life in a variety of strange ways. Years after his death, I struck up an email correspondence with his remarkable widow Joan, who completed a couple of his unfinished manuscripts for posthumous publication, before she died in 1999. The baton was passed to Joan's sister and brother-in-law, Lecia and Peter Foston, with whom I have had the pleasure of developing a delightful friendship over two decades.

Meanwhile, I hassled Bagley's publisher, David Brawn of HarperCollins, with a view to writing a biography (the brief book-cover rubric hardly does his extraordinary story justice). I wrote a two-part screen adaptation of *The Tightrope Men*, entitled simply *Tightrope* – which has yet to be made, if any producers are looking in. I followed with enthusiasm

Nigel Alefounder, whose website desmondbagley.co.uk reveals the fine work he has done over many years to keep the Bagley flame alive.

My heartfelt thanks and appreciation for their commitment and support go to all these people and more – including, of course, my own 'Joan', Tricia, to whom this book is dedicated.

And then came the discovery of a 'new' Bagley manuscript among his papers, written in 1972 and subsequently archived in Boston, Massachusetts. Investigative researcher Philip Eastwood – who hosts the website thebagleybrief. com – found the novel there in the form of a typed first draft with extensive handwritten annotations by the author and his original editor, Bob Knittel. In addition, correspondence between the two showed in some detail the plans Bagley had for a second draft.

I couldn't be more thrilled and honoured to have been invited by David Brawn to implement those plans. Permissions and assistance have been very kindly forthcoming from the trustees of the Bagley estate, the Howard Gotlieb Archival Research Center in Boston, and Sam Matthews and Leishia-Jade Finigan of Moore Stephens in Guernsey, without whose co-operation this book would not have seen the light of day.

What follows is, unquestionably, a Desmond Bagley novel. The emendations may be mine; the brilliance is his.

**Michael Davies**

*For Tricia – who else?*

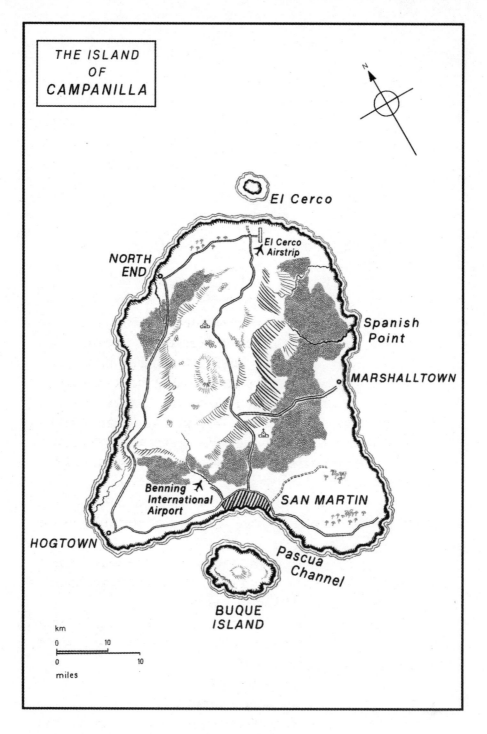

The island of Campanilla

# ONE

## I

I was late into the office that morning and Mrs Hadley, the receptionist, told me that Jolly wanted to see me. 'It's urgent,' she said. 'He's been ringing like a fire alarm.'

Jolly might have been his name, but jolly he certainly was not. He was a thin, dyspeptic man with a face like a prune and a nature as sour as a lemon. He had a way of authorising the payment of claims as though the money was coming out of his own pocket, which was probably not a bad trait for a man in his job.

He looked up as I walked in and said irascibly, 'Where the devil have you been? I've been trying to find you for hours.'

I did not have to account to Jolly for the way I spent my time so I ignored that and said, 'What's your problem?'

'A man called David Salton has died.'

That didn't surprise me. People are always dying and you hear of the fact more often in an insurance office than in most other places. I sat down.

'How much is he into you for?'

'Half a million of personal insurance.'

That was enough to make even me wince: God knows what it was doing to Jolly's ulcer.

'What's the snag?'

He tried – and failed – to suppress the look of pain on his face. 'This one is all snag. Salton first came to us twenty-five years ago and took out £10,000 worth of insurance on his life. Over the years he built it up to a quarter-million. Just over a year ago he suddenly doubled it; the reason he gave was galloping inflation.'

'So on the last quarter-million he only paid two premiums,' I observed. I could see what was needling Jolly: the company was going to lose badly on this one. 'How old was Salton?'

'Fifty-two.'

'Who gets the loot?'

'I imagine it will be the widow,' said Jolly. 'The terms of his will aren't known yet. The thing that bothers me is the way he died. He was found dead in a small boat fifteen miles from land.'

'Alone?'

'Yes.'

I looked past him out of the window at the snowflakes drifting from a leaden London sky. 'I assume there was an inquest? What did the coroner say?'

'Death from natural causes. The medical certificate states a heart attack.' Jolly grimaced. 'That might be debatable. The body was badly decomposed.'

'Decomposed? How long had he been out there?'

'Four days. But it wasn't so much the time as the heat.'

I stared at Jolly. 'What heat?'

'Oh, it happened in the Caribbean,' he said, as though I ought to have known. 'Salton's boat was found off the island of Campanilla – he lived there.'

I sighed. Jolly's problem was making him incoherent. 'What about starting at the beginning?' I suggested. 'And then tell me what you'd like me to do.'

The way Jolly told it, Salton was a native-born, white Campanillan. In his youth he emigrated to the United States, where he made his pile and took out US citizenship. His money had come from building houses for returned soldiers just after the war and he'd done very well at it. But he never forgot his roots and went back to Campanilla from time to time, buying some land on the island and building himself a home, which he used for holidays. About three years ago he'd moved back permanently and began to do a lot for the island community. He built a couple of hospitals, was the mainstay of higher education and had an interest in providing low-cost housing for the populace – something he'd become expert at in his Stateside days.

Then he died in a small boat at sea.

'Campanilla is British, isn't it?'

'It was,' said Jolly. 'Not any more. After Harold Wilson's "Bay of Piglets" PR disaster in Anguilla, we were all too happy to let them slip away. They even opted out of the Commonwealth.' He looked me in the eye. 'That's one of the problems, of course.'

I didn't really understand why that was a problem, but then I didn't know anything of Campanilla. Jolly said, 'Another problem is that the company invested money in Salton's house-building schemes. Now he's dead we want to make sure the money's safe.'

Wheels within wheels. 'How much?'

'A little over three million. You'll have to talk to Costello about that.'

I knew Ken Costello a little. He and Jolly were the proverbial two hands that didn't let the other know what each was doing; Jolly was the insurance man and Costello the investment whizz-kid. They didn't like one another much. While Jolly was a good company man, he wasn't worried about Costello's troubles. The half-million potential pay-out loomed larger in his mind than the shaky future of Costello's three million. But there was something else gnawing at the back of my mind. I knew the company would still pay out in the event of suicide, but not until two years after the death. The idea was to deter any sudden impulse to leave the wife and kids in good financial shape. The realisation that you are worth more dead than alive can be positively unhinging to some men, but the two-year gap helped keep the door from falling off.

I said, 'Was the usual suicide clause in Salton's policies?'

Jolly looked hurt. 'Of course,' he said peevishly.

'Then what's biting you?' As though I didn't know.

He tented his fingers and looked magisterial. 'I'm not too happy about that inquest. The law in these banana republics can be slipshod, to say the least of it.'

'Do you suspect funny business?'

'If there is any funny business we ought to know about it.'

'And that's where I come in. When do I leave?'

He gave me a knowing look and then smiled. Jolly's infrequent smiles were unnerving. 'You'd better wait until you've seen the chairman.' He glanced at his watch. 'You have an appointment with him at eleven.'

During my ten years offering expert consultation to this company, I had met the chairman exactly ten times and I'd already had my ration for the year. 'What does he want?'

'Ah!' said Jolly, and smiled again. 'Mrs Salton is the chairman's niece.'

Lord Hosmer was perturbed. He waffled on for fifteen minutes without stopping, repeating himself many times, and it all boiled down to the fact that he was exceedingly and understandably perturbed. I was to investigate the situation directly and personally and not to rely on any of my minions; I was to investigate the situation and report to him immediately, if not before; I was to proceed to Campanilla starting, if possible, yesterday, and what was I waiting for?

Yes, sir; yes, sir; three bags full, sir.

There was one question I really wanted to ask: what angle should I take? Did he want me to look for a reason to invalidate the claim – in which case Jill Salton, niece to the chairman, would be justifiably annoyed? Or should I work the other side of the street and let the company catch a £500,000 draught? But that's not a question to put lightly to the chief executive of an insurance company. Hosmer was neatly impaled on the horns of a dilemma and it would be tactless to embarrass him by asking awkward questions which should properly be put to an underling, who would instead look at the entrails of a chicken at dead of night and interpret the Great Man's mind.

So I went back to friend Jolly and put the awkward question to him.

He was affronted. 'You're to find out the truth, Kemp,' he said pompously.

Ken Costello was a much happier man. Although he juggled hundreds of millions of pounds, he didn't let the awesomeness of it worry him unduly. He was a big, boisterous extrovert given to practical joking in the infantile Stock Exchange manner and equipped with an enormous fund of dirty stories also culled from former colleagues on the trading floor. When I walked into his office he lifted an enquiring eyebrow.

'Salton,' I said.

'Ha!' His eyes rolled. 'Is Jolly worried?'

'More to the point, are you?'

He shrugged. 'Not much – yet.'

I sat down. 'Okay, I'm listening.'

Costello leaned back in his chair and adopted the cheerful air of a tolerant college tutor happily indoctrinating his students. 'Campanilla is snowballing,' he said. 'More particularly, there's a building boom. They're putting up hotels so fast that if your bedroom isn't built when you check in, you still sleep sound that night. Money is flowing like champagne and caviar has become a staple food. That's what happens when the palsied hand of the British Raj is shrugged off.'

'Never mind the economics lecture,' I said acidly. 'Where did Salton come in?'

'He was a property man through and through – that's how he made his fortune in America. He got himself some nice tracts of land and started to cover them with ticky-tacky. He needed development capital, which we supplied. End of story.'

'It is for Salton. What about you – how safe is your money now?'

'Reasonably safe. Salton wasn't a fly-by-nighter, and he was building for the locals, not the speculative stuff for middling-rich, middle-class immigrants who want a place in the sun to retire to. Although it wouldn't have been altogether a bad thing if he'd tried that. We wouldn't have touched it, though.'

'Who runs things now that Salton is dead?'

'That *is* a bit worrying,' admitted Costello. 'He was always a loner – kept things very much in his own hands – although he had a good manager, a man called Idle.'

'My God,' I said. 'That name doesn't sound too promising.'

Costello chuckled. 'It isn't as bad as it sounds. I took the trouble to look it up. It's from the Welsh, *Ithel*, meaning "Lord Bountiful".'

'Could be worse.'

He grinned. 'Idle, Mrs Salton and a firm of lawyers are running the show now. They're not doing too badly so far.'

'How far? When did Salton die?'

'The boat was discovered two weeks ago. You going out there?'

'The chairman insists. What fuels this economic miracle on Campanilla?'

'Much as I regret to say,' said Costello, not looking regretful at all, 'it's gambling. Of course, there are a lot of other angles, too. Campanilla has turned itself into an off-shore financial paradise with a set of fiscal laws that make the Cayman Islands look positively restrictive. You've heard of Bay Street in Nassau?'

'The mecca of the Bahamas.'

'Capital is leaving there so fast that the bankers are catching pneumonia from the draught. Campanilla has its very own version: Cardew Street.'

'And you put three million of the company's money into Cardew Street?' I said.

'Safe as houses, dear boy,' said Costello. 'As long as they were Salton's houses.'

## II

Eight hours later I was on a 747 taking off from Heathrow and heading for Campanilla by way of Miami. I travelled first-class, of course; it was written into my service agreement with the company. Somewhere behind me, in the back of this flying barn and jostled by the common ruck of economy flight passengers, was Owen Ogilvie, the official representative of Western and Continental Insurance Co. Ltd. To an eye untainted by suspicion, he was the company man sent out to enquire into the death of David Salton. He would do the expected and leave me to a quiet and restful anonymity.

Jolly disapproved of my service agreement; it offended his sense of the fitness of things. There was nothing he could do about it though, since I negotiated directly with the board.

During the flight I studied Salton's policies. They were all fairly standard and with no trick clauses and I couldn't see how Jolly could weasel his way out of paying. Whether Salton had died naturally, been murdered or committed suicide, the payment would have to be made. All that was at issue was the timescale and the most that Jolly could

extract would be the interest on £500,000 for two years –
say £90,000, or thereabouts.

Not finding much there, I went up to the bar which the
airline thoughtfully provides for those of the jet set who
can afford first-class passage. I took with me a handbook
on Campanilla, which the efficient Mrs Hadley had dug up
from somewhere. It offered interesting reading over a drink.

The highlights of this Caribbean jewel appeared to be the
climate, the swimming, the sailing, the fishing, the cuisine
and the tax structure. Especially the tax structure. The main
feature of the tax structure was that there wasn't much of
it. If the United States was the Empire State Building, then
Campanilla was a marquee – all roof with nothing much
to hold it up, and vulnerable to financial gales.

I examined the historical section. Campanilla was originally Spanish, colonised in the sixteenth century. The British
took over in 1710 during one of the fast shuffles of the War
of the Spanish Succession and stayed until the twentieth
century, when to have colonies offended world opinion.
During this period it was called Bell Island but, on attaining
independence, it reverted to the Spanish name of Campanilla.
Probably some public relations geek thought it a more exotic
and fitting name for a tropical paradise.

The fold-out map at the back of the handbook showed
that the island really was bell-shaped. The lower rim of the
bell was scooped out in a huge bay and the clapper was
formed by Buque Island, separated from the main island by
Pascua Channel. Opposite Buque Island was the capital of
San Martin. Two misshapen peninsulas on opposite coasts
represented the trunnions by which the bell would be hung.
Northwards, at the top of the 'bell', was a coral formation,
almost atoll-like, forming a perfect ring called El Cerco, which
represented the ring to which the bell rope would be
attached. Nature was imitating art in a big way.

Further study was profitless so I slept.

# III

My hotel in San Martin grandly called itself the Royal Caribbean. It was new, which just goes to show that there is no one more royalist than a good republican. The foyer was lined with one-armed bandits which, on inspection, proved to be fuelled by silver dollars. All around could be heard the cadences of American speech from the guests and the slurred English of the Campanillans who worked there.

On my way in from Benning, the island's international airport, two things had struck me: the smell of prosperity and the oppression of the heat. Both were almost tangible. San Martin, a clean and well-scrubbed town, was fringed on the skyline with cranes as new high-rise buildings went up. The traffic in the streets was heavy – flashy American cars driving incongruously on the left, British-style. The shops in the main streets were opulent and the crowds thronging the pavements were, on the whole, well-dressed. As for the heat, it had hit me like a wall as soon as I stepped off the plane. Even at this time of year, it was enough to make a pallid Englishman gasp.

I checked in at the hotel, showered off the stickiness, and went down again to sniff some more atmosphere. On the way out I stopped at the desk, and asked, 'I suppose you have a newspaper here?'

'Yes, sir; the *Chronicle*. You can buy a copy at the news stand there.'

'Where is the *Chronicle* office?'

'Cardew Street, sir. Two blocks along and turn right.'

There is nothing like reading the local paper for picking up a quick feel of a place. A newspaper is a tribal notice-board which tells you what people are doing and, to a certain extent, thinking and saying. I'm a behaviourist myself and take more notice of what people do rather than what they say. The old saw 'actions speak louder than words' is truer than most proverbs, and I wanted to find out what people had been doing round about the time Salton had died.

I walked along the street in the hot sun and stopped at the first men's outfitters I came to. I bought a light, linen suit more in tune with the climate than the one I was wearing, and paid for it by credit card, which was accepted without question. I wore the new suit and asked that the old one be sent to the hotel. Then I carried on towards the *Chronicle* office.

It looked and smelled like newspaper offices all over the world, a composite of library paste, newsprint, ink and suppressed tension. A press rumbled somewhere in the bowels of the building. When I asked to see the back file for the previous month, I was shown into a glass-walled office and seated in front of a scarred deal table. Presently the file was put before me. On its front was a pasted notice promising unimaginable punishments for anyone criminal enough to clip items from the pages.

I opened it and took a random sampling. Prices were high generally and food prices exceptionally so. The price of housing made me blink a little. Cigarettes, liquor and petrol were cheaper than in England but clothing was more expensive. That I already knew; the cost of my linen suit had been damn near the Savile Row level and the quality not a tenth as good.

I turned to the employment columns and did a quick rundown of wage levels. What I found didn't look good: while prices rose above North American levels, wages were lower than European, which didn't leave much scope for gracious living on the part of the working populace.

This was reflected in the political pages. It seemed there was an election coming up in a month or so and the government party appeared beleaguered. A small extreme left-wing party made up for shortage of numbers by a lot of noise, and a larger and more central opposition party threatened reform when it came to power. Meanwhile the Prime Minister made soothing sounds and concessions.

Pretty soon the name of Salton popped up, making a pugnacious speech against the ruling party:

*'This toadying government must stop licking the boots of foreigners for the sake of private profit. There must be an end to cheap concessions by which foreign gangsters can make their fortunes while our schools are understaffed. There must be an end to the pernicious system whereby foreign companies can filter untold millions of dollars through our country at no cost to themselves, while our own hospitals are neglected. There must be an end to the continual rise in prices at a time when the wage structure is depressed. I promise the Prime Minister that he will know the true mind of Campanilla during the forthcoming election, despite the activities of his hired bully boys.'*

Evidently Salton had caught it from both sides. The Prime Minster, the Honourable Walden P. Conyers, responded smoothly: 'It has been brought to my notice by the Department of Immigration that Mr Salton has not given up his American citizenship. He would be advised to do so before complaining about those enlightened foreign companies who have done so much to bring prosperity to this island.'

On the other side, a left-winger snarled acidly about two-faced millionaires who wrote wishy-washy liberal speeches while sipping martinis on the terraces of their expensive villas as their well-paid overseers were grinding the faces of the native poor. That sounded familiar, as did the call for instant revolution by the down-trodden proletariat.

I flicked through some more recent editions and came to a big splash story, emblazoned with a full-page picture of Salton. He must have been a really big wheel for his death to have made the commotion it did. The first thing I felt was the sense of shock that permeated the initial accounts; it seemed as though the reporter couldn't really believe what he was writing. Then the accusations began to fly, each wilder than the last, while riots broke out on the streets and the police had their hands full.

It was hard to reconcile these accounts of civil unrest with the well-oiled gentility I'd seen outside on Cardew Street, but I soon found out the reason. The inquest had quietened things down considerably and the rioting stopped on the day that Dr Winstanley stood in the witness box and announced that Salton had died of natural causes. When asked if he was sure about that, he replied stiffly that he had performed the post-mortem examination himself and he was quite certain.

Mrs Salton gave evidence that her husband had had heart trouble six months earlier. This was corroborated by Dr Collins, his personal physician. When Mrs Salton was asked if her husband habitually went out by himself in a small dinghy, she replied that after his heart attack she had asked him not to continue this practice, but that he had not given up sailing alone.

The verdict, as Jolly had informed me back in London, was death by natural causes.

Salton's funeral was attended by all the island dignitaries and a few thousand of the common people. Conyers made a speech, sickening in its hypocrisy, in which he mourned the loss of a noble fellow-countryman. After that, Salton pretty much dropped out of the news except for an occasional reference, usually in the financial pages, concerning the activities of his companies. No one can be forgotten quicker than a dead man.

I turned back to the obituary and was making a few notes

when I became aware that someone had come into the room. I looked up and saw a podgy, balding man watching me intently. He blinked rapidly behind thick-rimmed glasses and said, 'Interesting reading?'

'For those who find it interesting,' I said. A tautology is a good way of evading an issue; that's something I've learned from listening to too many politicians.

'You're an off-islander,' he said abruptly. 'You've not been here long.'

I leaned back in the chair. 'How do you know?'

'No tan. Just out from England?'

I looked at him thoughtfully. 'Yes. I'm interested in local conditions.'

'By reading about a dead man?' His voice was flat but the irony was not lost. 'Taking notes, too.'

'Is it illegal?'

He suddenly smiled. 'I guess not. My name's Jackson.' He waved his hand. 'I get into the habit of asking too many questions. I work here.'

'A reporter?'

'Sort of.' He gestured at Salton's obituary. 'I wrote that.'

'You write well,' I said politely.

'You're a liar,' said Jackson without rancour. 'If I did I wouldn't be in this crummy place. What's the interest in Salton?'

'You do ask questions,' I said.

Unapologetically he said, 'It's my job. You don't have to answer. I can find out another way if I have to.'

'You didn't come in by accident and find me here.'

He grinned. 'Mary Josephine tipped me off. The girl at the desk. We like to know who checks our files. It's routine.' He paused. 'Sometimes it even pays off. Not often, though.'

All that was quite possibly true. I said cautiously, 'Well, Mr Jackson, if you were interested in the future of the late Mr

Salton's companies, wouldn't you be interested in knowing how he died?'

'I guess so.' He looked at my notebook. 'You don't have to take notes. I'll give you a copy of anything you want.'

'In exchange for what?'

'No strings,' he said. 'It's in the public domain. But if you turn anything up – anything unusual – I'd be glad to know.'

I smiled at him. 'I don't think my principals would like publicity. Is anything unusual likely to turn up?'

Jackson shrugged. 'If a guy turns over enough stones he's sure to find something nasty some place.'

'And you think there's something nasty to be found by looking under Mr Salton's stones. That's very interesting. What sort of a man was Salton?'

'No worse than any other son-of-a-bitch.'

My eyebrows rose. 'You didn't like him?'

'He was a gold-plated bastard.'

I glanced down at the obituary. 'You're a better writer than you think, Mr Jackson. It doesn't show here.'

'Company policy,' said Jackson. 'Mrs Salton owns the *Chronicle*.'

That was a new one on me but I didn't let him know that. I said, 'If you talk like this to strangers you're not likely to be on the payroll much longer. How do you know I'm not a friend of Mrs Salton's?'

'You're not her friend,' said Jackson. 'You're an insurance investigator. We've been expecting you to show up, Mr Ogilvie.'

He had the wrong man but the right occupation and I wondered how that had come about. I decided to let him have his cheap triumph for the time being and said evenly, 'So?'

'So she's sticking your people for a lot of dough. You wouldn't be human if you admitted to liking her for it.'

I looked down at the obituary. 'Granting there's a certain amount of bias here, Salton still doesn't measure up to your personal description of him. What about the two hospitals he built, the university foundation, the low-cost housing? Those are facts.'

'Sure,' said Jackson. 'He's been buying votes. Was successful at it, too. A very popular guy. You should have seen his funeral.'

'I've seen the photographs,' I said.

'That cheap housing was a surefire vote-catcher.' Jackson leaned forward and rested his hands on the table. 'Have you any idea of the cost of housing on this island? You'll be damned lucky to get away with £10 a square foot. So he cut a lot of corners – he built cheap and he built nasty and he didn't sell a single goddamn house he built.'

'I don't understand. If he didn't sell any houses, where did he make his profit?' I thought of Costello and the three millions and wondered if his ears were burning.

'He didn't,' said Jackson. 'He was losing like crazy. He rented those houses and the return was completely uneconomic. But it gave him a solid vote.'

'He must have been rich,' I commented. 'That's an expensive route to politics.'

'He had a lot of dough,' conceded Jackson. 'But not that much. Mr Black was behind him with a slush fund.'

I sighed. 'And who is Mr Black?'

Jackson stared at me. 'Don't you know *anything* about what goes on here? You'd better learn fast. Gerry Negrini is Mr Big in the casino crowd.'

'Negrini?'

'Negrini – Mr Black, get it?'

'Oh, I see. But where do casinos come into it?'

'Negrini represents certain New York and Chicago interests who are bucking Las Vegas and Reno.'

I still couldn't see the connection. 'But why should he support a liberal like Salton?' I tapped the file. 'I've read Salton's speeches.'

'You need a crash course in local politics,' said Jackson earnestly. He was getting into his stride, teaching this dumb foreigner how things worked around here, and I wasn't about to stop the flow. 'Look, Mr Ogilvie, this island is wide open and a buck moves faster here than any other place in the world. Mr Black and his boys have got the whole thing sewn up – they've put Campanilla on the map for the jet set and all the well-heeled suckers who go for gambling.'

He hesitated. There was evidently more to come.

'But there's another angle. The bankers and the big corporations have also got it made here, and they don't like gambling and the associations that go with it. They don't want the off-shore trust funds confused with the spin of a roulette wheel. That's bad for business.'

'I can see their point.'

'So they made sure they had their own man – Conyers. He was their boy, and he had his instructions: get the election out of the way and then crack down on the gambling. Mr Black *had* to pick an opposition leader and he picked Salton.'

'Salton? But he'd only been back on the island five minutes.'

Jackson shrugged. 'You can make a lot of noise in five minutes, Mr Ogilvie. Especially with someone like that behind you.'

'So the cheap housing was just an expensive red herring.'

'Make no mistake about it: if Salton had lived he'd almost certainly have been the next Prime Minister.' Jackson waved airily at the file. 'But all that flapdoodle in his speeches was for the suckers. You can bet that as soon as he got into power those house rents would have been raised pretty swiftly.'

He was on a roll so I kept up the masquerade. 'I've been reading the account of the inquest. Do you believe Salton died of natural causes?'

Jackson sat down opposite me at the table and leaned back: he looked like he was settling in for the duration. 'Winstanley is a doddering old fool at the best of times but even if he was the best pathologist in the world I doubt he could have made much of what was left of Salton.' He grimaced. 'I saw the body when he was brought in.'

'He'd been out there for days, hadn't he? Wasn't anyone looking for him? Didn't Mrs Salton raise the alarm?'

'Which of those questions would you like me to answer?' said Jackson. There was more than a hint of condescension in his voice. 'No. The first anyone knew about it was when the body was found.' He stared at me. 'Don't you find that strange?'

'She must have had an explanation that was acceptable to the police.'

'The police?' Jackson snorted. 'They're in Conyers's pocket, from Commissioner Barstow down to the last man on the beat.'

'That's an interesting take, Mr Jackson. In fact, you've raised a lot of interesting points.'

'Glad to be of help, Mr Ogilvie,' he said genially. 'You'll be visiting Mrs Salton?'

'Probably tomorrow.'

'You'd better telephone first,' he advised. 'No one gets to El Cerco without an invitation.'

'Have you got a telephone directory?'

He grinned. 'You won't find the number in there. It's unlisted.' He picked up my notebook and scribbled in it. 'That'll find her.'

As I stood up to go, I asked casually, 'How did you know I was Ogilvie?'

'I have a pipeline into the Department of Immigration at the airport. I knew that Western and Continental Insurance would be sending a man so I put out the word.'

So that was how Ogilvie had been tagged. 'That's all very well, but how did you know *I* was Ogilvie? It's not tattooed on my forehead.'

'Hell, I knew you'd be coming in here to check the files so I had Mary Josephine tip me off. Then there was this.' He lifted my notebook and grinned at me. Stamped on its cover in gilt were the words *Western and Continental Insurance Co. Ltd*. 'I didn't need to be Sherlock Holmes.'

'No,' I agreed. 'You didn't.' I took the notebook from him and put it away.

Jackson heaved himself to his feet and said, 'I'd be very much obliged if you let me know anything you turn up, Mr Ogilvie.'

'I don't think I will,' I said. 'You see, I told the truth when I said I was only interested in Mr Salton's companies in a business way. I have no connection with this insurance company beyond having taken out a policy with them, and my name is not Ogilvie – it's Kemp.' I smiled. 'The notebook was a handout. Western and Continental lash them out to all their clients.'

Jackson's eyes flickered. 'I don't believe you,' he said flatly.

I took out my passport and handed it to him. *William Kemp, business consultant*. 'But thanks for the tutorial. It was most interesting.'

Jackson seemed to have had the wind knocked out of him as I took back the passport and pocketed it. He said, 'Hell, anyone can make a mistake – and you went along with it.'

I nodded. 'I go along with most things as long as it suits me, Mr Jackson.' I walked to the door and turned. 'By the way, I *will* be seeing Mrs Salton tomorrow. I'll give her your regards.'

'Hey, Mr Kemp, you won't tell her . . . I mean . . . you won't repeat what I've said?' He was shaken right down to his liver and obviously terrified of losing his job.

I smiled. 'I'll reserve judgement on that – as long as it suits me.' I gave him a curt nod and walked out of the room, leaving a shocked man. I don't know who he thought I was, but I reckoned I'd given him enough of a fright to keep his nose out of my affairs.

I went back to the Royal Caribbean and telephoned Ogilvie. It was a long time before he answered and when he did his voice was grumpy. 'Kemp here,' I said.

'You've woken me up,' he complained. 'I'm dead on my feet.'

I knew how he felt. Air travel is tiring and my time sense was shot to pieces because of the transatlantic flight. 'Just something for you to do tomorrow,' I said. 'Go to the *Chronicle* office in Cardew Street and ask to see the back issues for the last month. You'll find a lot of interesting stuff about Salton.'

'What's the point if you've already done it?'

'You'll probably be contacted by a creep called Jackson. Don't try to hide who you are, but if he asks about me you're ignorant. Jackson is a bit hard to take, but disguise your finer feelings and get pally with him. He'll like you better if he thinks you're here to torpedo Mrs Salton's claim.'

'Well, aren't we?'

'Don't be cynical,' I said, and put down the telephone. If Jackson wanted to meet Ogilvie, who was I to stand in his way? Besides, there was always a chance his loose lips might give the company man something else we could work with.

I took out my notebook, checked the number Jackson had given me, and dialled. The call was answered immediately and a slurred Campanillan voice said, 'The Salton residence.'

'I'd like to speak to Mrs Salton,' I said. 'My name is Kemp.'

'What would it be about?'

'If she wants you to know she'll tell you.' I never have liked the nosy and over-protective underling.

There was a pause, some brief heavy breathing and then a rattle as the handset was laid down. Presently there was another rattle and a cool voice said, 'Jill Salton speaking.'

'My name is Kemp – William Kemp. Your uncle, Lord Hosmer, asked me to call and present his condolences.' He hadn't, but it made a good story.

'I see,' she said. 'Do you want to come here?'

'If that's all right with you. I'm free tomorrow, if it's convenient.'

'Would the morning suit you? Say at eleven?'

'That would be fine, Mrs Salton.'

'Very well, I'll expect you then. Good day, Mr Kemp.' There was a click and the connection was cut.

I called down to reception and made arrangements for hiring a car, to be ready in front of the hotel at nine the following morning.

Then I got undressed and fell asleep as though I'd been sandbagged.

# IV

At nine-fifteen next morning I was threading my way out of San Martin in a fire-engine-red Ford Mustang with an automatic shift that I didn't like. I prefer to change gear in a car when I want to, and not when a set of cogs thinks I should. Maybe I'm old-fashioned.

The road took me out along the coast for a way and through the outskirts of what was evidently a high-life area. Large and expensive-looking houses were set discreetly away from the road, some of them surrounded by high walls, and there were some plushy hotels with turquoise swimming pools of all shapes except rectangular. Those of the pools that I could see were surrounded by acres of bare skin, all tanning nicely. Here and there, uniformed waiters scurried around the poolsides with the first rum-and-coconut-milk of the day. *La dolce vita*, Caribbean-style.

I drove slowly, taking it all in. Even at this hour the sun was uncomfortably hot and the air pressed heavily on the open-top Mustang. Presently the road turned away from the sea and began to climb into a hilly and wooded area. The ambiance changed and the air cooled a little as I went inland. There were fewer white faces and more black, fewer bikinis and more cotton shifts, less concrete and glass and more corrugated iron. The tourists stuck close to the sea.

The landscape seemed poorly adaptable for agriculture. A thin soil clung to the bones of the hills but there were naked outcrops of limestone showing where the ground had eroded. Most of the afforested land was covered by a growth of spindly trees, which couldn't be of any economic significance, but occasional clearings opened up in which crops were apparently grown.

Nearly every clearing had its shacks – usually of the ubiquitous corrugated iron, although beaten-out kerosene tins were also to be seen. Around each shack were the children, meagrely dressed and grinning impudently as they waved at the car and shouted in shrill voices. I passed though a succession of villages, all with rudimentary church and classroom. The churches were marginally better built than the classrooms, which tended towards the shanty school of architecture, each with its dusty, pathetic area of playground.

As I came over the central ridge of the island, I pulled off the road and looked north towards the distant glint of the sea. Close by, a couple of Campanillans were hoeing a field and planting some sort of crop. I got out of the car and walked over to them. 'Am I on the right way to El Cerco?'

They stopped and looked at me, then the bigger one said, 'That's right, man.' His face was beaded with sweat. 'Just keep going.'

'Thanks.' I looked at the ground by his feet. 'What are you planting?'

'Corn.' He paused. 'You'd call it maize.' His accent wasn't the usual Campanillan drawl; he enunciated each consonant clearly. He didn't sound like your average peasant.

'It's hot,' I said, and took out a packet of fat, imported American cigarettes that I'd picked up on the plane.

He gave me a pitying smile. 'Not hot yet. Still winter.'

I tapped out a cigarette, then offered him the packet. 'Smoke?'

He hesitated, then said, 'Thanks, man,' and took a cigarette. The other man, older and with a seamed, lived-in face, ducked his head as he took one with gnarled fingers.

I took out my lighter and we lit up. 'This is a very nice island.'

The younger man stabbed his mattock into the ground with a sudden violence that made the muscles writhe in his brawny arm. 'Some think so.'

'But not you?'

'Would you like it if you were me, mister?' he asked.

I looked around at the arid field and shook my head. 'Probably not.'

He blew out a plume of smoke. 'You going to El Cerco? The Salton place?'

'That's right.'

'If you see Mrs Salton, you tell her McKittrick said hello.'

'Are you McKittrick?'

He nodded. 'Tell her I was sorry about Mr Salton.'

'I'll tell her,' I said. 'Do you know her well?'

He laughed. 'She probably won't remember me.' He took the cigarette and delicately nipped away the coal before dropping the stub into his shirt pocket. 'People forget.' He tugged the mattock out of the dust. 'This isn't getting the corn planted.'

'I'll pass on your message,' I said.

McKittrick made no answer but turned his back and bent to draw a furrow in the ground. I hesitated for a moment and then went back to the car.

I knew immediately what Jackson had meant about invitations when I arrived at El Cerco. I looked at the strong, meshed cyclone fence set on steel posts and at the two men at the gate. They wore what might or might not have been a uniform and, although they didn't seem to carry guns, they looked as though they should have done. One stayed by the gate; the other came up to the car and bent to look at me.

'My name is Kemp,' I said. 'Mrs Salton is expecting me.'

He straightened up, consulted a sheet of paper which he took from his pocket, and nodded. 'You're expected at the beach, Mr Kemp. The boat is waiting for you.' He waved at the other man, who opened the gate.

What boat?

I found out about two hundred yards down the road the other side of the gate, where the asphalt curved into a bend giving a view over the sea. El Cerco was breathtaking. The natural coral formation was a perfect circle about three-quarters of a mile in diameter. Outside, the steady trade wind heaped up waves which crashed on to the coral, sending up spouts of foam, but inside that magic circle the water was smooth and calm.

Right in the centre was a small island, not more than a hundred yards across, and on it was a building, a many-planed structure that curved and nestled close to the ground on which it was built. It seemed as though David Salton had created his own Shangri-la. It was a pity he wasn't around to enjoy it.

I drove on down the road, which descended steeply in a series of hairpin bends until it came to the edge of the lagoon. There was another house here and a row of garages with a big boathouse at the water's edge. A man was waiting for me. He waved the car into a garage and when I came out he said, 'This way, Mr Kemp,' and led me to a jetty where a fast-looking motor launch was moored. Less than five minutes later I stepped ashore on the island in the middle of El Cerco.

An elderly servant stood in attendance. He had grey hair and wore a white coat – a typical Caribbean waiter. When he spoke I thought I recognised the voice I had heard on the telephone when I called the previous day. He said, 'This way, Mr Kemp . . . sir.' There was just the right pause to make the insolence detectable but not enough to complain about. I grinned at the thought that the staff didn't like being ticked off by strangers.

The house had been designed by a master architect, so arranged that at times it was difficult to tell whether one was inside or outside. Lush tropical plants were everywhere and there were streams and fountains and the constant glint of light on pools. Most noticeably, the house was pleasantly cool in the steadily increasing heat.

We came into a quiet room and the old servant said softly, 'Mr Kemp, ma'am.'

She rose from a chair. 'Thank you, John.'

There was a man standing behind her but I ignored him because she was enough to fill the view. She was less than thirty, long of limb and with flaming red hair, green eyes and the kind of perfect complexion that goes with that combination. She was not at all what I had imagined as the widow of David Salton, fifty-two-year-old building tycoon.

A lot of thoughts chased through my mind very quickly but, out of the helter-skelter, two stayed with me. The first was that a woman like Jill Salton would be a handful for any man. Physical beauty is like a magnet and any husband married to this one could expect to be fighting off the competition with a club.

The second thought was that under no circumstance in law can a murderer benefit by inheritance from the person murdered.

Now why should I have thought that?

# TWO

## I

'Mr Kemp, glad to meet you,' said Mrs Salton. She showed no sign of being aware of my goggle-eyed reaction; perhaps to her it was standard from the human male. Her grip was pleasantly firm. 'This is Mr Stern.'

Reluctantly I shifted my gaze. Stern was a tall man somewhere in his mid-thirties. His features had the handsome regularity of a second-rank movie star. First-rank stars don't need it – just look at John Wayne. He smiled genially and stepped forward to shake my hand. I let him crush my fingers and looked expectantly at Mrs Salton. 'Mr Stern is my lawyer,' she said.

I allowed a twitch of an eyebrow to betray surprise as I was manoeuvred to a seat. Stern caught it and laughed. 'I invited myself over,' he said. 'Mrs Salton happened to mention your proposed visit when she telephoned me yesterday. I thought it advisable to be on hand.'

'To hear Lord Hosmer's expressions of regret?' I said ironically.

'Oh, come now,' said Stern. 'The chairman of Western and Continental didn't send a man across the Atlantic just for that. Besides, he has already spoken to Mrs Salton on the telephone.'

She was sitting opposite me, her hands in her lap smoothing the hem of the simple black dress she wore, and her eyes were downcast. I said, 'Will you accept my regrets, Mrs Salton? I've heard your husband spoken of highly.'

'Thank you, Mr Kemp,' she said quietly, and looked up. 'Can I offer you anything? We were just about to have coffee.'

'Coffee would be very nice.'

Stern was about to say something when John trundled a loaded tea trolley into the room. He had to do something with his open mouth so he said innocuously, 'Did you have a good flight?'

'As good as they ever are, I suppose.'

We stuck to trivialities while John was serving the coffee, and I studied Mrs Salton appraisingly. She was a very still woman and appeared to have no mannerisms of gesture, her voice was quiet and restful – educated and English – and I thought it would be most relaxing to spend time in her company. Her beauty did not come out of a Max Factor bottle but stemmed from good bone structure and sheer animal health.

John departed and Stern waited until he was out of earshot before he asked, 'Can we assume that the insurance claim will be met expeditiously?'

I studied him with interest. He seemed to be as jittery as Mrs Salton was placid, and he couldn't wait to bring up the subject. 'It will be handled as quickly as circumstances allow.'

He frowned. 'Do you mean that the circumstances are unusual?'

'I mean that the company, as yet, knows very little about the circumstances. There are one or two points to be clarified. That's why I'm here, rather than a loss adjuster.'

'I don't follow.'

'I'm an independent consultant,' I said. 'Rather different remit, you see.'

'What remit?' he demanded, almost aggressively.

I ignored the question and looked again at Mrs Salton, who was sitting watchfully with no expression at all on her face. I said, 'What was Mr Salton's departure point when he took the boat out that final time?'

She stirred. 'He sailed from here.'

'The boat was found four days later drifting off Buque Island – that's the other side of Campanilla. A long way.'

'That was gone into at the inquest,' said Stern. 'The wind direction and the current drift accounted for it satisfactorily.'

'Maybe, but I was looking at the sea as I came here. In whichever direction I looked there was a boat. There are a lot of yachts here and four days is a long time. It seems odd that Mr Salton's boat wasn't discovered earlier.'

'A matter of chance,' said Stern. 'And boats don't approach each other too closely anyway. Even at a hundred yards you couldn't tell . . .' He looked at Mrs Salton and stopped.

'But Mr Salton was missing for four days. Didn't anyone worry about that?'

Stern started to speak but Mrs Salton interrupted. 'I'll explain. I didn't know David was missing.' She paused. 'My husband and I had a quarrel – a rather bad one. He left the house in a fit of temper and went across to the main island. We have an airstrip there where we keep a plane.'

She must have noticed my reaction to this exemplar of the super-rich, because she added, 'My husband had many interests in the United States and it was convenient to run our own aircraft.'

I straightened out the expression on my face. 'Did he pilot it himself?'

'No. We have a pilot and an engineer. Shortly after David left here, the plane took off. I didn't think much of it at the time but when David didn't come back I went across to the airstrip. The plane wasn't there, of course, and I couldn't find Philips, the engineer. I went to see Mrs Haslam, the pilot's wife – Haslam and Philips both have houses on the estate. She said she had seen Haslam talking to my husband and they got into the plane. I assumed he had flown to the United States.'

'Just like that? Without packing a suitcase?'

'It wasn't necessary,' she said. 'He maintains a wardrobe in the apartment in New York.'

'What was he wearing when he left?'

She considered. 'A polo shirt, shorts and sandals.'

It was winter in the northern hemisphere. While the heat was borderline unbearable in the Caribbean, the snow could be drifting up to three feet thick in the streets of New York. This was straining my credulity a bit too far. I said, 'He went to New York in midwinter in a polo shirt, shorts and sandals. Is that what you're telling me, Mrs Salton?'

She smiled slightly. 'There was nothing odd about it, Mr Kemp. In flying long distances one can never be sure of ground conditions at the destination. Lightweight and heavy-weight business suits were always carried in the aircraft, together with shirts and other accessories.'

Millionaires *are* different from other people.

I accepted that and said, 'But he didn't go to New York, did he?'

'I didn't know that at the time. Look, it was a matter of dignity for me: I was waiting for him to call. But after two days I caved in and telephoned the apartment in New York. There was no answer so I telephoned the offices of his New York holding company. He hadn't been there.'

'So you contacted the police.'

She shook her head. 'I wasn't worried then – not in that way. I think I was more annoyed than anything else. There I was, all set to apologise, and I couldn't find him. Next day the plane came back.'

'That would be the third day?'

'Yes. That's when Haslam told me David hadn't been on the flight to the States. They talked together on the plane but David got off again before it took off.'

'Why *did* the plane go to the States, Mrs Salton?'

'It was due back at the manufacturer for a routine service.'

'I see. So what did you do?'

'I was very worried. David had just walked out of the house and if he hadn't gone to the States, then where was he? He certainly couldn't lose himself on Campanilla – he was too well known. I didn't know what to do. In the end I telephoned the police.'

Stern broke in. 'She also telephoned me.'

'Before or after contacting the police?'

Mrs Salton's lips compressed slightly and Stern said evenly, 'She wanted my advice. I told her to get in touch with the police immediately.'

'I telephoned Commissioner Barstow,' she said.

Another millionaire touch: if you want something, go right to the top. I said, 'He sent someone to find out what was happening?'

'He came himself.'

Of course. Let a millionaire vanish and the chief cop would arrive in a sprint. 'What was his reaction?'

Stern said, 'What you'd expect. His first thought was that David had been kidnapped. He alerted all his men and they began to investigate.'

'There was a lot of talk that went on and on that evening. Some of Barstow's plain-clothes men even attached a tape recorder to the telephone in case any kidnappers got in touch.' There was a note of weariness in Mrs Salton's voice – perhaps an echo of the weariness of that night. 'I had a headache and went to my room to rest and I was looking across the water towards the mainland when I suddenly thought of the boat. It's kept in a boathouse over there.'

I nodded. 'I've seen the boathouse.'

'I told Barstow and he had the boathouse checked. The boat wasn't there.' She paused, then said, 'It was exactly midnight.'

'So your husband's body was discovered as a result of a sea search?'

'No,' she said. 'A fisherman out of Hogtown discovered the boat early next morning and towed it into San Martin.'

I thought about it for a while. Stern fidgeted in the silence but Mrs Salton was as composed as ever. It all seemed to hang together and explained why there had been no hue and cry as soon as Salton went missing. Perhaps it hung together too well, but suspicion is an occupational disease in my trade. I said, 'What do you think really happened, Mrs Salton?'

'Substantially what was said at the inquest. I think that David was very angry when he left here, and to cool down he took the boat out. I think he had a heart attack and died at sea.'

'What was your quarrel about?'

Stern jerked himself erect. Mrs Salton said, 'It was about a personal matter which I don't care to go into.'

Stern subsided, but not much. I said carefully, 'So your husband was very angry – angry enough that you weren't surprised he'd flown to the States, apparently in a fit of pique?'

She looked down at the back of her hands. 'He was very upset,' she said in a low voice.

'Upset enough to take his own life?'

'Don't answer that,' said Stern sharply. He glared at me and said frostily, 'That's a most improper question.'

'Under the circumstances I think not.'

'I'll answer it,' said Mrs Salton. 'My husband would never commit suicide, Mr Kemp. He was not that kind of man.'

'The idea of David Salton committing suicide is laughable to anyone who knew him,' said Stern.

'I had to ask the question,' I said. 'I'm sorry if it distressed you in any way.'

'I understand, Mr Kemp,' she said. 'You must do your job.' The way she said it made me wish I had a different job.

'Strictly speaking, it's not my affair,' I said, and Stern stared at me in surprise. 'A Mr Ogilvie is dealing with the matter of the claim. I'll see him and pass on the information you've given me so that you won't have to go through all this again. I expect he'll be coming to see you quite soon but if you wish he can deal through Mr Stern.'

'He certainly must deal through me,' said Stern. 'But what are *you* here for?'

'Oh, I'm here on an entirely different matter,' I said blandly. 'I'm representing Mr Costello, the company's investment analyst. Not unnaturally, he is interested in the future of Salton Estates Ltd.'

'What has Western and Continental got to do with Salton Estates?' asked Mrs Salton.

'They invested money in the firm,' I said. 'Over three million pounds.'

'Eight million dollars,' said Stern. 'Mr Salton tended to think in dollars. He lived over there a long time.'

I watched the frown mar Mrs Salton's lovely face. 'Didn't you know about your husband's business affairs?'

'Some,' she said. 'But I didn't think he'd borrow that much. It *was* a loan? He always said he'd never give away a piece of the action.'

I suppressed a smile at the uncharacteristic slang in the well-modulated English tone. 'Yes, it was a long-term loan at two per cent over bank rate. He's been paying the interest regularly – that comes to £288,000 a year. He was due to begin paying off the principal in a couple of years' time.'

'I didn't know,' she said.

'It was just an ordinary business deal,' said Stern.

I shrugged. 'Mr Salton may have been a very good businessman but he appears to have played a lone hand. Now that he's . . . no longer around, Mr Costello is wondering if Salton Estates will continue to be run along the lines laid down by Mr Salton.' I smiled in what I hoped looked like sympathy. 'It's not that we're very worried but we'd just like to make sure.'

'And how are you going to make sure?' asked Stern. He seemed unaccountably hostile.

'I'd like to run my eye over the books – check the cash flow, the reserves, things like that.'

'Are you empowered to do that?'

I leaned back in my chair. 'If you think I'm not then I suggest you telephone Lord Hosmer immediately.'

'Of course you can look at the books,' said Mrs Salton. 'As far as I know Salton Estates is doing marvellously.' She glanced at Stern. 'Maybe you could take Mr Kemp to the office this afternoon, introduce him to Martin Idle.'

Stern nodded curtly. 'Very well.'

'Meanwhile, perhaps you'd care to stay for lunch, Mr Kemp?'

'Thank you,' I said politely.

The house had a series of internal courts or rooms without roofs – the atrium of Roman architecture, modified for the Caribbean – and we had lunch in one of these. Over the crawfish I remembered the man from the dusty cornfield and said, 'I met someone who sends you his regards – a Mr McKittrick.'

Mrs Salton seemed confused. 'McKittrick?'

'Tall, well-built.'

Her brow cleared. 'Oh, *Doctor* McKittrick.'

I sampled the nutty-flavoured white flesh of the crawfish. 'He didn't look like a doctor to me. When I saw him he was planting corn.'

Mrs Salton smiled. 'Dr McKittrick has unorthodox ideas of what constitutes medical practice.'

'Very unorthodox,' said Stern. 'He's a troublemaker.'

'I haven't seen Jake McKittrick for nearly two years,' said Mrs Salton.

'He said he was sorry to hear of what happened to your husband.'

'Sorry?' said Stern. 'I'd have thought he'd be cheering.'

'Just because he and David had a quarrel doesn't mean . . .' She stopped, then said, 'I must drop him a line.'

'I wouldn't,' said Stern. 'The elections are coming up. As your lawyer I advise you to put nothing in writing to Jacob McKittrick. It could be misinterpreted – no matter what you write.'

I waited for Mrs Salton to reply but she said nothing, apparently content to drop the issue. I added McKittrick's name to the list on my mental file and dropped another stone into the conversational pool. 'A man called Jackson gave me some interesting information on local affairs. You may know him, Mrs Salton. An American on the staff of the *Chronicle*.'

'On the staff? He's the editor.'

Jackson may have been miles away on the other side of the island, but he was still capable of pulling surprises.

'He told me you own the *Chronicle*.'

'I suppose I do, now that David is dead.'

'Don Jackson's a sound man,' pronounced Stern. 'A very good editor.'

And a very good backstabber, I thought. It was not news to me that a newspaperman's personal politics need have no relationship to the political views of the paper for which he works – it's probably why journalists have a reputation for cynicism – but Jackson's naked hostility towards Salton and his wife seemed to be different and based on something other than politics. I sensed that if Western and Continental torpedoed Mrs Salton's claim, then Jackson would be very pleased. He was a dog in the manger and there must be a reason.

Stern glanced at his watch. 'I have to be getting back.'

I suddenly changed my mind about investigating Salton Estates that afternoon. I wanted a chance to talk to Mrs Salton without Stern in the way – he was a repressive influence. 'I'd like to talk to Haslam while I'm here,' I said. 'If I get it all wrapped up it will save Mr Ogilvie a journey.'

'He's available,' said Mrs Salton. 'The plane's not been used since . . .' She stood up. 'I'll talk to him.'

She went away and Stern said, 'It seems to me that Western and Continental are being unduly zealous, Mr Kemp. I should have thought that the inquest made the situation quite clear.'

I smiled at him. 'Inquests have been known to be wrong. As I'm sure you know, insurance companies are regarded as fair game by a lot of otherwise legally-minded people. To cheat an insurance company is viewed as a minor infringement, like smuggling an extra bottle of booze through Customs. So they tend to be zealous as a matter of routine.'

Stern nodded acceptance. 'I suppose you're right. And you have your job to do – whatever that is. But if you're not coming to San Martin with me now, when do you want to look at the books?'

'Maybe tomorrow. I'll phone first.'

Mrs Salton came back. 'You can see Haslam any time.'

'No time like the present,' said Stern jovially. 'You can cross to the mainland with me. I'd like to have a word with you on the way.'

So my plan was stymied, and Stern and I crossed to the mainland together. Whatever word he'd wanted to have with me I never found out because he didn't tell me. I concluded that the sole aim of his manoeuvres was to make sure that I was never alone with Mrs Salton. I could have been wrong, but that was the way it worked out.

## II

Haslam lived in a neat little house next to the airstrip. He was a tall, spare Canadian with not enough meat on his bones for his height. His eyes were a faded blue, networked around with the wrinkles of middle age, so that he gave the impression of being worried about something. Maybe he was.

His wife was a frizzy blonde, pouchy under the eyes and burnt nearly black from too much sun so that her hair made a startling contrast to her leathery skin. And she showed a lot of skin.

I found them sitting beside a small swimming pool behind the house. Haslam stood up as I approached. 'Mr Kemp?'

'Yes,' I said.

'Mrs Salton said you'd be coming. She told me to tell you anything you want to know.'

Haslam's wife looked up at me and indicated a jug on the deck table beside her. 'Drink, Mr Kemp? Margarita.'

I felt the mid-afternoon sun searing my scalp and the roof of my mouth was dry. 'It would be appreciated.'

She got to her feet. 'I'll go get a glass while you talk business with Jim. Then we can all have another drink.'

She appeared to have had too many already – the perils of a sedentary life in paradise, perhaps. I said, 'I'll be wanting to speak to you, too, Mrs Haslam.'

She lifted her eyebrows. 'Okay. Be back soon.' She tottered unsteadily towards the house.

I turned to Haslam and took the cane chair he indicated. 'Suppose you tell me everything that happened just before Mr Salton died.'

He shrugged. 'I can't tell you any more than I've told already.'

'Humour me,' I said. 'I'm a stranger round here.'

So he told me, and there was nothing in his account that was any different from that of Mrs Salton. While he was speaking, his wife came back with a glass and a refilled jug, sat by the pool and poured me a drink, as well as one for herself. Haslam was not drinking. I sipped my margarita while listening to him and discovered that Mrs Haslam was uncomfortably heavy with the tequila.

At last he finished. 'That's all I know, Mr Kemp.'

From the airstrip came the sudden howl of a jet engine winding up. I said, 'What's happening over there?'

'Les Philips is testing the engines. I'm taking her up this afternoon.'

'Oh, where are you going?'

'No place. Just around. There are a lot of moving parts in an airplane, Mr Kemp, and if they're left alone they get sticky. An airplane needs exercise, same as a man. She's not been up since . . . since we came back from the States.'

'How long will you be gone?'

'Maybe an hour.'

I said, 'I wanted to look at the plane. Maybe I'll come with you.'

He hesitated. 'That's all right with me, but maybe I'd better check with Mrs Salton.' He broke into an embarrassed laugh. 'It's her airplane. I'm just the hired driver.'

'Well, why don't you ask her if it's all right?'

'Sure, I'll do that.' He got up and walked towards the house.

Mrs Haslam reached for the jug and refilled her glass. 'You wanna ask me somethin'?' She was drinking too fast and her voice was slurred.

'Yes,' I said. 'On the day that Mrs Salton came up here to ask if you'd seen her husband, you told her that your husband and Mr Salton had gone into the plane and then the plane took off. Isn't that what you said?'

She looked at me owlishly. 'Sure, that's what I said.'

'But it wasn't so. Why did you say it?'

'It was so, too. You making me a liar, Mr Kemp?'

'I'm just trying to get things straightened out,' I said.

'It happened like I said. Mr Salton got into the airplane with Jim. The plane took off.' She looked up. 'But I wasn't looking at that airplane the whole damn time.'

I said carefully, 'You mean that Mr Salton might have left the aircraft without you seeing him, before it took off?'

'Sure.' She drank from her glass and a dribble of liquid ran from the corner of her mouth down her chin. She dabbed it with the back of a paw.

'But when it became clear that Mr Salton was missing, didn't it occur to you to tell someone?'

She shook her head muzzily. 'I didn't know David Salton was missing. And if Mrs Salton thought he was, then she kept her troubles to herself.'

That fitted. I couldn't see Mrs Salton confiding in a woman like this, the addled wife of her husband's employee. Haslam called from the house. I said, 'Excuse me,' to Mrs Haslam and went across.

'Mrs Salton would like to talk with you,' he said, and led me inside the house to the telephone.

I picked it up. 'Kemp here.'

Her voice was cool and pleasant. 'After your flight would you like to come back to the house and make use of the pool?'

'That would be very nice.' I paused. 'I have no trunks with me.'

She sounded amused. 'I think we can find something for you. In about an hour, then.'

I put down the telephone and went back to Haslam. 'Would you like to go right away?' he asked.

'If you're ready,' I said.

He nodded abruptly and went back to the pool. He had a few words with his wife and then came back. I fell into step with him and we walked across the airstrip towards the distant hangar. He was silent and seemed to be brooding about something. At last he said, 'Bette . . . my wife . . . She's not usually like that. It's just that she's upset.'

'About Mr Salton?'

He shrugged. 'In a way. She's worried about me.'

'I don't see that you can be blamed for anything,' I said.

Haslam stopped in mid-stride and turned to me. 'It's not that. She's worried about my job. Mrs Salton doesn't use the airplane much – it was his baby – and Bette thinks I may be out of a job pretty soon. She may be right, at that.'

'Did you like working for Mr Salton?'

'Hell, yes. He was a real nice guy. Very considerate, not like some bosses I've had. Wherever we went – and we went to some weird places – he always saw that the aircrew were okay before he went about his business.'

We began to walk again, and I said, 'How many in the crew?'

'There's me as pilot, and Les Philips. He's the engineer and does the routine ground servicing but he has his pilot's ticket too, so he comes along as co-pilot. I do the navigating. House servants are on board as stewards – one or two, depending on the number of passengers. And there was usually Mr Salton's secretary.'

'Who was?'

'Mrs Forsyth.'

'Is she around here now?'

Haslam shook his head. 'She used to live here at El Cerco but she's now working with Mr Idle in San Martin.'

I thought of the rambling house on the island in the lagoon. 'Does Mrs Salton now live entirely alone in the house? I mean, apart from servants.'

Haslam looked at me consideringly for a moment, then said briefly, 'I wouldn't know.'

We'd been walking for several minutes and it suddenly

struck me that this was an indecently large airstrip to accom-
modate a relatively small plane. I asked Haslam about it.

'I thought the same thing when I first came here. What
you have to remember is that it wasn't built by Mr Salton.
The strip predates that lagoon house by many years.'

That surprised me. The northern tip of the island was
remote by any standards, and it seemed unlikely that anyone
would put a random airstrip – especially one as big as this
– so far away from the island's residential centres.

'It was actually built by you Brits in the war,' said Haslam.
'Transport station for most of the Caribbean. The Yanks had
squadrons here too. After they all shipped out, it was used
occasionally for local traffic. But then Mr Salton bought it
up when he moved back to the island. Now it's just his
plane that flies out of here.'

'How long is the runway?'

'Pretty long. Six thousand and two feet, if you want to
be exact. They could run commercial flights from here just
as easily as from Benning, if ever they decided to develop
this end of the island. But I guess with Mr Salton gone,
that's not going to happen any time soon.'

I smiled wryly. 'Oh, I'm not sure about that. I know a
man in London who's very interested in keeping Mr Salton's
investment plans alive.'

We turned the corner of the hangar and I saw the aircraft:
a Lear executive jet, about half a million dollars' worth of
luxurious machinery. Its purpose was to transport a busy
man about his empire. But the man was dead and his wife
apparently not air-minded. No wonder Haslam looked
worried: it was odds-on that Mrs Salton would cash in this
white elephant and divert the proceeds to something more
useful.

He introduced me to Philips, a short, stocky man with a
London accent – not Cockney, but unmistakeably metro-
politan. We exchanged brief greetings and then Philips

engaged Haslam in a technical conversation. I stood looking
at the plane for a while, then butted in. 'Do you mind if I
go aboard?'

'That's okay,' said Haslam. 'Just don't smoke while we're
on the ground.'

I climbed the boarding ladder and entered the fuselage
to find a flying office complete with all modern conveni-
ences, most of them built-in. There were two desks, one
with an electronic calculator and a recording machine, the
other fitted with a typewriter, another tape recorder and a
photocopier. I guessed that was Mrs Forsyth's post. I opened
a filing cabinet nearby; it was empty.

I moved aft and opened a door in a bulkhead. There was
a corridor leading to the tail. I went along it and found
myself in the galley, gleaming in stainless steel. I checked a
cupboard at random and found what would have been a
well-stocked cocktail cabinet had there been any bottles in
it. Of course, if the aircraft had been due to go back to the
manufacturers, the booze would have been tactfully removed.

The galley was spotless but there was not a scrap of food
in it. Even the refrigerator was empty. I pulled down a flap
and found myself looking into a microwave oven. After
another glance around I decided there wasn't anything for
me here so I went forward again along the corridor.

There was a door on the starboard side which led into a
sleeping cabin with accommodation for two. The beds were
narrow but comfortable, as I found by testing, and they
were made up ready for use. I slid open a wardrobe door
and found three suits in various weights of cloth. When I
checked the pockets I found nothing, not even a shred of
lint. Whoever valeted Salton knew their job.

I drew a blank in the dressing table too. Neatly folded
double-cuff shirts, underwear, ties, shoes, socks and nothing
much else. All clean and tidy. But there was something
missing and I couldn't put my finger on what it was.

When I got back to the main cabin, Haslam was climbing aboard. 'What do you think of it?' he asked.

'Where's the ticker tape and the teletype?' I asked jokingly.

He grinned. 'It wasn't for the want of trying.'

Something clicked. 'There's something else missing,' I said. 'There are shirts back there but no cufflinks; ties but no tiepins.'

'Mr Salton's personal jewellery is kept in the safe,' said Haslam.

'A safe? I'd like to see inside that. Can you open it?' He hesitated, so I said, 'It's all right, you won't get into trouble. And you can breathe down my neck.'

The safe was well hidden under the floor. It had a good combination lock and if you'd wanted to extract the whole contraption you'd have had to take the plane apart to do it. Haslam opened it and stood aside. I said, 'How come you have the combination?'

'There's currency of different sorts in there,' he said. 'At most airfields we can operate on credit, but at some of the smaller ones – particularly in South America – we have to pay cash for gas, servicing and airfield charges. Sometimes Mr Salton wasn't aboard, so he gave me the combination.'

That sounded reasonable. I dug into the safe and produced several sheafs of foreign currency – American dollars, Brazilian cruzeiros, Ecuadorian sucres, Bolivian pesos, Peruvian soles and so on. It was quite a wad, even if it did look like Monopoly money. There were no Campanillan pounds but then those wouldn't be needed.

There were several objects in protective wallets: two cigarette lighters, one of gold and the other of what appeared to be stainless steel but was probably platinum, and two cigarette cases likewise. Four sets of cufflinks and four tiepins, two signet rings and an American silver dollar with a hole bored through it – a good luck piece?

Nothing else.

I put it all back then looked at Haslam. 'Was all this stuff here when you took the plane back to the manufacturer?'

The expression on his face was a mixture of shock and surprise. 'You know, no one even thought of it. Mr Salton didn't mention it and it never occurred to me.' He smiled ruefully. 'I guess we've got to thinking of it as part of the standard equipment of the airplane – like the radio, say. Mr Salton's clothes weren't taken off, either.'

'But the alcohol was,' I said.

Haslam shrugged. 'The galley is cleaned out as a matter of course after every flight.'

When I stopped to think about the kind of man I was investigating, it all sounded completely logical. The very rich are not just folks like the rest of us. One of the super-rich once said in surprise, 'You know, a man with five million dollars can live just as though he were a rich man.' That's pretty high-level philosophy.

'Anything else, Mr Kemp?'

'No,' I said. 'Not for the moment.'

Haslam went forward to join Philips in the cockpit or the flight deck or whatever fancy name they give it in planes that size. I sat down and began to go through drawers. I didn't really expect to find anything, but old habits die hard. There's a curious fascination about going through a man's effects, delving into the minutiae of his life – not that there was much to find about Salton because the cupboard was bare apart from blank stationery, office knick-knacks and the like. Everything personal had been cleared out, presumably by the efficient Mrs Forsyth.

Presently the plane began to move. We taxied up the runway and then turned. A loudspeaker over my head crackled and Haslam said, 'Fasten your seatbelt, Mr Kemp.'

I snapped the seatbelt closed and the plane roared off, climbing rapidly. It levelled off and the warning lights went out. Haslam said over the speaker, 'Okay, Mr Kemp, you can come forward if you want to.'

I found Philips at the controls and Haslam chatting to someone on the radio. He signed off and I said, 'Who were you talking to?'

'Air traffic control at Benning Airport.'

'Do you have to do that, even on a flight like this?'

'They like to know what's in the air,' he said. 'It's mostly for the benefit of the missile tracking station at Fort Edward. We're down-range of Cape Canaveral and they don't like unforeseen blips on their radar.' He put his hands on the controls. 'I'll take her, Les.'

I studied Philips. 'You're a long way from home, Mr Philips.'

He half-turned in his seat so as to face me and somehow combined the movement with a shrug. 'If you're in the flying business you get around.'

'Have you been working for Mr Salton long?'

'Three years.'

'Me too,' said Haslam. 'Ever since he moved back to Campanilla permanently.'

We chatted for a while. Both Haslam and Philips seemed depressed by the death of Salton and their depression seemed to be an amalgam of worry about their jobs and a genuine regret for the death of their employer: they had both liked Salton and thought him a good boss.

We flew a triangular course and came back to El Cerco flying low over the lagoon. By then I was back in the cabin with my belt fastened for landing, and I had a good view of the house on the tiny island.

I could even see the swimming pool and a diving board on which was a tiny figure that must have been Mrs Salton. As the plane went over, she dived and I caught the splash as she hit the water. Then the plane had passed and I lost sight of her.

Back on the runway I said to Haslam, 'Thanks for the flip.'

'Did you find everything you wanted to know?' he asked.

I grinned at him. 'Who does?' I nodded pleasantly and walked away.

He called out, 'Okay, Les, let's get the bird back into the nest.' I turned and looked back to find him staring at me. I waved and he waved back, then I turned the corner of the hangar and looked out over El Cerco.

# THREE

## I

'Kemp,' said Mrs Salton lazily. 'Is that Celtic, Norse?'

'English of the English,' I assured her. 'There was a Will Kemp in Burbage's company at the Globe Theatre. I like to think I have an ancestor who, perhaps, acted with Shakespeare.'

'Did Shakespeare act?'

'He's supposed to have played the ghost in Hamlet.'

We were sitting in voluptuous chairs by the swimming pool and sipping something cool and alcoholic from tall glasses. I had swum six lengths of the pool, paced easily by Mrs Salton, and then had flopped thankfully ashore trying not to feel ashamed of my winter-white English skin. The heat dried the bubbles of moisture from my torso even as I watched.

I was waiting for her to come to the point, to come out with what she wanted to ask me. She wanted something or she wouldn't have invited me back to the house.

'Kemp,' she repeated. 'William Kemp. What do your friends call you?'

I turned my head and looked at her. She filled her bikini rather better than Mrs Haslam, I thought uncharitably, but then she had youth on her side. 'I'm known as Bill.'

'And I'm Jill.' She stretched out a hand, which I reached

for amiably. It was a little late for this kind of introduction, but I went along with her.

'On Campanilla we're more informal than in England, especially when lounging by a pool.' She put down her glass with a click. 'Mr Stern is a wee bit stuffy but he means well. He's trying to look after my interests.'

'I'm sure he is,' I said, not feeling at all sure. A widow with as much money as she had could prove to be quite a temptation.

'You said you spoke to Don Jackson at the *Chronicle*. What did he tell you?'

'This and that,' I said offhandedly. 'Political stuff, mostly. Background material.'

'About David?'

'Apparently he was on course to be the next Prime Minister.'

She nodded. 'It was very likely.'

'I read one of your husband's speeches,' I said. 'He was having quite a go at the government. But there was one reference I didn't understand – he said something about hired bully boys. What would he have meant by that?'

'Merely political rhetoric.'

'No basis in fact?'

'Maybe a little,' she admitted. 'The elections were coming closer and tempers were rising. Politics can be rougher here than in England, Bill.'

'I can understand the bully boys,' I said. 'But what about the hired bit?'

'David was a politician,' she said. 'He used words like weapons.'

'And to hell with the truth. Is that it?'

'No, it isn't,' she said, with force in her voice. She took a deep breath. 'I see that Jackson has been dropping poison in your ear.'

'Is that what you think? You don't seem to like Jackson.'

'I don't.' She was silent and I waited for what she had to say next. At last she said, 'All right. He once behaved towards me . . . rather objectionably.'

'He made a pass at you?'

'If you want to put it that way.'

'It must have been a heavy pass,' I said. 'Why didn't you have him fired?'

She stared at me. 'Good heavens! It's not a criminal offence to make a pass at the boss's wife. Besides, he's a good editor for the *Chronicle*.'

'Did your husband know about this?'

'No. And after that I kept out of Jackson's way. I haven't given him another chance.' She picked up her glass. 'So what did he really tell you?'

'Nothing about you,' I said, and wondered whether to pursue the matter. Conceivably I might have a further use for Jackson and if I didn't tattle-tale to Jill Salton then I'd have a club to hold over his head. 'Let's talk about someone else. Do you know of a man called Negrini?'

She sat up. 'Mr Black – who doesn't? But, for a stranger, you've been getting around.'

'Not really,' I said modestly. 'It's just that I'm exceptionally brilliant at my job. Do you know him personally?'

'Yes.'

'And did your husband?'

'Of course. Gerry is very much a part of the social life of this island.'

'Good. I'd like to meet him.'

'Now that might be difficult, Bill. You see, Gerry is not available to all. He picks and chooses very carefully those with whom he associates. I doubt if you'd get near him. What do you want to see him about?'

'I can't tell you that,' I said honestly. 'It's a private matter.' I didn't want to tell her that I was investigating her husband's connections with the gambling interests. If she didn't know about it the news might come as a shock, because she had given all the indications of believing him to be a genuine liberal.

'Does it concern David?'

'No,' I lied. 'It's about something that came up just before I left England.' Lying was something else that went with the job.

'Is it urgent?'

'Yes, in the sense that I have very little time on Campanilla.'

'All right, I'll introduce you. Would tonight be soon enough?' She was smiling.

'You can do it as quickly as that?'

'Why not? All we have to do is to go into San Martin – to the Blue Water Casino. We'll have dinner here first – I'll even cook it myself. I don't get into the kitchen nearly enough.'

John came down to the poolside carrying a telephone. 'A call for Mr Kemp,' he said.

That was Ogilvie. I had rung his hotel to find he was out so I had left the Salton number for him to call. As John bent to plug the telephone jack into a socket in the wall of the house, I said quickly, 'I'd rather take it inside.'

Jill sighed. 'Oh, more secrets!' She turned to John. 'Mr Kemp will use an inside phone – and tell Anna she needn't stay on.'

'Very well, ma'am.'

'And you can go off yourself, John, at any time.'

John gave me a look of pure dislike and said evenly, 'Thank you, ma'am.'

I followed him into a hall where he picked up a receiver, spoke into the mouthpiece, and then held it out. 'Your call,' he said. 'Sir.'

'Thank you,' I said, and watched his upright back disappear among the greenery. 'Kemp here.'

'You wanted me?' Ogilvie asked.

'What's new on the Rialto?'

'I wish you'd stop quoting,' said Ogilvie peevishly. He sounded tired. 'Especially when you misquote. I've been talking to the police. They think the inquest went off fine.'

'No foul play?'

'None that was detectable. Winstanley's report ought to be printed in *Punch*, though.'

'The pathologist? Why – is it unreliable?'

'I wouldn't bet heavily on it, let's put it that way. The body was in a bad condition but from what I hear, Winstanley is worse. Seventy and shaky.'

'But highly respected,' I said. 'What happened to Salton – buried or burned?'

'Buried. Are you thinking of poison?'

'I'm not thinking of anything much. Did you see Jackson?'

'I saw him. As you said, a creep. But an informative creep. He'll lose his job if he doesn't stop that sudden rush of words to the mouth.'

Ogilvie told me what Jackson had said, which didn't add anything to what I knew already.

'I'd better tell you how I've been doing here.'

'Where's here?' asked Ogilvie. 'All I have is a telephone number.'

'El Cerco – the Salton place.' I brought him up to date and he said, 'Bill, do you suspect murder?'

'I don't know yet.'

'Look, you're the boss but does it make any difference to us? We pay out anyway.'

'It all depends on who has done the murdering.'

His voice was incredulous. 'Mrs Salton?'

'I didn't say that,' I said. 'Not out loud, anyway. Do some checking on the political side if you can. I'll tackle the Salton Estates end tomorrow. Tonight I'll be at the Blue Water Casino tying up Mr Black. I'll be there pretty late, say, about ten o'clock. I'm having dinner here. Mrs Salton is preparing it with her own fair hands.'

'If you're thinking what I think you're thinking, you'd better watch for the arsenic in the artichokes. What's she like, anyway?'

I considered before I spoke. 'She's fiftyish, runs to about two hundred pounds on the hoof, sallow complexion, dark moustache. You'll be seeing her tonight at the casino.'

'Ouch!' said Ogilvie. 'Bill, you work bloody hard for your money. See you later.'

He rang off and I grinned as I put down the telephone. But he was right; I do work bloody hard for my money. There was more to this than the possibility of a plain old insurance scam. My reputation as the best consultant in the business was at stake.

Back at the pool there was no one around so I sat down and contemplated the water. I had waited for Jill Salton to come to the point and all she had come up with was Jackson. Very curious. I thought of Jackson and Jill Salton, separately and in conjunction, and came to no conclusion.

Presently John came along. 'Mrs Salton says to tell you she's in the kitchen if you'd like to go along there.'

'Where's the kitchen?'

He told me. He had taken off his white coat and was dressed neatly in smart civvies. 'Are you going off duty now, John?'

'Yes, sir,' he said stolidly.

'Were you here the day Mr Salton walked out – the last day he was seen alive?'

'Yes, sir.'

'Do you know what Mr and Mrs Salton talked about just before he left?'

There was a sudden widening of his eyes, a movement quickly cancelled. He said quietly, 'I don't talk about the doings of my employer, sir.'

One in the eye for Kemp. I ought to have known not to pump the servants. Christ, what a lousy job I had. He stared at me steadily with defiant brown eyes, daring me to make something of it. He knew, all right! He knew what the Saltons had quarrelled about. But he wasn't telling.

I said, 'That's good, John. Keep it that way.'

'Is that all, sir?'

'Yes.' He turned away and I said, 'How long have you worked for the Saltons?'

He was walking away as he said without turning his head, 'Twenty-two years. It's twenty-two years since I started with Mr Salton.'

I watched him until he was out of sight and thought what a right bastard I was, then I went into the changing room, showered, dressed and headed for the kitchen.

It was exactly what you'd expect to find in a house like that: a lot of stainless steel, eye-level ovens, islanded preparation counters, all gleaming and clean as a whistle. Jill Salton had changed, too. She was wearing a short frock, a simple little number you can buy anywhere for $1,000. As I arrived she said, 'How do you like your martinis?'

I'm not a martini mystic. I shrugged and said, 'As they come.'

'You must get a lot of different martinis that way,' she observed, and poured a healthy slug from a gin bottle into a shaker.

'I like variety.'

She mixed the drinks and poured them, strained through cracked ice into chilled glasses taken from the refrigerator. 'How often do you see my uncle?'

I smiled. 'As little as possible. We don't exactly rub shoulders.'

She handed me a glass. 'He thinks a lot of you. He said so this afternoon.'

I sipped the martini. It was very good. 'Face to face?'

'Via satellite. He sang your praises a lot. He says you're the best man in the business.'

'I'll have to remember that when I negotiate my next contract.'

She lifted her glass and her cool, green eyes appraised me over the rim. 'What business would that be?'

'What else but insurance? I'm a money man at heart.'

She smiled. 'I doubt that. Are you married?'

'Not at present.'

'You sound as though you've been burned. You were married?'

I hooked over a chair with my foot and sat down. 'Twice. My first wife died and my second divorced me.'

'I'm sorry to hear about the first, and surprised at the second.'

'Surprised?'

'I can't see how a woman in her right mind would let you get away.'

I thought she was joking but she seemed serious enough. Abruptly she put down her glass and walked across the kitchen to open the lid of a big deep freezer. I played it lightly and said to her back, 'There was nothing to it. I didn't wriggle off the hook – she threw me back.'

'Why? Were you tomcatting?'

You ask some damn personal questions, Jill Salton, I thought, then reconsidered. Come to that, so did I. Perhaps this was her way of giving me a taste of my own medicine. 'No,' I said. 'She didn't like bigamy. I was married to the insurance industry.'

She took some packets to a counter and switched on an oven, then began to prepare the food. From what I could see, millionaires didn't eat any better than the rest of us – just the same old frozen garbage. 'Some women are fools,' she said. 'When I married David I knew what I was getting into. I knew he had his work and it would take up a lot of his time. But there's a certain type of woman who doesn't understand how important a man's work can be to him.' She paused with a knife upheld. 'I suppose it means as much as having a baby does to a woman.'

'You're not the liberated feminist type, then. When were you married?'

'Four years ago.' She got busy with the knife. 'Believe it or not, I was still a virgin at twenty-four.'

She was right – I did find it hard to believe. I wondered why the hell she was telling me all this. My acquaintance-ship with beautiful young heiresses was admittedly limited, but I'd come across a handful in the way of business and none had felt impelled to tell me the more intimate details of her life. Still, statistically, anything can happen given a long enough period of time, and maybe she'd get around to telling me about the quarrel with her husband.

She said, 'David was exactly twice as old as I was, give or take a couple of weeks. My family said it would never work.'

'Did it?'

She turned her head and looked at me. 'Oh yes, it worked. It worked marvellously. We were very happy.' She looked down at the counter again and wielded the knife. 'How was your first marriage?'

I looked back along the years. 'Good,' I said. 'Very good.'

'Tell me about her.'

'Nothing much to tell. We married young. I was a second lieutenant and she was an army wife.'

'So you were a soldier.'

'Until ten years ago, when I started working with Western and Continental. I'm still in the reserves.'

'What rank?'

'Colonel.'

She raised her eyebrows. 'You must have been good.'

I laughed. 'Good, but not good enough, tactically speaking.' I found myself telling her about it.

I had worked my way upwards from my green commission with a rapidity that pleased me until I found myself a half-colonel commanding a battalion in Germany. I did not get on very well with my superior officer, Brigadier Marston, and the bone of contention was that we disagreed on the role of the army. He was one of the old school, forever refighting World War II, and thought in terms of massed tank operations, parachute drops of entire divisions and all the rest of the junk that had been made obsolete by the *pax atomica*. For my part, I could see nothing in the future but an unending series of counter-insurgency operations such as in Malaya, Cyprus and Aden, and I argued – maybe a bit too forcibly – that the army lacked training for this particular tricky job.

When Marston wrote my annual report it turned out to be a beauty. There was nothing in it that was actionable; in fact, to the untrained eye the damned thing was laudatory. But to a hard-eyed general in the War House, skilled in the jargon of the old boys' network, the report said that Lt-Col William Kemp was not the soldier to put your money on. So I was promoted to colonel and I cursed Marston with all my heart. A colonel in the army is a fifth wheel, a dogsbody shunted off into an administrative post. My own sideline was intelligence, something at which I was particularly skilled, but my heart wasn't in it. After a couple of years I negotiated very good freelance terms with Western and Continental, who paid willingly for my expertise. I would still be pushing pieces of paper around various desks but I'd be getting £15,000 a year for doing it. Marston, meanwhile, was in Northern Ireland, up to his armpits in IRA terrorists and wondering what the hell to do with his useless tanks.

I finished my story and looked up at Jill, who was staring hard at me. My army experience had exposed me to some brutal interrogation techniques, but Jill Salton could give my instructors points. 'So that was it,' I said. 'I quit.'

'But your wife had died earlier.'

'I was stationed in Germany and my wife was flying out to meet me. The plane crashed.'

She said thoughtfully, 'You must have married your second wife *after* you left the army.'

'I did,' I said. 'But how did you figure that?'

'Any woman who can't stand the pace of living with a man who works for an insurance company would never be an army wife.' She put dishes into the oven and closed the door. 'Dinner in thirty minutes. Time for another drink.' She came over and picked up my glass. 'For you?'

'Thanks.'

As she mixed another shakerful of martinis, she said, 'What was it like when your wife died?'

'Bloody,' I said. 'It gave me a hell of a knock.'

'I know.' She was suddenly still and when she finally turned her head towards me her eyes were bright with unshed tears. 'I'm glad you're here, Bill. You understand.' She slammed down the shaker and said passionately, 'This damned house!'

The tears came, flowing freely, and I knew what the matter was. Plain loneliness. The reserve that stopped her communicating her inner feelings to her friends melted with a stranger. She was open with me because I would be gone within days and she would probably never see me again, never have to look into my eyes and know that I knew. People who travel receive a lot of confidences from total strangers who would never dream of relating the same stories to their friends.

But there was something else. As she said, I understood: I had been there too, and this made a common bond.

So she cried on my shoulder – literally. I held her in my arms and felt her body tense as she wept. I said the usual incoherent things one says on such an occasion, keeping my voice low and gentle, until the storm blew itself out and she looked up at me and said brokenly, 'I'm . . . I'm sorry, Bill. It just . . . happened suddenly.'

'I know,' I said.

I saw her become aware of where she was and what she was doing. Her arms, which had been about me, went limp and to save her embarrassment I released her. She stepped back a pace and touched her tear-stained face. 'I must look awful.'

I shook my head. 'Jill, you're beautiful.'

She summoned a smile from somewhere. 'I'll go and clean up and then we'll have dinner. Don't expect too much: I'm a terrible cook.'

She was right. She was the only woman I knew who could ruin a frozen meal. But it was another thing that made her more human.

## II

We drove into San Martin in my car, the headlights boring holes through the quick-fallen tropical night. She sat relaxed in the passenger seat and we talked casually about anything and everything that didn't concern her or her husband. She had come back after repairing the damage and we'd had another drink before dinner and neither of us referred to what had happened.

I turned a corner and nearly rammed a large vehicle approaching on the wrong side of the road. It was only strong wrists and quick action that saved us from a collision. The car scraped through a narrow gap which I thought would be impossible and then we were on the other side and safe.

I pulled to a halt. 'What the hell!' When I looked back I saw that whatever it was had not stopped.

'A jitney,' said Jill.

'A what?'

'A jitney – a local bus.' Her voice was composed. 'They're a law unto themselves.'

'Are they, by God?' I put the car into drive and set off again, turning the next corner more circumspectly. 'It was about here that I saw your friend, Dr McKittrick.'

'He lives quite close by.'

'Stern didn't seem to think much of him.'

'Abel Stern is a dyed-in-the-wool, pre-shrunk and pre-tested conservative. He thought even David was in danger of turning communist, so what do you think he makes of Jake McKittrick?'

'Is McKittrick left-wing?'

'Labels – how I hate them.' There was a new edge to her voice, something I hadn't heard before. 'He's a human being trying to make the best of things, as most of us are.'

I said, 'You mentioned a quarrel between your husband and McKittrick. What was it about?'

'That was years ago.'

'I'd like to hear about it.'

She stirred in her seat. 'Jake was a bright boy – lots of brains but no way to use them. He lived with his parents on a smallholding in North End but there wasn't much of a future in it. David got to know him, saw the potential and sent him to the States for his education. Jake chose medicine and when he'd done his internship and taken his degree, he came back here to practise.'

'That was very good of your husband.'

'He was always doing things like that,' she said. 'Jake and David were good friends for a while, until David took an interest in politics when he came back here to live. The trouble with Jake was that his ideals didn't match up to reality. He used to say his medical practice was actually all about economics, and what was the point of curing a man of an illness if he couldn't afford to eat? He reckoned not enough money was getting to the rural communities in Campanilla.'

'He sounds a good man too,' I commented.

'You say you saw him planting corn. He was probably helping someone out so that he wouldn't have to treat them for nutritional deficiencies this time next year. Jake's a great believer in preventative medicine.'

'So what went wrong with your husband?'

'I'm coming to that. Things were all right between him and David for a while. They both wanted to knock the government off its perch and install a more equitable system. But David wouldn't go fast enough for Jake and that led to friction. I can see Jake's point of view; he worked at the grassroots and saw things David didn't. But David had a more practical view of politics. Anyway, they pulled further and further apart until finally there was a huge bust-up – it was out at El Cerco, as a matter of fact. I wasn't involved in the conversation but you've seen the place: there was no way to keep an argument like that quiet. Jake called David a wishy-washy liberal, David called Jake a political illiterate, and that was that.'

'When was this?'

'A little over two years ago, I suppose.' She sighed. 'I don't think David and Jake spoke again after that. I ran into Jake from time to time. He told me things about this island that make me ashamed. But then we drifted apart.'

I said, 'What did you think of your husband's brand of politics? Did you go along with him?'

'Of course.' She seemed surprised that I should ask. 'This government is corrupt to the core – it must be toppled.'

'And you think your husband's approach was best?'

'It wasn't the best approach,' she said wearily. 'It was the only approach. No one wants a bloody revolution, not even Jake, but that's what will happen if he keeps heading the way he is.'

I thought of David Salton, the crusading liberal with his shining armour all nicely burnished, the man who would be next Prime Minister – with the help of Mafia gambling money, if Jackson was to be believed. Either Salton was an idealist who'd inexplicably compromised those ideals for a shot at the main prize, or he was an opportunistic chancer who'd somehow been able to fool his wife for years. It didn't make sense whichever way you added it up. And then Salton was suddenly dead – most conveniently so, from the point of view of Prime Minister Conyers and his government. The whole thing stank to high heaven.

I said, 'Did your husband have any business dealings with Gerry Negrini?'

Her voice rose. 'What business would David do with a gambler? Bill, you should read some of David's speeches some time. He was dead against the gambling interests moving in when independence came, and after the election he was all set to close the casinos.'

'And yet he was personally friendly with Negrini. That's a bit odd, isn't it?'

She was silent for a while, then she said quietly, 'I did wonder about that myself. But you should understand that Gerry Negrini is a genuinely nice man, and they can be in short supply in the kind of circles David moved in. I think he liked David personally and regarded the political thing as a chance he'd have to take. He is a gambler, after all.'

'You mean he viewed the whole thing as a game.'

'Something like that.'

'Do you really think your husband would have won the election?'

'I'm certain of it.'

I drove in silence for a long way before she said, 'Bill, you've been asking a lot of questions and I've just been adding them up.' Her voice was strained. 'The answers I'm getting are beginning to frighten me. Do you really think that David was m—?'

I cut in quickly before she said it. Once you say a thing

it's impossible to unsay it, and things once said acquire a reality of their own. 'I'm not thinking anything. I'm not a policeman, Jill, and I'll be leaving soon – probably the day after tomorrow. Let it lie and don't talk about it.'

'But—'

'Forget it,' I said harshly. 'Nothing can be proved now one way or the other, and loose talk might stir up a lot of grief for a lot of innocent people. If the *Chronicle* is anything to go by, it already has. Adding things up can be a dangerous pastime: there's an infinity of wrong answers but only one right answer. Making a mistake in a thing like this could have bad consequences.'

'My God,' she said. 'My God!'

She didn't speak again until we were in San Martin amid the glaring neon and the bustling traffic. I don't know what she was thinking, but I thought that David Salton had turned out to be a very bad insurance risk.


# III


The Blue Water Casino was on Buque Island and the owners ran their own ferry service from San Martin free of charge. It was possibly the only free ride to be had on Campanilla. So the boat was crowded with tourists who grabbed at the opportunity of a sea trip *gratis* and who, in return, could be expected to drop a few dollars on the casino tables.

As we sat down I said to Jill, 'Maybe this isn't such a good idea. I mean, you coming here with your husband just dead. I wouldn't want to compromise your reputation.'

Her chin came up. 'I can look after my reputation,' she said coolly.

That settled that, so I turned to look out over the water as the boat left the quay. It didn't take long to cross Pascua Channel – maybe fifteen minutes – and the boat docked in a channel that ran right inside the casino. Even before stepping ashore we could see the crowds around the tables through plate glass walls.

We were escorted off the boat by men dressed in clothes of a vaguely nautical sort, and there were others in dinner jackets standing around, apparently doing nothing. All were broad-shouldered and tough-looking. As much money flows through a casino as through an average bank and the security must be at least as good. However, a casino is hampered by the fact that the security must not show. It would be hard to work up an atmosphere of merry, whirling high life in an environment of bulletproof glass, steel bars and tellers' cages, so security is by surveillance conducted as discreetly as possible. The hardboiled, dinner-jacketed gents were the front men, put up to show the wise that the security was indeed there. The real security would be less in evidence.

We drifted along with the crowd and, in the foyer, Jill ran into a man she knew from Salton's political group. The introductions were polite but cursory, and she only stayed for a few words. Then we went on towards the main hall and I looked back to see the man reaching for a telephone.

Business was thriving. Apart from the one-armed bandits around the walls, the casino offered roulette, blackjack, baccarat and craps, and all the tables were busy. I'm not a gambler because I'm numerate enough to know that the odds are rigged and if you play the tables consistently you'll be the loser in the long run. There are others who think differently and they're a nutty crowd.

At least the kids were losing their money with abandon, the secretaries and junior-grade executives on their first vacation outside the States who were prepared to risk a few dollars in order to buy a glamorous experience to tell the folks back home. They were having fun.

Not so the older gamblers, who placed their bets unsmilingly and, win or lose, never relaxed the passivity of their closed faces. Among these were the system players, each with his ballpoint pen and notebook close to hand, who recorded every play and bet according to whatever system they were using. These were the mathematical ignoramuses who seem to believe that the wheel has a memory and remembers what it has just done. All were serious, for gambling is a serious business with nothing funny about it, and these were the people who kept men like Gerry Negrini in Havana cigars.

We stood and watched for a while, then Jill said, 'Let's go into the bar.'

She led the way and we passed a glass cage where a teller was dispensing chips to a voluble American woman. I noted the wad of dollar bills she pushed at him, and said, 'Is American currency valid here?'

'Any currency is valid here. Have you ever known a casino turn away money?'

I grinned. 'Not often.'

We went into the bar and I saw Ogilvie perched on a stool at the far end. He saw me too but he made no move. He knew I'd give him a signal if I wanted him. Jill and I claimed a couple of newly vacated stools and ordered drinks and I blinked when the bartender told me what they cost. Sending a couple of men to Campanilla could bankrupt Western and Continental.

I jerked my head to signal to Ogilvie as Jill said, 'I can't stop thinking.'

'Relax,' I advised. 'You're making too much of it. When I'm doing a survey like this I ask lots of questions. Wait until all the returns are in before jumping to conclusions.' Ogilvie came up and I said, 'Mrs Salton, I'd like you to meet Owen Ogilvie, my associate.' I saw a bewildered look come into Ogilvie's eyes as he cottoned on, and added, 'In the office he's known as double-O seven.'

'I was christened long before James Bond was invented,' said Ogilvie. 'Nice to meet you, Mrs Salton. Mr Kemp described you to me over the telephone.'

Jill smiled. 'Do I match his description?'

'Mr Kemp has a very graphic imagination,' said Ogilvie diplomatically.

Jill looked over Ogilvie's shoulder and her face altered in recognition of someone. I swung round on my stool and saw a tall man approaching. He held out both hands. 'Jill, I'm delighted to see you. I'm sorry I was out when you phoned, but I got the message.' He lowered his voice. 'I can't tell you how shocked I am about David.'

'I know, Gerry,' Jill said. 'And thank you for your letter. It was very kind.' She indicated me. 'This is Mr Kemp and his associate, Mr Ogilvie.'

We shook hands. Negrini was very American and not at all Italianate, despite his name. His voice was cultured and his manners smooth and he bore himself with an easy assurance. I could see how he would attract women and why the Saltons had liked him. We chatted for a few minutes and I was polite about his casino. At last he said, 'I understand that you want to talk to me about something, Mr Kemp.'

'Very mysterious,' said Jill. 'He wouldn't tell me about it.' The muscles of her face tautened slightly and I knew that she was looking at Negrini in a different way from before. Suspicion is the most corrosive of all thought patterns and warps the vision so that white becomes black and black white. I would have to make sure I let her off that insidious hook before I left Campanilla.

Negrini said, 'Well, I suggest we use my office.'

'Fine.' I slid off the stool. 'Owen, will you entertain Mrs Salton until I get back?' I smiled at her. 'Don't lose too much on the tables.'

'I won't,' she promised. 'I don't play – I'm not allowed to.'

'Not allowed to – why on earth not?'

'I'm a Campanillan resident,' she said. 'There's a fine of £100 for every bet I place in a casino. That's the law.'

I went with Negrini to his office. As we threaded our way through the crowd in the gambling hall, I asked, 'Is that a fact that Campanillans aren't allowed to gamble in the casinos?'

'It is,' said Negrini. 'What Jill didn't tell you is that for every bet she places I'm fined £100 too. Neither of us can buck those odds.' We came out into the foyer. 'And you know who came up with that little legislative gem? My own friend, David Salton.'

I probed a bit. 'You must have been annoyed.'

'I was – but not too much. The natives wouldn't bring in huge sums compared with the tourists, and anyway it makes us look good. Even a gambler worries about his image.' He stopped before a door. 'Here we are.'

I noted the man lounging negligently in the corridor and was not surprised when Negrini didn't have to unlock the door. We went inside and he waved me to an easy chair. 'Drink?'

'Scotch, thanks.'

There was a sideboard with bottles and glasses laid out. He poured the drinks and said, 'In here you get it free. Out there you pay.'

'And pay and pay. You must be doing well.'

'I get along.' He handed me a glass. 'What can I do for you, Mr Kemp?'

'I represent the Western and Continental Insurance Company,' I said.

Negrini broke in. 'I have all the insurance I need.' He was smiling.

'No doubt, but I'm not selling. We insured David Salton for a lot of money. Now he's dead.'

'I see.' Negrini's eyes turned hard. 'And you're here to figure out a way of not paying.'

'Not at all. Insurance companies have been defrauded

before but not, I think, in this case. And, in any event, the chairman of the company I work for is Mrs Salton's uncle. He sent me here to look after her interests. At the present moment there is only one point at issue: did Salton commit suicide? If he did, there's a clause in the policy which precludes payment until two years after his death.'

Negrini was more relaxed. He lounged against his desk, drink in hand, and said thoughtfully, 'Yes, I can see the point of having a clause like that.'

I said, 'The circumstances being what they are, we might even waive that clause if necessary.'

'I can save you the trouble,' said Negrini. 'Salton didn't commit suicide.'

'Have you proof of that?'

He shook his head. 'No proof, but you can call me as a character witness. Salton would never take his own life – he wasn't that kind of man. He was a fighter.'

I pushed a little. 'Did he fight you?'

'What's that supposed to mean?'

'I've been reading his speeches. He didn't like casinos on Campanilla. He was tough about it, too.'

Negrini shrugged. 'All politicians have to make those sort of noises.'

'Do you think he'd have won the election, become prime minister?'

Negrini put his glass on the desk. 'I'm not a gambler, Mr Kemp. People who run casinos aren't gamblers because the edge is on their side and it's working for them all the time. Salton would have won the election, no question. To prove how certain I was of that, let me tell you that I was keeping £10,000 in that safe in easily moveable banknotes.'

'Why? What do you think he'd have done to you?'

'Judging by his speeches, I'd have been on the first plane back to the States,' said Negrini with a broad smile. 'Of course, when he died all bets were off.'

'So if Salton was . . . er . . . assisted in his death, you'd be a prime suspect.'

Negrini was no longer lounging. 'What the hell . . . ?'

'Calm down,' I said. I'd poked him a little too hard and I still had a tricky question to ask. 'How much did you contribute to his campaign funds?'

He stared at me with unfriendly eyes. 'You know, Mr Kemp, I have to admire your gall. What makes you think I gave Salton a nickel?' He snorted. 'Why should I, when he was going to run me out of the country?'

'That's what I want to know,' I said, smiling. 'It's been puzzling the hell out of me.'

Negrini grinned faintly and picked up his glass. He sipped the whisky and said, 'Who told you?'

'Does it matter? The point I'm making is that if you had something to lose by Salton's death then you wouldn't be a suspect if it turned out that he'd been murdered.'

'I get the point,' said Negrini. 'But was he murdered?'

'He died in suspicious circumstances and he had a lot of enemies.'

He pondered a little, then crossed the room and pulled up another armchair. 'All right, what do you want to know?'

'Why did you contribute to his political campaign, and how did you get him to accept? From all accounts, Salton was a fine, upstanding fellow of impeccable morals, so why did he take your filthy gambling lucre?'

Negrini narrowed his eyes. 'You can't be as naïve as all that.'

'I'm a stranger around here. Just spell it out in easy words.'

He spread his hands. 'All right, it's really quite simple. The big corporations, the off-shore funds, the banks – the whole Cardew Street crowd – they pack a lot of clout, and Conyers is their boy. They don't like the aura that comes with gambling and Campanilla has been getting itself a bit of a reputation in that regard. They thought it was starting to taint their image, and no banker likes to be thought of as a gambler. That's why they build all those marble halls to look like churches.'

I nodded. It checked out precisely with what Jackson had said. Negrini said, 'The word around town was that as soon as the election was over, Conyers was going to get his instructions to crack down on the casinos. Anti-gambling legislation was going to be pushed through and I'd be out. I had to find a horse of my own and the only one available who looked like a realistic runner was Salton. It *had* to be him.'

'So you'd actually have been squeezed by Conyers if he'd won the election.' That explained the £10,000 in banknotes: the casino owner was hedging his bets. 'But how did you persuade Salton to see things your way?'

'Salton was a realist. He didn't mind gambling as long as it was controlled. He knew that if you don't have legal gambling, you'll have illegal gambling. And he was a tough negotiator – he was going to double the gambling tax. I went along with that on the basis of half a loaf being better than none, and all that jazz. There was going to be plenty left over.'

I shook my head. 'I still don't understand why Salton fell in with you.'

'Because he wasn't after me. He was gunning for the striped-pants boys on Cardew Street.' He paused, watching to see if I was keeping up with him. 'Do you know how many Euro-dollars are funnelled through this island every year?'

'I haven't given it much thought.'

'I don't think anyone really knows,' said Negrini. 'But the lowest estimate I've heard is seven billion, and the highest was ten billion. You come to this island and all you see are tourists. There are a hell of a lot of them and that's the way I make my money. But the tourists are just the froth on the top. Any government must raise taxes, so this government taxes imports and exports. Goods are taxed coming in and people are taxed going out. You can get on to this island free but you have to pay to leave. There's a departure tax of two pounds a head for tourists and residents alike. If you buy a car here – say, an American car – you'll pay a thirty per cent tax on top of the American price. They even tax the freight charges to bring the car from the States at thirty per cent.'

I shrugged. 'So?'

'So you have a high cost of living here and a low wage structure. Salton didn't like that and wanted to change things around. He wanted to cut the import taxes on food altogether so that people could at least afford three square meals a day. To do that, he'd have to tax something else. There are billions of dollars going through here and they don't leave a cent behind in taxation – and that's why you find a couple of new banks opening up every week.'

I didn't need a degree in economics to see that this would be an attractive prospect to a certain kind of investor.

Negrini chuckled. 'You ought to hear the Cardew Street crowd talk about Salton. You'd think he was a million miles to the left of Chairman Mao. There's no one so righteous as a corporation lawyer attacked in the bottom line. Salton was going to slap a tax on the corporations, the banks and the trust funds – not enough to make them pull out, but just enough to get the money he needed for his political programme. It would be a pin-prick compared with what they pay anywhere else, but Cardew Street regarded him as a banana republic dictator about to nationalise the lot of them.'

'And you financed him.'

'For my own good.' He shrugged. 'And because I like to hear the sweet sound of corporations squealing. But God knows what's going to happen now Salton's dead. There's nobody else in the party good enough to step into his shoes.'

'Sounds like he was something of a one-man band.'

'Not quite. But the political group he built around him since coming back to the island is full of young idealists, and none of them has any real experience outside of Campanilla. It was the money that put him in pole position – without that, he wouldn't have had a look-in, especially as a white islander who'd been away for so long.'

'So Conyers wins after all.'

'Maybe – you never know with elections.'

'Thanks for everything you've told me,' I said. 'It's cleared my mind about a lot of things.'

He stood up. 'That crack you made about Salton being murdered. Do you believe that, or did you just say it to open me up?'

'I don't know,' I said slowly. I tapped the side of my head. 'There's a little man who lives in here and every so often he gives me a kick in the hunch-box. I've found him very useful in the past because he's right a lot more times than he's wrong.'

'I don't run down that kind of talent,' said Negrini thoughtfully. 'Out there on the tables I have an edge. In roulette I have a steady 5.71 per cent advantage so I know I'll come out on the right side in the long run. But there are some people who can come in and buck the tide consistently. I don't mind that either because it's good for trade – a winner encourages others to play. But they scare me because I don't know how they do it.'

'I don't suppose they do themselves. I know I don't.'

'And your little man says Salton was murdered?'

I got to my feet. 'Every time I think of Salton and murder, something goes clang. It's nothing to do with the insurance. Mrs Salton gets paid out come what may.'

Negrini was acute. 'If she didn't do it.'

'That makes no difference to us in the end. Someone

gets paid. In the event that Mrs Salton killed her husband – which, incidentally, I think highly improbable – then the money would go to the next heir after Mrs Salton. I presume he has a family.'

Negrini nodded. 'There's an older sister.' He looked me in the eye. 'I'm glad your little man doesn't think Jill did it. David was a good man and Jill is a good woman.' He took me by the arm. 'Shall we join the lady?'

'There's just one more thing,' I said. 'I've been asking a lot of awkward questions and Mrs Salton picked up the drift. To pack it small, it's possible she thinks that you were responsible for the death of her husband. I haven't told her about your contributions to Salton's fighting fund because I don't think she knew about it.'

'She didn't,' said Negrini. 'David said she wouldn't understand.'

'So from her perspective, you're an obvious candidate,' I said. 'I'll attempt to disabuse her of the notion. In case you were wondering, my little man is silent about you. You had too much to lose.'

'You're an impressive man,' said Negrini. 'Do you know that? I have a feeling about you. I have a feeling that you're a really hard-nosed bastard; that if you thought I'd killed David Salton you'd stop at nothing to pin it on me. Consequently, I'm glad you think otherwise. And you'll have my thanks if you put it right with Jill. I value our friendship.'

I liked Negrini – I liked him very much – but I had to ask out of purely personal curiosity. 'One last question,' I said. 'Are you really a front man for the Mafia?'

He smiled genially. 'If I were, would you really want to know?'

I grinned. It was an answer of sorts, and more than I had expected to get.

## IV

It was going to be a long night: I drove Jill Salton back to El Cerco. I'd expected Negrini to offer her transport but he didn't, so I was left with the job of chauffeur, a service which she blandly accepted as of right. It was a hell of a long way to El Cerco and back and I felt decidedly sour.

We talked very little during the drive. I was busy going over what Negrini had told me and she seemed to be wrapped up in her own thoughts. It was only when I stopped the car outside the gates of El Cerco and waited for a sleepy guard to open them that I said, 'That conclusion you jumped to on the drive out.'

'What about it?'

'You can scratch Mr Black.'

'Are you certain?'

'Positive. He's quite a man, isn't he?'

'I've always liked him. He and David were good friends.'

I drove through the gateway. 'Is he married?'

'To the eyeballs,' she said. 'A wife and six children.'

Most uxorious. It seemed funny to think of a Mafia chief living in domestic bliss, bringing up a string of little Negrinis and worrying about their education, just like any bowler-hatted City nine-to-fiver. Still, people don't actually live in casinos, do they?

I drove down to the little quay. As the car stopped, a man was already in the launch and starting the engine. Jill got out of the car and, after a moment's hesitation, so did I. She called out to the servant in the launch, 'I'll take her across.' He nodded and climbed up on to the quay.

She turned to me and said, 'You don't have to go back to San Martin, Bill. It's a long drive and you must be tired.'

'I must admit I wasn't looking forward to it,' I said.

'You can stay in the guest cottage – it's ready for you. It's where David and I lived while we were building the house on the island.' She turned her head and said to the servant, 'Show Mr Kemp to the cottage.'

She jumped lightly into the boat and looked back. 'I'll see you tomorrow, Bill.' Then she cast off and the boat curved away into the darkness.

I looked after it thoughtfully and turned to find the servant looking at me with veiled amusement. There wasn't much I could do about that, so I said, 'Lead on, MacDuff.'

'The name is Raymond, sir,' he said. 'This way.'

Whatever it was, it certainly wasn't a cottage – at least not the kind with the thatched roof and roses around the door. Had it been put on the property market in Britain it would have been described, in the curious English affected by estate agents, as 'a commodious gentleman's residence situated in delightful surroundings'.

There was a refreshing lack of expensive gimmickry: the beds were rectangular and not circular, the chairs were of wood and woollen fabric and not plastic stretched over chromed gas-piping, and the bath was normality itself and not carved from a single hunk of mother-of-pearl. Pyjamas and a dressing gown were laid out and there was a new toothbrush still sealed in its container.

There was also an imposing array of bottles and fresh ice in the ice bucket, so I poured myself a whisky and undressed slowly. It had been a long day. I put on the dressing gown and stood at the window, sipping the whisky and looking out over El Cerco. There was a single light shining from the house on the island and it flickered as someone moved in front of it. Presently it went out, so I finished the whisky and went to bed.

I was woken by the distant sound of an aircraft engine. Sunlight flooded the bedroom and reflections danced on the ceiling from the waters of the lagoon. The noise grew louder. It sounded as though the Lear was taking off so I got up and put on the dressing gown. By the time I reached the window it was overhead and its shadow flicked at me. I watched it climb over the sea and curve to the north. Then it went out of sight.

Somebody tapped gently at the door so I opened it and found John looking at me. He said, 'Mrs Salton asked me to look after you, sir. She hopes you slept well.'

'I slept very well.'

'Would you care for coffee, sir? And what would you like for breakfast?'

We discussed the menu gravely and then he said, 'When would you like it served, sir?'

'Shall we say half an hour?'

'Very well, sir.' He paused. 'Mrs Salton regrets that she can't see you today. She has had to go away.'

Involuntarily I looked towards the window and the sky. 'In the jet?'

'Yes, sir.'

'You don't know where she's gone?'

'No, sir.'

'All right,' I said. 'Breakfast in half an hour.'

While splashing in the shower, I wondered why Jill had found it necessary to jump off for points unknown at an unreasonably early hour after her last words had been that she would see me on the morrow. It was fairly certain that she had left Campanilla: not even a millionaire uses a Learjet for local commuting. That would be like going from London to Paris by space rocket.

I used the electric shaver thoughtfully provided, dressed and went in search of breakfast. I had just broken the yolk of a fried egg when John came in with a telephone. 'You are wanted,' he said, plugged in the instrument and laid it on the breakfast table.

I picked it up. 'William Kemp here.'

'Detective Superintendent Hanna. I understand Mrs Salton is absent from El Cerco.'

'That's right.'

'Have you any idea where she has gone, Mr Kemp?'

'I haven't.'

'I see.' He paused and I could hear a murmur of voices as he consulted with someone. He spoke again. 'A man was severely assaulted in San Martin last night. A notebook in his pocket contained your name and a telephone number. The number proved to be Mrs Salton's, unlisted.'

'Who is the man?' I noted that my knuckles had whitened as I gripped the telephone.

'He appears to be a Mr Owen Ogilvie. Do you know him?'

'Yes. I'll be in your office as soon as possible. What's your address?'

I skipped breakfast that morning. Within three minutes I was on the road to San Martin.

# FOUR

## I

Detective Superintendent Hanna was a tall, lanky local with a thin face and sleepy eyes. Though the hour was early, his Palm Beach suit was wrinkled and tired. Hanna himself looked exhausted and I suspected he had not been to bed that night. He lit a long cheroot and said, 'Is Ogilvie a friend of yours?'

'I suppose I'm his boss.' I told him what Ogilvie had been doing and why and, as I spoke, I could see that he was becoming increasingly worried. To him, this sounded as though it might be political, and good policemen hate the taint of politics. There are too many abnormal pressures, too much interference from the top and a hell of a lot of thin ice to skate over.

'Do you know anything about his movements yesterday?'

I ignored the question: I had enough of my own. 'How is he?'

Hanna drew on his cheroot and inspected the end of it. 'He was very badly beaten. Some of his ribs are broken and so is his right arm, his skull is fractured and he has many bruises and contusions. He is in hospital.'

'And he's still unconscious, otherwise you wouldn't be asking me for an account of his movements.' Hanna nodded. 'He saw your people here; he went to the *Chronicle* office where he spoke to a man called Don Jackson; he saw Dr Winstanley, who conducted the post-mortem on Salton's body; and he saw Dr Collins, Salton's physician. I last saw him at the Blue Water Casino at about midnight.'

Hanna grabbed for that one. 'Was he winning?'

I shook my head. 'He wasn't gambling.' It wasn't going to be as easy as that for Hanna. There could be many reasons for the attack on Ogilvie but he certainly wasn't mugged and robbed because he'd made a killing at the casino.

'Why did he want to see Winstanley?'

'To hear what he had to say.'

'But he knew what he'd say.' Hanna ticked off points on his fingers. 'When he came here, Ogilvie saw Inspector Rose, who showed him the police report, the pathologist's report and a transcript of the inquest. All Winstanley's evidence was there.'

'Do you believe everything that's said at an inquest? Some day, I'd like to hear your opinion of Winstanley's professional qualifications and his fitness to be a pathologist. In fact, I wouldn't mind hearing it now. That body was far gone and Winstanley was a damned sight too certain in his evidence.'

'Is that what Ogilvie thought?'

'He thought the pathologist's report was a joke,' I said flatly. 'What did you think?'

'What I think doesn't matter,' said Hanna.

'It should matter,' I retorted. 'If you had anything to do with the investigation.'

'I was called in when David Salton's body was discovered.' He spoke reluctantly. 'The fisherman who found it passed downwind of Salton's boat – he *smelled* the body. That's what made him investigate. Yes, Mr Kemp, the body was far gone, as you say.'

'And you let Winstanley get away with that?'

'I don't control the conduct of inquests and I'm not

responsible for their findings. Dr Winstanley's testimony was given under oath.'

I leaned forward with my hands flat on Hanna's desk and said, 'Do you know what I think? I think the idea was to get rid of Salton fast – rush the inquest, stop the rioting in the streets and bury Salton so he could be forgotten. And you know damned well that a policeman is not bound by the findings of an inquest. That's one legacy the English legal system has left you.'

He said stiffly, 'I obey the orders of my superiors.'

'Oh yes – Commissioner Barstow, who has Prime Minister Conyers breathing down his neck. Were you actually ordered not to press too hard?'

'I don't have to account to you for anything.' Hanna looked at me with dislike. 'And I don't see that this has anything to do with the assault on Ogilvie.'

'Then you must be bloody blind,' I said. 'Or are you deliberately not seeing? The man who might have been your next Prime Minister is found dead in mysterious circumstances, another man investigating his death is assaulted, and you don't see any connection! How did you get to become superintendent?'

Hanna took a deep breath and then relaxed. 'You can't insult me, Mr Kemp. You say you saw Ogilvie at the Blue Water Casino last night. What was he doing there?'

'He was there to see me.' I hesitated. I didn't want to bring Jill Salton into this but Hanna was sure to find out she was there and he would wonder why I hadn't mentioned it. Thus is suspicion born where none should exist. 'I was there with Mrs Salton. We had driven over from El Cerco.'

'What were you doing – gambling?'

'No. We had a few drinks in the bar.'

Hanna was politely incredulous. 'You drove all the way across Campanilla just to have a few drinks in the bar of the Blue Water Casino?'

'Not at all. I went to see Ogilvie.' Again I hesitated, but I decided that Mr Black was very well equipped to look after himself. 'And to see Mr Negrini.'

'Negrini? What about?'

'About the manner of Salton's death.'

'Would he know about that?'

'He might.'

'Yes, he might,' agreed Hanna. 'But did he?' He looked with disgust at the stub of his cheroot and extinguished it in the ashtray. 'You needn't answer that. He wouldn't tell you if he did. But I find it interesting that you should think it necessary to ask him. Did Ogilvie talk to Negrini?'

'A few words on introduction, that's all. This isn't getting us far, is it, Superintendent?'

'I'm doing all right,' he said placidly. 'Who did you see yesterday, Mr Kemp?'

'Am *I* being investigated?'

He smiled wickedly and leaned forward. 'You should never antagonise a policeman, Mr Kemp. Failure to answer reasonable questions can be construed as obstructing the police in their duties. For a foreigner, this can lead to summary expulsion from Campanilla. You wouldn't want that, would you?'

'No,' I said resignedly. He was right and I shouldn't have pushed him so hard. A copper has too many ways of hitting back – and they're all legal. 'I saw Don Jackson at the *Chronicle*, Mrs Salton, her lawyer Mr Stern, a few house servants and the pilot and engineer of Salton's plane.' I paused, remembering. 'And the pilot's wife.' I paused again and came up with one more name. 'And Jake McKittrick.'

That brought a reaction. 'Jake McKittrick! Why did you talk to him?'

I grinned. 'I asked him the way to El Cerco. He wanted me to present his condolences to Mrs Salton – that's how I know his name.'

'That's all?' Hanna was suspicious.

'That's all.'

He thought for a few moments. 'You and Ogilvie both saw Don Jackson. Together or separately?'

'Separately.'

'Why see him at all?'

'Oh, for God's sake! He runs a newspaper. It's a good source of information.'

Hanna pondered. 'All right, Mr Kemp, that will be all for the moment. I must ask you to keep yourself available for further questioning. Where are you staying? The Royal Caribbean or El Cerco?'

'The Royal Caribbean. Where can I find Ogilvie?'

Hanna scribbled on a notepad, tore off the sheet and handed it to me. 'That's the hospital. One more thing – where did Mrs Salton go this morning?'

'She didn't tell me.'

He shrugged. 'It doesn't matter. I can find out from Benning.'

'How would they know?' I asked curiously.

'All aircraft leaving Campanilla must depart from a state-licensed airport. That usually means Benning International.' He smiled. 'We have to collect the departure tax, you know.'

Plus it makes a handy method of police control, I thought. I stood up and said, 'I'll get along to the hospital.'

'There's not much point,' said Hanna. 'He's still unconscious and you probably won't be allowed to see him.'

'I'll go anyway,' I said, and left his office.

The *Chronicle*'s editor had implied that the police were unreliable in this case, being corrupted by the government. Hanna had reinforced this impression: although he declined to say so outright, he had as much as told me that Barstow, under pressure from Conyers, had soft-pedalled on the investigation. Yet there was room for hope in the lines of Hanna's questioning. He knew damned well that Salton's death was a factor to be considered when looking at poor Ogilvie.

And then there was his interest in Jill Salton's sudden flight. Twice he had asked me where she had gone, once on the telephone and again in an apparent fit of absent-mindedness that didn't fool me for a minute. It struck me that Hanna might be a fundamentally good copper who would go on doing his job in spite of instructions to the contrary from above.

I found Ogilvie looking like something recently excavated from a sarcophagus. The bits of him that weren't bandaged were blue with bruising. He breathed stertorously, but then he was lucky to be breathing at all. He was still unconscious.

The doctor in attendance was professionally cautious. When I asked him the outcome, he said, 'It's difficult to say at this stage, Mr Kemp.'

'Try to put a percentage on it.'

He shrugged slightly. 'Call it fifty-fifty.'

Fifty-fifty – a toss of a coin as to whether a man lived or died. 'I know you'll do your best, doctor.' I looked down at Ogilvie. 'He's a friend.'

## II

A blind man has no trouble finding his way about his own house because he knows from experience where the furniture is placed. Put him in a strange house and he'll stumble around, barking his shins. I was a blind man in a strange house and I needed a seeing-eye dog. So I went to see Mr Black.

I told him of Ogilvie and of my session with Hanna. He heard me out, then said disagreeably, 'So you put me in the middle.'

'You *are* in the middle. If Hanna checks on me and Ogilvie, he's certain to find out I talked to you last night. I just cut a corner by telling him before he asked.'

Negrini nodded gloomily. 'Is Hanna reopening the investigation on Salton?'

'I don't know. But if I have anything to do with it, the investigation into the assault on Ogilvie won't have a soft core, and if it leads to Salton then the chips will have to fall where they may. I need help. I need someone who knows Campanilla, who knows where the bodies are buried. I need information.'

Negrini was sour. 'And you've elected me.'

'I could have gone to Jackson at the *Chronicle*,' I said. 'But I don't like him and I don't trust him.'

'And you trust me?' Negrini laughed. 'That's one for the books. All right – what do you want to know?'

'I could stand knowing where Mrs Salton is.'

Negrini looked faintly alarmed. 'She's missing?'

'She flew the coop early this morning. Hanna said the plane would have to put into Benning before proceeding. Could you check and find out the destination?'

'I can do that. Anything else?'

'When Haslam and Philips took the plane to be serviced, they'd have to do the same. Maybe check on that flight, too.'

'That was a while ago, but it should be on record.' Negrini looked at me curiously. 'You think there's something funny about it?'

'I don't know. The devil about this kind of business is that you don't know which questions to ask, so you have to ask them all.'

I stood up and he said, 'What are you going to do now?'

'Report back to London, tell the boss that fifty per cent of the Campanillan task force is out of action.'

'Yes,' said Negrini. 'Break the news that they might have to pay out on his insurance, too.'

'That's not funny,' I said. 'Owen Ogilvie has a young wife and a one-year-old son.'

'I guess it wasn't funny at that,' he said. 'I'm sorry.'

# III

Things began to break. People came to me instead of me having to go to them, which is always a good sign. In the next two hours I had two telephone calls, both anonymous, and two callers.

I left the Blue Water Casino and went back to the hotel, where I put in a call to London and broke the news to Jolly. He even sounded dyspeptic on the phone but absorbed what had happened to Ogilvie without apparently incurring much pain, the cold-hearted bastard. He dismissed the occurrence with a few curt words and said, 'What are your findings on Salton?'

'I'm recommending immediate payment. If he committed suicide you'll never be able to prove it now and, anyway, the verdict of the inquest was death by natural causes.'

'All right,' he said because he couldn't say anything else. 'I'll have the cheque drawn. When are you coming back? We need you here.'

'When the police will let me,' I said. 'Otherwise, when I feel like it.'

'I said we need you in London.'

'And Ogilvie needs me here. What am I supposed to do? Leave him here unconscious in hospital and forget him? Besides, I haven't finished the investigation.'

His voice was acid. 'You have as far as I'm concerned. And I don't like the tone of your voice.'

'So have me fired – if you can.' He couldn't and he knew it. 'You can tell Costello that I'm looking into Salton Estates Ltd.'

I put down the telephone before he could say anything else, and fumed for a while. Then the phone rang and caused me to simmer in quite a different way.

A man said, 'Keep your nose out of what doesn't concern

you or you'll get what your friend Ogilvie got.' There was a click and then silence on the line and I listened to it for a long time, hearing only the surge of blood in my inner ear.

Gently I laid the telephone on to its cradle. The chips were down and the game had started. Up to then, everything had been misty and conjectural. Hypothetically, Ogilvie could have been hammered in a street brawl that had nothing to do with the Salton case. But now I knew that someone had something to hide, someone with flesh which would bruise as readily as Ogilvie's had. I was ready and prepared to do the bruising.

The phone rang again and I picked it up. The receptionist said, 'There's a gentleman here to see you, Mr Kemp. A Mr Roker.'

'Put him on the line.'

The earpiece clicked and buzzed, and then a man said, 'You don't know me, Mr Kemp. My name is Roker. I'm with the Caribbean Banking Corporation here in San Martin. I'd like to have a few words with you in private.'

'What about?'

'About the . . . er . . . investigation you are apparently making here,' he said delicately.

'You'd better come up.'

I went into the bathroom and splashed cold water on my face. I didn't bother wondering what Roker wanted; he'd tell me soon enough. I was drying off when there was a knock at the door and I opened it to find a smiling man dressed in the ubiquitous linen suit and carrying a panama hat. 'Roker,' he said.

'Come in, Mr Roker.' I swung open the door and continued to dry my hands. 'Take a seat – I'll be right back.' I took the towel into the bathroom and when I returned Roker was standing at the window looking down into the street.

I joined him as he said, 'More trouble.' He had lost his smile.

Down in the street there was a procession of sorts, a straggling line of people – mostly men but with a few women, some carrying banners and placards. There were a handful of white faces among the black, and they all seemed poorly dressed. They set up a rhythmic chanting but I couldn't distinguish the words.

'What's going on?'

'Politics is what's going on, Mr Kemp.' Roker's accent was American of the flat mid-west brand. 'Politics, Campanilla-style. I expect it'll get rough down there pretty soon.'

We watched in silence as the scene unfolded. The marchers were shouting at passers-by on the pavement and gesturing at them to join in. The head of the procession stopped and the street quickly became packed with a dense crowd behind him. I crossed to another window to see if I could find out the reason for the halt and saw a line of policemen strung across the road, each armed with a long baton and carrying a riot shield. The crowd remained at a distance and were chanting at the police.

I said, 'Why would the police stop a political procession?'

'Because it's illegal,' said Roker. 'Those people are breaking the law.' He joined me. 'Open the window and listen to what they're shouting.'

I did as he said and the noise swelled instantly. The crowd was shouting one word over and over and over again.

'Sal-ton, Sal-ton, Sal-ton, SAL-TON.'

Then a missile flew and I saw a couple of policemen duck. Two more followed, and suddenly the blue line charged, batons flailing, and the chanting turned into screams. More police appeared from somewhere, several carrying big-barrelled guns. The air was ripped with a series of sharp cracks, blooms of white smoke appeared and the tear gas tore holes in the thick crowd.

In minutes the street was empty, except for four still figures lying in the roadway. I couldn't tell if they were dead or not.

From behind me, Roker said, 'You were responsible for that, Mr Kemp.'

I turned and stared at him. 'How do you make that out, for God's sake?'

'I'll get to that,' he said.

'What do you mean, you'll get to that? Who the hell are you, anyway?'

'I represent the Caribbean Banking Corporation and you are working for Western and Continental Insurance of London. Right?'

'And?'

'Western and Continental own thirty per cent of Caribbean Banking, so you could say we're working for the same people.'

'I suppose you want me to welcome a new colleague,' I said sarcastically. 'You're clearly after something, so why don't you tell me what I can do for you?'

He sat down uninvited in an armchair and said blandly, 'You can go back to London.'

I studied him silently for a while, then said, 'Why should I?'

'You're a bit of grit in the works. The machine isn't running so smoothly any more.'

'You'll have to come out with something plainer than a bad metaphor,' I said.

He jerked his head at the window. 'Those people out there believe that David Salton was murdered. After he died there were riots like that, but because of the findings at the inquest things quietened down. Now someone is stirring things up again – and that someone is you.'

'How in hell would a crowd like that know about me?' I demanded. 'I've only been here two days.'

'Two days too long,' said Roker bitterly. 'The word is that

Mr Kemp says David Salton was murdered. And the word is spreading like a prairie fire.'

'I don't know who has the long ears,' I said. 'But whoever he is, he's got it wrong. Admittedly, in a couple of private conversations I might have mentioned the possibility of murder – along with a few other hypotheses such as suicide, accident and natural causes. I suppose you believe Salton wasn't murdered.'

'I don't know a goddamn thing about it,' said Roker. He spread his hands. 'But I do know what was found at the inquest. Go home, Kemp. You're rocking the boat.'

'Who sent you?'

'Does it matter? Look, Kemp, it's delicate here in Campanilla, like sitting on top of an atom bomb. If it goes off, a lot of people could get hurt.' He pointed to the window. 'You saw what just happened.'

'You make me sick,' I said. 'You're not worried about people being hurt. You just don't want anyone stabbing you in the wallet. You've got a sweet set-up here and you don't want someone messing about with the laws.'

'It makes no difference what my reasons are,' he said equably. 'You are going back to London.'

'And how are you going to make me do that?'

Roker became exasperated. 'Haven't you been listening to a single word I've been saying? Your company owns a big piece of mine. Our interests are the same. It's your duty to quit.'

'When I need a lesson in ethics I won't come to you,' I said.

Roker looked at me in wonder. 'Well, for Christ's sake!' he said softly. 'A goddamn knight in shining armour. It makes no difference. I can have you pulled out of here.'

I walked across the room, picked up the telephone and dumped it in front of him. 'You'll be just in time to catch the London office before it closes.'

He looked at the telephone but made no move to pick it up. 'Jesus!' he said. 'I can have you fired, you know.'

'There's the telephone – try it. Go back to Cardew Street and tell the gang it hasn't worked. Now, will you leave by the door or do I have to toss you out of the window?'

Roker wasn't scared, I'll say that for him. 'You're nuts,' he said. 'A crazy man – a genuine crazy man. Don't you know we can have you deported?'

I smiled. 'I wouldn't do that. You can tell Conyers that we have some very good newspapers back in the United Kingdom. A Prime Minister suppressing an investigation into the possible murder of the leader of the opposition would be just their meat. I'm surprised they haven't got on to it already. And when they get their teeth into a thing like this, they spend money like water and put a really big team on to it. They'd roast Conyers alive, and you can bet those people in the street would get to hear of it. You'd get a few burns too.'

Roker stood up. 'You're a guy who can think fast on his feet,' he conceded. 'But why you're being so hard-nosed about it I don't know.'

'If you don't know now you'll never know,' I said.

He paused at the door, twirling his hat in his hand. 'Be reasonable, Kemp. Okay, maybe I've gone about this the wrong way. But suppose I said we could do something for you? Suppose that something was the offer of a good job at maybe double your present freelance rate?'

'Since it's a supposition I'll pretend you didn't say it. Because if you did say it, I'd be inclined to break your bloody neck. Now get out.'

He shook his head and opened the door. 'They'll never believe this.'

'Wait a minute,' I said, and he turned back eagerly. 'Did you or your Cardew Street boys instigate Salton's murder?'

He flinched. 'Christ!' he said. 'You're a *really* dangerous man. You'd better watch it.' The door slammed.

I stood there looking at the closed door then slowly lifted my hands and found they were trembling. I picked up the telephone and put it back where it lived and then, on impulse, picked up the handset and rang Negrini.

'Anything for me?'

His voice was pained. 'Give me time.'

'There's something else. When next we meet – and I don't know when that will be – I'll want to know everything there is to know about a man called Roker of the Caribbean Banking Corporation. Can do?'

'Okay, Mr Kemp,' he said resignedly.

I smiled. 'Since we're going to be working together you can call me Bill.'

He burlesqued a Western accent. 'Well, Bill, I'll allow that's mighty nice of you.'

I smiled again as I put down the handset and picked up my coat; I could get along with Negrini. As I was leaving the room the phone rang again. I don't know what Bill Kemp was doing to the political life of Campanilla but he was certainly increasing the profits of the Campanilla Telephone Company.

I went back. 'Kemp here.'

'Well now, Mr Kemp, would you like to know a little thing about David Salton?' The voice was deep, rumbling and American, but not very cultured.

'What about him?'

'Come on, man, you must surely be bugged,' he said reproachfully. 'And that's why you don't get no name, neither.'

I hadn't thought about anyone bugging the telephone but I certainly wouldn't put it past Hanna. I said, 'So it's a stand-off.'

'It's hot today, man. Supposin' you took a walk, you'd raise quite a sweat and maybe get thirsty. Now, if you were around the Rainbow Rooms near the market on the water-front, you'd likely drop in for a nice cool drink – say, a Cuba Libre. I hear the Rainbow Rooms are real popular.'

'All right,' I said. 'When?'

'Say now? I get thirsty too, so you order two drinks.' The voice sharpened. 'But if you've been tailed, man, you'll have to drink them both.'

'I'll be there,' I promised, and put down the phone.

## IV

I seemed to be gaining a degree of popularity. When I reached the hotel lobby, I was hailed by Jake McKittrick. He had lost the look of a field labourer and appeared to be what he really was: a professional man. He wore the standard linen suit and carried a black bag.

'Mr Kemp, I was hoping to find you.'

'What can I do for you, Dr McKittrick?' I glanced at my watch. 'I have an appointment – rather urgent.'

'I won't keep you long,' he said.

I peered into the lounge, which seemed moderately empty. 'All right. Let's go in there.'

We sat at a table and McKittrick said, 'So you talked about me to Mrs Salton.'

'I passed on your message.'

'And she told you about me?'

'As did Mr Stern,' I said dryly.

McKittrick smiled ruefully. 'I can guess what he said. What was Mrs Salton's attitude?'

'You'll have to ask her,' I said. 'I'm not one to pass on gossip.'

He nodded. 'That's an honest answer. I had that coming.'

He paused. 'The word is going around that you think David Salton was murdered. True?'

I wagged my head wearily: he'd obviously been talking to the same snitch as Roker. 'Untrue. It was just one of a number of suggestions that happened to come up. The medical evidence at the inquest was hardly satisfactory.'

'I can accept that, I suppose.'

'I don't give a hoot in hell whether you accept it or not,' I said feelingly, adding, 'And I'd like to know who's been eavesdropping on my private conversations.'

'It's immaterial, of course,' said McKittrick. 'What matters is what people *think* you think. That must be straightened out or there's going to be trouble. Suppose you make a statement to the *Chronicle* that Salton wasn't murdered?'

I stared at him. 'I can't do that.'

'Why not?

'Because I don't know that he wasn't. There's no evidence one way or the other.'

McKittrick was waspish. 'There's such a thing as being too honest.' He leaned forward and said urgently, 'Mr Kemp, there's trouble coming and people are going to die on the streets. Campanilla is coming to the boil because of this rumour. There's already been violence.'

'I saw some of it,' I said, and pointed to the window. 'Just out there.' It had crossed my mind that Roker might somehow have laid that little performance on especially for my benefit, but now another thought occurred to me. 'I don't suppose you stirred that one up, did you?'

McKittrick appeared genuinely shocked. 'I'm a doctor,' he said. 'My job is to heal people, not to get them killed or hurt. Where did you get that idea – from Stern?'

'No, but Mrs Salton told me of your quarrel with her husband and said that since then you'd gone even further towards radicalism. In fact, she called it a bloody revolution.'

That hit him. 'She said that of *me*?'

I offered him a concession. 'She said it might not be what you wanted, but you were heading that way despite yourself, maybe.'

'Nobody wants that kind of revolution – well, I don't, at least.'

'But there are some who do?' I studied him. 'It seems to me you've got yourself into a trap, Dr McKittrick. You'd have done better staying with Salton. If he'd lived, he'd have been the leader of the next government, by all accounts. His way *was* better than yours. And now you're out on a limb.'

'Let's forget about me,' he said tightly. 'And keep to the point at issue.'

'Look, I can do this much for you,' I said. 'I spoke to London this morning and recommended that Mrs Salton's claim be met immediately. The cheque is being drawn now. If I gave that fact to the press, perhaps it would cool things a bit.'

'Would you do that now?' he said eagerly.

'I don't see why not. I'll tell Jackson straight away.'

Jackson was acid on the phone. 'No connection with Western and Continental, Mr Kemp. Isn't that what you told me? You had me fooled there for quite a while – until I heard a couple of things last night. Seen the *Chronicle* this morning?'

'I haven't had time.' I picked idly at the printed telephone instructions pasted up in the hotel lobby booth.

'I'll bet you haven't,' he said. 'But it makes good reading. What do you want now?'

'I called to tell you that I've recommended Mrs Salton's claim be met in full. Western and Continental in London agree and are following through.'

'Can I quote you on that?' he asked quickly.

'Mr Jackson, I wouldn't tell you anything you couldn't quote.'

'Is that so?' He sighed. 'So Jill Salton's the richer by a

million and a quarter bucks. The rich get richer and the poor get poorer, ain't that so, Mr Kemp?'

'Cracker barrel philosophy doesn't suit you,' I said.

I was about to put down the phone when Jackson said hurriedly, 'Don't hang up, Kemp. Stay on the line a second.' There was a clatter and a babble of background voices for a couple of minutes, then Jackson said, 'Perhaps you'd like to give me your views on something, Mr Kemp?'

'Depends on what it is,' I said cautiously.

'Perhaps you'd like to comment on the death of your assistant, Ogilvie?'

I felt as though someone had belted me in the stomach. For a few seconds I couldn't speak. 'When did it happen?'

'About ten minutes ago. I had a man at the hospital and it's just come through.' He waited for me to speak and, when I said nothing, he quacked, 'Well, Mr Kemp, anything for attribution?'

'You can say I expressed my deep regrets,' I said. 'Apart from that, no comment.'

I put down the phone and stared at the printed instructions. Ogilvie had been married less than two years and I had introduced him to his wife Janet, the daughter of an old family friend I'd become reacquainted with after quitting the army. They had been totally and ridiculously happy, a salving balm to those like me who had not found happiness in marriage. Only six days earlier I'd had dinner with them – Janet taking special care because of my influence at Owen's workplace – and she had talked about the future, the large and happy future that stretched ahead.

I don't know how long I stared blindly and bitterly at that oddly meaningless set of words, but presently McKittrick opened the glass door and said anxiously, 'Are you all right, Mr Kemp?'

I turned and stepped out of the booth. 'A friend has just died.'

'Mr Ogilvie? I'm sorry.'

'What do you know about it, McKittrick?' My voice was edgy.

'Nothing,' he said. 'Nothing at all.'

'You'd better be right,' I said coldly. 'For your own sake.'

# FIVE

## I

By the time I got down to the market, the feeling of numbness was beginning to wear off, replaced by a growing anger. Owen Ogilvie had died because Salton had died, and people were trying to push me around, to manipulate me. Roker tried it, McKittrick tried it and, I suspected, Hanna would try it next time I saw him. It only needed Stern to attempt a bit of leverage and that would more-or-less complete the roster. And apparently they all had different motives.

The only people who hadn't twisted my arm were Negrini and Mrs Salton – and she wasn't around to try.

The market sold local produce. At one time it was probably a practicable proposition, but with the rise of the supermarket it had declined into a tourist trap. There were more stalls selling gimcrack souvenirs than there were selling tomatoes, and more tourists than grocery shoppers. Still, it made a bustling spectacle for any traveller's camera.

I found the Rainbow Rooms, a series of cool caverns, dim after the hard sunlight. About half the tables were occupied; I selected an empty one with two chairs and sat down. A waiter bustled up. 'Yes, sir?'

'Rum and coke – twice.'

He brought the drinks in tall, ice-tinkling glasses and I sipped the cold liquid, spinning it out over, perhaps, fifteen minutes and brooding over my next move. I still had to look into the affairs of Salton Estates Ltd, which would mean coming up against Stern again.

I had just about given up on my mysterious telephonous friend and was reaching over for the other glass when the waiter whisked it from the table. 'This way, sir,' he said, and I got up and followed him into the dark recesses. He stopped at a shadowed alcove and put the glass on a table.

A bass voice rumbled, 'Another drink for Mr Kemp.'

The waiter went away and I sat down facing a giant of a man. 'I guess you thought I wouldn't make the scene,' he said. 'You were clear – no tail.'

I looked around at nearby tables and realised we were isolated from view, but I was somewhat reassured by his chubby face and merry, twinkling eyes, and he wore a red shirt patterned with white flamingoes. Then he leaned forward and suddenly his eyes were not so merry. 'But you were rapping with Jake McKittrick. What about?'

'Why the hell should I tell you?' I asked equably.

He laughed and his eyes twinkled again. 'Good question. You been causing quite a stir on this little old island.'

'You're not the first to tell me that.'

'I guess not. You were with the fuzz this morning. Give you much grief?'

'I didn't come here to discuss my affairs with you. What's this about Salton?'

'Well, man, that's like . . . delicate. What about a bill?'

'Sorry, I don't know what you're talking about.'

'I'm talking about bread, man – dough. One hundred dollars.' He stopped. 'Christ, I forget where I am. This British money'll send me nuts. Forty British quids.' He flashed me a grin. 'You do say quids?'

'It's usually in the singular,' I said. 'But not this time.' I began to get up. 'I receive information but I don't pay cash for it – especially not to someone I don't know.'

He leaned forward and put a meaty hand on my shoulder. 'Fold the gams, man.' I assumed he meant I was to sit back down, so I did. 'Make social. You can call me Joe.'

The waiter put a glass in front of me. He didn't wait to be paid but went without asking. Joe said, 'They're converting into dollars here next year. Will I be glad.'

I sipped from the glass and said, 'Salton.'

He looked up at the ceiling. 'Pesky as that blue-ass fly.' Suddenly he became brisk. 'Okay, Mr Kemp, I'll give you a freebie just because I like you. You go see Leotta Tomsson, ask *her* what she knew about David Salton. Ask her who pays the rent on that silk-lined pad.'

'Leotta Tomsson. What address?'

'For one bill, man?'

I laughed. 'Nothing doing.'

'A hard-nosed Britisher is worse than any damn Yankee,' he complained, but he didn't seem too put out. 'Maybe I'll tell you. Let's talk a while first.'

'What about?'

'About what you think you're doing here.'

'Investigating an insurance case,' I said. 'I've just about finished.'

'True?'

'Read about it in the *Chronicle* tomorrow.'

'I wouldn't believe a thing in that piece of . . .' He tailed off, then took a slug from his glass. 'You level about Salton being croaked?'

'For God's sake!' I said. 'I don't know where all this has come from. This bloody island is worse than an echo chamber.'

'Folks are getting stirred up,' he observed.

'There was a riot outside my hotel this morning. Did you have anything to do with that?'

He laughed richly. 'Why should I beat a drum for a liberal like Salton – a white one, at that?'

'There *was* a murder,' I said. 'But it wasn't Salton.'

'Ogilvie? That cat's died?'

So he knew about the attack on Owen. I stared into the red depths of my glass. 'This morning. Anything to tell me about it?'

'Nix.' He paused and nodded his head across the room. 'That guy might tell you something if you ask him nice. I told you this place was real popular.'

I looked over at a small group on the other side, fussing around a central figure. 'Who is it?'

'Conyers. The big ugly guy in the middle.'

The Prime Minister of Campanilla was tall and imposing and had the telltale belly of the prosperous man. His acolytes had significant bulges under their armpits. I said, 'You don't approve?'

Joe sighed. 'He's lived in Government House so long he's become part of the establishment. He's what the liberals call a successful member of the native intelligentsia.'

Joe's voice was sardonic and suddenly more cultured, and I wondered about him. 'And he's owned. Man, is he owned!' His bitterness seemed to etch the dark air.

'Cardew Street?'

Joe nodded and took another drink.

I said, 'I was reading one of Salton's speeches. He talked about Conyers and his hired bully boys. Do you know anything about that?'

'Conyers don't need no heavy gang – he's got the whole of the fuzz.' I noted that Joe had reverted to type. 'But it's like this, man. If it's a matter of leaning on a guy when the fuzz can't do it, then the word goes out. Not that Conyers has a private army or anything – just enough to be useful.'

'You think that's what happened to Ogilvie?'

Joe shrugged. 'Don't ask me. Ask that cat over there.'

'Maybe I will,' I said grimly.

'And maybe you'll wind up in marble city with Ogilvie and Salton. Mr Kemp, why don't you go home?'

'I thought you wanted me to see this woman, Leotta Tomsson?'

'A guy can change his mind, can't he? Look, for a pinko you seem to be a nice guy. You don't stand for no shit and you don't give none. I'd hate to have to send white lilies.'

'It doesn't matter,' I said. 'I can find her from her name.'

The waiter trotted by and snapped his napkin so that it cracked softly. Joe stood up. 'I gotta go,' he said. 'The heat's arrived. Gregory Plaza, number 432. Marshalltown.'

It seemed impossible that so big a man could move so quickly and quietly. I stood up and looked around but he had disappeared, so I moved towards the street, where a car was pulling up outside. It looked official and I laid a bet with myself, which I won when the rear door opened and Superintendent Hanna got out.

He straightened up, then saw me and beckoned, so I went to meet him. 'You can be a hard man to find,' he said.

'I didn't know you were looking. Have you come to tell me about Ogilvie?'

'You know?'

'Jackson told me.'

'He probably knew before I did,' said Hanna sourly. He took a big handkerchief from his pocket and mopped his brow. 'I want to talk to you and I might as well do it here. I could do with a drink.'

'All right,' I said, so he signalled to the driver of the car and we went inside and found a table. Hanna's eyes were even sleepier and he seemed drawn. 'You look tired.'

'My wife's not seeing much of me,' he said.

'Got any kids?'

'Three – two boys and a girl.' He looked out into the street at the empty space where his car had been. 'Sorry about Ogilvie. About the arrangements: there'll have to be a post-mortem.'

'It had better not be Winstanley,' I said coldly.

'It won't be. What about afterwards?'

'The body had better be shipped back to England. Western and Continental will pick up the tab.'

'I can see to that,' he said.

'Have you got any further in finding out who did it?'

'Not much.' He pointed. 'It happened just there.' I looked at the pavement 'He came back on Negrini's private ferry just before one in the morning. He walked up past here and then he was attacked. There were no witnesses but I'd say it was a gang bust – no one man could do that to another.'

'Any ideas of who or why?'

'No evidence of anything.'

'That wasn't my question,' I said. 'I asked if you had any ideas.'

Hanna looked at me with lazy, half-closed eyes, then turned as the waiter came up. 'I'll have a cold beer,' he said. I ordered another rum and coke. When the waiter went away Hanna said abruptly, 'You're keeping bad company, Mr Kemp.'

'Who?' I asked, and jerked my thumb over my shoulder. 'Conyers?'

Hanna turned and surveyed the room, then looked at me. 'You've been talking to Joe Hawke,' he said. 'Gerry Negrini may be Mr Black but Joseph Leroy Hawke is Mr Black Power. What did he want?'

'He seemed to think I'd proved that Salton was murdered,' I said. 'I disillusioned him.'

'Lots of people seem to have got that idea. It's causing us trouble.'

'I saw some of it this morning outside the hotel. Your policemen weren't very nice.'

'Those people were breaking the law,' said Hanna. 'Do you approve of lawbreakers?'

'No,' I said. 'But I think there are some damn fool laws.'

Hanna nodded. 'I'm a cop and I'm employed to uphold the law – all of it. I can't uphold those bits and pieces I approve of and let the rest go. Sure, there are foolish laws and I like them less than the average man because they cause me personal trouble. If I don't like a law, I have to act like an ordinary citizen – use my vote to get rid of the politician who made it and elect another to change it.'

I said carefully, 'It seemed to me that the coppers I saw this morning were working on a hair trigger. There was no real violence before they started in on the crowd. It looked to me like what is known in Chicago as a police riot.'

'You're right,' said Hanna tiredly. 'There are good cops and bad cops. But don't blame me for it.'

'I'm not,' I said. 'I'm just making light conversation until I find out why the hell I'm sitting here.'

The waiter came with the drinks and I paid him. Hanna said, 'Joe Hawke.'

'All right, let's talk about Joe Hawke. He didn't seem much to me.'

Hanna smiled sleepily. 'So he gave you his Harlem soul brother routine. He likes to appear stupid but he's about as stupid as Albert Einstein. He's a good lawyer but he doesn't practise here because he has no local qualifications. He's a revolutionary – not one of your talk-talk boys, but an activist.'

'Why don't you deport him back to the States?'

'Can't. He's a Campanillan citizen. Went to the States when he was eight years old. The State Department tossed him back when he got too troublesome. So I'm stuck with him and I have him on a list.'

'What's he done to be on a list?'

'Not a thing,' said Hanna, and took a deep draught of

cold beer. 'I have him there on principle.' He put down the glass. 'What do you know of our local politics?'

'I seem to be learning more by the hour. Where is Joe Hawke on the political spectrum?'

'Look, things have changed since you Brits gave up on the empire. There's just as much radicalism in the colonies as anywhere else.'

'Former colonies.'

'Former colonies,' he conceded. 'Hawke is a radical, fiercely anti-government. He joined the People's Party and went up fast. The PP was pretty radical before, but he's pushing it towards revolution. That's why he's on my list – because revolutions mean blood. Besides,' he added ironically, 'they're against the law.'

I thought about that, and about Hanna. The police uphold the laws, which means upholding the *status quo*. Those who want to break the mould of things as they are and shape what they perceive to be a better world tend to come into conflict with the police and regard them as enemies. The police, naturally enough, resent being called fascist pigs and there is an instant polarisation. I suppose in the event of civil disturbance in Moscow, the police engaged in defending the Communist *status quo* would also be called fascist pigs. A funny thought.

I said, 'What about McKittrick?'

'He was with Salton and the Campanillan Liberal Party. But he fell out with Salton and joined the PP at about the same time as Hawke. He and Hawke don't get on too well: McKittrick thinks he's too much of a wild man, while Hawke regards McKittrick as soft.'

'And Conyers?'

Hanna smiled. 'Conyers leads a conservative government – the businessmen's party. The corporate interests would much rather deal with him than with the Liberals.' He shrugged. 'What did Joe Hawke really want?'

'It's a funny thing about Joe,' I said. 'I've come under pressure from some people suggesting I leave. One of them was pretty insistent about it. But you know what? I do believe Joe Hawke wants me to stay. How do you account for that?'

'Because you mean trouble,' said Hanna. 'And he thrives on it. Those people on the streets this morning were the Liberals. They think Salton was murdered and they want to pin it on someone – preferably Conyers. Hawke doesn't mind that at all.' He scratched the side of his jaw. 'At the same time, now that Salton's dead, Conyers will win the election – and that'll suit Joe Hawke too. He'd much rather there was a right-wing government to have a go at.'

'Doesn't his own party have a chance?'

'Not a hope. Despite the name, there's not enough popular support. There might be, though, given a few more years of Conyers. The opposition will have to come from somewhere – the Liberal Party's a spent force without Salton.'

There was a sudden burst of laughter and cheering from the Conyers table and Hanna glanced across at them. Then he downed the last of his beer and gave me a meaningful look. 'Policemen aren't supposed to talk politics, and I haven't been talking politics. Peace-keeping is my job and, as a realist, I've been assessing the situation. You understand what I mean?'

'I understand.' I felt better about Hanna. 'Roker threatened me with deportation. Does he have that much pull?'

'Oh, sure. You're an embarrassment to the government.'

'And how do you feel about that?'

'What I said this morning still stands. I'm conducting an investigation into murder, and you're to hold yourself available for further questioning.'

'In spite of what Commissioner Barstow may say?'

Hanna frowned. 'Leave Barstow to me.'

I took a deep breath. 'Thanks.'

'For what? I've not done a thing.'

I grinned at him. 'Thanks, anyway.' My instinct had been right. Hanna was a good copper who rebelled at seeing an investigation swept under the rug for political reasons. But I wouldn't give a bent penny for his chances of promotion.

He stood up. 'Thanks for the drink, Mr Kemp. I'll buy the next when I have more time.'

I walked out with him and we stood on the pavement outside the Rainbow Rooms. 'Tell me,' I said. 'Did you discover where Mrs Salton went?'

'New York,' he said simply. 'What are you going to do now?'

'I've already advised my office to settle with Mrs Salton, so that's out of the way. Now I have to check into Salton Estates Ltd. My firm has a big stake in the business.'

He nodded. 'As long as you stick to that, Mr Kemp, you'll be all right. But don't get underfoot on this Ogilvie thing – that's my job.'

'Okay, Superintendent. But if I stumble over the bastard by chance, you're likely to have another corpse on your hands.'

His eyes flickered and he shook his head deliberately. 'No. You shout "copper" and I'll come running. Promise?'

'All right, I promise.' I took the business card he handed me.

'I wouldn't want to take you in for breaking the law,' he said, and turned on his heel and walked away, leaving me standing in the hot sun.


## II


Marshalltown was a plushy development at the base of Spanish Point, the eastern trunnion of Campanilla's bell. The houses were big and stood in well-manicured grounds and looked as though they'd been plumbed for hot and cold running champagne. The school here was no corrugated iron shack but a modern building, pleasantly tree-shaded. Most of the kids on the green playing fields had white faces.

Gregory Plaza was a spanking-new high-rise apartment block with its own golf course on one side and a private beach on the other. I parked the car and went in, through the foyer and out the other side to the beach. The long white combers surged up on to the pink sand with a soft roar, bearing with them the joyous surf-riders. I looked at the recumbent figures scattered over the beach, each flanked by the inevitable bottle of sun tan oil. Any one of them could have been Leotta Tomsson.

I went back into the foyer and pressed the button for the lift and then instructed it to take me to the fourth floor. Number 432 was an uninformative door with a bell push which I pressed to hear soft chimes. It was pleasantly cool in the corridor and there was nothing to be heard but the soft and expensive sighing of the air conditioning.

There was a click and the door opened three inches. 'Yes?' enquired a warm, female voice.

'Miss Tomsson. My name is Kemp. I'd like to see you for a few minutes.' She was invisible behind the door, which was secured by a burglar chain.

'What about?'

'I represent a London insurance company and . . .'

'I have enough insurance.' The door began to close.

I rammed the palm of my hand flat against it. 'Hold it! I'm not selling.' The door began to open again and stopped with a jerk at the regulation distance of three inches as the chain tightened. 'I want to talk to you about something else.'

'What?'

'David Salton, to start with.'

There was nothing but silence from the other side of the door. I waited a while then said, 'Miss Tomsson?'

'What about David Salton?'

'You tell me.' I glanced up and down the quiet corridor. 'But maybe you'd prefer to do it in private.'

There was another calculating pause. 'All right,' she said, and the chain rattled as she took it off. I pushed gently on the door and it swung open and I saw Leotta Tomsson walking away, silhouetted against the light from a big window overlooking the sea. I closed the door and followed her.

When she swung around to face me she took my breath away. Six feet of unadulterated loveliness – copper-gold skin, tawny-streaked blonde hair, hazel eyes and the physique of an athlete. She was as unlike Jill Salton as it was possible to be. Although both were beautiful, to compare them would be ridiculous, like asking which is the more beautiful, a perfect tree or a perfect sunset. I was learning a lot about David Salton and I gave him full marks for his taste. I also suspected I was looking at the cause of the quarrel with his wife on the day he disappeared.

Leotta wore a short white robe and fidgeted nervously with the belt. 'What did you say your name was?'

'Kemp. William Kemp.' I looked at her consideringly. 'Don't the jungle drums reach this far? You must be the only person on Campanilla not to have heard of me.'

'I haven't been out for a couple of days,' she said. 'There wasn't anything on the radio.'

I smiled. 'I haven't got that far, Miss Tomsson, but I dare say I will.'

Her fingers plucked at the belt. 'Well,' she said. 'What do you want?'

I looked around the apartment, which was big and simply furnished in an austerely expensive way. I thought I could detect a sort of incense – the scent of burning five-pound notes – but I always have that illusion in the vicinity of the rich. 'May I sit down?'

'I'm sorry,' she said. 'Of course.'

She sat on the edge of a settee while I sank into a starkly simple chair. 'I represent the Western and Continental Insurance Company of London. I'm here to look into the death of David Salton because a lot of money is involved. This is just routine, you understand.'

She nodded. 'But why come to me? I'm not a beneficiary.'

'Not with Western and Continental,' I said. 'I know that. But I wondered if, perhaps, Mr Salton had taken out insurance with another company in your favour.'

There was a flash of something that may have been anger in her eyes.

'So you thought that, did you?'

'You were friendly with Mr Salton?'

The corners of her generous mouth quirked for a moment, then she said stonily, 'I was.'

I said, 'Miss Tomsson, don't get me wrong. I have no interest in this matter other than safeguarding the insurance company. I leave moral judgements to others. Your association with Mr Salton is irrelevant to me – unless it had something to do with the cause of his death. How do you think he died?'

She bent her head and looked down at her hands. 'Foully,' she whispered.

'Do you mean foul play?'

'I mean the way it happened.' She lifted her head and her face was paler. 'To die like that. To die and to rot adrift at sea.' She looked out of the window at the sharply etched blue horizon. 'I haven't swum in the sea since it happened.'

I kept my voice casual. 'Do you know Mrs Salton?'

She kept her face averted. 'I've not met her. I've seen her around.'

'Did she know about you?'

'I don't know. I don't think so. David wasn't likely to tell her.' She turned her face towards me. 'David was a *good* man,' she said quietly. 'I wouldn't want his reputation dragged through the dirt. Must this come out into the open?'

'Not through me,' I said. 'Others I can't tell about.'

She looked a little surprised, and then frowned. 'By the way, how did you know about me?' she asked. 'Who told you?'

'A man called Joe Hawke.'

She rose abruptly and walked to the window, where she stood looking down at the beach. 'Hawke will use it,' she said flatly. 'He always hated David and everything he stood for. He'll use this when it suits him.'

'Why should he?'

'It's a weapon, a political weapon. He'll use it to smear David.'

'But David Salton's dead.'

'What difference does that make? Mud sticks. It will stick to anybody who was close to David. It will stick to the party.'

I nodded. Perhaps that was the way it was. And Hawke was using me as a stalking horse: it would be better for him if the disclosure came from someone who wasn't Joe Hawke – someone already looking into Salton's affairs and known to be politically neutral. If news of a moral flaw in the great David Salton was leaked by Hawke, then it would tend to be discounted because everyone knew Hawke had an axe to grind. But if it came from someone else entirely, someone who had never even met the Prime Minister-in-waiting, then it would pack a much stronger punch.

I decided then and there that Hawke was going to be unlucky, because I was going to keep my mouth shut. No one was going to use me as a patsy.

'When did you get to know Salton?' I asked.

'Five years ago, in New York. He helped me to find a job.'

'What sort of job?'

'He introduced me to the head of a modelling agency.'

She would make a good model. 'Five years ago?' I raised my eyebrows. 'That was before he was married.'

She returned to the settee and sat down with a fluid grace. 'He met me and Jill Salton – Jill Pedlar, as she was then – in the same week.' With a curious gesture of resignation she said, 'He *married* her.'

She reached out to the table beside the settee and picked up a soft pack of cigarettes. She didn't offer them, but took one out and lit it with a heavy gold lighter, which she then snapped shut with a jerk of her wrist.

'I got this,' she said, waving the lighter dismissively. 'The inscription is particularly touching.'

She tossed it in my direction and I caught it one-handed. It was as heavy as it looked. I inspected the inscription; it read, '*L – Always yours. D.*'

I didn't know what to say to that so I leaned forward and put the lighter down on the table again. The comment about the inscription had been sarcastic, but other than that, I couldn't detect any bitterness towards her lover who had married someone else.

I said, 'Are you a Campanillan?' She nodded assent. 'When did you come back here?'

'Two years ago.' The corners of her mouth turned down. 'Maybe you think I shouldn't have come running when he called.'

'I'm not thinking anything,' I said. 'I'm just trying to see the situation as a whole.'

'David was a hell of a man,' she said. 'So when he whistled I broke into a gallop, even though I knew it would do no good in the end. I loved that man. When I heard he was dead I broke down and cried for two days.' She looked at me dry-eyed. 'Did Mrs Salton cry for him?'

I looked down at the carpet. 'I've seen her cry.'

'I used to watch her,' said Leotta. 'I knew about her but

she didn't know about me. That was something I used to hug to myself, a sort of cheap triumph.' She looked a little sick as she gazed inside herself. 'So I watched her, cool as ice, and tried to figure what David saw in her and what he saw in me. In the early days I used to ask him about her but he wouldn't talk. He never talked of her, so I stopped asking.'

'So you still think she doesn't know about you?'

'She might, she might not. I don't care either way.'

'And what opinions do you have on Salton's death?'

'I think it was as they said at the inquest. He had a heart attack.'

'Did you know he'd had one before?'

She looked at me for a moment, startled, then stubbed out the cigarette. She waved her hand about the apartment. 'He had it here – in the bedroom. I thought my heart was going to stop too.'

I frowned and thought that must have been awkward for her. 'What did you do?'

'I telephoned his doctor, of course. What else could I do?' She narrowed her eyes. 'Oh, I see what you mean. Well, it was a bit tricky and we had to skirt round the edges a bit. Before the doctor arrived, David was able to talk so I got some clothes on him and we made up the story that he'd had the attack in the elevator. I stopped it at my floor and got him into this apartment. It was the only thing we could think of.'

'Ingenious,' I commented. 'But what would he be doing here at all?'

'Going up to the eighth floor, of course. To see Mr Stern, his lawyer.'

It was my turn to be startled. 'Stern lives here? Does *he* know about you?'

'I don't know,' she said. 'Most likely not. David wouldn't have talked about me.'

I thought about it, then said, 'And Mrs Salton – what about her?'

'I took good care not to be around when she got here,' said Leotta. 'I stood the other side of the golf course and watched them take David away in the ambulance, and I only came back when everyone had gone. She telephoned me three or four times but I put on an accent and pretended I was the maid and that Miss Tomsson was out. Miss Tomsson was always out when Mrs Salton called. Then she wrote me a letter thanking me for helping David and after that I heard nothing more.'

'I see.'

'That was the last time I saw David.'

I stared at her. 'You mean you haven't seen him for nearly eight months?'

'That's right. He phoned me a few times but I didn't see him. We both figured it wouldn't be any good for either of us.'

I said uncertainly, 'I don't quite understand.'

'You're not that dumb,' she said. 'David didn't bring me from New York just for my beautiful brains. When he had that heart attack we were – you know – making love. After it happened, Dr Collins told him to cut out sex for a while.' She smiled thinly. 'I often wondered how his wife felt about that. I knew how I felt.' She shrugged. 'Anyway, David thought that if he came here he wouldn't be able to help himself and it was best to keep away.'

'You've been very frank, Miss Tomsson,' I said. 'Thank you.'

I stood up and she said, 'There's no point in telling lies now, is there, Mr . . . I'm sorry, I've forgotten your name already. I'm no good at names.'

'Kemp.' As she walked with me to the door I said, 'What are you going to do now?'

'The rent's paid on the apartment until the end of the

quarter. I might stay until then. I might go back to the States, although I think not. I might go to London – I've never been over there.' She drooped a little. 'There are too many memories here and in New York.'

I took out my wallet and extracted a card. 'If you come to England, look me up,' I said. 'I know some people in the modelling game who might help you.' I didn't, but I would by the time she landed at Heathrow. 'No strings, Miss Tomsson.'

She took the card. 'Thank you, Mr Kemp. I appreciate the gesture and I might take you up on it.'

I regarded her. Like Jill Salton, she was a physically healthy specimen glowing with vitality but again, as in Jill Salton, I detected a weariness of spirit, a guttering of the inner flame. Abruptly, I said, 'How many times have you been out of the apartment in the last three weeks?'

'A couple of times, to get groceries. Why do you ask?'

'Listen – what's done is done,' I said. 'I don't pretend to know what happens to the dead, but I do know that the living must go on living. Get out of here, Miss Tomsson. Get out and live a little. You'll find it comes easier with practice.'

'You're a nice man, Mr Kemp,' she said. 'Do you know that? Not everyone would have that much regard for a person like me.' There was an undertone of self-contempt and her eyes had gone misty.

'For Christ's sake!' I said. 'All you did was to make a man a little happier. Monogamy doesn't suit some men. We might try to blink it but it's one of the facts of life, and it seems that David Salton was one of those men. You did the decent thing and you didn't flaunt yourself before Mrs Salton and so nobody got hurt. Don't blame yourself for anything.'

She put her hand on my arm. 'You are a nice man. Maybe I will look you up in London.' She was as tall as I am and her eyes were level with mine. She blinked a few times and then turned away, ostensibly to open the door.

I left her apartment and went down to the ground floor, where I paused for a few minutes to look out over the beach. The surfers were still relentlessly riding the waves and the bronzed bodies were still lying in the same positions under the hot sun. The only change was that the level of sun tan oil in the bottles had gone down a quarter-inch.

# III

'Mr Salton owned quite a bit of land on Campanilla,' said Idle. He pointed to a large map on the wall of his office behind a chair occupied by Stern. 'The parts that are shaded in colour.'

Idle was about thirty-five, an amiable Englishman with a Guard's moustache and a slight limp. Neither the moustache nor the limp were indicative of army life, he'd been quick to explain when I asked: the moustache was fortuitous and the limp a result of childhood polio.

I walked over to study the map, forcing Stern to shift his chair out of the way. I wasn't too sure why Mrs Salton's lawyer was even there, unless he wanted to keep a close eye on me. 'Why three colours?'

Stern said, 'Blue is for Salton Estates Ltd, red is the Campanillan Land Company, and green is Jildav Ltd. That's the holding company which represents Salton's personal fortune.'

The map was splashed with blue and red in roughly equal proportions. El Cerco was coloured green, as was a small area of Marshalltown. Idle said, 'The Campanillan Land Company is purely commercial – organised to make money. It's doing very well. Salton Estates Ltd was, I suppose, Mr Salton's private charity and dedicated to the building of low-cost housing. It also financed hospitals and contributed to educational needs.'

'How does it really work?' I said.

Idle limped over and stood beside me, looking at the map. 'Mr Salton bought land steadily for about twenty-five years, mostly in small parcels as they became available. Naturally he bought as cheaply as he could and he had a keen eye to values. He split the holdings roughly equally between the Campanillan Land Company and Salton Estates. When the boom started, the price of land rose appreciably and he was on to a good thing.'

He pointed to a tract of blue on the coast. 'He bought this bit for two million dollars just before the boom. When we went to Western and Continental for a loan it was put up as collateral and valued at five million. Last week I was offered eight and three-quarter million for it. That more than covers the loan, of course. We turned it down.'

I did a quick mental calculation. 'That's an appreciation of about fifteen per cent a year.'

Idle grinned. 'That's why we borrowed money. We could have got it by selling land, but the value of the land is rising faster than the interest we're paying you people for your money. It pays us to borrow.'

It surely did. I surveyed the map. 'What's the total value of the Salton holdings?'

Idle shrugged. 'Difficult to say. Maybe about forty million dollars right now. The way things are going, in ten years' time you could put it at a hundred million.' He stretched out his hand and indicated areas. 'These are the tracts that were put up as collateral for the loan and valued at eight million dollars. I could get twelve million for them now.'

It seemed as though Costello didn't have to worry too much about the security of his money. 'Do you always work in dollars?' I asked.

Stern said, 'Mr Salton lived in the United States a long

time and thinking in dollars came easier to him. But Campanilla is converting its currency within the year, moving from Campanillan pounds to Campanillan dollars on a par with American dollars.'

Idle laughed. 'The changeover will be easier in this office than in most.'

I said, 'Tell me about the low-cost housing project.'

'A few years ago Mr Salton came across a Canadian architect who had some good ideas about low-cost housing,' said Idle. 'On a pilot scheme the ideas worked and so he went to Western and Continental for development capital. We've built nearly a thousand houses and, at the moment, we're completing them at the rate of about five a week.'

'I hear they're rented and not sold,' I said, and Idle nodded. 'How does that affect your cash flow?'

'It doesn't make things particularly easy,' Idle admitted. 'But we get by.'

'Are the rents economic?'

He grimaced. 'Just economic. We might make a one per cent profit.'

I said carefully, 'Someone suggested to me that the rents weren't economic and that Salton was building houses to buy votes.'

Idle flushed and said hotly, 'Whoever said that is a damned liar. The rents are low because we keep our overheads down and because of the architect's smart ideas. We're not out to make a profit, but we're not out to make a loss either.'

I turned to Stern. 'Since Salton Estates is primarily a charitable organisation, I'd have thought it would be better established as a trust, with a proper board of trustees.'

'Mr Salton was thinking of doing just that,' said Stern. 'His death interfered with those plans.'

'What's the situation now?'

'We had a directors' meeting. Mr Idle – who was general manager – was made managing director. I'm chairman.'

'And Mrs Salton?'

'She's on the board.'

I thought about it and I didn't like what I was thinking. This was altogether too loose. Business trust is a frail flower and the best way of encouraging it is to ensure that there is no scope at all for larceny. Idle and Stern were probably pillars of mercantile rectitude, but there was an outside chance that they were otherwise, and that was a chance that had to be covered.

I said deliberately, 'It seems to me that, pending the formation of a trust, Western and Continental should have a representative on the board of directors. We have a lot of money invested here – about a quarter of Salton Estates' fundings.'

Stern said stiffly, 'There's been no suggestion of that before.'

'Circumstances alter cases,' I said. 'I'll be making that recommendation to Mr Costello. It's up to him if he follows through or not.'

Stern's mouth was a tightly compressed line. He could see very well what I was getting at, and he didn't like it. I couldn't blame him – no one relishes the idea of a personal watchdog, as I was discovering with him. 'Very well,' he said.

I was an intelligence consultant and not an accountant, so there was no point in me going through the books, even though I'd told Stern I wanted to. Figures, whether in a ledger or on a computer print-out, were just a lot of chicken tracks to me. I let him off the hook. 'Well,' I said genially. 'I don't think there's much more I can do here, except one thing – I'd like to see Mrs Forsyth, Mr Salton's secretary. I believe she works here now.'

'Of course,' said Idle. 'I'll send for her.'

'I'd rather see her alone,' I said.

He nodded. 'I'll take you to her office.'

Stern stood up. 'You won't be needing me, Mr Kemp. I'll get back to Marshalltown. Work doesn't stop just because one isn't in the office.' Mrs Forsyth was evidently too low-grade to require his presence. He paused at the door on his way out. 'I can't tell you how shocked I was to hear of the assault on Mr Ogilvie. I truly hope he recovers.'

I shook my head. 'Too late for that, Mr Stern. He died this morning.'

His face went pale. 'My God, I'm sorry to hear that. Have the police found out who did it?'

'They're still looking,' I said. 'I don't think they have much hope of success, though.'

'That's terrible,' he said. 'Terrible.' He made a fluttering gesture with his hands. 'I don't know what to say, Mr Kemp.'

'There's nothing much anyone can say.' I looked at my watch. 'I'll come over to your office after I've seen Mrs Forsyth, if that's convenient. There's a small problem I'd like to talk over with you privately.'

## IV

I didn't get much out of Mrs Forsyth. She was about sixty, extremely slight and with a brisk, no-nonsense air about her. Yes, she had cleared Mr Salton's effects from the office in the Learjet. No, she had not touched his suits – they were none of her affair. No, she hadn't found anything unusual in Mr Salton's desk drawers in the aircraft. Anywhere else? His office at El Cerco? Anywhere at all? No, nothing at all, Mr Kemp.

Thank you very much, Mrs Forsyth. For nothing.

I drove to Stern's office and waited twenty minutes while he disposed of a client. Then I was admitted and sat down. He put the tips of his fingers together. 'You spoke of a small problem, Mr Kemp.'

'Not really a problem, more of a delicate situation,' I said.

'When a man dies, his executors sometimes come across strange things. It might be discovered that a pillar of the church has amassed the finest collection of hardcore pornography in the world, for example. What did you find out about Salton?'

'Nothing at all,' he said, but his eyes were watchful.

'You are Salton's executor,' I said. 'So you must have checked on Jildav Ltd. Isn't that right?'

'That is correct.'

'And Jildav Ltd owns property here in Marshalltown – the only place it does on the island, besides El Cerco. Isn't that correct?'

'Yes,' he said. 'But what of it?'

'Would I be right in saying that Jildav owns Gregory Plaza?'

Stern stood up and went to the window. He stared into the street for a moment then swung around and faced me. 'Yes,' he said. 'And I repeat – what of it?'

'You live there, don't you? On the eighth floor.'

'I do, but I don't see what that's got to do with anything.'

I smiled. 'Do you pay an economic rent, Mr Stern?'

'That's a damned insulting question,' he said. 'I pay the going rate, the same as anyone else who lives there. If you're implying that . . .'

I held up my hand. 'I'm not implying anything, Mr Stern. Just trying to get at some facts. Do you still say that you haven't found anything about Salton that might prove to be a matter of some delicacy?'

He moved uneasily. 'I don't follow you.'

'All right, I'll spell it out. Who pays the rent on apartment 432?'

'How would I know? I don't know anything about apartment 432.'

'Oh, come off it, Stern. That's where Salton had his first heart attack.'

He sat down suddenly as though the strength had gone out of his legs. 'So you've got that far, have you?'

'It wasn't hard. Did you know about her before Salton died?'

He shook his head. 'I suspected something, but I wasn't certain. After his heart attack I kept a check but he never went near the place so I decided I was wrong. It was only when he died and I went through his accounts that I discovered he was paying the rent.'

'He'd have to pay the rent. He couldn't just let her live there rent-free even though he owned the place. That would be too obvious. Did Mrs Salton know about Miss Tomsson before Salton died?'

'No, not to my knowledge.'

'Does she know now?'

'I haven't told her,' he said. 'And I don't intend to. These peccadilloes in a man's life shouldn't be given a public airing after his death. If Mrs Salton doesn't already know, there is nothing to be gained by telling her. It would hurt her dreadfully and unnecessarily.'

'I agree,' I said. 'And I don't intend to tell her. But someone else knows.'

'Who?'

'Joe Hawke. What are the odds on his blowing the gaff?'

'My God!' said Stern. 'That's something he'll use. That bastard has no principles at all.' The uncharacteristic language showed that he was perturbed. 'How do you know that Hawke knows?'

'Because he tipped me off about it. What are you doing about Miss Tomsson?'

'What do you mean? What should I do?'

I said, 'Are you looking after her interests in any way?'

'Looking after her interests?' He was plainly baffled. 'A woman like that?' he said distastefully.

'A woman like what?' I demanded. 'Don't be such a

bloody puritan. She was good enough for Salton, wasn't she? I'd have thought he'd want her looked after – discreetly, of course.' I stared at him. 'Do you mean to tell me that you're just letting the rent run to the end of the quarter and then leaving her to fend for herself?'

'There is no legal obligation,' he said primly.

'No, there isn't,' I said through gritted teeth. 'She could blackmail the hell out of Mrs Salton but, if I'm any judge of character, she's made no move to do so. How much would it be worth to Mrs Salton to prevent a story like that breaking? Do you think a man like Salton would shack up with any floozy? She's a straightforward and honest woman and she deserves better.'

'I don't see what this has got to do with you,' Stern said acidly.

'I don't either,' I said. 'I just don't like seeing anyone knocked down. But think this one over, Mr Stern. David Salton had a quarrel with his wife just before he was found dead in most mysterious circumstances. You know it, I know it and Superintendent Hanna knows it. If it should prove that the quarrel was about Miss Tomsson, then Hanna is going to be putting two and two together to make five. Jill Salton wouldn't be the first jealous wife to kill her husband. Very few people are murdered by strangers – it's your nearest and dearest you have to watch out for.'

Stern moistened his lips. 'That's a ridiculous hypothesis. And the inquest findings . . .'

'That post-mortem was a joke. Besides, a policeman is not bound by the findings of an inquest.'

'So what do you suggest I do about Miss Tomsson?'

'Whatever it is, it will have to be very discreet. She wants to go to England, I believe, which should suit you. Paying her air fare and giving her a stake to live on until she settles down might not be a bad idea. But do it carefully and through a third party.'

Stern grimaced. 'I'm a lawyer and an officer of the court. Are you asking that I become accessory to a felony?'

'What felony? As you said, it's just a hypothesis, interesting and perhaps ridiculous. Maybe you'd better ask Hanna which of those descriptions he prefers.'

I walked to the door and Stern came from behind the desk, rather more meek than I had seen him before. 'I have to thank you for pointing out the delicacy of the situation, Mr Kemp. I must say that I hadn't thought the thing through quite as cogently as you have. I might take some such action as you have outlined.'

As I went down to the street I speculated about Stern. He knew on which side his bread was buttered and I suspected he liked the butter spread thick. Running an apartment in Gregory Plaza wasn't cheap, even for a successful lawyer, and he had the wit to know that Mrs Salton was his meal ticket. If she was removed from the scene, then it was likely that he would no longer be chairman of Salton Estates Ltd and he could lose his other directorships in the lucrative Salton empire. I rather thought his legal ethics wouldn't stand in the way of extending a welcoming arm to help Leotta Tomsson.

I crossed the pavement and got into my car. The interior was like an oven so I wound down both side windows to allow the air to circulate. I took the key from my pocket and, as I moved my hand to put it in the ignition, it slipped from my fingers. I stooped to pick it up from the floor and something brushed the nape of my neck.

I straightened, put the key in the lock and then felt the back of my neck. My fingers came away red with blood.

The pain came later.

# SIX

## I

'You think someone took a shot at you?' said Superintendent Hanna.

I winced as the doctor did something to the back of my neck. 'Either that or you've got bloody big mosquitoes here. Ask the expert if you don't believe me.'

The hotel doctor was competent enough at administering first aid, given the constraints of my suite. I had rung Hanna immediately and, as he had promised, he came running. He looked sleepier than ever.

'Well, doctor?' he asked.

'It looks like a bullet graze,' said the doctor. 'There's nothing to say it isn't. It certainly isn't a mosquito bite.'

'Very funny,' said Hanna. 'Did you hear the shot?'

'No,' I said. 'But there was a lot of traffic noise.'

'Which direction did the bullet come from?'

'How the hell would I know?' I said. 'I didn't even feel it at first.'

'I think I can tell you that,' said the doctor. 'From the way the tissue is torn, I'd say it came from left to right.' He pressed firmly. 'That dressing should hold, Mr Kemp. You can lift your head now.'

'That's something,' said Hanna. 'Do you remember where the car was parked?'

I straightened and flexed my neck. 'Of course.' Suddenly I shuddered.

Hanna leaned forward and stared at me. 'What's the matter?'

'The thought just came into my mind of what would have happened if I hadn't dropped the key.' I lowered my head a little and then raised it. Touching the side of my neck, I said, 'The bullet would have entered just about here. It would have cut through the carotid and I'd have bled to death in about two minutes.'

I began to laugh as the hysteria kicked in, and the doctor shook out a couple of tablets from a bottle. 'Take these.'

'What are they?'

'Just a sedative,' he said soothingly. 'You're a bit uptight right now.' He went into the bathroom and came back with a glass of water and I took the tablets. 'I'd stay in your room tonight,' he said. 'Rest as much as you can. I'll see you tomorrow morning.'

As the doctor packed his bag, Hanna said, 'Don't talk about this to anyone, doctor. It's police business.'

'I never talk about my patients.' The doctor went away.

'So someone took a shot at you,' said Hanna. 'Why?'

'I don't know,' I said, and then a thought struck me. 'How do you suppose alcohol would combine with a sedative?'

'No idea.'

I crossed the room and picked up the telephone. 'Get me the hotel doctor.'

'People don't shoot at people for no reason,' said Hanna.

'They don't necessarily give a reason.' I listened to what the telephone said. 'I know, he's only just left my suite. Ask him to give me a ring when he gets in, would you? The name is Kemp.' I hung up the phone and lay on the bed.

'First Ogilvie and now you,' said Hanna.

'First Salton,' I corrected him. 'Ogilvie came later.'

'The connection between you and Ogilvie is obvious – maybe a little too obvious,' said Hanna. 'But it's the methods. I don't like the variety of methods. Ogilvie was beaten up and you were shot.'

'It comes to the same thing in the end,' I said. The telephone rang and I picked it up.

'Ogilvie could have survived,' said Hanna. 'The attempt on you was intended to be more final.' He shook his head irritably.

I said into the telephone, 'Hello, doctor. How would alcohol mix with the sedative you gave me?'

'You mean you want a drink?' He paused. 'It should be all right, provided you don't drink the whole bottle.'

'Thanks. I'll do the same for you some day.' I put down the phone and said to Hanna, 'There are glasses on the tray and scotch in the minibar. Do you mind?'

He sighed tiredly and got up from the chair in which he was sitting. 'You really think this is to do with Salton's death?'

'Don't you? It seems as though anyone asking about Salton runs into trouble.'

Hanna put down two glasses on the bedside table. 'No one has shot at me,' he said. I frowned as he uncapped a half-bottle of malt and poured the drinks. 'Who did you see today?'

'A man called Roker from the Caribbean Banking Corporation.'

'What did he want?'

'I don't have to tell you *all* my business,' I said.

Hanna smiled. 'Tell me something, even if it's only a lie. What did Roker want?'

'You remember me telling you that someone had been pretty insistent about me leaving – that was Roker. He wanted me to cease and desist. It seems I'm rocking his boat.'

'What did you tell him?'

'I told him what he could do with his suggestion. Then he tried to bribe me.'

'Who else?'

'Jake McKittrick, Joe Hawke, Abel Stern and Martin Idle of Salton Estates. Oh, and Mrs Forsyth, Salton's secretary. There was also an anonymous character on the telephone who said that if I didn't quit I'd get the same as Ogilvie.'

Hanna raised his eyebrows. 'You should have told me about that. Were those his words – *the same as Ogilvie* – is that what he said?'

'Exactly.'

'But you were shot. That's not the same as Ogilvie.'

'The manner of my death won't make any difference to me when I'm dead,' I said tartly.

Hanna sipped from his glass. 'Good whisky,' he said approvingly. 'You've left someone out, Mr Kemp. Leotta Tomsson, 432 Gregory Plaza, Marshalltown.'

Hanna was a crafty devil and not nearly as sleepy as he looked. 'You know about her?'

'I work on the political detail, Mr Kemp – seeing that visiting dignitaries don't get shot full of too many holes, that sort of thing. To do that, I have to know who is likely to do the shooting. So we keep an eye on everybody. We ran security checks on Salton as a matter of routine after he came back to Campanilla. We came across Leotta Tomsson eighteen months ago.'

I could see David Salton's secret leaking out even as we talked. 'I bet Prime Minister Conyers finds your files fascinating,' I said.

Hanna looked hurt. 'Conyers doesn't know. This is state security, not party political stuff. If anyone wants to see the files he has to get past me.'

I regarded him thoughtfully. This was the age-old problem with police work, when loyalties become divided, motives strained and the best of good intentions lead directly to hell.

Still, if you had to have a watchdog, Hanna might be a good one and relatively incorruptible.

'So what about Leotta Tomsson?' I said.

'Nothing much – nothing political, anyway. Why did you see her?'

'Joe Hawke seemed to think it was a good idea.'

'Did he indeed? And what happened?'

'Nothing,' I said blankly. 'I just confirmed her relationship with Salton, that's all.'

'The eternal triangle,' mused Hanna, looking down into his glass. 'Salton, Mrs Salton and Leotta Tomsson.'

'I asked Miss Tomsson if Jill Salton knew about her. She said she didn't think so.'

'And yet there was a quarrel between Salton and his wife. Interesting.'

'Not that interesting, otherwise you'd have followed it up before now.'

He drained his glass and set it down. 'I can't sit around drinking with you all hours of the day, Mr Kemp. I have work to do.'

'I'll try not to drag you away from it again.' The telephone rang. 'Stick around for a minute: I put in a call to London and this may be it. The boss might want to talk to the authorities. I suppose you qualify?'

Hanna closed his eyes tiredly as I picked up the telephone. 'I suppose I do,' he said despondently.

After a lot of snapping, crackling and popping, Costello came on the line. He sounded irritable because I'd called his home. Because of the time differential, the London office was closed and I'd called him direct. 'For God's sake!' he said. 'I'm in the middle of a dinner party. I have a house full of people here.'

'Pity you couldn't have invited Ogilvie,' I said.

'What? Oh yes. I was sorry to hear about the assault. Look, Mrs Ogilvie is coming over on the next plane to look after him. We had a conference and the chairman thought it was the thing to do. He's flying out himself and bringing her with him.'

'You'd better stop him,' I said. 'It's too late. Ogilvie died this morning.'

'I'm sorry,' said Costello. 'I didn't get that. There's a crackle on the line.'

I repeated what I had said and there was a silence. At last Costello said in a disbelieving voice, 'Dead?'

'He was very badly beaten up. Didn't Jolly tell you?'

'He told me Ogilvie had been attacked but he appeared to overlook the severity.'

I said, 'I have Detective Superintendent Hanna with me. He's investigating the case. Do you want to talk to him?'

'Put him on,' said Costello, and I handed the telephone to Hanna and then went to pour myself another drink. I didn't pay much attention to what Hanna was saying. It would be the usual soothing syrup for administration on these occasions. I got some water from the bathroom and then went back and lay on the bed. Hanna handed me the telephone and I put it to my ear and made a noise. 'This is a hell of a mess,' said Costello. 'Hanna says you've been wounded.'

'I'll live.' I took a sip of peaty malt whisky. 'I'll be sending you a report on Salton Estates. I don't think you have much to worry about but I'm recommending we have a seat on the board. That's it in a nutshell, but I'll dress it up in the report.'

'What are you going to do now?'

I yawned. 'Go to bed.'

'Don't be funny,' snarled Costello. 'I have to get on to the chairman to stop him taking Mrs Ogilvie to Campanilla. What do I tell him about you?'

'You can tell him I'm helping the police with their inquiries,' I said, and put down the telephone.

Hanna looked down at me. 'You don't take much from anyone, do you?'

'I'm no pushover,' I agreed.

'I don't suppose you're ready to go to the scene of the crime?'

'You heard the doctor. He advocated complete rest until tomorrow.'

'All right, tomorrow after breakfast.' He picked up his straw hat and walked to the door. 'Have a good rest. If you move outside this room I'll know about it.' The door closed behind him.

I lay there, drinking whisky and trying to think, but found that my brains had seized up. The faces of all the people I had interviewed wheeled in front of my eyes as if in a kaleidoscope, and little bits of conversation reverberated in my skull as though it were an empty cavern. After a while I decided it *was* an empty cavern. I ordered a light meal from room service, undressed wearily and went to bed.

## II

Hanna sat next to me in the car and looked at me in disgust. 'So you had to break the law and park illegally,' he said, and pointed to the right. 'You parked in front of this alley and now, I suppose, you expect us to find the bullet.'

I grinned at him cheerfully. 'So that's it. I got shot for illegal parking.' I was feeling pretty chipper: twelve hours' sleep and a hearty breakfast had made a lot of difference. The pain at the back of my neck had dulled into a generalised ache and I only winced when I moved my head sharply.

Hanna tapped the side window of the car. 'Why didn't this get broken?' He was looking better, too. The lines of strain about his eyes had smoothed out.

'The car had been out in the sun. I opened both windows to get some air circulating.'

He nodded and opened the door. 'All right, let's have a look.'

In the alley we were joined by two of Hanna's men and he told them what to look for. I didn't think they'd find anything and even if they did it wouldn't be enough to matter. It struck me that Hanna was merely going through the motions of police procedure.

Fifteen minutes later, one of Hanna's boys gave a shout and we went to see what he had found. It was a streak of bright metal about six inches long on the side of a brick wall. Hanna stooped to look at it. 'A soft-nosed bullet – that would have made quite a hole in you.'

'Murderers aren't bound by the Geneva Convention.' I peered at the smear of the bullet, about three and a half feet from the ground. 'You're not going to get much from that – you certainly won't match it to a gun.'

Hanna squatted on his heels. 'No, but forensics will still have to try. We can weigh the lead, for instance, and that will tell us a lot about the gun it *wasn't* fired from.' He turned his head and stared down the alley at my car. 'I'd say it was fired from another car. It's at just the right height.'

'Great!' I said. 'So we have a murderer on wheels.'

Hanna stood up. 'It all helps,' he said mildly. 'And what makes you think he's a murderer? You're not dead – yet.'

'Ogilvie is.'

'There's no evidence that the two attacks are related. Is your car in the exact position it was yesterday?' When I nodded he said, 'I'd be obliged if you'd leave it there for a couple of hours. Our forensic people will want to measure sight lines.'

'That's all right as long as I don't get a parking ticket. How will measuring sight lines help?'

'I don't know,' he said. 'But in police work you go by

the book, and the book says we measure sight lines. Police procedure goes by its own book, not by the lucky guesses of detective story writers. I haven't read a detective story yet where the evidence would stand up in court.' He pointed to my car. 'I may have to testify and the defending counsel will say, "Superintendent Hanna, did you measure the sight lines?" and if I hadn't, he'd say, "Why not?" and there'd be a big question left in the minds of the jury, irrespective of whether sight lines came into the evidence at all.'

'So you measure sight lines,' I said.

'We do a lot of unnecessary work just to protect ourselves. There are too many people ready to think ill of the police.'

We walked down the alley towards the street. Hanna said, 'What are you going to do now?'

'That's up to you,' I said. 'My work is finished. Do you still want me around for questioning?'

We arrived in the street and paused on the pavement. A motorcycle pulled up behind my car and a uniformed policeman climbed off it. Hanna glanced at him and turned to face me. 'How do you feel about staying?' he asked. 'It might be dangerous – someone has already taken a shot at you.' He held up his hand as I opened my mouth to answer. 'I don't mind telling you that there is pressure on me to get you off Campanilla. If it came to the crunch, I couldn't stop you leaving if you wanted to.'

'Do you want me to stay?'

He smiled faintly. 'Things happen when you're around, Mr Kemp. It would certainly strengthen my hand if you stayed.'

I said, 'I told you yesterday I'm no pushover. People have been pushing me, wanting me to leave, and that alone makes me inclined to stay. And then there's Ogilvie. I'd like to get to the bottom of that.'

The policeman from the motorcycle came over and gave Hanna an envelope. Hanna said, 'I'll let you know if there's an answer,' then turned back to me. 'All right, but stay out of dark corners and let me know where you are at every minute of the day. And let's have no secrets, shall we? Cases like this aren't solved by inspired amateurs.'

He ripped open the flap of the envelope and took out a memo sheet. He read the few lines of typescript and then folded the sheet precisely. Glancing at me he hesitated before saying, 'Mrs Salton is back at El Cerco.'

'Is she, by God?' I could do with seeing her again. 'I'm afraid I'll need my car.'

'No,' said Hanna. 'Remember the sight lines.' He frowned and I noticed that the lines of strain were beginning to re-appear. Apparently he was juggling with a decision. 'As far as I'm concerned, Mrs Salton is one of the most delicate areas of this investigation. I have to walk very soft-footed at El Cerco.' He chewed his lower lip. 'That's why I'm going to let you go out there. You can ask questions which I can't.'

'What do you want to know?'

'I want to know about the quarrel the Saltons had. Maybe you can surprise it out of her.'

'I can try.' I wasn't too keen on the idea of doing Hanna's dirty work for him, but my own curiosity was raging in my brain.

He dug his hand in his pocket and produced a car key. 'Take my car. We're still going by the book.'

'Thanks,' I said, and turned away.

'One more thing,' he said. 'When you're at El Cerco, remember that pressure I mentioned.'

For a straightforward copper who did things by the book, he could be bloody enigmatic.

As I pulled Hanna's car away from the kerb, I glanced in the rear-view mirror and saw him talking to the policeman, who had remounted his motorcycle. The policeman followed me all the way to the northern tip of the island at a tactful distance of two hundred yards.

At El Cerco the gates were closed and the same two men on duty. The one on the outside came forward and stooped to look at me. 'Mr Kemp to see Mrs Salton,' I said.

He straightened and took a sheet of paper from his breast pocket. After scanning it, he said. 'You're not on the list.'

'Have you a telephone? I'd like to speak to Mrs Salton.'

He gave me a long unsmiling look. 'Wait here.' He walked back to the gate and spoke to the man inside. I turned my head and looked back along the road. The policeman on the motorcycle had stopped two hundred yards back and was waiting quietly.

Presently the gates opened and the guard waved me through. As I stepped on the accelerator I checked the mirror. The policeman made no move but waited unobtrusively. It seemed as though I had a guard of my own.

Down at the quay, Raymond was waiting in the launch with the engine already turning over. There was one thing you had to say about El Cerco: the place ran with machine-like efficiency. I dropped into the boat, and said, 'Thanks, Raymond,' and we shot off across the lagoon.

John was waiting on the island. 'Mrs Salton is engaged at the moment. She asks you to wait a few minutes.'

'All right,' I said.

'This way, sir.'

I followed him through that quiet and beautiful house to one of the indoor patios, where I found my principal employer just finishing what could have been breakfast. Lord Hosmer looked very tired – flights across time zones hit older people very hard. He looked up as I arrived. 'Didn't expect to see you so soon. I left a message at your hotel only an hour ago.'

I hadn't expected to see him at all. Costello had given me the impression that Hosmer would call off his trip. 'I didn't get your message,' I said. 'I was coming here anyway.'

He looked up at me, sharpness in his faded blue eyes. 'Why?'

I recalled that he was Jill Salton's uncle. 'Just to say goodbye to Mrs Salton.'

'You've finished your work here?'

'Yes. I just have to write a report for Costello.'

'Good. Then there's nothing to keep you here.' He flicked his hand at a chair. 'Sit down, Kemp. Bad business, this – about Ogilvie, I mean.'

'How did Mrs Ogilvie take it?'

He dabbed at his mouth with a napkin. 'Not well. We had some trouble in persuading her not to come. What arrangements are being made about the . . . er . . . the body?'

'It will be released after the inquest, say, in two or three days. I suggest it should be flown to England, not shipped. There's no point in dragging things out for Mrs Ogilvie.'

He nodded. 'Very wise. Before you leave, you'd better see a local undertaker. You can do that this afternoon, I suppose. And you can leave tomorrow.'

Hosmer seemed to be taking a lot for granted. I said, 'I may not be able to leave that soon. The police want me to stay. They think I can help them.'

'Would that be Superintendent Hanna?'

'Yes.' Hosmer seemed to be clued up about the local force.

He flapped his napkin. 'Forget about him,' he said tersely. 'I'll handle that end at a higher level.'

I studied the old man thoughtfully. 'Don't you think it would be better if I stayed? If the police think I might be some help in finding out who killed Ogilvie, then I think I should stay. Apart from anything else, it's good public relations.'

'I don't give a damn about public relations. You're needed back in London.'

I remembered Hanna's parting words. *When you're at El*

*Cerco, remember that pressure I mentioned*. He must have known that Lord Hosmer was here and guessed what his line was likely to be.

I pushed a little. 'Why am I needed back in London?'

'I don't know. Something Jolly's in a flap about.'

I shrugged. 'Jolly's panics don't usually amount to much. The last time he got his knickers in a twist, it was about someone stealing from the petty cash in the Edinburgh office.'

'I should think you'd be glad to leave,' said Hosmer irascibly. 'Costello tells me you've been wounded yourself.' He surveyed me. 'It doesn't show.'

'Just a scratch,' I said modestly.

'Well, it doesn't matter. I suggest you go back to London by the first flight tomorrow.'

The crunch had come. I either had to go meekly back to London or lay my contract on the line. It was a fine contract and I enjoyed my job. I was bloody good at it too, but I didn't deceive myself into thinking I could walk away with no consequence. I might have been the best intelligence consultant outside Whitehall, but Hosmer had enough pull in the insurance world to blackball me from London to Hong Kong – both ways around the world. A lot of my kind of work depends on trust and once Hosmer dropped the acid I'd be history. He wouldn't even have to tell the truth: a vague hint would be enough.

I said, 'You know, I don't think I have finished here. I'm still not satisfied with the manner of Salton's death.'

He looked at me from under shaggy brows and, for the first time, I noticed he had boar's eyes. A dangerous man to cross. 'What the hell do you mean by that?' he demanded. 'You were satisfied enough to tell Jolly to draw a cheque.'

'Some new evidence came in after I talked to Jolly.'

'What evidence?'

'A man called Roker came to see me.'

I waited for Hosmer to say something. He obliged. 'Never heard of him.'

'An American,' I said. 'He came from the Caribbean Banking Corporation – which, he informed me, is one-third owned by Western and Continental. Is that true?'

'Near enough,' said Hosmer. 'We have a thirty per cent stake.'

'He wanted me to quit. He tried to blackmail me first and when that failed he tried a bribe. Then he said he'd get me deported. I advised against it. I think he took my advice.'

'You *advised* against it,' said Hosmer heavily. 'What form did your advice take?'

'I said I'd blow the story to the British press, who would be delighted to climb in. I think he took the point.' I hoped Hosmer also took the point.

He looked at me for a long time in silence. I once thought that I wouldn't give a bent penny for Hanna's career prospects. Right then, I wouldn't have given even that much for my own. Hosmer wasn't a pleasant sight. He was thinking hard, figuring out all the angles and testing one chance against another. I knew damned well that Roker, or whoever was behind him, had telephoned London to tell Hosmer to bring his dog to heel. And Hosmer had come running.

He put his hand to his breast pocket and took out a cigar case. Extracting a long cigar, he clipped the end with a gold cutter and then lit it carefully. When he had it going to his satisfaction, he blew a steady plume of smoke. 'You're playing a dangerous game, Kemp,' he said.

I leaned forward. 'What is it to you who gets in power here?'

'Commitments,' he said. 'Mutual obligations.' His voice was hard. 'When does your contract run out?'

'About eight months. Why?'

'Time enough,' he said. 'In eight months all this will have

blown over. No newspaper will listen to you then. What editor likes an eight-month-old story? Don't expect your contract to be renewed.'

There it was, the flat threat. 'So do I stay?' I asked.

He grunted. 'Please yourself.'

I said, 'The story might get out anyway. I'm surprised it hasn't already. There's a smart man called Jackson at the *Chronicle*.'

'Jackson is gagged.'

A cool voice behind us said, 'Who gagged him?'

We both turned round. Jill Salton was standing half-hidden by some shrubbery. I don't think either of us knew how long she had been there or how much she had heard. She came forward and said to Hosmer, 'If Mr Kemp needs a job in eight months' time, I'm sure he'll be welcome in one of my group of companies. He has impressed me very much.'

Hosmer was quicker than I to recover. 'You know nothing about him.'

'I know enough to trust him more than I trust you,' she said cuttingly. 'That wasn't a pretty conversation I heard. And don't think I knew nothing of the pressure you were putting on David. He told me everything, all about your tie-in with Cardew Street, your attempted bribes disguised as business deals, your threats to withdraw the loan from Salton Estates.'

'Jill, you don't understand about business,' he said. 'Whatever David told you, he must have misunderstood.'

Her voice was as cold as ice and hard as a diamond. 'You are not welcome in this house,' she said. 'There will be a car to take you to San Martin.' She turned on her heel and walked away.

I thought Hosmer would have a heart attack. His face turned a blotchy mixture of white and pink and a vein throbbed heavily in his temple. The cigar dropped from his fingers and lay disregarded on the paving, sending up a thin stream of light blue smoke. He stared at nothing for a long time and then began to lever himself out of the chair, pushing himself up with trembling arms. Suddenly he was a very old man.

He ignored me completely. I watched him walk slowly away and somehow felt sorry for the old bastard. If I had been spoken to with such utter contempt as there had been in Jill Salton's voice, I'd have been able to walk under a snake's belly wearing a top hat. If there was one thing she could do, it was to cut a man down to size. Aristocratically.

When he had gone, I sat in sheer wonder at the unasked-for display of feminine chivalry. Dame Jill Salton galloping to the rescue with lance poised and sharpened to kill was something I hadn't expected, and I didn't know whether I cared for it very much. Not because I was too proud to have assistance in fighting my battles, but because I would soon be asking her questions on behalf of Hanna – questions cunningly designed to find out whether or not she had killed her husband. I didn't seriously believe she had: all the evidence indicated otherwise, and her rage at Hosmer on behalf of her husband had been utterly convincing. But, as Hanna had said, police routine means going by the book and *all* the questions must be asked. And answered.

I stooped and picked up Hosmer's cigar and laid it gently in the ashtray, being careful not to break the ash.

## III

John said gravely, 'Mrs Salton will see you now, sir.'

I had been waiting on the patio for nearly an hour, making lists of people and what they'd said, and matching one conversation with another. It was what I had tried to do the previous evening before my brains went mushy. My brains were in better condition on that bright morning but the result was the same. I got nowhere. So I was happy to follow John into the same room where I had first met Mrs Salton.

Her face was pale and I thought she must have been crying. She said unsmilingly, 'Sit down, Bill. I'm sorry about that little scene.'

I sat down. 'Don't be sorry on my account.'

'I meant what I said about the job. You'd be very welcome.'

'I might take you up on it, if necessary. How much of the conversation did you hear?'

'Nearly all of it, I think. He's an evil and vicious old man, Bill. You've made a dangerous enemy. He won't extend your contract.' She folded her hands in her lap. 'Hadn't you better tell me what's going on?'

'Before I do that I'd like to ask you a couple of questions just to get things straight in my own mind. Was that true, what you said to Hosmer about the pressure he put on your husband?'

'He never liked David,' she said. 'Remember I told you my family was against the marriage? He was the one who caused most of the trouble.'

'You'll get more trouble from him now,' I said. 'He'll call in the loan on Salton Estates.'

'The contract is cast iron and if he tries to fight it I can employ as many lawyers as he can. If I lose I can stand it.'

Forty million dollars makes a comfortable cushion. I could stop worrying about the future of Jill Salton. 'Why did you go to New York so suddenly?' I asked.

'To see David's sister. Something came up about the estate that she was worried about. What of it?'

I grinned. 'I think you had Superintendent Hanna a little worried. I suspect he was wondering if you were going to come back.'

Her eyes widened. 'I don't see why he should.' She stopped and drew in her breath.

'Precisely,' I said. 'He's still investigating your husband's death.'

'Commissioner Barstow told me the case was closed.'

'Barstow may think he runs Hanna. Hanna has other views.' I leaned forward. 'Jill, the air needs clearing. An important question has come up and only you can answer it. What did you and your husband quarrel about on the day he went missing?'

'Am I under suspicion?' she said in a thin voice.

'In a case like this, nobody is above suspicion.'

'My God!' She stood up and paced the room. 'All I have to do is call Barstow and Hanna will be put firmly in his place.'

'That would look really iffy,' I observed. 'You do that, and Hanna will definitely believe you have something to hide. Have you, Jill?'

'Don't be ridiculous.'

'Then why all the fuss? Just a simple answer to a simple question will get Hanna off your back.'

She said primly, 'I refuse to parade my private life before the world.'

'You wouldn't be doing that. Coppers can keep secrets.' I thought about that and added, 'So can insurance investigators.' I watched her stalk angrily up and down the room. 'Let me try to make it easier for you. Was it about Leotta Tomsson?'

She stopped in mid-pace and whirled around to face me. 'What do you know about her?'

'She was your husband's mistress. When did *you* find out?'

Her face was white. 'I didn't – not really. Just suspicions.'

'Hanna knew eighteen months ago,' I said. 'As I told you, coppers can keep secrets. Was she the cause of the quarrel?'

Jill nodded miserably. 'I was stupid. I tackled him about it before I had any real proof. He never lied to me, so he admitted it. But he said he'd broken with her, that he hadn't seen her for six months. I told him I didn't believe him.'

'Even though he never lied to you?'

'What was his mistress but a constant, unexpressed lie?' cried Jill passionately.

'It so happens he was telling the truth.' In a sad, sad way, I thought. 'They didn't see each other in the last six months.'

She sank into a chair and her face was now paper white so that a dusting of freckles stood out against her skin. She looked bleakly into the past and her hand went nervously to her mouth as she breathed, 'My God!'

'You'll have to talk to Hanna,' I said.

'I can't do that. David mustn't be dragged down.'

'He's dead, Jill,' I said gently. 'It won't matter to him now.'

'It will to his name, to his reputation.'

My recent run-in with Hosmer had reminded me of the power of reputation, but this was different. 'It's too late, Jill. David's political opponents already know. This thing must be cleared up once and for all, especially after what happened to Owen Ogilvie.'

She looked at me blankly. 'What about Ogilvie?'

'Don't you know? He was killed – murdered – just after he left Negrini's casino.'

She closed her eyes and I thought she was going to faint. 'Oh, that poor young man,' she whispered. 'He showed me a picture of his wife and child in his wallet. He was so proud of them.' She opened her eyes. 'Why was he killed?'

'Because he was going about asking questions about how David Salton died.'

Her hands were trembling. 'It could have happened to you, Bill.'

'It nearly did,' I said grimly. 'They had a go at me yesterday afternoon.' I told her about it.

'But why?' she said helplessly. 'What was it about David's death?' She stood up again and walked to the window. 'You're right. This business must be cleared up. I'll talk to Hanna.' She paused uncertainly. 'It gives me a motive, doesn't it? It makes me a suspect. Hell hath no fury . . .' Her voice tailed away.

'You can't be suspected of Ogilvie's death,' I said. 'You were with me when he was attacked. And the two go together – they must. You weren't even in the country when they took a crack at me.' Uneasily I wondered how many murders could be commissioned with forty million dollars. As I said before, suspicion is corrosive.

John came into the room, walking cat-footed. 'You are wanted on the telephone, sir.'

'Thanks.' That could only be Hanna. I excused myself to Jill and followed John to the telephone. He was learning fast: he hadn't brought along a portable to be plugged in.

He handed me the receiver and went away, stiff-backed. One thing he hadn't learned was to like me. 'Kemp here.'

'This is McKittrick. I'd like to see you, Mr Kemp.'

I was surprised. 'How did you know where to find me?'

'Does it matter? It's important that I see you.'

'When?'

'As soon as possible.'

'Where?'

There was a pause for thought before he said, 'Remember the field I was planting with corn? I'll see you there. It's close to my home.'

'I'd still like to know how you found me.'

'You haven't exactly been hiding,' he said.

Neither had I been broadcasting my movements to all and

sundry. Only Hanna and the copper on the motorcycle knew where I was. And Lord Hosmer. And Jill Salton. And . . . 'All right,' I said. 'Give me an hour.'

I put down the telephone and went in search of John, who was polishing silver in a pantry next to the kitchen. He rose to his feet as soon as he saw me. 'Sir?'

'Do you listen to every telephone call in this house?' I asked bluntly.

Not a muscle in his seamed face moved but there was an almost imperceptible widening of the eyes. 'Sir?' he said, apparently in surprise.

'The last time I was here I had a private telephone call during which I discussed certain theoretical matters with a Mr Ogilvie. The next day rumours of that discussion were all over this bloody island and Ogilvie was dead.'

John's face turned an unhealthy grey and he swayed on his feet. The polishing cloth dropped from his fingers. 'Dead?'

'Dead. And I was nearly dead, but I was lucky. Did you just tell McKittrick I was here?'

He leaned on the table. 'Excuse me, sir.' He eased himself shakily into the chair, looked uncomprehendingly at the fork he was holding, and then dropped it with a clatter.

I raised my voice. 'Did you tell McKittrick?'

He was stricken. He lifted his head and his lower lip trembled. 'I didn't mean anything by it, sir. I was just passing on a message.'

'Was it to McKittrick?'

'Yes, sir.'

I took a deep breath. 'Right, let me get this straight. You told Dr McKittrick the details of my telephone call with Mr Ogilvie? Is that right?' He nodded tremulously. 'There were riots in San Martin the next day,' I said. 'People were hurt because of that. All because of your meddling.'

'I didn't mean that to happen.'

'What I don't understand is why you did it. Why tell McKittrick?'

'He's my grandson,' said John simply.

# IV

McKittrick was waiting by the roadside, the field behind him all neat and tidy. As I pulled the car to a halt, he stepped forward and then stopped to look back along the road. I glanced into the mirror and saw the copper on the motorcycle come to a halt, the regulation two hundred yards behind. Dust rose in the hot air.

McKittrick bent down and said through the window, 'Why did you bring him?'

'I didn't,' I said. 'He's fastened to the back of the car with an invisible length of rope. Whither I go, he goeth. I suppose he's some kind of bodyguard.'

'Do you need one?'

'Superintendent Hanna seems to think so. Someone took a shot at me yesterday. Gave me a real pain in the neck.'

McKittrick looked back at the motorcycle. He seemed worried. 'Let's go to my place,' he said, and opened the door. He settled in the seat and I set off. 'Who would want to kill you?'

I looked sideways at him. 'Don't you know?'

He jerked. 'How would I know?'

'You've got a hell of a lot to answer for,' I said. 'I've just had a fast talk with your grandfather. Jesus, when I talked to you the other day I thought you were all right. Now I don't know if you're a damned fool or a raving maniac.'

He was silent, then he said, 'Turn right here.' I wheeled the car around the corner and checked the mirror to see if

Old Faithful was still with me. He was. McKittrick said, 'It's Joe Hawke – he's pushing hard.'

'Why don't you leave him?'

'Where would I go? Join Conyers and his mob?' He sounded sick.

'You could always go back to the Liberals. Now Salton is dead they need leadership.'

'I left them once. I doubt if they'd have me back. I've been thinking over what you said. Salton was right and I was wrong.' He shook his head. 'But it's too late now.'

'I don't think so,' I said. 'Better men than you have turned their coats twice. Churchill did it, went from the Conservatives to the Liberals and back to the Conservatives again to become leader of the party.' I smiled grimly. 'He said that anyone can rat once, but it takes a man to rat twice.'

'I'll think about it.' His tone was unconvincing.

I said, 'Whoever set up that political demonstration was looking for trouble. The police were waiting.'

'That's Joe,' said McKittrick. 'He's trying to make as much political capital out of Salton's death as he can. After the inquest things cooled down but when you came, he saw the chance to stoke the fire again. There was another riot today.'

'For God's sake, why did you pass on your grandfather's message to Hawke? Leaving aside the ethics of it, it was a bloody foolish thing to do if you really feel as you say you do.'

'Joe was there when the call came through. I saw no reason not to tell him. He went off like a fire cracker.' McKittrick pointed ahead. 'That's the house.'

It was not very large but neat and of modern design. When we got out of the car McKittrick said, 'I'm still living in a Salton Estates house too, and that doesn't make me feel any better.'

I thought that McKittrick needed a swift kick in the pants to bring him out of his self-abasement, but I didn't say anything. We went into the house and he introduced me to his wife, a pretty young woman called Lena. She said, 'Make yourself at home, Mr Kemp. Would you like a cold beer?'

'That would be very nice.'

She went away and I looked around the room. It was well furnished but did not reek of money, as a lot of other rooms had that I'd visited recently. There were a lot of books. My gaze returned to McKittrick, who was slumped in an armchair. 'What do you want to see me about?'

His voice was low. 'Later.'

I sat down and Lena came back with glasses and cans of beer on a metal tray. As she put it down, I noticed four glasses on the tray. My confusion was shortlived: Joe Hawke came out of the kitchen, a thunderous frown on his face. 'What did you bring the fuzz for? And that's a cop car you're driving.'

'Hertz and Avis have got competition,' I said. 'Would you believe the Campanillan Police Force?'

'Don't crack wise, peckerwood.'

'I'll tell you what,' I said. 'I'll talk English if you will. That phoney lingo makes my ears hurt.'

He grinned and the twinkle returned to his eyes. 'Someone's been talking out of school. Could it have been my friend Superintendent Hanna?' His voice was now cool and well-modulated eastern States. He handed me a glass and a can of beer. 'All right, we've had our fun, so let's get down to business. That cop outside – what's he there for?'

'To see that I come to no harm.'

'It figures,' Hawke said to McKittrick. 'Someone tried to shoot Kemp yesterday.'

That was curious: McKittrick hadn't known but Hawke did. I made a mental note to tell Hanna that Hawke might have a pipeline into his department. 'They didn't try,' I said.

'They succeeded. I can still feel the pain. Any idea who it was, Joe?'

'No. I put out the word but got no answer.' He filled his glass carefully. 'What did you think of Leotta Tomsson?'

'Nice girl.'

'That all?'

'What else is there?'

Hawke laughed shortly. 'Cagey, aren't you?'

'It's just that I'm not on your side,' I said, and tasted the beer. It was cold and bitter on the tongue.

'I know you don't like me, Mr Kemp, but I'm still going to help you. I've tried once and I'll try again.'

'I can hardly wait.'

'Now, this is a hot one,' he said. 'You know Raymond White?'

'Never heard of him.'

'He works at El Cerco – keeps the boats in order, things like that.'

'Oh yes, I've met him.'

'You remember the testimony at the inquest. Mrs Salton said her husband left the house and she thought he'd taken a plane flight. The plane took off at eleven in the morning. Right?'

'That's right.'

'Then, when the plane came back and she discovered he had never been on it, she telephoned the police. While they were at El Cerco she remembered about the boat and it was found missing. The assumption was that Salton had taken it to sea, had a heart attack and died.'

'All correct so far.'

Hawke leaned comfortably back in his chair and twinkled at me. 'What if somebody came forward and said that the boat was in the boathouse at three in the morning the day after Salton was last seen? And what if he said that it was missing an hour later?'

'Is someone saying that?'

'Why don't you ask Ray White?' He smiled at me. 'I've handed it to you on a platter.' He put up a finger. 'What the hell was Salton doing between eleven in the morning and four the next morning wearing only shorts and a polo shirt?' A second finger. 'White will say that a woman took the boat away.' A third finger. 'So where the hell does that leave Mrs Salton?'

I glanced at McKittrick. He had not said a word since Hawke came into the room. He just looked sick.

# SEVEN

## I

I telephoned Hanna from McKittrick's house and told him about it. This was something for the police to handle: Hanna wouldn't thank me if I played the amateur detective and interrogated White, however skilfully I might do it. With several pairs of ears in the room, I told the story baldly, sticking to the facts and avoiding the speculation with which Hawke had embroidered it.

A long silence bored into my ear, and I said, 'Are you there?'

'I'm thinking,' said Hanna testily. 'Someone on this case has got to think some time. Hawke told you all this?'

'That's right. Wasn't White questioned during the original investigation?'

'I don't know,' said Hanna. 'Barstow handled the El Cerco end personally. Wait a minute – I'll check the report.'

As I waited I stared at McKittrick, who was still slumped in the chair gazing into space. I looked around the room. Lena McKittrick was finishing her beer but there was no sign of Hawke. 'Where's Joe?'

She put down the glass. 'He's gone.' She smiled slightly. 'He's got work to do.'

'I'll bet he has,' I said. 'The revolution must go on.' I wondered how he'd use this latest development.

Lena looked at her husband. 'At least he does something.' Was that a touch of contempt in her voice?

Hanna came back on the line. 'There's nothing in the report about White being questioned. Looks like Barstow botched it. Is that patrolman still with you?'

'Yes. I'm not sure why, though.'

'To stop you getting your head blown off,' said Hanna irritably. 'I told you to let me know where you were every minute of the day. You didn't tell me you were going to the McKittrick place.'

'It came up suddenly,' I said.

'What are you going to do now?'

'I think I'll go back to El Cerco.'

'I'll meet you there,' said Hanna. 'But don't do a damn thing until I see you. Especially don't talk about this to anyone. That goes for McKittrick and Hawke, too.'

'Hawke isn't here,' I said. 'Apparently he had business to attend to.'

'Christ!' said Hanna. 'More trouble. Something interesting has happened here. I'll tell you about it when I see you.' He hung up.

I put down the telephone and said, 'Superintendent Hanna wants you to keep quiet about this, at least until he's had a chance to see what White has to say.'

McKittrick stirred. 'Sure. Don't cause trouble, keep the temperature down. That's all the police think of.'

I said, 'I don't understand you, McKittrick – or Hawke, either. As far as I can see, you Campanillans have got it made. Independence without any conditions, a booming economy with few legal restrictions, and an island paradise to enjoy it all. So what's Hawke doing, trying to stir up revolution? Is it just a hangover from his Black Power days in the States?'

'You don't know much about us, do you?' McKittrick
stood up. 'Let me show you something.'

I followed him out of the house. The police patrolman
sat astride his cycle a little way down the road; he appeared
to be manicuring his nails. When we came out of the house
he put away the file and laid his hands on the controls in
readiness for a quick start. McKittrick ignored him and
pointed across the valley. 'See that house there?'

It was a shanty, half fieldstone and half corrugated iron.
'That belongs to Amos Shadlow,' said McKittrick. 'Let me
tell you about Amos. Not long ago we were a British colony
with all the trimmings, including a governor in a feathered
cocked hat. We had colonial police to oppress us and the
economy was stagnant. We thought we were hard done by.
But Amos could make a living – not a good living, but a
living. The only thing you British ever did for us was to
educate some of us, and what good was that? What good
was education on a stinking poor island like this? It just
led to trouble and trouble we had in plenty, so the British
walked away and we got our freedom.'

He threw his arms wide. 'Freedom! We all thought we'd
been given the promised land, but what did we actually
get? We got Conyers.'

'You got self-rule,' I said. 'The government you wanted.'

'We got a government,' said McKittrick. 'But not the one
we wanted. Unnoticed by anybody, that education the
British gave us led to a prosperous middle class, and let me
tell you, Mr Kemp, that rule by the prosperous middle class
is ten times worse than colonial rule. Amos Shadlow over
there isn't oppressed any more, he's just ignored. He's an
irrelevance to the fat cats in government. Conyers made a
deal with Cardew Street and the money poured in, but
none of it reaches Amos. His wages haven't gone up in the
last five years but the price of his food has risen by forty-
four per cent. Housing costs are up fifty-four per cent, so

when Amos wanted to repair his house he couldn't afford it. He had to patch it up with corrugated iron.'

'This is nothing new,' I said unsympathetically. 'Most politics boil down to economics.'

'Right!' said McKittrick. 'And that's why Joe Hawke is trying to stir up revolution, as you put it. So there is Amos Shadlow: his house is draughty and leaks, so he gets sick. His sickness hits him harder than it should because he isn't getting enough of the right food. And I'm expected to cure him.'

'When I saw you planting corn – the man you were with was Amos?'

McKittrick nodded. 'I do what I can. Corn meal mush is not a good diet but it's better than nothing. Meanwhile, Conyers has just bought himself a Mercedes 600, every member of the Cabinet runs a car at the public's expense and they're all directors of Cardew Street companies.' He spat into the dust of the road. 'This government is corrupt to the core.'

'Salton seemed to have the answer,' I said. 'At least a better answer than Joe. Hawke's a destroyer, McKittrick – that's all he understands. He wants to pull down the government.'

'Nothing wrong with that. Salton wanted it too.'

'True. But Hawke wants to destroy Cardew Street, and what the hell does he propose to put in its place? From what I've learned about Salton, he was enough of a politician to realise that the system exists and has to be lived with. It's the source of economic power and he wanted government to control it, instead of being controlled by it. But Hawke wants to destroy it and I'd hate to see what would happen here then. Campanilla would sink to the level of Haiti.'

McKittrick nodded gloomily. 'But Salton is dead,' he said flatly. 'And that means the Liberal Party is too. So what else is there? Someone has to do something about those fat bastards guzzling at the public trough, and the only runner in sight is Joe Hawke.'

'Not if you're in the race,' I said. 'Think about it. Think damned hard. Joe Hawke is only tough if no one stands up to him.' I checked the time. 'I'd better be going.'

McKittrick turned on his heel and went back into the house without saying a word. I stared at the closed door for a moment and then got into my car. As I did so, I heard the patrolman start his engine with a crackling roar. I turned the car and came abreast of him. 'El Cerco,' I shouted, and he nodded briefly.

## II

I had no trouble getting past the gate at El Cerco but my escort tactfully stayed outside. Apparently I had some kind of a day pass. I drove down to the quay and parked the car. Ray White was polishing the metalwork on one of the boats but I ignored him, following Hanna's instructions. I could have gone across to the island but I didn't feel like talking to Jill Salton right then – I might have given something away. I stood about for a while and, in the end, went up to the airstrip for something to do.

The Haslams were sitting by the swimming pool at the side of their house, very much as they had been on my first visit. It would appear that they, especially Mrs Haslam, lived in a sort of alcohol-induced nirvana, a lotus existence of the type usually found only in the travel advertisements of the glossier Sunday supplements. It was a surprise to remember that Haslam had been to New York and back in the interim.

He got to his feet as I walked over. He looked more worried than ever. 'Hi, Mr Kemp. What can I do for you?'

I smiled. 'You can offer me a drink,' I suggested. 'It's another hot day.'

'Sure,' he said, and turned to his wife. 'Bette, how's the jug doing?'

'See for yourself,' she said without looking up. 'I'm not your slave.' There was an edginess in her voice I hadn't heard the last time I was there.

Haslam peered into the jug. 'Room for one more.' He pulled over a cane chair. 'Take a seat.'

I took the chair and placed it so that I could see the gate to the estate in the distance across the airstrip. I wanted to know when Hanna arrived. 'How did the flight to the States go?' I asked.

'Not bad. No trouble to speak of.'

'Where did you go?'

'Philadelphia. Mrs Salton went to see her sister-in-law.' He handed me a glass.

'Thanks. Did she say anything about her plans for the plane?' Haslam shook his head and the lines about his eyes deepened. 'Maybe you'd better ask her,' I said.

'Hell, no! I don't want to buy trouble.' He was drinking this time and took a deep slug from his glass.

'At least you'd know one way or the other,' I said. 'You'd be able to make plans.'

He shrugged. 'I don't want to put ideas into her head. Maybe she hasn't even thought about it. I'd be a damned fool if I gave her the notion.'

Bette Haslam snorted. 'No, you don't want to give Mrs Salton any ideas. Any ideas at all.' She was tipsy again – not incapably so, but in that alcoholic haze which the heavy drinker is able to maintain indefinitely.

'Shut up, Bette,' said Haslam. He said it with a lack of force and a little tiredly, as though it was something he said automatically and without thinking. A routine reprimand. 'You want anything in particular, Mr Kemp?'

I looked over at the gate. 'Not really,' I said. 'Just taking the air and sitting in the sun.' I stretched out my legs. 'Somebody told me that whenever the plane leaves this island, you have to call in at Benning.'

'That's right. We get nicked for the departure tax.'

'Aircrew, too?'

'Everybody,' he said firmly. 'No exceptions.'

'Sounds like a profitable tax,' I said. 'What about coming back? I suppose you fly directly here.' I didn't really want to know: I was just making conversation.

'No. We have to land at Benning for a Customs check.' He grinned. 'They get us coming and going.'

'Even millionaires? What would they be smuggling?'

'The Saltons wouldn't be smuggling anything,' said Haslam. 'Mr Salton was very hot on that type of thing. Every-thing was declared if he was bringing anything in, and he paid the duty on the nail. A man in his position, it wouldn't be worth his while to be caught avoiding Customs duty.' He tapped himself on the chest. 'Aircrew are different. You'd be surprised at what aircrew can get away with. And don't the Customs boys know it: they always give us a real going over.'

'Looking for what?'

He shrugged. 'Drugs, most likely. They've never found anything on us. Mr Salton gave me strict orders about that type of thing and nothing got on that plane that I didn't know about. But the Customs had to check just the same.'

'In the line of duty,' I said. 'I know what you mean. A pity people have to be so suspicious.'

Bette Haslam said, 'You can't trust anyone these days. But God, the things I saw when I was a hostess.'

'You were an air hostess?'

'Sure,' she said. 'A flying waitress. It's not so glamorous, not like they make out. You spend your life wiping off snotty-nosed kids and holding vomit bags and fending off passes from drunks – especially first-class drunks, where the booze is free. They still get plenty of suckers for the job but I was glad to get out.' She poked her glass in the direc-tion of her husband. 'That's when I met this big clunk.'

There was a car at the gate. I finished my drink and said, 'Thanks for the cooler. Do you ever get into San Martin?'

'Sometimes,' said Haslam.

'Maybe we can get together. I'd like to repay your hospitality.'

'What's a couple of drinks?' said Haslam. 'But thanks all the same, Mr Kemp. Maybe we'll do that.'

I got up, said goodbye and went away with nothing gained but a margarita. When I got down to the quay, a car was just pulling to a halt with my friend on the motorcycle as an outrider. Hanna got out of the car, pulled out a large handkerchief and mopped his brow. I went over to him and said, 'You made good time.'

'I'm a demon driver when aroused.' He glanced at the launch, where Raymond was still polishing the brightwork. 'Would that be White?'

'Yes,' I said.

'Tell me it again,' said Hanna. 'I want to check if I've got it right.'

So I told him, and he took a deep breath and stared at White. 'If this is true, I ought to slap him so that his head spins. I won't, though. Let's see what a little honey will do before we resort to vinegar.'

He walked over to the edge of the quay and looked down into the launch. 'You Raymond White?'

White looked up at him. 'Yes, sir. Do you want to go over to the island, sir? I didn't get a call about that.'

'No,' said Hanna. 'It's you I've come to see. Do you mind stepping up here?' His voice was smooth and soft.

White climbed up on to the quayside. 'You've come to see me, sir?' He appeared to be bewildered as he looked past Hanna towards me.

'I'm a police officer,' said Hanna. 'And I want to ask you a few questions. Nothing to worry about if you tell the truth.'

White's face closed up. 'Questions! What about?'

'Suppose you show me Mr Salton's boat – the one he was found in. It's here, isn't it?'

'In the boathouse. This way.' White led the way to the boathouse and we went inside. There was a big cabin cruiser about forty feet long and equipped for game fishing, there was a thirty-foot sailing boat with the mast unstepped, and there were three dinghies. White pointed. 'That's the one – the Flying Fifteen.'

It didn't look to me as though it could fly but then I know nothing about dinghies. Hanna said, 'How did it get back here from San Martin?'

'Mrs Salton told me to go over and sail her back round after the police had finished with her,' said White.

'That must have been about ten days ago.'

'Yes, sir.'

'And when did you last see it before that?' asked Hanna. His voice was casual.

'I . . .' White stopped and started again. 'That was before Mr Salton took her out.'

Hanna took out a notebook and a pen. 'The date?'

White's face wore a hunted look. 'That's not easy, sir. It was a while ago.'

'All right, tell me this. When did Mr Salton disappear?'

'I don't know, sir. Not really. It was all a mix-up, wasn't it?'

'You must have read the papers,' said Hanna. 'Didn't you see the account of the inquest?' White stood mute, so Hanna said, 'According to Mrs Salton's evidence, he disappeared on the ninth of January at about eleven in the morning. You read about that, didn't you?'

'No, sir.'

Hanna frowned. 'You didn't? Weren't you interested? Your boss dies in a strange way and you weren't interested enough to wonder how it happened? I find that hard to believe, especially since it was your job to look after the boat in which he was found.'

'I may have read it,' said White sullenly. 'I've forgotten.'

Hanna said gently, 'Are you afraid of something, Mr White? You've no need to be afraid if you tell the truth. But you have every reason to be afraid if you lie to me. Now, I'm going to ask you a straight question and I want a straight answer. When did you last see that boat before you brought it back from San Martin?'

White shuffled his feet and said in a low voice, 'On the tenth. Early morning.'

'Speak up,' said Hanna. His voice was a whiplash. 'I didn't hear that.'

'All right,' said White. 'I saw her on the morning of the tenth of January, about three in the morning.'

'Where was the boat?'

'Here, right where she's lying now.'

'And what were you doing down here at three in the morning?'

'I'd been night fishing,' said White. 'Mr Salton didn't mind – I asked his permission. He said it was all right so long as I got enough sleep to do my work. He said if I made a good catch I should give him some fish.'

'How often did you go out?'

'One night a week, maybe. Sometimes two.'

'Which boat did you take?'

'Most times I'd take the work boat,' said White. 'The twenty-footer next to the launch out there.'

'What time did you go out on this occasion?'

White reflected for a moment, then said, 'About ten o'clock on the night of the ninth. I got back five hours later.'

'At three o'clock on the morning of the tenth,' said Hanna. 'And you saw this boat here. Weren't you surprised?'

'Why should I be surprised?' demanded White. 'She was where she was meant to be.'

'But Mr Salton had disappeared.'

White shrugged. 'I didn't know that.'

'All right,' said Hanna. 'Now, when did you find the boat had gone?'

'An hour later,' said White after a long pause.

'You came back to the boathouse at four in the morning. Why?'

'I was worried about the work boat. I couldn't remember if I'd moored her properly so I came back to check. It was one of those things – you know, you leave your house and you can't remember if you've turned off the oven so you go back and check. I cleaned the fish and had a beer and I came down to check the work boat before I went to bed.'

'And what did you find?'

White said, 'Is this important?'

'Very important,' said Hanna.

White swallowed. 'I saw the dinghy in the lagoon, heading towards the pass in the reef.'

'It was night time. Could you see it clearly?'

'There was a moon,' said White. 'It was a good light.'

'Could you see who was in it?'

'A woman,' said White. 'She was sailed by a woman.'

'White or black?'

'Hard to tell. It was a fair way. But she had pale hair.'

'So what did you do?'

'Do?' said White. 'I did nothing.'

Hanna stared at him. 'Someone was sailing away in one of your employer's boats and you did nothing. Isn't that strange?'

'What the hell!' said White. 'I thought it was Mrs Salton. She likes night sailing.'


## III


'Like extracting teeth one by one,' said Hanna. We stood by his car and roasted in the sun. White had been sent home under the guard of the patrolman until he could be taken into San Martin for further questioning. 'I've got other things to do right now,' said Hanna.

'Such as questioning Mrs Salton?'

'Maybe.' He stared over the water at the island. 'White is a damned fool with a misplaced sense of loyalty. He knew his evidence was important but he was trying to protect Mrs Salton.'

'How do you suppose Hawke got wind of it?'

Hanna shrugged. 'I don't know. Maybe White got drunk one night and opened his mouth a bit wide. There's not much on this island that Hawke doesn't know about. Sometimes I think his intelligence service is better than mine.'

I nodded. 'He knew I'd been shot,' I said. 'McKittrick didn't.'

'If I find the leak in my department, they'll be fired so fast they'll think it was from a cannon,' said Hanna grimly. He leaned inside his car and came out with a large envelope. 'This came for you.'

It looked official and was of heavy and expensive cream laid stationery, addressed to me at the Royal Caribbean Hotel.

'How did you get your hands on it?' I asked.

Hanna smiled. 'That's the kind of question you don't ask a policeman. I just thought you might like to see it sooner rather than later.'

I looked at the envelope. Embossed on the flap was a coat of arms. I had difficulty ripping it open because it seemed to be constructed on the lines of a bank vault. Hanna said, 'You've been invited to a cocktail party.'

I took the card from the envelope and found that it was so. The Honourable Walden P. Conyers, Prime Minister of Campanilla, took pleasure in requesting the attendance of Mr William Kemp at a reception at Government House, 5 p.m. to 7 p.m. that very evening, dress informal.

I turned suspiciously to Hanna. 'You must have X-ray eyes. How did you know what was in here?'

'I've got one, too,' he said. 'Interesting, isn't it?'

I looked down at my suit. I had been wearing it continuously since I had arrived on Campanilla and it was beginning to show the strain. It looked grubby and there were dark sweat stains under the arms. 'I don't know how far your protocol takes informality,' I said. 'But this is the only lightweight suit I have, and I'd boil to death in my English suit.'

Hanna gave me a measuring look, like an undertaker at a resident in an old people's home. 'I've just got a couple of suits back from the cleaners,' he said. 'I'd say you're about my size. You can come back with me and have a fitting if you like.'

'That's very accommodating of you,' I said.

He smiled warmly and said, 'I think we'll leave Mrs Salton for tomorrow. White has been salted away so he can't talk to anyone.' He checked his watch. 'We just have time to go home and change before the party.'

'It's as late as that? I didn't have lunch – I forgot.'

'I didn't either,' he said. 'But it wasn't for want of remembering. My wife will fix us something.' He tapped the card I still held in my hand. 'I think the Honourable Walden P. Conyers is about to let the boom down on you, Mr Kemp. Heavy pressure.'

'Don't worry about me,' I said. 'But if Commissioner Barstow gives you a direct order to drop this case, what will you do?'

'I don't know, not right now. But I will know the moment he gives that order.'

I turned it over in my mind as we got into the car. If anybody knew where the political bodies were buried, it would be the head of the political police. But perhaps Barstow would be afraid of tangling too directly with Hanna. I hoped so.

# IV

I felt cleaner and less sticky when we got to Government House. Hanna had a charming wife and three delightful children, all of whom climbed over him as soon as we arrived. Mrs Hanna came out of the scrimmage and apologised cheerfully: 'It's just that we don't see enough of him, Mr Kemp.'

I grinned. 'I think I may be seeing too much of your husband.'

The house was bright and well furnished but the careful eye could see the evidence of making-do: the neatly mended upholstery of a chair, the small patch in the tablecloth, the place where a piece had been let into a carpet. If a superintendent of police had to make do and mend, what chance was there for a working-class man? What McKittrick had said was brought home forcibly.

I showered and changed into one of Hanna's suits, which fitted as though made to measure, and Mrs Hanna provided a light snack. Then we went on our way and arrived at Government House dead on time.

The imposing white stone building overlooked Fleming Square, at the heart of San Martin's administrative quarter, and the district was buzzing with cars and people, presumably heading for the same cocktail party as we were. Hanna parked facing the square and said, 'This is going to be interesting. That's one of Salton's cars.' He nodded towards a Cadillac.

We went inside to find cut-glass chandeliers and marble walls. As we climbed a wide staircase to the first floor, Hanna caught my eye and said sardonically, 'Built to impress the natives in colonial times. The Governor used to live here.'

The reception was held in a large mirrored ballroom along

the front of the building, oppressively heavy with ornate gilding and convoluted plasterwork on the ceiling. There was the usual hum of voices from the early minutes of a cocktail party. As time went on and more drinks were consumed, the noise would become louder until reasonable conversation was impossible. All over the world these parties are the same: the drinks are too warm or, if you put ice in them, they become too dilute; the faces become dissociated from the hurried given names; the canapés curl at the edges because of the heat and, in the end, all that are left are the few regular drunks who have to be tactfully eased out.

I handed my card to a flunkey in knee-breeches, who bellowed, 'Mr William Kemp.'

No one seemed to take much notice so I went in. A man stepped forward with his hand outstretched and a deep voice said, 'Glad you could come, Mr Kemp.'

I took the offered hand and looked into the charismatic face. 'It was kind of you to invite me, Mr Prime Minister.'

'Let me introduce you to my wife,' said Conyers. 'Darling, this is Mr Kemp from London. You may remember that he's employed by Lord Hosmer.'

As I shook hands with the middle-aged woman in the Balmain gown, I reflected that Conyers had put me firmly into place. *Employed by Lord Hosmer.* God bless Lord Hosmer and his relations and keep us in our proper stations.

Mrs Conyers mumbled something I couldn't hear so I smiled and passed on.

I captured a scotch from a passing tray-carrier and turned to look for Hanna, but he wasn't there and neither had the flunkey boomed his name. I suspected that the tactician in him had decided we should not make our entrance together. Guilt by association is a political disease he didn't care to catch.

Drink in hand, I surveyed the throng. Everyone looked prosperous and well fed, and from the names of the arriving guests that were bawled from the door, this seemed to be a meeting of the ruling class with an admixture of influential foreigners. Subtle lapel badges on various guests revealed the national flags of the United States and other countries sharing diplomatic ties with Campanilla, while a thick Russian accent near me betrayed a broad-cheeked Soviet, apparently part of a visiting trade contingent. Elsewhere there seemed to be dignitaries, civic worthies and a few high-ranking army and police officers, including one I assumed from his uniform to be Commissioner Barstow. I sipped my drink and wondered why I was there.

Knee-breeches shouted, 'Mr Henry Roker.' There was a crowd between me and the reception line at the door so I couldn't immediately see him, but my brain cells began tingling when the next call came: 'Lord Hosmer.'

A voice behind me said, 'Well, Bill, I didn't expect to see you here.'

I turned and found Negrini. 'Hello, Gerry.'

'Are you here by invitation?' His voice expressed incredulity.

'I haven't got leprosy,' I said.

'You've got the social equivalent, from what I hear,' he said. 'You are not too popular with Conyers.'

'Maybe I've been invited to be the principal guest at a lynching.' Roker and Hosmer strolled by, their heads close together. They were talking in short, jerky sentences and both faces were unsmiling. I indicated Roker. 'That's the chap I asked you to check on.'

'Roker,' said Negrini. 'There's a kind of Chamber of Commerce – not the official one but a sort of inner club of the big boys. Very private and by invitation only. Roker seems to be a trouble-shooter and hatchet man. Who's the other guy?'

'Lord Hosmer, my employer – for a short while. He's going to fire me.'

'*Going* to fire you!' Negrini was baffled. 'Why the hell doesn't he do it now?'

'I've got him by the balls,' I said. 'But I can't hang on long. Besides, I was present when someone reamed him out. He's not going to forget that.'

'You lead an interesting life,' said Negrini.

'What are *you* doing here?' I asked. 'You told me Conyers is going to chase you off the island after the election. You're not too popular, either.'

He grinned. 'It's the old political game of pretending we're all gentlemen. Besides, it's easier to stab a man when you're shaking his hand.'

I looked across the room and saw Hanna talking to the uniform I'd seen earlier. 'Who is that with Hanna?'

'His boss, Commissioner Barstow.' He laughed. 'Do you see Jackson just behind them trying to eavesdrop?' He tapped me on the arm. 'What the hell is going on at El Cerco? Jill Salton tells me that Hanna has arrested someone from the estate.'

'Not arrested,' I said. 'Just held for questioning. When did she tell you that?'

'About five minutes ago.'

'She's here then?'

Negrini nodded across the room. 'Over in the far corner.'

'I'll see you later,' I said, and moved off through the crowd. It seemed as though the gang was all here and they must have been assembled for a reason. Any man who gets to become Prime Minister is no fool, and I wondered what was in Conyers's mind.

Jill was talking to a short, balding guest but she saw me coming, excused herself and came to meet me. She wasted no time. 'What does Hanna think he's doing?' she demanded in a low voice. 'Why has he arrested Raymond White?'

'He hasn't,' I said. 'White is helping the police with their inquiries.'

'You know damned well that's a newspaper euphemism,' she said.

'But it's true this time. Barstow blundered when he went to El Cerco. He neglected to question White. Hanna is just doing a follow-up.'

'What has White been saying?'

I shook my head. 'I can't tell you that, Jill. Why don't you ask Hanna?' I turned my head and indicated him. 'He's over there talking to Barstow.'

'I might do that,' she said.

'Actually, don't. Not yet, anyway. Can I suggest you refrain from talking to Hanna unless you've got Stern there? You might need him.'

For a moment she was speechless, then she recovered her breath. 'You mean to say that he really suspects *me*?'

'White could be potentially damaging,' I said soberly. 'Don't talk to Hanna without Stern present. It's as bad as that.'

'For God's sake! What did Raymond say?'

I mentally tossed a coin. Should I tell her or not? I was getting on well with Hanna and I didn't want to jeopardise that relationship. On the other hand, I didn't think Jill Salton had killed her husband. But that was a private and personal opinion, which could possibly be wrong.

I was saved from answering by no less a personage than the Honourable Walden P. Conyers, Prime Minister of Campanilla. As he approached, all the danger signals went up because, hanging on his arm, was Leotta Tomsson.

'Good evening, Mr Kemp, Mrs Salton. I trust you are enjoying yourselves.'

I stared at Leotta, who looked back at me with a blank face. 'Yes,' I said. 'It's a good party.'

'But your glass is empty,' said Conyers. He snapped his fingers and a waiter dashed up.

I took a fresh drink and adjusted my position slightly so I could see Hanna. For the first time since I'd met him, he didn't have that deceptive sleepy look. He was angry. He regarded Leotta Tomsson with wide eyes and looked mad enough to bite a snake, then he turned to Barstow and snapped out a curt phrase. Barstow appeared to respond soothingly and put his hand on Hanna's arm. Hanna shook it off with a distasteful gesture and again said something short and bitter. It must have been bitter because Barstow began to get angry too.

I switched my attention back to Conyers. 'Mrs Salton,' he said. 'I don't think you've met Miss Tomsson. I believe she was a very old friend of your husband's.'

Leotta Tomsson's face was still as blank as if she'd been drugged, but Jill Salton had gone white, and pink spots burned in her cheeks. There was going to be an almighty explosion if someone didn't do something quickly and the only someone around was me, because Conyers was clearly relishing the situation.

Deliberately I tilted my glass and poured the entire contents down the front of Jill's dress. She let out an involuntary squeak as the ice-cold drink hit her stomach. 'Oh, I'm sorry. How clumsy of me.' I flipped a handkerchief from my pocket and dabbed ineffectually at her. She shrank away from my hand and slipped on a piece of ice, and the only reason she didn't go down was because I grabbed her arm and kept her upright. In another age I could have earned a living with Mack Sennett.

Jill looked down at her dress and gave me a cold look. 'Excuse me,' she said to Conyers. 'I must sort this out.' She walked away quickly in the direction of the door.

I grinned weakly at Conyers. 'Now I do need another drink.'

'Of course, Mr Kemp.' His voice was affable but his face was hard. 'I understand you're already acquainted with Miss Tomsson.'

'We've met,' I said. 'Once.'

'Then perhaps you will entertain her for a few minutes.' He inclined his head courteously and walked away, abandoning Leotta, who had served her purpose.

A waiter shoved a tray under my nose. I waved him away and said to Leotta, 'Just what the hell do you think you're doing here?'

'I didn't want to come,' she said. 'They brought me.'

'Who did?'

'The police. Commissioner Barstow.'

Hanna was at my elbow. I turned to him and said, 'You ought to keep those files of yours in a vault. What the devil does Barstow think he's doing?'

'He's playing politics,' said Hanna tiredly. 'You'd better go home, Miss Tomsson.'

'What about Mr Barstow?'

'He won't trouble you now.'

Leotta hesitated. 'I'm sorry if I caused trouble. I didn't know I was going to meet Mrs Salton. I wouldn't want to cause her any hurt.'

Hanna sighed. 'The damage has been done.'

'Maybe if I talked to her . . .'

'No,' I said. 'Keep away from Mrs Salton. You won't do any good and you might do more harm.' I turned my head and saw Jackson threading his way through the crowd. 'And for Christ's sake, don't talk to the press.' Hosmer might have gagged Jackson but I didn't know how effective the gag was.

'Very well,' she said as Jackson came up. 'I'll do as you say.'

She moved away gracefully and I grabbed Jackson by the elbow as he turned to follow her. 'Superintendent Hanna wants to talk to you, Mr Jackson.'

Hanna looked surprised but caught on and picked up his cue. 'Yes, about the riots today.'

'Oh,' said Jackson. 'Who was that?'

I shrugged. 'I don't know. A friend of Conyers, name of . . . er . . . Samson, I think.'

'Simpson,' said Hanna with a straight face.

'She's quite a looker,' commented Jackson. 'What about the riots, Superintendent?'

Hanna took his arm. 'I don't think you are giving the police a fair shake in your coverage.'

I left them to it because I had seen Stern on the other side of the room. Halfway across I was button-holed by Roker. 'Hold on a minute, Kemp.'

'What do you want?' I said brusquely.

'Just a friendly chat.'

'I pick my friends carefully,' I said.

'What's the point of insulting me?' he asked. 'I understand Mrs Salton offered you a job. You won't get it. You'll find she'll withdraw the offer.'

'You seem to know a lot about what Mrs Salton will or won't do.'

'I know exactly,' he said flatly. 'And you're through as far as she is concerned. You already know what Lord Hosmer thinks of you. You might as well quit. If you do, then Hosmer promises he'll reconsider.'

'Big of him,' I said. 'What's your leverage on Mrs Salton?'

'You were just talking to it. Conyers says that if you're still here at midday tomorrow, he'll break the story of Salton's mistress. There's someone putting Mrs Salton in the picture right now. I'd say that she's going to hate your guts if you're still here tomorrow afternoon.'

I glanced around the room. 'I don't imagine there's been a bigger crowd of bastards collected in one place since the Nuremberg trials.'

'Quit wailing,' said Roker. 'Look, you can come out of this on top. You can make things right with Hosmer and still be in good with Mrs Salton. Doing her a favour like that could get you quite a piece of change.'

'You asked me a question just now,' I said. 'You wanted to know what was the point of my insulting you. I insult you with words because I'm prohibited at the moment from insulting you with my fist.' I tapped him on the chest. 'But only at the moment. If you approach me with any of your smart-alec suggestions again, I'll drive your teeth through the back of your neck.'

'Big talk!' He sneered at me.

'You'd better hope so,' I said, and left him.

Stern had disappeared while I was talking to Roker but I didn't bother looking for him because I wanted to find out who was talking to Jill Salton. As I might have expected, it was Hosmer: he had her corralled in a corner of the marble hall and was yapping at her.

I walked up and said, 'Having trouble?'

She looked at me and her eyes flickered away. A bad sign. Hosmer said, 'I don't think Mrs Salton wants you to stay on Campanilla.'

'Is that right, Jill?' I asked deliberately.

'It's that woman,' she said. 'I've just been told that if you don't leave by noon tomorrow Conyers will tell the press about her and David.'

'The age of chivalry is dead, Jill.'

'But David's reputation . . .'

I cut in. 'And what about Ogilvie? Am I supposed to forget that?'

'Why so stubborn?' asked Hosmer.

'That's a quality you've paid for highly in the past,' I said. 'Don't knock it now. Jill, let me get one thing straight. Is Conyers willing to guarantee that if I leave by noon tomorrow, the story won't get into the press?'

'Of course,' said Hosmer quickly.

'Then he's a liar, because he's promising something he can't deliver. Hawke knows about it and you can be sure he'll break the story in his own good time, and there's nothing Conyers can do about that. This is going to come out anyway, Jill, and right now you're being conned by Conyers, the con man. I just wanted you to understand that before telling you that I wouldn't have left anyway.'

I glanced at Hosmer, who was moistening his lips, and added, 'If you don't believe me, look at your precious uncle and you'll see it written all over his face. Lord Hosmer, common blackmailer.'

His face purpled. 'Now, see here . . .'

'Shut up!' I said. 'And keep that bastard Roker away from me or I'll break his neck.'

I walked away feeling a dreary satisfaction at having been able to speak my mind for once. This whole damned business was beginning to get me down and for the first time I seriously questioned my own motives for staying. I knew the answer, of course. I was exactly what Hosmer had said: stubborn. Obstinate, pigheaded, obdurate – all to the point of wilfulness. That was the real reason I'd come a cropper in my army career.

But I didn't like being pushed and I didn't like being manipulated, and there were too many people trying to do both. My reaction to being pushed was to push back, but this case was so bloody amorphous that I didn't know who or where to do the pushing. Slamming at Hosmer only gave me small satisfaction – it was hard to imagine he had anything to do with Ogilvie's death, either directly or indirectly. The Hosmers of this world aren't murderers. They don't kill a man; just his spirit. But somebody had killed Ogilvie, and somebody had taken a shot at me, and there was still a hell of a stench surrounding Salton's death. My biggest frustration right now – apart from the feeling of being unwillingly backed into a corner – was that the whole mystery was shrouded in a fog against which it was futile to push.

I headed back to the party to find that the noise level had reached the optimum decibel rating, marginally less than that of Concorde taking off. Negrini was near the door. He took one look at my face and said, 'You look as though you've just swallowed a lemon. Cheer up and have a drink.'

'Not now.' I looked about the room. 'Seen Hanna?'

Negrini grinned. 'I saw him talking to Barstow a few minutes ago. It looked like the opening shots in a civil war. I'd say there's a schism developing in the police force.'

I said, 'How safe is Hanna if it comes to a power struggle with Barstow?'

'I wouldn't know. He's a clever guy, and don't you be deceived by that sleepy look of his.' He shook his head. 'But Barstow has Conyers behind him.'

I saw Hanna on the other side of the room, standing with his head cocked on one side as if listening to something. I said, 'I think we're about to find out how safe he is. The earthquake is coming, Gerry.'

I went across to Hanna and said, 'They're trying to black-mail her. Me too.'

He blinked at me. 'Who and who?'

'Conyers, Hosmer and Roker want me absent. They threatened to blow the story of Salton and Leotta Tomsson if I don't leave. I think I spiked it – for now.'

'As I said before, things happen when you're around. There's a word for it. You're a catalyst.' He frowned and cocked his head on one side again. 'Something's going on.'

'What?'

'Listen.'

A woman near me was yelling at her escort in a high-pitched soprano. 'For God's sake!' I said. 'What am I supposed to hear in the middle of this?' But obediently I listened and found that there was a different quality to the noise, an underlying rhythm of varying intensity, which seemed to beat in waves.

Hanna jerked his head at me and I followed him to the window. He pulled aside the curtain and we looked out over Fleming Square. Dusk was falling and it was packed with people, a shimmering mosaic of shouting heads and waving arms in the fading light. There must have been a couple of thousand out there and they were all shouting the same thing.

*Sal-ton*. Sal-ton. *SAL-TON*. SAL-TON.

As Hanna dropped the curtain I saw the first of the riot squads arrive on the other side of the square. He said, 'That's no rentacrowd – that's the real thing. They mean business.' He looked around and beckoned to Barstow.

I parted the curtain again and looked out over the square. The contrast between the colonial rococo inside and the raw street outside, between the urbane civilities of the cocktail hour and those clenched fists, made me realise what the Czar and his family must have felt just before the mob stormed the Winter Palace.

Someone out there must have seen the chink of light at the upper-storey window. I caught a brief glimpse of something thrown and there was a smash of glass just to my left. I dropped the curtain quickly and stepped back. The drapery had prevented shattered glass from spraying into the room, but the missile lay on the carpet: a jagged half-brick.

Out of the corner of my eye I saw Hanna and Barstow making a quick exit and then Conyers was coming towards the window. 'What's going on out there?'

'It's the voice of a dead man,' I said. 'You can't fight that, Mr Prime Minister.'

# EIGHT

## I

Although Joe Hawke had not been invited to the Prime Minister's cocktail party, he was undoubtedly present, in spirit if not in body. The crowd out in the square might have been yelling the name of Salton, but they were puppets manipulated by Hawke. He was milking the situation for all it was worth.

The reaction in the ballroom could best be described as modified panic. As another window smashed, the noisy conversation gave way to the roar of the crowd outside and, for a tantalising moment, everyone stood still. The mob, a manifold wild beast, sounded like something out of a zoo baying with a rage that held everyone in a strange paralysis.

Then a woman screamed and the spell was broken. Conyers swung on his heel and elbowed his way through the crowd, which had begun to scurry about in a chaotic manner. Women were gathering up their handbags and already the quicker-witted were slipping away. I saw Conyers approach a red-tabbed army officer and speak to him urgently. The officer nodded, picked up his braided cap and a swagger stick, and shouldered his way to the door.

I didn't like the look of that. If sending in the army was Conyers's instinctive response to a civil disturbance, it suggested he was losing his grip. The use of armed force against civilians is not a good indication of a clear-headed statesman.

A third window smashed and I decided it was time to make a move. The crowd had thinned appreciably – there would be no last-minute drunks at this party – and I made my way across the room. Negrini grabbed my arm. 'Seen Jill Salton?'

'The last time I saw her she was out there.' I nodded towards the door.

'Good,' he said. 'She'll have got a head start.' He grimaced. 'What do you think's blown the lid off?'

'Someone told me it was me,' I said, and ignored his look of surprise. 'What's the best way out of here?'

'You saw out front: how does it look?'

'The square's jammed with people.'

'Damn,' he said. 'My car's out there. Maybe the back door's our best bet.'

The rear of Government House was a rabbit warren of service rooms. The architectural splendour diminished as we went on. We passed through a kitchen and then came into a long corridor with dull marmalade-coloured walls. Negrini pointed. 'Looks like an exit.'

We came out on to a cul-de-sac that was used for deliveries. In the dying light I saw a row of dustbins and a scrawny cat, which fled as we appeared. At the end of the cul-de-sac, people were running and shouting, and the chanting of the crowd from the square on the other side of the building was intense.

A rush of people burst out of the door behind us, spooked by the noise from the square. It had taken them longer than us to realise that the best way out of Government House was the rear, but there were a lot of them – not only guests from the party, but also servants in white jackets and other staff – and we were pushed back against the opposite wall. From what I could see of their faces in the light from the corridor, panic was really setting in. The wide eyes, open mouths and meaningless noises brought sharply to mind a batch of raw recruits I'd commanded in Korea as a young officer. Terror in human beings is never a pretty sight.

I grabbed a passing figure by the arm. 'What's happening back there?'

It was the balding man I had seen talking to Jill at the party. 'They're breaking down the front door,' he said breathlessly.

He tore himself loose and ran away. When I turned to speak to Negrini I found he had gone, jostled aside in the crowd, and the narrow alley was full of running people. In the distance I heard the wailing of sirens.

I flattened myself against the wall again and let them go by. When the first spate had gone, I followed towards the end of the cul-de-sac. In front of me was the limping figure of a woman and when I reached her I saw it was Leotta Tomsson. 'I thought you left earlier,' I said.

'I saw the crowd coming into the square,' she said. 'So I turned back.'

'What's the matter with your leg?'

'Nothing. Just my shoe – the damned heel's come off.' She stopped suddenly. 'The hell with it!' She stooped and took off her shoes. 'Tonight's a time to run,' she said.

We approached the corner. 'Could be,' I said. 'Let's go carefully here.'

The cul-de-sac opened out on to a street that led to Fleming Square along the side of Government House. I peered around the corner to the left, towards the square, and saw a writhing mob of people. The noise was a solid wall of sound. A quick glance the other way showed more trouble. Several lines of police were strung across the road, the street lights gleaming off their plastic face shields. Behind them loomed an armoured car, from which projected the ugly snout of a water cannon. At least, I hoped it was a water cannon.

'This is not a good place to be,' I said.

'Is that the police up there?'

'Yes.'

'They're on the move,' she said. 'Let's get back.' I saw the line of policemen move forward, their batons raised.

'Good idea.' I was thinking of the pitched battle I had witnessed from my hotel window. If that was a sample of Campanillan police work, I didn't want to encounter it at the sharp end. And that was a mere skirmish compared to what was brewing now.

We moved a little way back down the cul-de-sac and stood against the wall, waiting for the police to go by. When they appeared they were already moving at a trot. The first line went by and then a second, and then they must have hit the crowd in the square because a shout went up, interspersed with screams. Another line of police went past the entrance to the cul-de-sac and then a squad of six veered off and came running directly towards us.

I grabbed Leotta and pulled her into the alcove of the exit, now dark with its door closed once more. We flattened against it and they didn't see us in the gathering gloom, their boots clattering past in the alley. They got to the blind end and paused. Two of them went into Government House through another door further down, and the other four came back more slowly. I had the sudden impression they were looking for something. Or someone.

All hell seemed to be breaking loose in the square. The armoured car rumbled past and I heard the detonations as gas canisters were discharged. But I was less interested in that than in the fact that two of the coppers had produced powerful flashlights and were giving the alley a thorough inspection.

They came closer and the nearer light settled on me. 'Sergeant.'

I was blinded and put up a hand to my eyes as I heard

the thud of boots running up. They clattered to a halt. 'That's him. Right!'

I twisted sideways as a baton flailed out and hit the wall by my head. Leotta screamed in a piercing wail as I ducked out of the revealing light. Something, probably another baton, hit me in the side with enough force to have cracked ribs if I hadn't been moving away from it fast. I kicked out high with my foot and the flashlight went flying.

It had been a long time since I'd practised unarmed combat – too long. And even so, odds of four to one were too much, especially as these men were prepared for action. They wore helmets and their faces were covered, they had riot shields and those damned batons, and their boots were heavy. It was the boots I was afraid of. I knew that if I went down, it would be all over. They could stomp me right into the ground.

Leotta screamed again and a hoarse voice shouted, 'Leave the girl!' One of the coppers came at me: I whirled and his stroke missed. I chopped sideways at his neck and connected, but another of them got in a good blow to my shoulder as I did so and my whole right arm went numb. Then another came in lower and thrust his baton between my legs so that I stumbled and fell.

As I pitched forward I had a sudden vision of Ogilvie as I had last seen him, his face and body purple with bruises, and I knew it was going to happen to me. When I hit the ground I rolled away desperately, but not quickly enough. I was booted hard in the thigh at the same time as a baton cracked down heavily on my back.

I knew I had to protect my head and stomach so I squirmed into a ball with my knees up and my head bent over covered with my hands, trying to imitate a hedgehog – or a foetus. A boot cracked against my shin and blows rained down. The men were silent except for their heavy breathing and occasional grunts.

Then a voice yelled *'Sergeant!'*, there was a final blow and the beating mercifully stopped.

That last stroke of the baton had been over my kidneys and a wave of dizziness washed over me. I heard the voice again, cold with authority and crackling with tension. 'Sergeant, just what do you think you're doing?' A light played over me. 'What's your name, Sergeant?'

'Taylor.'

'Taylor – what?'

'Taylor, sir.'

'Post?'

'Hogtown, sir.'

'Well, Taylor, you will take these men and report to my office immediately. You will turn in those weapons and you will report to Inspector Rose and tell him that you are under arrest pending an inquiry. If he is not there, you will wait for him or for me. Is that understood?'

There was a pause. 'Well?'

'Yes, sir.'

The voice was soft with menace and I suddenly realised it was Hanna. I had never heard him sound like that before. 'If you are not there when I get back, Campanilla will not be big enough to hold you. Now get out of here.'

I unfurled myself cautiously and Hanna squatted on his heels. He held the flashlight on me and said, 'How are you, Mr Kemp?'

I couldn't help laughing. 'As well as you might expect.' I stopped laughing when I found it hurt.

Someone else knelt down and I looked into the eyes of Leotta Tomsson. 'Are you hurt bad?' Her dress was torn.

'They didn't get my head,' I said, and tried to sit up.

'Wait,' she said, and I felt her hands on me, pressing on my chest. 'Does that hurt?'

'Not much,' I said. 'Just sore.'

'I don't think they broke any ribs,' she said, and smiled

at my enquiring look. 'I was a nurse before I was a model. I know what a broken rib feels like.

Someone came running over. 'What the hell happened, Bill?' said Negrini. 'I lost you.'

'I was the victim of a police riot.' I eased myself up so I was sitting, with Leotta supporting me.

'They'll be disciplined,' said Hanna in a hard voice.

'You're missing the point,' I said. 'It was premeditated. They knew me, Hanna. They identified me before they attacked. It was the sergeant who knew what I looked like.'

Hanna looked bleak. 'Are you sure?'

'It's true,' said Leotta. 'They shone the light then called the sergeant, and he said, "That's him." Then they attacked.'

Hanna took a long shuddering breath. I said, 'I think you now hold four suspects for the murder of Owen Ogilvie. His injuries were consistent with what they tried to do to me. I'm glad you were around, Hanna.'

'It will be investigated,' he said, and stood up. 'We ought to get you to a hospital.'

'That's not an option,' I said. 'I don't want to be lying helpless in a hospital bed when someone slips me a mickey. Same goes for the hotel. I'm a witness, Hanna, and so is Miss Tomsson.'

Negrini said, 'We have a house doctor at the casino. How about that?'

'That'll do fine,' I said. 'As long as I don't have to walk there. Help me up, someone.'

Negrini and Hanna hauled me to my feet. Hanna said, 'You'd have a police guard in hospital.'

'Don't make me laugh,' I said. 'It hurts too much. I've just about had enough of your bloody police force.' I saw the sadness in his eyes and said quickly, 'Present company excepted. But you know what I mean.'

'Yes,' he said heavily. 'I'll find you a car. Fleming Square isn't safe yet. Wait here.'

He went away carrying an aura of depression almost like a visible cloud. I stood there testing various bits of my anatomy and found that I hurt in the damnedest places. Negrini said, 'I don't know what the hell's going on, but you'll be safe at my place.' He paused. 'I keep some strongarm boys on the premises, so if you need a bodyguard just shout.'

'Thanks,' I said, and looked at Leotta. 'Could you extend your hospitality to Miss Tomsson here? She's as much at risk as I am.'

'Sure,' said Negrini. 'Be glad to have you, Miss Tomsson.'

She hesitated and I said quickly, 'I wouldn't go back to Marshalltown for a while. As I said to Hanna, you're a witness and I wouldn't want Commissioner Barstow tracking you down. He's the wrong sort of copper, like Sergeant Taylor.'

'All right,' she said, and I breathed easier.

Presently Hanna came back with a police car and I hobbled into it. Hanna said, 'I'll see you tomorrow. I'm busy right now.'

That sounded like the understatement of the year.

Negrini drove the car and Leotta and I sat in the back. He had to drive the long way round, avoiding Fleming Square and its immediate vicinity. There were police everywhere and several streets were barricaded. 'What's the pitch?' said Negrini.

I glanced at Leotta. 'I'll tell you later when I feel more in the mood.'

As we turned on to the sea front, Negrini whistled and put on the brakes. A convoy of army trucks passed, including several Land Rovers with machine-guns already mounted. The soldiers appeared to be armed. 'What does Conyers think he's doing? Martial law?'

'He seems to be over-reacting,' I said. 'I'd say he's panicking.'

'I felt pretty panicky myself,' said Negrini. 'What a hell of a way to break up a party.'

He drove to the ferry and the three of us went over

alone, jumping the queue. I suppose that was the boss's prerogative. Not that there was much of a queue – the riot seemed to have put a damper on festivities. In the casino we took the lift up to a penthouse, which Negrini told us was his private quarters whenever he stayed in town. 'I have a house over in Marshalltown,' he said. 'A casino is no place to bring up kids.'

Within ten minutes he had a doctor in attendance and I was sipping a scotch while the quack probed into the sore places. Leotta helped him and he glanced at her. 'You've done this before,' he commented.

She nodded but said nothing, and he didn't pursue it.

On the other side of the room, Negrini was on the telephone. 'Sure, honey, I'm all right. I don't care what it said on the radio, I'm still all right. Look, I'll be staying here tonight. Lock up tight, you hear?'

The doctor was content to let Leotta strap me up tightly in bandages. Negrini said, 'Who's that? Charisse? Hello, honey-bun.' He made oochy-coochy noises for a while, then put down the telephone. 'Kids!' he said. 'I love 'em.'

The doctor went away and Leotta fingered her torn dress. 'Would your establishment run to a needle and thread, Mr Negrini?'

'Better than that,' he said. 'We can find a new dress.'

He picked up the telephone and presently a young lady appeared who made commiserating noises and whisked Leotta away. Negrini stared at the closing door and said, 'That's a hell of a beautiful woman. Who is she?'

'She was David Salton's mistress.'

He choked over his drink. 'The randy old goat! You mean that he . . . and she . . .' He put down his glass. 'Did Jill know?'

'She does now. Conyers was blackmailing her with it.' I told him about it.

'Conyers,' said Negrini disgustedly. 'He's so crooked I bet

he uses marked cards when he's playing solitaire.' He shook his head sadly. 'Jesus, you never know what a man will do.' He held up two fingers close together. 'I thought Jill and David were like that.'

'Maybe they were,' I said. 'I think they were.'

He nodded slowly. 'I know what you mean. It would take some woman to equal Jill, but maybe this Tomsson girl does that.'

I felt suddenly weak and tired. The doctor had doped me with something and all I wanted was a bed. I looked at the jacket I had been wearing. One of the pockets had been torn right off and the rest of it didn't look too good. It appeared I owed Hanna a new suit. That and my life.

Negrini looked closely at me. 'You're nearly asleep. We'll get you into bed.'

He helped me into the bedroom and stood around while I undressed and then assisted me into pyjamas and saw me settled. It was the first time I'd been tucked into bed since I was a child. As he straightened up he said, 'By the way, you wanted to know something about Salton's plane on the day he vanished. It went to Benning all right, and took off for New York at eight in the evening. Hope it helps.'

He switched off the light and closed the door and I lay there trying to think about that and what made it so important. But my head was buzzing with drugs and fatigue – there is nothing in the world so tiring as being beaten up – and I slid into the depths of sleep while trying to grasp hold of something significant but very slippery.

II

I awoke to sunshine flooding the bedroom. At first I was disoriented and didn't know where I was, but then I moved in the bed and the bundle of assorted aches brought recollection crashing back – the cocktail party, the rioting, the assault. The pain wasn't too bad considering everything. I had been lucky that Hanna had turned up when he did.

The bedroom door opened and Negrini stuck his head around it, saw that I was awake and came in. 'How are you feeling? What about breakfast in bed?'

I sat up, unfastened the pyjama jacket and looked at the broad bandages strapping my chest. I prodded myself experimentally and said, 'No, I'll get up. Just point me in the direction of the bathroom before you leave.'

'Okay. Breakfast in half an hour. It's nine o'clock now and Hanna says he'll be here at ten.'

I got out of bed slowly. 'What happened to Jill Salton last night?'

'She's okay,' said Negrini. 'I checked after we'd sorted you out. She holed up at Abel Stern's place. Said she's going back to El Cerco this morning.'

Breakfast was most pleasant. The table was set before a floor-to-ceiling window, which gave a panoramic view of Buque Island, Pascua Channel and a part of San Martin. The sun shone in a cloudless sky, the breakers rolled in from the blue sea and already the first of the brown sun-worshippers were relaxing on the beaches below. The scene was as bright as a picture postcard and it was hard to associate it with rioting and police violence. But Leotta Tomsson was at the breakfast table and her presence – and my aching back – made the reality abundantly clear.

Her dress was a simple shantung sheath and I said, 'That's nice.'

'Mr Negrini was optimistic when he said he could find me a dress,' she said. 'I'm six feet tall. One of his secretaries went over to Marshalltown and brought back a selection of my own clothes.' She poured herself coffee. 'She said the police arrived at Gregory Plaza just as she was leaving.'

I hesitated with my fork poised in the air. 'Did they, by God? Did they question her?'

'She passed them in the lobby. They didn't stop her but she noticed they went up to the fourth floor. She got out of there quickly.'

'It's just as well you didn't go back. I wouldn't want to be responsible for losing you too.'

Negrini arrived with a newspaper and sat down. 'The *Chronicle* is interesting this morning.' He passed it to me.

Jackson had gone to town. The headlines were big and black and there was a centrefold of nothing but pictures. One was of Jackson himself. He had a black eye. The front page asked a question in 120-point capitals – 'MARTIAL LAW?' – and below it was a picture of a soldier behind a machine-gun. Other pictures showed policemen charging beneath the unequivocal headline 'POLICE BRUTALITY'.

I turned to the editorial, which said, in the measured prose peculiar to leader writers, that this time the government had gone too far, that there was no necessity for the death of fourteen Campanillan citizens and the maiming of dozens of others, and that the disturbance – a justifiable outburst of the people's rage against a wicked government – could have been contained without the bloodshed of a police riot.

It seemed that Hosmer's gag on Jackson had slipped. Up to the time of Salton's death the *Chronicle* had been the organ of the Liberal Party, which was natural enough since Salton led the Liberals and owned the *Chronicle*. Since his death it had been curiously non-committal – the result, I assumed, of Hosmer's gag. But there was nothing non-committal about this coverage of last night's events.

I said, 'Jackson seems to have changed his tune.'

Negrini grinned. 'When the editor is given a black eye by a cop, you can't expect him to be on the cop's side. But there's more to it than that. Jill told me last night that she'd ordered Jackson to pull out all the stops, to go for the police and Conyers. Did you have anything to do with that?'

I put down my coffee cup. 'I might have done. I showed her that Conyers couldn't deliver on the promises he'd made to her.'

'She isn't as interested in the political side as David was,' said Negrini. 'But something must have made her mad last night. Even with a black eye Jackson wasn't too enthusiastic about going along with her, apparently. Until she threatened to fire him on the spot.'

I smiled. So that was why he'd spat out the gag. And once he'd done that, once he knew he had the support of his employer, there would be other consequences. Nothing I'd seen so far suggested that Jackson wasn't actually a decent journalist, so the next step would follow logically. I guessed he'd already sent a cable to the *Sunday Times* in London, alerting them to the fact that there was more to the rioting on Campanilla than met the foreign eye. Within two days, the *Insight* team would be probing into the situation. There was nothing Conyers could do about it, except declare journalists *personae non gratae* – and that would shout to the world that there was something rotten in the state of Campanilla.

Negrini stood up. 'This isn't putting money in the bank. I have work to do.' He pulled down the corners of his mouth. 'All this is hardly conducive to the smooth operation of the tourist trade. Business is going to be lousy over the next few weeks.' He shrugged and walked towards the door, then turned. 'I'll send up Hanna as soon as he arrives.'

I said to Leotta, 'Are you still thinking of leaving?'

'I couldn't stay here now,' she said. 'Not after what's happened.'

'No,' I said pensively. 'No, you couldn't. Still thinking of trying England?'

'I might. What's it like over there? All I can picture are big smoking chimneys and factories. I wouldn't like that.'

I smiled. 'Neither would I. I live in London but I have a little cottage down in Devon, between Dartmoor and the sea. Not many factory chimneys in Devon. Whenever I get uptight in London I go to the sea to smooth the wrinkles out of my psyche.'

'What's it like?'

'The cottage or Devon?'

'Both.'

'The cottage is thatched, believe it or not. A woman from the village keeps it in order for me. Devon is rolling hills and narrow country roads with hedges between the sea and the moor. I do some fishing and I have a little sailing cruiser moored in the Dart – that's the river. Sometimes, in the evenings, I go down to the pub and chat with the locals in the four-ale bar. They're not very fast-moving but they're shrewd in their country way. Not much gets past them. They're just not very interested in the city rat-race – so maybe they're the really smart ones.'

'It sounds nice,' she said.

'If you ever get to England, I'll take you there.'

The door slammed and I turned to see Hanna. He was rumpled but, for a change, not at all sleepy-looking, although he must have been out late – possibly all night. His movements were stiff and jerky and I wondered if he had pepped himself up with pills.

He came over and said abruptly, 'How are you feeling?'

'A bit stiff, that's all. Thanks for last night.'

'You were lucky,' he said. 'I was passing that alley at a run. If I hadn't glanced sideways I wouldn't have seen you. And I didn't know it was you until I shone the light.' Even his speech was jerky.

'What did the sergeant have to say?'

Hanna came out with a stream of foul obscenities which crisped my ears. I glanced at Leotta.

He stopped as suddenly as he had started. 'Sorry,' he said.

'So what happened?'

'It was late when I got back to the office,' he said. 'All hell was breaking loose in the city. When I got back, I saw Inspector Rose. He told me that the men had turned themselves in as I ordered. And then Barstow came in and took them away. Rose couldn't do anything about it. Barstow countermanded my order and took them away.' Hanna suddenly sat down.

'What are you going to do?'

He glared at me. 'What do you expect me to do? Arrest Barstow?'

That was hardly likely. I said, 'The police raided Gregory Plaza last night.' I explained how I knew.

'What can you do?' said Hanna in despair. 'No, tell me: what can I do? That son-of-a-bitch is playing politics. He's taking the whole damned police force into the political arena. Did you see the *Chronicle* this morning?'

'I saw it.' I thought of something else. 'Does Barstow know about Raymond White?'

'I shouldn't think so,' said Hanna. 'I have him in custody at a police station up in North End.'

'He might know by now,' I said. 'Gerry Negrini knew last night. Mrs Salton was making no secret of it. She wanted to know why he'd been arrested.'

Hanna jerked upright. 'She might even have asked Barstow. Where's a telephone?'

Leotta pointed. 'Over there.'

Hanna crossed the room and I settled down to think of the consequences of Barstow knowing what White had said. With the *Chronicle* coming out against Conyers quite openly, Barstow might reckon it a good move to make a snap arrest of Jill Salton so as to discredit the *Chronicle* and the Liberals. It would also take the heat off as far as the riots went. After all, they'd happened essentially because of the uncertainty about Salton's death, so if it could be made to look like a squalid jealousy killing, then Conyers would be laughing.

No wonder Hanna wanted a telephone fast.

He came back. 'It's all right. White's still there and no one from headquarters has asked any questions. I've given instructions that he be taken back to El Cerco. It's time I had a talk with Mrs Salton.'

'Yes,' I said. 'I think so, too.'

'Are you fit to travel?'

I looked at him in surprise. 'You want me along?'

'As I said, you're a catalyst. You start reactions going.'

'Not a catalyst,' I said. 'If you look at the proper defini-tion, a catalyst comes out of a chemical reaction unchanged. I think I've changed a lot since I came to Campanilla.'

'Never mind that,' he said impatiently. 'Can you come?'

I felt the constriction around my chest. 'If I took off these bandages I'd probably fall apart, but I reckon I'm okay if I can pick up another suit. You won't be getting yours back, I'm afraid.' I grinned at him. 'I'll put it on my expense account and Hosmer can pay.'

## III

Leotta stayed at the casino with instructions not to move out of the penthouse and Negrini agreed that if the police came looking for her, he'd keep her safe and out of the way. Hanna looked as though he was being torn in two. The conflict between his loyalties was in danger of breaking him. I watched him tell Negrini to keep Leotta out of police hands and it was positively painful.

I dosed myself up with painkillers and then Hanna and I went into town, to the shop where I had bought a suit previously, and I picked up another off the peg and paid by credit card. San Martin showed evidence of stress. The tailor's shop had a broken window. The police and the army were highly visible and the populace subdued. Even the

thronging tourists appeared to be sombre, but I reflected
that if I'd booked a fortnight in the sun and arrived to find
the place in violent uproar, I might feel a bit sombre too.

We came out of the shop and were crossing the pavement
to the car when we were intercepted by a uniformed police
officer. 'Superintendent Hanna?'

'Yes, Inspector?'

The officer indicated me. 'Is this Mr Kemp?'

'I'm Kemp,' I said.

'Commissioner Barstow would like to see you.'

'What about?'

'He didn't tell me.'

Hanna said, 'It's all right, Inspector. Mr Kemp is in my
charge.'

The inspector said, 'Commissioner Barstow wants to see
Mr Kemp as soon as possible.'

'Yes, you've given me the message,' said Hanna icily.

'The Commissioner said immediately,' insisted the inspector.

'I heard you the first time,' said Hanna. 'Is there anything
more?'

The inspector hesitated. 'No,' he said. 'That's all.'

Hanna said softly, 'Inspector, how have you been trained
to address superior officers?'

'That's all . . . sir.'

Hanna nodded and we got into the car, leaving the
inspector on the pavement. He seemed to be uncertain
about what to do. I said, 'What now?'

Hanna put the car into gear and inserted himself in the
traffic stream. 'Two can play at that game. Barstow did it
last night and I'm doing it now. To hell with him.'

'We go to El Cerco?'

'We go to El Cerco,' agreed Hanna. 'And we go fast.'

Hanna was laying his career on the chopping block. I
couldn't see him surviving in his job for very long if he
went on this way. It was all right bucking a junior officer

who probably didn't know which end was up anyway, but when Barstow caught up with him it could be different. On the other hand, perhaps Hanna knew exactly what he was doing. Perhaps.

Once out of town, he started to drive really fast. Sometimes there would be a jitney ahead, a beaten-up bus painted gaily and with slogans scrawled across it. The jitneys were the lords of the road and usually drove plumb in the middle, straddling the white line. But a touch of a button set the siren wailing, and the jitney would veer over, usually to bump heavily on the hard shoulder.

I said, 'When I talked to Joe Hawke in the Rainbow Rooms, he told me something of Conyers's methods.'

Hanna was sardonic. 'Did you believe him?'

'Not entirely. But he implied that Conyers, as well as controlling the police, sometimes used means of enforcement that were, shall we say, outside the normal legal channels.'

'You're thinking of the attack on Ogilvie,' said Hanna, and he sighed. 'That sergeant last night – I checked back. He and the three other men were all off-duty the night Ogilvie was attacked.'

'Does that mean something?'

'I think they were told to lean on Ogilvie a bit, to scare him. There's nothing takes the guts out of a man more than a physical hammering. I doubt if they intended to kill him. That was an accident. But if he'd claimed that four cops had beaten the hell out of him, then there'd be trouble. So it had to be done when they were in plain clothes. That way, even if Ogilvie yapped, there'd be no comeback.'

'What about me? They were in uniform when they attacked me.'

'You were different,' said Hanna patiently. 'You were caught up in a riot. Somebody took a chance and hoped to get away with it.'

I said, 'Who would have given the order for Ogilvie?'

'It's not a matter of orders,' said Hanna. 'Look, someone in Cardew Street mentions to Conyers that Ogilvie's asking questions, and isn't that awkward. Conyers expresses the same sentiments to Barstow, and so it goes down the line. Then someone, somehow, does something about it. No direct orders beyond, maybe, a wink.' His voice hardened. 'But no one had the guts to wink at me.'

I thought of the anonymous caller who threatened me and realised how important it had been that I'd made very clear what I would do if my movements were hampered. I had laid it on the line with both Roker and Hosmer and that had saved me. For a while.

I said, 'But who shot me?'

'That one has me worried,' said Hanna. 'It doesn't fit.' He cornered with a squeal of tyres. 'But we'll come to it in time.' He swung the wheel violently the other way. 'If I'm given the time,' he added grimly.

'And if no one takes another shot at me,' I said. 'They may not miss next time.'

As we approached El Cerco, I saw that the gates stood open and a uniformed policeman was at the entrance instead of the two estate guards. Hanna stopped and said, 'Is White here?'

'Yes, sir.'

'All right.' He smiled tightly. 'Don't announce me.' I saw that the sleepy look had come back and I felt a bit more cheerful.

We drove down to the quay and got out of the car. 'There's no one to take us over,' said Hanna and pointed to the launch. 'But I think I can drive that thing.'

Hanna was good at driving a car; at piloting a boat he was terrible. When we got to the island he rammed the bows into some stonework with a crunch. I grabbed a mooring ring and held on, and we tethered the painter to it. As we climbed from the launch, John appeared. He seemed perturbed by the fact that someone had come through the gate and reached the island unannounced.

'Superintendent Hanna to see Mrs Salton.'

'I don't think Mrs Salton is receiving,' said John.

Hanna speared him with a gimlet eye. 'She'd better,' he said. 'See to it.'

John vanished into the house. Hanna said, 'Loyalty is one thing. Common sense is another.'

I looked at him sideways, thinking of the spot he'd put himself in. 'You ought to know,' I said.

John came back in jig time. 'Mrs Salton will see you, sir.'

'Of course she will,' said Hanna with a trace of triumphalism.

'Come this way.'

Hanna grunted in his throat. 'That grandson of yours; you tell him he's a damned fool. Tell him from me that if he keeps running with Joe Hawke, he'll be in big trouble.'

John's eyes were steady. 'I've already told him, sir. But I'll pass on your message.' He turned and led us into the house.

Jill Salton had been swimming or sun-bathing. She wore a white robe very like the one Leotta had worn when I first saw her. I marvelled again how two women could rival each other in loveliness and yet be so different. Behind her stood Stern. Just as I'd advised. She said, 'Hello, Bill. Inspector, what can I do for you?'

'Superintendent,' said Hanna flatly. 'The time has come for you to answer some questions, Mrs Salton.'

'And if I don't?'

'Then I'll have to take you to San Martin and hope you'll answer them there.'

'Now wait a minute,' said Stern. 'You can't do that.'

Hanna turned on him. 'Why not?' he said, and there was a whipcrack in his voice that made Stern flinch. 'I've questioned others in San Martin. Why not Mrs Salton?'

Stern said stiffly, 'I think you should pay due regard to Mrs Salton's position. And besides . . .'

Hanna cut in fast. 'I'm not impressed with money,' he said uncompromisingly. 'Well, Mrs Salton?'

'This is outrag—' Stern spluttered.

'Oh, stop it, Abel,' said Jill. 'I'll answer the Superintendent's questions.' She looked at me. 'I said I would.'

I chipped in. 'Can I suggest we all sit down?'

So we sat down while Stern chuntered on. I think he really did regard the ownership of a lot of money as a qualification for special treatment. In general he may have been right, but it wasn't what was written in Hanna's book, and Hanna always went by the book. Even if he had to write parts of it himself, as he had been doing recently.

Hanna said, 'Let's get the simpler questions disposed of first. We know about Miss Tomsson. When did you find out about her, Mrs Salton?'

Stern said, 'Don't answer that. Are you accusing Mrs Salton of anything, Superintendent?'

'This is just a preliminary inquiry,' said Hanna. He looked at Stern thoughtfully. 'It is entirely up to Mrs Salton whether she answers any questions at all. If she does not do so, I will draw the appropriate conclusions and take the steps that I deem to be necessary. Do I make myself quite clear?'

Stern looked baffled. What Hanna had said was quite true but it didn't mean a damned thing. Jill laughed shortly. 'Abel, you're a fool. Just keep quiet and let's get this over with.'

Stern looked hurt. Jill said, 'I first learned about Miss Tomsson on the day my husband disappeared. David and I quarrelled about her.'

'How could that happen when you didn't know about her?'

'I suspected something,' said Jill. 'I challenged David with it and he admitted it. So there was a quarrel – as you can imagine. I actually met Miss Tomsson for the first time last night.'

'I'm sorry about that,' said Hanna regretfully. 'My files were not as protected as I imagined.'

'Yes, how did that happen?' asked Stern.

Hanna seemed even sleepier than usual. Perhaps the riotous night was catching up with him. 'I suggest you ask Commissioner Barstow.'

'Barstow,' said Jill. 'Of course.' .

'And after the quarrel, what happened?'

'David went off in a rage and I didn't see him again. Ever.'

'You assumed he'd flown to the States. But that wasn't right. Then, when it was discovered that the dinghy was missing, you thought your husband had taken it.'

'He had,' said Jill. 'He was found dead in it.'

'Can you give the exact time your husband left you?'

'Yes. It was just after ten o'clock on the morning of the ninth.'

Hanna's voice was solemn. 'I have firm evidence that the dinghy was still in the boathouse at three o'clock on the morning of the tenth.' Stern shot bolt upright. 'Can you suggest what your husband was doing during those seventeen hours?'

'But that can't be,' said Jill.

'Impossible!' exploded Stern simultaneously.

'What's impossible about it?' asked Hanna testily. 'Did you examine the boathouse at any time, Mr Stern?'

'No, of course not. I wasn't here.'

'Then you'll oblige me by keeping quiet when matters of fact you know nothing about are under consideration. If you have any hard evidence, I'll be interested to hear it later. Mrs Salton, did you check the boathouse?'

'Only when I thought of it, when Commissioner Barstow was here.'

'And that was on the evening of the thirteenth,' mused

Hanna. 'The dinghy had gone.' He stirred, then put his hand to his breast pocket. 'Do you mind if I smoke, Mrs Salton?'

'Not at all.'

Hanna took out a cheroot and lit it. He examined the glowing end and said, 'Do you like sailing at night, Mrs Salton?'

'Sometimes, yes. David and I used to take a boat out at night occasionally. He liked night fishing.'

'Always in a dinghy?'

'Generally. David liked to sail. We have a big fishing cruiser but David rarely used it. He wasn't much of a man for power boats.'

'What about you, Mrs Salton? Did you ever take the dinghy out by yourself?'

'I have done.'

'At night?'

'No, never at night. I wouldn't go out alone at night. David was always with me then.' She frowned. 'Am I supposed to have taken the dinghy to sea at three in the morning? If Raymond said that he's mistaken.'

'Possibly. May I use your telephone?'

'Of course. You'll find one in the hall.'

Hanna stood up and jerked his head at me, so I followed him into the hall. He said, 'Mr Kemp, I like you very much but I don't want you talking to Mrs Salton at this stage of the investigation. You might not give anything away deliberately, but you could let a chance word slip.'

I grinned and said, 'There's the telephone.'

He picked it up and got through to the shore, speaking in a low voice. Presently he put it down and said, 'They're bringing White across.'

'But we've got the launch on this side.'

'There are other boats,' he said without interest, and lapsed into thoughtful silence.

We waited half an hour in the hall, during which time

John came and silently laid a tray of tea on a side table. He was going away when he turned and said to Hanna, 'I told Jake what you said.'

'Any answer?'

John looked at me. 'He said Mr Kemp knows all about it.' He went away.

Hanna said, 'What was that about?'

'I don't know,' I said. What was I supposed to know about?

Eventually White was brought into the hall, escorted by a uniformed policeman. Hanna looked at him levelly for a long time, then said, 'Remember what you told me when we met last?'

'Yes, sir.'

'Right. You saw a woman taking out that dinghy at four in the morning.'

'Yes, sir.'

'Who was it?'

'I don't know, sir.'

'You said you *thought* it was Mrs Salton.'

'Who else would it be?' White shuffled his feet embarrassedly.

'How long have you worked here?'

'Ever since Mr David built the place.'

'And you've always looked after the boats?'

'Yes, sir. Mr David – he said I looked after them well. That's when he gave me a raise.'

'Now, listen carefully to this question. Have you ever known Mrs Salton take out a dinghy alone at night?'

White frowned and his feet jiggled around some more. At last, after evidently painful thought, he said, 'No, sir. I don't recollect any time she did that.'

Hanna permitted himself a snort of exasperation. 'But this time you thought it was Mrs Salton. Why?'

'Well, who else would take it?' His brows knitted together. 'I thought it was all right if Mr David was there.'

Hanna was momentarily speechless, then he spluttered, 'Salton was there?'

'I don't know, sir. I didn't see him.'

I thought Hanna was going to explode, so I touched his arm. 'Hang on a minute.' To White, I said gently, 'Let's get this straight, Raymond. You saw a woman in the dinghy in the moonlight. You couldn't identify her for sure, but you thought it was Mrs Salton. And because you thought it was Mrs Salton, you assumed that Mr Salton was in the boat as well. Is that what you're saying?'

White's brow cleared. 'Yes, sir,' he said eagerly. 'That's it exactly.'

'But you didn't actually see Mr Salton?'

'No, sir.'

'Or any other man?'

'No, sir.'

I said to Hanna, 'I think that's it.'

Hanna made a sign to the waiting policeman. 'Take him away,' he said disgustedly. 'Keep an eye on him, though.' To me, he said, 'Not just loyal, but stupid.'

'What now?'

'We talk to Mrs Salton again.'

We went back and found Stern giving Jill the length of his tongue. He was saying, '. . . and if you ignore my advice like this ever again, I shall have to think seriously about representing you.' He looked up as we came in and shut his mouth like a steel trap.

Hanna said, 'Forgive me, Mrs Salton. I am obliged to put this question to you formally. Did you kill your husband?'

Stern was horrified. 'Superintendent!'

'Shut up, Abel,' said Jill, and stood up and faced Hanna. 'No, I did not kill my husband.'

'Did you take the dinghy from the boathouse on the morning of the tenth?'

'No, I did not.'

Hanna suddenly broke into a smile. 'I shall be glad to accept those answers, Mrs Salton. I'm sorry to have put you through a trying time. However, I have to warn you that you may be questioned again.'

'I'll be ready,' she said.

'Thank you,' said Hanna, and made as if to go. Apparently as an afterthought, he turned back and said, 'By the way, are there any other women here?'

Jill considered for a moment. 'There's the maid and the housekeeper, and Anna, of course.'

'Your cook?' I said. She nodded.

'Do they live in the house?' asked Hanna.

Jill shook her head. 'No, they all go home when their work is done for the day. Mrs Forsyth used to live here. Until . . .'

'Salton's secretary,' I reminded him. 'About sixty.'

'What about on the rest of the estate?' said Hanna.

'No,' said Jill. 'Oh yes, there's Mrs Haslam, the pilot's wife.'

Mrs Haslam. Something went off at the back of my mind – something I'd heard recently. I thought about it but nothing came, nothing except a ferocious headache exactly like the one I'd had the previous evening.

# NINE

## I

We drove back to San Martin. Hanna didn't want to talk
to Mrs Haslam. 'I don't know enough yet,' he said.

'Enough about what?'

He looked thoughtful. 'Have you ever been to a criminal
trial?'

'No,' I said, wrestling with my headache.

'A good counsel never asks a question unless he knows
at least ninety per cent of the answer. I'd like to know a
little more about this woman before I interrogate her.'

I suppose it made sense. He didn't even know what
questions to ask. I said, 'All I know is that she was an air
hostess. That's how she met her husband.'

'Did she tell you that?'

'Yes.'

Hanna snorted and seemed to discard the information.

He dropped me at the casino ferry and said, 'Stay out of
sight until I tell you to come out. I don't want you running
around where Barstow can get you.'

'You're taking a hell of a chance. What about that
inspector this morning?'

'I can handle that.' His tone was confident but I didn't

think he was. 'Stay invisible,' he said. 'And that goes for Miss Tomsson.'

He watched me walk on to the ferry, waited until it got to the other side, then drove away. I went up to the penthouse. Leotta took one look at me and said, 'You need the doctor.' I eased my bruises into a comfortable chair while she telephoned.

The doctor was minatory. 'You shouldn't have gone out this morning.' His finger jabbed into me and I winced. 'You should be in bed. You're all bruise and no brains.'

He was right. My torso was coming out in lovely colours – iridescent blues and purples, like a sunset in reverse – and my head throbbed as I searched for that elusive bit of information I had mislaid.

'He won't go out again,' said Leotta. She sounded like a nurse. She helped the doctor strap me up again after he had been liberal with the liniment and I smelt like a football locker-room. Then he went away and she said firmly, 'Bed!'

I grinned at her. 'Thanks for the invitation but I ache too much right now.' To my surprise she blushed. 'Sorry,' I said, and changed the subject. 'Is that a chaise longue on the patio out there?'

So I lay out there in the sun and, after a few desultory bites of lunch, I slept. Ever since I had arrived on Campanilla I had been on the hoof, as busy as a bee but gathering very little nectar. The usual reason for going to Campanilla is to relax, lie in the sun and soak up the vitamin D, to get that exact shade of bronze which the discerning eye knows does not come from a sun tan lamp in winter, the badge of the jet set. Instead, I had been threatened, manipulated, beaten up and shot. I thought it was about time I behaved like a tourist. Besides, I had nothing else to do.

I slept for two hours and when I woke up Leotta was beside me, stretched on a beach towel and taking in the sun. She rolled over as I stirred. 'Did you sleep well?'

'Marvellous,' I said dreamily.

'You snore,' she said, and began applying sun tan oil to her arms.

'It doesn't worry me,' I said, and picked up the bottle of oil. 'I'll do your back.'

'All right.' She lay prone and unfastened her bikini top. I massaged the oil into her silky skin and she lay with her head pillowed on her arms, her eyes closed. Presently she said, 'What do you think will happen?'

'About what?'

'About us.'

I wasn't quite sure what she meant. Was she talking about our respective circumstances on this exotic island, both caught up in deadly political manoeuvrings that neither of us had sought out? Or was she hinting at something more personal, something I couldn't deny that I felt, but which seemed curiously inappropriate given the present situation?

'We could leave,' I said. 'There's nothing to stop us. That might put Hanna in a jam, though. I was assaulted by the police and you're a witness to it. He needs us for evidence.'

'But he can't find those four men.'

'He's looking,' I said. 'If he finds them and we're not around to tell the tale, he could be for the chop.'

'And after that, you'll be going to England?'

'That's right.'

'To Devon?'

I smiled. 'I could do with a month in Devon. There's probably some snow about this time of year.'

'I don't like snow.'

I stopped myself from saying that I wasn't offering her any. 'The first snowdrops will be coming up, and then the crocuses and daffodils. And the birds will start singing. You ought to hear our English birdsong.'

She opened her eyes and twisted her head to look at me. 'You sound quite poetic.'

'I'm a country boy at heart. You know, I haven't heard a bird sing all the time I've been here. Hell, even in London the birds sing.'

'It must be nice,' she said softly, and closed her eyes again.

The telephone jangled a foot from my head, startling me so that my fingers dug into Leotta's flank. 'Ouch!'

'Sorry.' I picked up the telephone and found I was listening to Negrini. 'Bill, I have Jill Salton on another line. She's been phoning around trying to get you – your hotel, the Salton Estates office and now here. I said I'd have you paged. Do you want to talk to her?'

'Okay,' I said. 'Put her on.'

Leotta was kneeling up, fastening her bikini strap. Jill said, 'Bill?'

'Speaking.'

'I didn't have a chance to talk to you this morning.' I could sense a wry smile as she spoke. 'I had to reserve all my attention for Superintendent Hanna.'

'I'm sorry if you found it tough.'

'It was hard to take,' she said sombrely. Her voice brightened. 'But I'd like to see you. Could you come to El Cerco this evening? Wait a moment before you answer,' she went on quickly. 'I'd like you to bring Miss Tomsson with you, if she'll come.'

I glanced at Leotta. 'What do you want to do, scratch her eyes out?'

Jill said, 'I loved David, you know that, Bill. But more than that, I respected him and I respected his judgement. If he saw something in her, I'd like to find out what it was for myself.'

'Wait a moment.' I put my hand over the mouthpiece. Leotta was doing things to her hair. 'Jill Salton wants me to go out to El Cerco. She's invited you too.'

'Why?'

I shrugged. 'To chop your head off, to choke you with

cream, to measure the one-time opposition. How the hell would I know? I'm no connoisseur of the female mind.'

Leotta was very still, then she nodded her head gravely. 'Very well.'

I uncovered the mouthpiece. 'Okay, Jill. But not tonight. My doctor wouldn't approve.'

'Doctor? What's wrong, Bill?'

'I ran into a slight riot last night.'

'But you seemed all right this morning.'

'Pills and willpower,' I said. 'But they didn't last. I am really bushed, Jill, but I'll be all right tomorrow.'

'Come whenever you like,' she said. 'I'll be here. And in the meantime, look after yourself. Stay out of riots.'

'Just one thing,' I said. 'Don't tell anyone where I am. And anyone really means anyone. It could be important.'

'All right,' she said, and rang off leaving me wondering what that was all about. I supposed she might even have been telling the truth.

Negrini did not sleep in the penthouse that night but went home to Marshalltown and connubial domesticity. Leotta and I had dinner served by a uniformed waiter direct from the restaurant below. The stars hung on the other side of the huge window like a theatrical backdrop and there was a gibbous moon to add to the romantic atmosphere.

We talked, but not about Campanilla or anything to do with why we were there. I learned a lot about Leotta and, I suppose, she learned a lot about me in those few hours. She told me something of her early life and why she had left Campanilla to go to New York. The reasons were economic, mainly – the islands of the Caribbean are generally not paradises for those who have to live there. She'd studied nursing and worked at it for a few years before she was discovered as a model. 'Shortly after that I met David,' she said, but was silent about it thereafter.

Over coffee and brandy I smoked one of Negrini's Havana cigars and felt rich and contented. I told Leotta about England and everything I thought she'd need to know if she was going to live there. She was still interested in Devon and made me describe the land and its people. By the stars in her eyes, I judged she regarded it as some kind of heaven. Perhaps it would be to one such as Leotta.

'But there's not much call for modelling in Devon,' I warned.

'You have hospitals, don't you? I can work.'

'You might have to go to school again,' I said.

She nodded contemplatively. 'I was thinking of doing that, anyway. Do you think I could be a doctor?'

'It would take hard work and a long time.'

She merely inclined her head in acceptance of that and said no more.

That evening was to prove the happiest and most relaxing time I had on Campanilla. We turned in early – about ten o'clock – and I considered making a pass at Leotta. But I didn't because I was scared that she would turn it down, and even more scared that she would fall into bed with me. We didn't know each other well enough for it to be anything other than a one-night stand, and suddenly I found that I wanted more than that.

I went to bed alone.


## II


Negrini showed up for breakfast. 'How are you kids going?' He wore a broad grin.

I looked at him sourly because I had spent a restless night, and not the kind of restless night he evidently had in mind. I said, 'Why so cheerful?'

'Seen the *Chronicle*?' He tossed it on the breakfast table. 'Things are starting to jump.'

I picked up the newspaper and shook the folds out. The headline slammed at me and I began to smile. My sour mood vanished and I felt a pulse of excitement. 'What is it?' asked Leotta.

I held up the newspaper so she could see the headline: 'McKITTRICK GOES LIB!'

'He's done it,' I said. 'So that's what John meant.'

'Who is John?' asked Negrini.

'McKittrick's grandfather.'

I scanned the story, which led off:

*In a dramatic move yesterday, Dr Jacob McKittrick broke with Joe Hawke and the People's Party to return to the fold of the Campanillan Liberal Party. He is now expected to defend the seat of North End, currently vacant due to the recent death of David Salton.*

*Leaders of the CLP unanimously welcomed the move at a meeting yesterday. A reshuffle is expected to take place in the upper echelons of the party hierarchy, with Dr McKittrick tipped for a role in Cabinet if the Liberals win the election. Some rumours suggest he could even be in line for the Premiership.*

*Following the announcement last night, Dr McKittrick wasted no time in laying out his political agenda, including the promise of a complete overhaul of the police force. He also launched a scathing attack on his former colleagues, claiming: 'The citizens of this country are being misled by the demagogues of the People's Party. I know because I watched it happen. I was there. Joe Hawke wants to lead Campanilla along the road to revolution – but it's the road to hell, poverty and ruin.'*

*He pledged full allegiance to the policies of the CLP and, in a moving tribute to the late leader of the opposition, admitted: 'There was a time when I disagreed with the ideas of David Salton. But I was wrong and David Salton was right. I believe he was the greatest man this nation has produced, and I commit myself unreservedly to the realisation of his political plans.'*

*Dr McKittrick's dramatic switch took onlookers by surprise and is sure to transform the political landscape just weeks before a critical election. The walkover that was predicted for the Conservative Party after the death of Mr Salton now looks far from certain.*

*In an exclusive interview with the* Chronicle, *Dr McKittrick said: 'I think the CLP has a good chance of winning – maybe not the chance it had when David Salton was alive, but a good chance nevertheless. If Mr Conyers wants to remain Prime Minister and to continue to mismanage the economy, he will have to fight harder than he has fought in his life.'*

*The Prime Minister was not available for comment, but Mr Hawke, leader of the People's Party, said: 'How can the honest people of this country believe a man who has been a traitor not once but twice? Any man who will turn his coat again and again for political advantage is clearly not to be trusted.'*

*(Cont. p.2; Editorial p.12)*

I said, 'Well, well. So he did it after all.'

'Did you know about this?' asked Negrini.

'A little,' I said. I didn't feel like going into the details, that I had advised McKittrick to do this and it might never have happened without me. It gave me a strange feeling to realise that perhaps I had altered the destiny of a country, even one as small as Campanilla, with just a few persuasive words.

I looked up at Negrini. 'Will you be contributing to McKittrick's fighting fund?'

'If he'll take the dough. He might not.' He smiled. 'He's more of an idealist than Salton was.'

'He's learning,' I said. 'If I see him I'll talk to him – tactfully, of course.' I leaned back in my chair. 'Looks like Joe Hawke over-reached himself.'

'How do you mean?'

'He was drumming up all this unrest by exploiting the name of Salton, but the leadership of the CLP were too naive to take advantage. McKittrick may be many things but he isn't naive. He'll also flog the name of Salton.' I tapped the paper. 'He's already started. He'll cream off everything Hawke has done for the benefit of the CLP. But unlike Hawke, I think he means it.'

'You could be right at that,' said Negrini. 'But I wish the goddamn elections were over. Politics are bad for business.'

He went away to do whatever casino operators do first thing in the morning. As I turned to page twelve to read the editorial, Leotta said, 'Aren't we supposed to be going to El Cerco?'

'I've been thinking about that and I don't know if Hanna would like it very much. Jaunting across Campanilla in broad daylight isn't exactly staying out of sight. I'll ring him at a more civilised hour.' I returned to the editorial, which was decidedly euphoric.

As it happened I didn't ring Hanna, because Negrini returned and said, 'Hanna wants to see you in his office. He wants to talk to you.'

'What's wrong with the telephone?'

Negrini twitched a sheet of paper in his fingers. 'He thinks his phone is bugged, and mine might be. That's why he sent a letter by hand. He wants me to take you in my car.'

I looked at Leotta and shrugged. 'Why not?'

We didn't use the main lift but a dingy service lift at the rear of the building, emerging into a garage. Negrini nodded towards a Cadillac. 'That's mine.' We went over and he opened the boot. 'Jump in.'

'For God's sake!'

'This is the way Hanna wants it,' said Negrini sharply. 'He doesn't want you out in the open.'

'I'm sorry,' I said. 'I left my cloak and dagger upstairs.' Negrini made an impatient noise so I obediently got into the boot and he slammed down the lid. There's one thing about big American cars: they have plenty of luggage space, so I wasn't cramped at all. I was glad Negrini didn't drive a Volkswagen.

I lay there for more than twenty minutes and amused myself by trying to estimate just where the car was at every stage of the journey. We crossed to the mainland on the ferry and then went along the waterfront and past the market. After that I got lost. Eventually, after an unexpected swooping passage that reminded my stomach of a roller-coaster, the engine stopped and presently Negrini opened the boot.

I climbed out stiffly and stretched. We were in an underground garage in what was presumably police headquarters. There was a line of Black Marias and, in a far corner, a couple of armoured cars equipped with water cannon. A man in plain clothes was standing by. He said quietly, 'This way, Mr Kemp,' and led us to a lift.

As we went up, I said to Negrini, 'I have a nasty feeling I'm on the verge of being arrested for something.'

He grinned. 'Broken any laws lately?'

'None that I can think of, but I'm not at all sure that's necessary here.'

The lift stopped and the door opened. Standing in the corridor was a uniformed policeman, who nodded briefly to our escort. 'Move quickly, Mr Kemp,' said the man at my side, and emphasised his words with a push.

We walked along the corridor and around a corner. I noticed what seemed to be a relay team of police stationed at strategic points and we were hastened along by a series of nods and beckoning arms. At last we went past a door, through an outer office and into Hanna's sanctum. The lights were on and the venetian blinds were drawn.

Hanna looked up, waved away our escort, and said, 'I

suggest you leave and have a cup of coffee, Mr Negrini. Come back in half an hour.'

'Goddamn it!' said Negrini. 'What am I? A chauffeur service for the cops?'

'Your services are appreciated, of course,' said Hanna. 'But there are things which Mr Kemp and I must discuss in private.'

'I get it,' said Negrini. 'What I don't know won't hurt you. Okay, Bill, I'll be back in half an hour.'

He left, and Hanna snapped a switch. 'No one is to come into my office unless I say so. I repeat, no one at all. If anyone wants me, tell me.' He switched off the intercom, leaned back in his chair, and said, 'Sit down, Mr Kemp.'

I took the chair on the other side of his desk and studied him. He appeared to be screwed up to a pitch of tautness I had not seen before. His eyes were exceptionally bright and his movements precise and controlled to the point of being finicky. He said, 'It is now more essential than ever that you stay out of the hands of the police, especially the uniformed branch. I would hate to lose you – or Miss Tomsson – at this stage.'

I stretched out my legs and smiled at him. 'I'm right in the middle of police headquarters. A funny place to be.'

'The police are hardly likely to look for you here,' he said casually, and took a file from a drawer. 'Let me explain the importance of all this.' He opened the file. 'The men who attacked you – Sergeant Taylor and Constables Whitley, Villegas and Robertson – dropped out of sight. When Commissioner Barstow countermanded my orders and took them from here, those four officers neither reported to their posts in Hogtown nor did they go to their homes. What do you make of that?'

'I'd say Barstow is covering something up.'

Hanna nodded. 'I've had the forensic laboratory working around the clock. I took it on myself to have the homes of all four men raided and their civilian clothing impounded for examination. On the clothing of Taylor and Villegas we found blood specks of the same blood group as Ogilvie. On one of Robertson's boots we found a thread caught up in a projecting nail. The thread is of the same material as Ogilvie's trousers and is not of a type usually found in Campanilla. Nothing was found to implicate Whitley in Ogilvie's murder, but we're still looking.'

I took a deep breath. 'That's a damn fine bit of work.'

'Normal police procedure,' said Hanna impassively. He put his hands on the desk and leaned forward. 'Mr Kemp, I must emphasise that as far as you are concerned, the position has changed. There is a lot going on in the uniformed branch of the police force that I don't like and I am afraid for your safety, and for that of Miss Tomsson. The fact is that a man cannot be convicted on a blood group specimen and Mr Ogilvie's blood grouping was not uncommon. So we're not going to be able to charge them with that – yet. But you and Miss Tomsson can give evidence against Taylor and his men on the matter of the direct assault on you. And that is why you must stay out of sight until I clear up this matter.'

'I see your point. I don't like your police thugs, either.'

I was curious to know why I'd been brought to police headquarters, but not Leotta. Surely if I was to be kept safe, then she should be too?

'Because she's probably better off where she is for the moment. Nobody knows she's there, apart from you, me and Mr Negrini. As I said, Mr Kemp, I want you both beyond the reach of the police.'

'Then why bring me here? Why didn't you go to Negrini's?'

'I was coming to that,' said Hanna. 'There is something else I must tell you. In the early hours of this morning I arrested Commissioner Barstow.'

For a moment I didn't register what he had said. Then I felt my hair stand on end. 'You've *what?*'

'I arrested the Commissioner,' he said with a grim smile. 'My superior officer.'

Now I understood his tautness. 'Do you expect to get away with that?'

He squared up the file in front of him. 'Four police officers cannot just disappear on Campanilla. Not when I'm looking for them. I began to wonder whether Barstow would be such a damned fool as to put them in his own home. As soon as the positive results came from forensic I had his house watched. They were there. Barstow went home last night as usual and I had the house raided at four this morning and arrested the lot of them.'

'What's the charge on Barstow, for God's sake?'

'Conspiracy to pervert the course of justice. He's in a cell now. The Prime Minister should be finding out any time, if he hasn't already. I'm expecting a loud scream.'

'They'll cut your throat,' I said. 'Conyers won't stand for it.'

'It doesn't make any difference,' said Hanna. 'I was finished anyway. The things I've been doing in the Salton case won't help my promotion. If I had just stood by, Barstow would be asking for my resignation within a fortnight.' He took a newspaper from his drawer and tossed it on to the desk. 'Have you seen this?'

I looked at the headline. 'I've seen it.' I bent my head to peer at the heavily underlined words on the page: *complete overhaul of the police force.*

I looked at Hanna. 'You're taking a hell of a chance. What if the CLP doesn't win the election?'

'Then Conyers won't have to cut my throat,' he said. 'I'll have done it myself. But either way, he'll have a lot of trouble explaining away Barstow.'

I said thoughtfully, 'You ought to write a book. How to

make enemies and influence people. Who knows about this so far?'

'Not many.'

'Conyers might try to hush it up,' I said. 'What you need is a press conference.'

He shook his head. 'I'm not a public relations cop. But it will get out.' The telephone rang and he picked it up. He listened, then said, 'Stall him for five minutes, then let him in.' He smiled at me as he replaced the telephone. 'And this is why I needed to be here, rather than making house calls at the casino. The Honourable Leon A. Shillabeer, our esteemed Attorney-General. I'll bet the steam is coming out of his ears.'

'I shouldn't be here.'

He stood up. 'It's all right. I'd like a witness. Discreetly, of course.' He opened a door in the wall behind his desk. 'This way.'

I followed him into a small room where he twitched away a curtain from a window. I looked through the window into his office. 'One-way glass,' he said. 'There's a mirror on the other side. Everyone assumes I'm vain. Sit here and keep quiet. Don't turn on the light or he might see it.'

He went back into his office and I sat down. Looking through the one-way glass was not as good as looking through an ordinary clear sheet but it was not far short of it. I wondered what other tricks Hanna had and found out immediately: before picking up the telephone he opened a drawer and switched on a tape recorder.

Shillabeer came in fast. He was a jowly man of middle height whom I remembered seeing at Conyers's party. Even before he was through the doorway he was talking. 'What the devil is going on, Hanna?'

'About what?' said Hanna.

'Is it true you've arrested Commissioner Barstow?'

'Oh, that,' said Hanna. 'Yes, it's true, Mr Shillabeer.'

That brought the Attorney-General up short. He had come to a halt because he could go no further and now he sat in the chair I had just vacated.

'Are you out of your mind? What's the charge?'

'Conspiracy to pervert the course of justice,' said Hanna. 'He was hiding four suspected murderers in his house.'

Shillabeer gobbled. 'But . . . but . . .' He started again. 'What suspected murderers?'

'Their names are Taylor, Whitley, Villegas and Robertson. I arrested them myself on another charge of assault but they were freed by Barstow.'

'And who are they suspected of murdering?'

'An Englishman called Ogilvie.'

Shillabeer opened his mouth and closed it again. He appeared suddenly evasive. 'Do you have evidence for this?'

'Enough to charge them. So I have.' Hanna was really sticking his neck out and I hoped Shillabeer hadn't brought a chopper.

'And because of this you arrested Commissioner Barstow. This is unheard of, Hanna. You realise this should have gone through my office first. I'll tell you who you can arrest and who you can't arrest.'

Hanna shook his head tolerantly. 'Conspiracy Act, 1965,' he quoted. 'The consent of the Attorney-General is necessary for proceedings, but this shall not prevent an arrest.' He thought for a moment, then added, 'Not that it makes any difference here.'

'I certainly won't consent to any proceedings,' said Shillabeer savagely. He stopped and looked at Hanna uncertainly. 'What do you mean, it makes no difference here?'

Hanna put his head back and looked at the ceiling. 'Conspiracy Act, 1965; Section 4. In the event of a High Court warrant made out by the Chief Justice, proceedings shall be taken automatically.' He lowered his head. 'You'll have to talk to Chief Justice Micklethwaite.'

Shillabeer was taken aback. 'Micklethwaite made out a High Court warrant for the arrest of Barstow?' he whispered.

'I was very worried last night,' said Hanna matter-of-factly. 'If I had to catch Barstow I had to catch him in the act, as it were – I had to catch him in the presence of the four men and in his own home. I tried to reach you but you were not available, Mr Shillabeer. I telephoned several times from about eight o'clock onwards.'

Shillabeer's eyes narrowed. 'I was away from home.'

'At about ten o'clock I happened to look out of this window and saw Chief Justice Micklethwaite going into his club – the Albemarle, just across the road – do you know it? I was unhappy about arresting Commissioner Barstow on my own account so I popped over there and asked Micklethwaite's advice. I told him I was worried Commissioner Barstow might try to get the men out of his house overnight so he suggested that he make out a court warrant for Barstow's arrest. I don't mind telling you, Mr Shillabeer, I was much relieved.'

I nearly laughed aloud. Hanna sounded about as relieved as a shark that has just bitten off a swimmer's leg. He said, 'Fortunately, no time was wasted as the Court House is next door to the Albemarle.'

Shillabeer licked his lips; his face had gone grey. 'You damned fool, Hanna,' he said. He stood up suddenly, knocking the chair over. 'You'll hear more of this.' He went out even more quickly than he had come in.

Hanna righted the chair and closed the office door, then came up to the one-way glass and straightened his tie in the mirror. 'You can come out now, Mr Kemp,' he said.

I joined him in his office. 'Is that right what you said about the court warrant? That proceedings will have to be taken?'

He seemed much more relaxed. 'I know my statutes,' he said. 'And Micklethwaite is no friend of Barstow. Our Chief Justice is as straight as a ramrod and he's appointed for life, which means he isn't afraid of politicians. I'd heard that he was worried about the activities of the police lately – the overreaction during the riots, for instance. Not that he'd said anything to me personally.'

'But you knew he'd sign a court warrant,' I said. 'Did you really just see him by chance going into the club?'

Hanna smiled. 'No, of course not. I telephoned him earlier in the evening, filled him in on some of the broad facts, and arranged to meet him there at ten.'

'And I suppose you just happened to know that Shillabeer would be away from home last night.'

'Mr Roker was giving a party,' said Hanna. 'Mr and Mrs Shillabeer were among the guests. They got home at two this morning.' He looked earnest. 'I did call his home several times last night, giving my name and saying that Mr Shillabeer must get in touch with me.' He shrugged. 'He rang here at two-thirty and my home soon after that. By that time, I was at Barstow's place supervising the snatch.'

'It's copper-bottomed,' I said. 'But Conyers will never believe it.'

'I don't care if he does or not,' said Hanna, sounding positively cheerful. 'But it will stand up in court if I have to give evidence.' He stopped smiling. 'Now, about you. I'm not sure how long the casino will remain a safe haven. I'm having an eye kept on it and there's been police activity there. I think you should move.'

'Mrs Salton wants me to visit her at El Cerco.'

He considered that. 'That might be all right, but it doesn't solve the problem of Miss Tomsson.'

'She's invited, too.'

Hanna was astounded. *'Invited?'*

'There won't be another murder,' I said dryly. 'I'll keep them apart.'

He wagged his head in a baffled way. 'It might work. Who would look for Miss Tomsson at El Cerco? The problem is getting you both there safely.'

He switched on the intercom. 'Has Mr Negrini come back yet?'

'He's here, sir.'

'Send him in.'

As we waited I said to Hanna, 'What have you discovered about Mrs Haslam?'

He gave me a frown and said, 'It's in the works.'

Negrini came in and Hanna swung his chair. 'Ah, Mr Negrini. How would you like another chauffeuring job?'

'Maybe I should charge expenses.' Negrini winked at me. 'A Caddy costs a lot to run.'

'I wasn't thinking of a car,' said Hanna. 'You have a boat – that over-engined so-called fishing boat of yours.'

'It's a speedboat,' said Negrini testily. 'I don't get much time to fish so I like to get in and out real quick. What about it?'

'I was wondering if you would like to take Mr Kemp and Miss Tomsson to El Cerco.'

Without waiting for an answer, Hanna opened a file on the desk in front of him. With his head bent he said, 'And watch out for the harbour police.'


# III


Negrini's boat looked fast. Standing still in his boathouse it seemed to be doing twenty knots. He slapped its side affectionately. 'Designed by Renato Levi and Italian-built. I have to support my old homeland. Jump aboard.'

Leotta dropped lightly into the cockpit and I followed. Negrini said, 'Better go into the cabin until we're at sea. There are too many eyes in the harbour.'

This was no boat for an extended cruise. The cabin, while being well fitted out, was small, with two bunks, a galley and a folding table. I suspected that a disproportionate amount of boat was taken up by engines. This guess was confirmed when Negrini started them up: the boat shook gently as they ticked over while he went through his cockpit drill. The low rumble spoke of raw power.

'Okay, folks, off we go,' he said, and the boat nosed gently out of the boathouse and into the harbour. I looked through a window and found that I seemed to be too close to the water. Negrini bent down so he could see me. 'Bill.'

'Yes.'

'Hanna was right. There's a police launch to starboard that seems to be taking an interest in us. It's heading this way on an intercepting course.'

I glanced at Leotta. It seemed that Hanna had called this one wrong. 'So what do we do?'

Negrini laughed. 'This,' he said, and there was a bellowing roar from the engines and the whole boat seemed to lift bodily from the water. He yelled, 'I've got forty-five knots out of this baby in smooth water. If that tub tries to match my speed, her engines will blow up.'

The view from the window had changed. The water level was way down because the boat was now planing and the harbour was zipping past at a dizzying speed. I shut my eyes. This was a bit different from taking a sailing cruiser out of the Dart.

'We're leaving her standing,' shouted Negrini. 'In a couple of minutes we'll be out of Pascua Channel and in the open sea. You'd better hang on to something and keep loose. Some of these trade wind rollers might break the dishes.'

The designer had thoughtfully fitted grab handles so I grabbed and held on. Negrini was right. The boat pitched alarmingly and if I hadn't been gripping tightly I'd have been thrown across the cabin and into Leotta's lap – which wouldn't have been a bad breakfall. I grinned at her and then noticed she was turning a delicate shade of dirty green, which clashed badly with the ice-blue of her trouser suit.

'Hold on,' I shouted. 'This won't last long.' I hoped I was right.

We pounded on for another fifteen minutes and then the note of the engines changed as Negrini slackened speed. His head appeared as he stooped to look into the cabin. 'They've given up,' he said. 'They're four miles back and turning around. I'll keep on this heading for a while – going no place – and then we'll swing around and head for El Cerco as soon as we're out of radar range. Okay?'

I nodded. 'Leotta isn't feeling too good.'

'Another quarter-hour and you can both come up,' he said.

Now that the motion of the boat was easier, Leotta wasn't getting any worse – though I wouldn't say she was getting any better. In twenty minutes Negrini told us it was all right to go into the cockpit, and Leotta made a dash for it. When I got up there she was being violently sick over the side. Negrini grinned at me genially. 'You want to shoot the cat, too?'

'It's not all that funny,' I said. I had been seasick at times and I knew how she felt.

'I guess not,' said Negrini, 'Sorry, Leotta.'

She flopped back on the stern cushions. 'I'm a lousy sailor.' But her colour was better.

I looked outboard and saw land to starboard about five miles away. We were leaving it at an angle. I said, 'I didn't expect you to go this way. I thought you'd go roundabout the other way.'

'It's not the easiest way to El Cerco,' agreed Negrini. 'But when you've had someone on your tail it's the best. I don't think those guys back there think we're going to El Cerco.'

'How long will it take?'

'Maybe six hours. Make yourselves comfortable.'

In spite of Negrini's advice it was definitely not a comfort-able journey. High-speed craft tend to be bouncy, which might be all right in the short run but not for six hours. Negrini held away from the land until it was lost in the heat haze and then he came around in a wide sweep to the north.

He was right about the time. It was almost exactly six hours after leaving San Martin when we threaded our way through the pass in the coral reef and into the lagoon of El Cerco. We were tired because of the movement and hungry because there had been nothing to eat on the boat, and I was deeply thankful when we drifted to the quay on the central island and moored the boat in stillness.

As we went ashore Jill Salton appeared. 'Glad you could come,' she said. 'But I didn't expect you by boat. I didn't expect you at all, Gerry.'

Negrini laughed. 'I just came along for the ride. I hope your kitchen's working because we're all hungry.'

Jill frowned. 'The kitchen's all right but there's no staff. The cook went to the mainland – her son was in a motor accident.' She smiled. 'Never mind. I'll get something ready.'

I wished she wouldn't: I'd already had a sample of her cooking.

Leotta stepped forward and said, 'I'll help out.'

Jill, cool and pristine in a crisp white dress, looked at Leotta, who was still recovering from the trip and not as *soignée* as I had seen her. She'd taken off her suit jacket and the halter-neck chemise underneath was looking decidedly creased. She and Jill were both taut and, like two strange animals, had unconsciously taken up almost identical offensive-defensive stances.

There was a prickly moment of stand-off before Jill relaxed and permitted herself a small smile. 'I think you need the bathroom before the kitchen,' she said. 'Let's go inside and sort you out.'

They went into the house and Negrini nodded after them. 'We'll be lucky if they don't barbecue each other. What say we build us a couple of drinks?'

It sounded a damned good idea so I went with him into the house. He did things with rum, sugar and fresh lime juice. It proved to be a most soothing concoction and I was just beginning to appreciate it when John appeared. 'Could I speak to you for a moment, sir?' He seemed worried about something.

'What is it?' John cast a side glance at Negrini, so I added, 'That's all right. Say what you want.'

'It's the servants, sir. They've all left.'

'So?'

'There were three telephone calls. Mrs Salton's maid – her father was ill. The housekeeper said she had to collect a parcel. And the cook . . .'

'I know about the cook,' I said. 'What's worrying you, John?'

He looked troubled. 'I'm not sure, sir. But the telephone is dead. I haven't been able to put through a call to the outside.'

'How can it be dead when you've been receiving calls?'

He shook his head. 'I don't know. And now there's just been a call for me to tell me that Jake wants to see me at his home immediately.'

'From anyone you know?'

'A stranger, sir.' His seamed face was puzzled. 'And I know Jake is in San Martin today.'

'That's odd,' said Negrini.

I felt a prickling unease and I had the overpowering feeling that something had escaped me. Abruptly I stood up. 'Let's check the telephone.'

We went into the hall and I picked up the handset. Not a cheep came through and the line seemed dead. I turned to John. 'How does this work? Is it a direct line?'

'No, sir. The estate exchange is on the mainland.'

Negrini said, 'Have you told Mrs Salton about this?'

'No,' said John. 'Not yet.'

Suddenly the sound of a jet engine winding up came keening across the water from the mainland and something exploded in my head. I grabbed Negrini's arm.

'Gerry, what did you tell me about Salton's plane leaving Benning Airport the day he disappeared?'

'It took off for New York,' he said.

'What time?'

'Eight in the evening.'

'For Christ's sake!' I said. 'I was muzzy when you told me and it slipped by. The plane left here at eleven in the morning.'

'So?'

'So what the hell was the crew doing during those nine hours?'

Negrini frowned. 'Is it important?'

'And what was Mrs Haslam doing taking out the dinghy at four the next morning?'

'Who the hell is Mrs Haslam?'

'The pilot's wife.' I stared at the silent telephone. 'Calls coming in, none going out. People being drawn off this island. I have a feeling we're being isolated.'

'*We* are?' queried Negrini. 'But nobody knows we're here.'

'All right then, Jill Salton's being isolated.' I bit my lip. 'I don't like this.'

Negrini said softly, 'That little guy who lives in your head?'

'Yes.' The jet engine howled again. 'And what are they doing over there on the airstrip? Jill isn't going anywhere in the plane, and they can't be testing it all the time.' I shook my head irritably. 'I wonder if there are any weapons in the house.'

'Sure,' said Negrini. His hand dipped inside his jacket and emerged full of automatic pistol. 'It's a habit,' he said, a little apologetically. He put the gun away. 'But we're not isolated.'

'The bloody telephone's not working.'

'The hell with that,' said Negrini. 'There's a radio telephone in the boat. We can call anyone we want.'

'Then I want to call Hanna.'

We left the hall, leaving John staring after us, and went
back to the quay where the boat was moored. Another boat
had just pulled in behind and Mrs Haslam was stepping
ashore. She came towards us and the first thing I noticed
was a gun held negligently at her side.

Behind her Philips, the engineer, was climbing aboard
Negrini's boat.

She said casually, 'Hi, Mr Kemp.'

Philips went into the cabin and there came a crunching
sound. 'What the hell!' said Negrini, and stepped forward.

'Take it easy, buster,' warned Mrs Haslam, but Negrini
ignored her. He made as if to lunge past her, to get to his
boat, and she lifted the pistol and shot him twice.

The first bullet stopped him in his tracks. The second
flung him backwards and sideways into some low bushes.
Although he thrashed around a bit while he was down, he
was dead before he hit the ground and the convulsive
movements were merely automatic nervous reactions.
When he finally lay still, I saw two red blotches on his
white shirt, about two inches apart and directly over his
heart.

# TEN

## I

The gun was pointing at me and it was rock steady. My mouth was as dry as a bone and I stayed very still. More destructive noises came from the boat and then Philips came up into the cockpit. 'They won't be sending any messages from here.'

Bette Haslam never took her eyes off me. 'Round up the two women and that old servant,' she said. 'I want them all in the same place.'

From behind me, Jill Salton called, 'What's going on out there?' She didn't seem too alarmed.

Philips came up the quay and walked past me. He didn't look at me and I might not have been there. He said in a genial voice, 'Nothing to worry about, Mrs Salton. I'd like you to gather everybody together in the same place.'

'Why?' There was a pause. 'What's that in your hand?'

'It's only a gun, Mrs Salton. Nothing to worry about if you behave nicely.'

Bette Haslam said, 'Okay, Mr Kemp, turn around and follow my friend there.'

I turned around obediently and walked back towards the house. Jill was looking in glazed astonishment at Philips,

who said, 'Just step backwards into that room, Mrs Salton.'
Jill's eyes flickered towards me and beyond to Mrs Haslam.

I nodded, and said harshly, 'Do it, Jill. They've killed
Gerry.'

She caught her breath and stepped away and I walked
towards her slowly, very conscious of the gun at my back.
Bette Haslam said, 'Get the other two, and make it fast.
This room will do. I can see the other side of the lagoon
from here.'

Philips vanished from the periphery of my vision and I
walked slowly until the Haslam woman said, 'Stop! Sit there,
both of you.' I turned my head cautiously and saw her
indicating a settee positioned against the wall. I went and
sat down. My legs felt like rubber.

Jill sat next to me. 'What's going on?'

'Shut up!' said Mrs Haslam flatly. She raised her voice
for Philips to hear. 'Hurry it up, Les. You don't have much
time.' She was wearing a shirt, brief shorts and a linen
jacket with big patch pockets; a very different creature from
the last time I'd seen her. Beyond her, through the window,
I saw the body of Negrini lying supine among the flowering
bushes, then there was his boat and the waters of the lagoon
and, in the far distance, the mainland. I saw it all but I did
not perceive it. My mind was a blank.

Philips came back, herding Leotta and John at gunpoint.
John's face was expressionless but Leotta looked flaming
mad: her lips were drawn back and her teeth glinted in a
snarl of rage, and her eyes darted from side to side but held
on to Bette Haslam in a wide stare as soon as she saw her.

Bette indicated the settee. 'You sit there, bitch. And you,
grandad, sit on that chair and be real quiet.'

Leotta sat down on the other side of Jill and then leaned
forward to look at me. I shook my head slightly, not taking
my eyes off Bette Haslam.

Philips checked his watch. 'I'll be going,' he said. 'I won't be able to come and take you off myself. It'll either be Steve or Terry.'

'Okay,' she said. 'And if you hear me popping off, don't worry. I'll just be doing some target practice to impress the folks.' She looked at me and said ironically, 'Not that Mr Kemp needs impressing. He's had a demonstration.'

'All right,' said Philips. 'You'll be picked up at nightfall.' He left and, through the window, I saw him walk along the quay and then disappear as he dropped into his boat. There came the putter of a small outboard engine and the boat came into sight and went off towards the mainland.

Bette Haslam stood there, holding the gun in one hand and with the other in a jacket pocket. 'Well now,' she said. 'You're all comfortable, so I don't see why I shouldn't be. Grandad, there's a nice chair over behind you there. Bring it over here, but do it slow.'

John got up and did as he was instructed. She waved him back to his seat and inspected the chair he had brought. 'Nice enough chair, but a mite too low. If I sat in that I might not be able to get up in a hurry.'

She perched herself on the arm of the chair and I took my eyes off her for the first time to risk a glance sideways. Jill was sitting with her back pushed as far as she could go to the rear of the settee, as though she could somehow get away from the gun in front of her. Her face was chalk white and the slight band of freckles across her face stood out like the liver spots on the hands of an old man. She was scared out of her wits.

Leotta was tense and leaning forward, her arms resting on her knees and her hands curled into claws. She gave the impression of a sprinter waiting for the starting gun for the hundred-metre dash. But nobody can run faster than a bullet, so I said in a low voice, 'Take it easy, Leotta.'

'What was that?' Bette Haslam waved her gun. 'If you want to talk, speak up. I don't want any whispering. No secrets, you hear?' Her own voice was as clear as a bell, with no trace of an alcoholic drawl.

I said, 'What the hell is all this about?'

'You don't need to know. Now I want to show you folks something – particularly Miss Coiled Spring there, who looks like she could tear my eyes out. Who are you, anyway, sister?'

'My name is Tomsson,' said Leotta.

'And a friend of my friend, the limey.' Bette laughed. 'Now, see here, Tomsson. I don't have to impress Kemp because he's as sure as hell impressed already, but you look a mite uptight so I reckon you need a demonstration.' She waggled the pistol. 'Grandad, come here.'

John got up again and walked towards her. She said, 'See those glasses on the table? Straighten them up into a line.'

I looked at the table where Negrini had 'built me a drink'. There were five glasses. John walked over and lined them up.

'All right, grandad,' said Bette. 'Stand aside.'

The gun in her hand exploded in rapid fire and the glasses shattered into fragments. The explosions slammed into my ears and I counted them. *One . . . two . . . three . . . four . . .* Jill, beside me, was rigid and her eyes were tight closed.

Bette said conversationally, 'I worked in a circus when I was a kid. Wasn't much of a circus – we worked every whistle stop and hick town in the south-west – but I was the best thing in it. Annie Oakley the Second, they called me. I can shoot every pip out of a ten of spades in four seconds. With two guns, of course.'

The acrid stink of cordite drifted about the room. Six shots, I thought. Two into Negrini and four at the glasses.

'One glass left,' said Bette. 'Pick it up, grandad. Hold it out on the palm of your hand.' John hesitated as he bent, and she said, 'Go ahead. I won't hurt you.'

He picked up the glass and held it out at arm's length on the palm of his hand. The pistol slammed again and suddenly he wasn't holding a glass any more.

*Seven.*

John drew his arm in slowly and his fingers were trembling. He looked at his forefinger and then put it to his lips and sucked it. Bette laughed.

'Did poor old grandad cut himself?'

John walked over to her, still sucking his finger. 'I have a name,' he said, without a tremor in his voice. 'It's John.'

'My God!' she said. 'The old guy has more guts than the lot of you. Okay, Johnny boy, go back and sit down.'

I cleared my throat and said, 'You shoot well. What's the gun?'

'Smith and Wesson nine-millimetre parabellum,' she said concisely. 'Not many women can handle this much gun.' So she had a streak of vanity.

My lips tightened. That pistol held a magazine load of eight, so she had at least another up the spout. And she might have put one in the breech, which meant she would have two shots. The odds still weren't good enough, not when she could use the weapon like that. She had already proved she would shoot to kill.

Suddenly, with a metallic click, she slipped the magazine from the pistol and inserted another that she pulled deftly from her jacket pocket, driving it home with the heel of her hand. 'I saw you counting, Kemp,' she said cheerfully. 'I'm not that much of a goddamn fool, you know.'

*Nine*, I thought glumly.

Leotta no longer looked as though she was ready to leap into action. Her hands lay limply on her thighs and she had sunk deeper on to the settee instead of sitting on the edge. Jill still had her eyes closed and was muttering something to herself.

'All right, Mrs Haslam,' I said. 'What's your bloody game?

You've proved you can use a gun. Now tell me what you're using it for.'

'To scare you shitless,' she said sweetly, and added with a touch of malice, 'It seems to have worked on prissy Mrs Salton.'

This couldn't be about politics, I thought. It had nothing to do with any struggle for power in Campanilla. This was something else entirely.

I began to count again. Haslam, his wife, Philips: that was three. Plus Steve and Terry – whoever they were – made five. If there was a Steve and a Terry there was the possibility of a Tom, a Dick and a Harry. Certainly five, possibly more, precise number unknown. Tackle it some other way.

'It's a pity you broke the glasses,' I said. 'I could use a drink.'

'Well, why not?' said Bette. 'Johnny, are there any more glasses – in this room?'

'In that cupboard,' said John.

'Go get them. And bring that bottle of rum.'

John did as he was told and put the bottle and the glasses on a coffee table, which he placed in front of the settee. Unobtrusively, I nudged the coffee table further away with my foot; I didn't want to be hampered if I had to move quickly.

John also took some bottles of Coca-Cola from a concealed refrigerator and Bette said, 'I'll have a seltzer.' She grinned at me. 'You may be easy to fool, Kemp, but I'm not. If you're thinking of getting me drunk, forget it.'

I poured rum into a glass and added Coke. 'Leotta?'

'Not for me.'

'How about you, Jill?'

She opened her eyes. 'I want to leave here,' she said breathlessly, and started to get up.

I pushed her down smartly. 'Get a grip. You won't help by becoming hysterical.' I poured neat rum into a glass and wrapped her hand around it. 'Drink,' I said.

Like a child she obeyed and choked as the neat spirit hit her gullet. She blinked rapidly and some of the glaze seemed to leave her eyes. 'Just take it easy and sit quietly,' I said.

'Very touching,' said Bette. She looked over at John. 'Have a drink, Johnny boy. Your serving days are over and the booze is free.'

'I don't drink,' said John stolidly.

'Suit yourself.' She settled back, leaning against the chair as though preparing herself for a long wait.

Nightfall, I thought. Philips said that she would be picked up at nightfall. I sipped the weak rum and Coke and wondered what would happen at nightfall. An hour and a half to wait.

## II

In circumstances like that, ten minutes can seem like ten hours and the silence eventually got on Bette Haslam's nerves. She moved uncomfortably on the arm of the chair and said at last, 'What's the matter? Cat got your tongues?'

I looked at her over the rim of the glass. 'All right. Why are you here on El Cerco, and not over there on the mainland with your husband?'

She scowled. 'You're a pain in the ass, aren't you, Kemp? Have been ever since you arrived, and now here you are again. It was only supposed to be Mrs Salton out here, and we'd already cut her off from civilisation. Then we saw your flashy speedboat come in and we had to do something about it. So think of me as your babysitter.'

She fell into silence again so I tried another angle. 'Why did you kill David Salton?'

I felt Jill jerk and dug my elbow into her ribs to quieten her. Bette said, 'He was alive when I saw him last.'

'Which wasn't in the plane,' I said. 'It was in the dinghy.'

'What the hell are you talking about?'

'You were seen,' I said. 'You were seen taking out the dinghy at four o'clock on the morning of the tenth. The day after Salton disappeared.'

Her interest sharpened considerably. 'Who saw me?'

'Does it matter? Hanna knows about it. He's having you investigated.'

'What's to investigate?' Although she shrugged it off it seemed to trouble her. Her teeth worried her lower lip and she frowned. 'He was alive,' she said at last, but her tone was unconvincing.

'But not for long,' I said. 'He died in the dinghy.'

'How long has Hanna known?' I was silent and the muzzle of the gun swung around and centred on me. *'How long?'*

'The day before yesterday.'

'That's all right then,' she said. 'He's too late. He won't have time to check me out.'

'What is there to check?'

She chuckled. 'Oh, quite a bit, but the pieces are scattered. He'll never put them together in time.'

'In time for what?'

She didn't answer that but relapsed into silence. I waited a few more long, hot minutes before poking her again. 'But you did kill Salton.'

'I told you, he was still alive,' she said irritably. 'How many more times?'

There was something about the way she said it that caught my attention: *still alive*. I took a punt. 'When did he have his heart attack?'

'When he caught . . .' She stopped. 'There's such a thing as knowing too much, Kemp. A little learning can be a dangerous thing.'

'David Salton seemed to have learned something,' I said. 'Enough to bring on a heart attack. Were you scared he'd talk?'

'You're a fast man with a conclusion, Kemp,' she said. 'And the hell of it is that you're right.' Her teeth nibbled her lower lip again. 'He couldn't talk, though. The guy was paralysed. Christ, we thought he'd died on us. It might have been better if he had – we wouldn't have had you coming here and screwing everything up.'

'But you had to get rid of him,' I said. 'You couldn't have him taken to hospital and recovering enough to talk, to tell anyone what had brought on his heart attack.' I was jumping from conclusion to conclusion as a man jumps from boulder to boulder across a river; some of the boulders might move under foot and some are slippery with moss, and it's only by moving fast that the man can get across.

'Jesus,' she said, remembering. 'We thought Salton had loused everything up good.' She laughed. 'You wouldn't think it, but it was that dumb clunk of a husband of mine who came up with the idea.'

'So you put Salton in a boat and took him out to sea,' I said flatly. 'I suppose Haslam was waiting somewhere outside the lagoon to pick you up when you set the dinghy adrift.'

'Turns out he has his uses.'

I thought of Salton lying paralysed in the dinghy, drifting under the hot sun. Perhaps he was conscious for a time. I hoped not. Maybe he died of thirst. It would have been better for him if he'd had another heart attack to finish him off. That would be more merciful.

'That's murder,' I said.

'Who cares?' she said freely. 'It solved the problem. Took the heat off.'

I glanced at Jill Salton. Her eyes were wide open and she held Bette Haslam with an unwinking stare. Her body was rigid and her hands had begun to tremble. Leotta had become tense again too: she had slid forward on the settee and was sitting on the edge, ready to take off. I put down my glass with a sharp crack and she jerked her head towards me. There was a feral glare in her eyes, which dimmed a little as I shook my head in a negative gesture.

'That's right,' said Bette Haslam. 'Cool it!' The gun swung towards Leotta. 'I don't know what you're so uptight about, sister. What was David Salton to you?' Sudden comprehension came into her eyes and she burst into laughter. 'Oh no, don't tell me the saintly David Salton had a piece of ass on the side? Christ, wait till I tell the boys about this.'

Although she laughed heartily, I noticed that the gun in her hand stayed steady. Her chuckle died away and she said, 'And what does Mrs Salton think about that? Did the three of you go to bed together? Must have been real cosy.'

Jill said, 'Shut your foul mouth.' Her voice trembled.

'Don't talk to me like that, Salton,' said Bette, suddenly vicious. 'I don't like you and I never have. I don't like people who treat me like dirt. You never knew I existed, did you? You bought an airplane and you bought a man to fly it. They existed so that David Salton could fly around the world and do his wheeler-dealing. But the pilot's wife was just something that was around, something that didn't matter, something that could be ignored. I could have dropped dead and you wouldn't have known the difference. So don't put on any airs with me, Salton, or I might just put that little bit of extra pressure on this trigger. You hear me?'

Jill was mute and Bette said in a rage, 'I asked if you hear me, you frozen bitch?'

I nudged Jill and she said, 'I hear you.'

I needed to bring down the temperature: antagonising a person with a gun can be fatal. I said, 'Whatever it is you're doing must be bloody important.'

'It's the biggest,' Bette said curtly. 'The biggest, Kemp.'

'And it's something to do with Salton's plane?'

So far my poking was keeping her talking, but there was just a chance I'd push her too hard and she'd clam up. She twitched with irritation. 'That's another thing. You had to stick your nose in there too. You really wound me up when you talked about Mrs Salton selling it.'

I thought about that. What could they use an aircraft for? Smuggling? That was possible but somehow I didn't think so. There was no necessity to isolate the El Cerco estate for a smuggling job. In fact, the reverse would be better: smuggling is something you don't draw attention to. Of course, they could always steal the damn thing, but a Learjet is hardly the easiest of contraband to offload with a fence.

'The biggest?' I said, and put a sneer into my voice, an audible edge of doubt.

'Yes, Kemp,' said Bette. 'The biggest. You don't believe me, do you?'

I wondered just how vain Bette Haslam was. She was certainly vain about her prowess with a pistol and that might spill over into other things. I'd heard that criminals tend towards self-importance, which is why a lot of them get caught. They can't resist boasting and sometimes they boast to the wrong ears. Maybe this would be an opening wedge.

'Well, you've got to admit, it's quite hard to believe, isn't it?' I said. 'I mean, what the hell could be that big on a tuppenny island like this?'

'Oh, Christ!' she said. 'You don't know anything, do you? I thought you did once, but you're just dumb. Dumb and goddamn lucky.'

'Lucky?' I looked around at our situation and didn't feel at all lucky right at that moment. 'How am I lucky?'

'Because I took a shot at you and missed, and it's not often I do that. You're a real lucky guy – so far.'

Unconsciously my hand went up and rubbed the tape that was still on the back of my neck. 'That was you?'

'That was me,' she said.

'Why, for God's sake?'

'Oh, come on, it's not that hard to work out, surely? All right, Kemp, let me spell it out for you. I reckoned you'd caught on to us. I happened to be in the Salton Estate office when you were talking to Mrs Forsyth about the airplane and what she'd found in it. I didn't hear it all because she came around and closed the door but I thought you were on to us. So I got back in my car, waited until you came out, then followed you until I got a chance to take a crack at you.'

So all the painfully built-up theories about political corruption and police cover-ups came down to this. It turned out Hanna had been right when he sensed a difference between Ogilvie's murder and the attack on me. They'd had nothing to do with each other at all.

Or had they?

This woman and her confederates killed Salton because he discovered their criminal enterprise. But if Salton hadn't died, neither Ogilvie nor I would have come to Campanilla. And if we hadn't come to Campanilla, Ogilvie would still be alive. So in a way it could be said that Mrs Haslam and her crew killed Ogilvie. And they were responsible for a lot more than that, too. Because of them, fourteen Campanillans died in the Fleming Square mayhem. Because of them, the whole island was in turmoil. Because of them, Joe Hawke was inciting the people to riot. All because they had killed a man called David Salton.

It was a chilling illustration of the domino effect.

I said, 'Do you really have any idea what you've done?'

'We know what we're doing,' she said confidently. 'We can't lose.'

I shook my head. 'You'll lose this one, whatever it is. You've caused too many people too much trouble. Too many lives have been lost. I know of at least a dozen myself. And there'll be more.'

'What the hell are you talking about?' she demanded. 'We haven't killed a dozen people. You're crazy.'

'Don't you read the newspapers? Don't you know what's been going on?'

'Oh, that,' she said. 'The political stuff. That's nothing to do with us. It keeps the cops busy, though. That's a real bonus.'

'What are you going to do?' I said. 'Raid Mr Black's casino? Rob a bank in Cardew Street?'

She smiled. 'You really want to know, don't you? That curiosity is going to be the death of you. But I'll tell you this much, Kemp. You limeys hold the world record for the biggest ever theft. The Great Train Robbery was such a sweet job – nearly seven million dollars, and they got back peanuts.'

'And you think you can beat that?'

'I know we can beat it,' she said.

'Most of those robbers ended up in jail,' I said. 'Is it worth it?'

'That won't happen to us,' she said briskly. 'It's all planned. A lead-pipe cinch.'

Over seven million dollars. But from where? And how?

I said, 'I don't believe a bloody word of it. You've been drinking too many margaritas.'

'Two years in the planning, Kemp, and nothing is going to louse it up now. Today's the day.' She laughed delightedly. 'You might call it Instant Millionaire Day.'

'You're out of your mind. There's not that much money on the island.'

'Oh, but there is, Kemp. And it's not in any bank vault, either. It's out in the open where anyone can get at it. And you know what? Transport is already provided.'

It was coming. She was on the edge of spilling it. I pushed her again. 'For God's sake,' I said. 'No one leaves seven million dollars lying around like that. You're in cloud cuckoo land.'

'Who said anything about seven million dollars?' asked Bette. 'You've got to think big, Kemp. You've got to think of twelve million bucks.' She laughed when she saw the expression on my face. 'Twelve million. In cash. What do you think of that?'

'I think you're nuts.'

She grinned. 'Okay, you go on thinking that, Kemp. I'll just collect my dough.'

She was slipping away so I made a last desperate attempt to reel her in. This time I targeted vanity's close cousin, hubris. 'You couldn't handle a job that size, even if that kind of money really was ripe for the picking.'

She bristled. 'Let me tell you something, you arrogant bastard. I've been working this out for two years, ever since I came to this crappy island, ever since I saw the tourists in the casinos pushing handfuls of dollars at the cashiers. Of course, I wasn't allowed to gamble myself – the saintly Mr Salton had just made that illegal for residents – but I asked myself a question. You know what that question was?'

I had a good idea but I didn't say. I wasn't about to interrupt her flow. 'You tell me,' I said.

'I asked myself, where do all those greenbacks go? They're not legal currency here on Campanilla – residents don't use them – so what the hell happens to all those lovely bills?'

'Shipped back to the States?' I mused.

She shook her head violently. 'Oh no, not to the States. They're too valuable for that. I studied it, Kemp. I studied it real good. I learned about international economics and damn near twisted my mind into a pretzel. You know what a Euro-dollar is?'

'US currency that's held in European banks?'

'Damn right. Those places are stuffed full of American dollars – fifty-five billion of them, in fact. I hear Uncle Sam is real worried about that but I don't lose any sleep over it. Those Europeans are so anxious to get hold of American dollars that there's a thing called a Euro-dollar premium. You ever hear of that?'

I nodded. 'In certain circumstances a dollar outside the States is worth more than one inside.'

'You're on the ball,' she said. 'Sometimes up to thirty

per cent more. Now where the hell do you think all those Euro-dollars come from?'

I didn't answer because it was obviously a rhetorical question and she was going to tell me. 'They come in the billfolds of tourists,' she said. 'Maybe not much at a time – a dollar here, a ten-dollar bill there, maybe twenty dollars cashed for chips in a casino right here on Campanilla. But there are one hell of a lot of tourists, Kemp, and the dollar bills stack up.'

'How high do they stack on Campanilla?'

'Oh, brother,' she said. 'This place is real popular with Americans. Ten flights a day from Miami. In a year they leave behind maybe thirty million dollars in bills. Is that a high enough stack for you?'

I was surprised. I hadn't thought it would be that much, probably because I hadn't thought of it at all. Now that I did, I could see that it was probably true. Given enough of a tourist flow from the States, and given that every tourist had a few dollar bills in his wallet, then the dollars had to accumulate somewhere. I knew the Americans had a law about how much US currency could be taken out of the States – I had a feeling it was $100 a head – so Bette's estimate of $30,000,000 would require just 300,000 tourists a year. The reality was that Campanilla had more than twice as many American tourists as that. Bette's estimate could be low.

'So that's where your twelve million dollars are coming from,' I said.

She was getting excited. 'Imagine it. Twelve million bucks in currency. They can't record all those goddamn numbers – in fact, I know they don't. Singles, five-spots, ten-spots, twenty-spots – all spendable and untraceable.'

I said casually, 'How are you going to hoist it?'

Maybe I was too casual; maybe I should have joined in her excitement. She became wary. 'That's my business,' she snapped. 'You don't need to know.'

But she needed a plane, and that was a clue of sorts. What was Salton's plane to be used for? The getaway? Perhaps. But it was still here at El Cerco. I had heard the engines and it hadn't taken off, so it was still here. How were they going to transfer twelve million dollars to Salton's plane while it was still at El Cerco?

Jill said, 'So you killed my husband just for money.' Her voice was dead.

'Just for money,' said Bette. 'You can say that nice and easy, can't you? Money doesn't mean anything to you because you've never been without it. You ever wanted anything, you said, "David, dahlin', I want a fur coat, a diamond bracelet, a new sports car."' She did a bad parody of an English accent. 'And then David would say, "Sure, honey, just pick out what you want." You had everything a woman could want. So don't look at me with those freezer-green eyes and say "Just for money".'

'Why did Salton have a heart attack?' I asked.

Her mood was angry and she snapped at me. 'Oh, for God's sake, can't you just let it alone?'

'I think Jill has a right to know. And besides, what difference will telling us make now?'

'All right, Kemp, you win. You want to know the whole goddamn story, well here it is. Salton turned up while we were doing a dry run. We'd got everything figured – number of packages, weights and everything – and we practised like hell, because everything has to run real slick. We didn't know how long he'd been standing there, watching and listening. Time enough, I guess, because the crazy fool came right out and asked us what we thought we were doing. Les Philips told him straight and the old guy's heart went pop, right there and then. Next thing we knew, he was lying on the ground. That clear enough for you?'

Nobody said anything because there didn't seem much to say, and there was another long silence. I looked past Bette

Haslam at the body of Negrini – a bundle of rags casually tossed into the bushes outside the window.

Presently I said, 'I think you've made a mistake. A big mistake.'

The look of triumph left her face. 'What are you talking about?'

'The man you shot – out there. Do you know who he was?'

'No. And I don't care.'

'You'd better care. Ever heard of Mr Black?'

'Sure, everyone's heard of . . .' She stopped. 'You're saying that's . . . I don't believe you.'

'That's Gerry Negrini,' I said. 'And you've killed him. Shot him stone cold dead. You know who he was, of course, who was behind him? Chicago and New York, I understand. The Syndicate doesn't like it when their operations are interfered with by small-time killers. What are you going to do when the Families get after you?'

'What the hell would Negrini be doing at El Cerco?'

'Minding his own business, I suppose. He and David Salton got on very well together. Isn't that right, Mrs Salton?'

'They were great friends,' Jill said in a low voice.

'In fact, Negrini contributed to Salton's political fighting fund,' I said. 'They were that close. And now you've killed him. It's possible you might escape the police, though I doubt it. But even if you do, I wouldn't give tuppence for your chances. You see, the police need evidence that will stand up in court, but the Families don't work that way. They don't give a damn about that sort of evidence.'

'What are you trying to do, Kemp?' Bette's voice was suddenly shaky.

'Just trying to point out your mistake,' I said, keeping my voice even. 'As soon as those people in New York and Chicago figure out what's happened – and it won't take them long – you'll be judged and condemned. You know how they work. They'll put out a contract on you, a price on your head. So there'll be a whole lot of people on the lookout hoping to collect on you, and the way they collect is with a bullet. You'll be targeted by everyone from a Syndicate hitman to a doped-up kid with a mail-order pistol. And there are plenty of those around.'

'Shut up!' she yelled. 'You know what I think? You're conning me. That guy out there is no more Mr Black than grandad, here.' She pointed a shaky finger at John.

I shrugged and settled back. 'He'll carry identification, of course. Credit cards, things like that.'

I watched the indecision in her face. She struggled with the problem for a moment, then said sharply, 'Johnny, go out there and get the guy's wallet.'

John stood up and began to move, and then she saw the flaw in it. Once he was out there he was out of her control. 'Forget it,' she said. 'Sit down.'

He sat down again and Bette thought it over. Her thumb was in her mouth and I heard the faint sound as she clicked the nail against her teeth. All she had to do was to wait until Steve or Terry came across the lagoon, but I had given it to her too fast and she was confused – too confused, I hoped, to think straight.

She jerked the pistol at me. 'Kemp, if this is a con then you're dead for sure. Hear me?'

'I've told you the simple truth.'

'Okay.' Bette looked at Leotta. 'Tomkins, Tomsson, whatever the hell your name is, if you make one move out of place then Kemp gets it. Because I'll be right behind him. That goes for Salton, too. Tell them, Kemp: you'd better tell them good.'

'She means it,' I said. 'And I'd hate to get my head blown off. I still have a need for it. Don't do a bloody thing. That goes for you too, John.'

'Yes, sir,' he said.

'Leotta?'

She nodded. 'I won't move.'

'Jill?' She was silent. 'Jill, I want to hear it.'

'All right,' she said.

'She won't do anything,' Leotta said. 'I'll see to it.'

I looked at Bette and she nodded in satisfaction. 'Okay. Stand up and walk to the door. Don't break into a run.'

It was good to stand up again after sitting for so long. I creaked a little as I walked to the door and Bette moved behind me. 'Slow,' she said. 'Make it slow. No sudden movements. I get nervous about those.'

We walked outside into the fading light; nightfall was not far away. At a funereal pace, like the bandsmen of the Grenadier Guards doing a slow march, we proceeded until we stopped outside the big picture window under which the body of Negrini lay. I looked in through the window and saw a movement at the settee, which ceased even as I watched.

'Okay,' said Bette. 'Now make it slow and easy. Bend your knees.'

Negrini's body was at my feet. I bent my knees until I was squatting. 'Take out his wallet and hold it up over your head. Remember there's a gun not far from your skull.'

Carefully I felt inside Negrini's jacket until I found his inner breast pocket and the wallet that was in it. I took out the wallet and transferred it to my left hand and held it up. It was twitched from my fingers. 'Keep your hand there.'

My right hand, screened by my body, was busy. I found Negrini's automatic pistol, slid it from its holster and brought it close to my waist. From behind I heard Bette's breath come from her lips in a sudden hiss. 'All right, so you called that one.'

'Why would I lie?' I asked. I sucked in my belly and pushed the gun down the waistband of my trousers.

'Get up,' she ordered. 'As slowly as you went down.'

We went back into the house at the same pace and I sat

down again, being careful not to let my jacket swing open. Leotta, who had been sitting back, came forward again, and Jill lifted her left arm and began to rub it. It almost looked as though Leotta had been holding Jill's arm twisted behind her back, though I could have been wrong.

Bette was flipping through the wallet. 'It's Negrini, all right. Driving licence, club cards, credit cards.' She tossed the wallet on to the floor. 'So the guy's dead,' she said. 'It could happen to anybody.'

I could have built up her fright again but I didn't. It had served its purpose and I didn't want her frightened again: she was dangerous in that condition. I said, 'Two years' planning? Must have been a lot of work. I suppose your husband and Philips did most of it.'

Vanity again. Bette stared at me. 'Are you kidding? That pair of slobs are a waste of space. All they can do is fly airplanes. But that's all they need to do. That and provide the muscle.' She tapped herself on the chest. 'This one is all mine.'

I nodded judiciously. 'It's possible, I suppose.'

'Goddammit! What do you mean, possible?'

'Oh, don't misunderstand me,' I said. 'I'm no male chauvinist pig.' I shook my head. 'I just don't see how you're going to do it.'

'You wouldn't,' she said. 'You haven't done the homework I've done.'

'So?'

'So, the dough goes out four times a year, by plane to Europe. This flight'll be the heaviest because it's just after the season. Cute, hey?'

'Very thoughtful.' My breath was bated enough to strangle me. I might get it this time: that's why I'd taken the chance and needled her again.

'Flight LH713, Benning to Frankfurt non-stop.' She checked her watch. 'Takes off in less than an hour. But it'll never make it to Frankfurt.'

'You're going to hijack it?'

'Sure. Why not? Philips and my old man will be aboard. They'll take over the controls and then dive real fast down to sea level to get under the radar. In less than two hours, they'll be landing old LH713 right here at El Cerco.'

'They'll never get away with that,' I said disgustedly. 'There have been too many hijackings. How the hell are they going to get their guns aboard? They'll need guns, you know.'

'They won't have guns when they go aboard. They'll just walk past that tricksy magnetometer and it won't give a cheep because they'll be clean. I told you this was planned, Kemp. The guns are on board already – have been since two this afternoon. And hidden real well. You'd be surprised what a couple of flyers who have made friends at an airport can get done.'

My heart sank. It might just work. Stash the guns well before take-off, and those two wouldn't have any trouble getting aboard. And they were both pilots, which the average hijacker is not. I couldn't recall a case where a plane had been hijacked by someone who could fly it. This one could work.

'Of course, there aren't just two of them,' she said. 'Someone has to keep the passengers quiet.'

I felt my skin crawl. 'This is a routine passenger flight?' Even though we had been talking about Haslam and Philips going aboard, it hadn't sunk in that there would be other passengers.

'Sure. I think they figured no one would suspect all that dough being aboard a standard flight. It cost me plenty to get that information.'

'So the plane lands here. What happens to the passengers?'

'Nothing. What the hell do I care about the passengers? It's the dough I want.'

That was what was troubling me: what did she care about the passengers? Anyone trigger-happy enough to shoot

Negrini the way she had was not too sane, and ever since she had done little to convince me she was stable. The palms of my hands began to sweat.

'Hold on. You've got a plane full of people and cash parked on a remote airstrip in the middle of the Caribbean. What can you possibly do with that?'

'Ah, now that's the smart bit. The money is switched to the Lear – we can use the passengers to help with that – and then we have a really cute trick. When the boys take over LH713, they'll send out a Mayday call just before they take her down below the radar. That way, everyone thinks she's crashed. But after we've taken the money off her, Philips flies her off again in a big circle back to San Martin. Did you know he's a real good parachutist?'

'No,' I said tonelessly.

'Made over four hundred jumps. It's the way he gets his kicks. Anyway, he reckons he can crash that plane right in San Martin harbour. He'll get out, of course, and we'll have a boat waiting for him.' She waved her finger at me. 'So that, friend, is going to cause one hell of a lot of confusion. Here's a plane that's supposed to have crashed at sea, which suddenly comes back and crashes at San Martin. Everybody and his uncle are going to get their goddamn wires crossed and nobody is going to know what to think.'

She made a swooping motion with her hand. 'In the confusion, we take off from here in Salton's plane. That will crash too, but only when the money's safe. Good, huh?'

I licked dry lips. 'Very.' I didn't ask her where the passengers would be when LH713 crashed in San Martin harbour. I was afraid to hear the answer.

I heard a popping noise and Bette cocked her head on one side. The light was quite dim but I could see a boat coming across the lagoon. 'Not long now,' she said.

I glanced sideways at Leotta. I didn't know if she'd seen me take the gun from Negrini's body. She could have seen and I hoped she had. If I had to shoot, then everyone would have to move fast. I looked at Bette and contemplated taking a chance before the reinforcement arrived but one glance at the steady muzzle pointing unwaveringly at my sternum changed my mind. There was no way I would beat Annie Oakley the Second.

'Don't we need a babysitter any more?' I asked.

She shrugged. 'You're no danger to us now. There's nothing you could do to stop us. Not this late in the game.'

The boat came up to the quay and the engine stopped. Presently a young man walked past the window, glanced down at Negrini's body, and then moved on. He came into the room. 'Okay, Bette,' he said. 'Time to go.'

He was wearing a shirt, shorts and sandals, very tanned and with the callouses on his knees that only come from hundreds of hours on a surfboard. A typical beach bum.

'Am I glad you're here,' said Bette. 'Take care of this lot, will you? I'm tired of holding this gun.'

I had to make a fast decision and I'll never know if it was the right one or the wrong one. But she was lowering her gun and he was pulling one out, and I judged him to be the greater danger, in spite of Bette's demonstrable marksmanship. I could only hope that taking them by surprise would buy me vital moments.

In the instant that their guard was down I shot him, making sure by pumping three rounds into him.

Leotta, who had been poised like a hunting panther, was halfway across the room before the report of my first shot died away. Bette saw her coming and jerked up her pistol fast and it exploded with a stab of flame and a slam of sound. I got off the third shot at my boy and saw he was falling, and whirled around to see Leotta jerk like a marionette with a string suddenly cut. But she carried on and before Bette could pull the trigger again, her wrist was pushed aside and the next bullet went wide.

The athlete's body I had first admired in Leotta was now
revealing that it wasn't just for show. She literally picked
up Bette bodily, plucking her from the chair and holding
her by her head, despite her kicks. Leotta threw Bette
through the big picture window with a smash and a jangle
of glass. And then she collapsed.

I ran outside. I wanted to make certain of the hellcat,
but I needn't have troubled. She had gone through the
window frontally and a shard of glass had chopped through
the side of her neck so that her carotid spouted blood. There
was still comprehension in her eyes as I bent over her and
she tried to say something, but all that came out of her was
an empty, breathy sound. Then her eyes glazed as the blood
supply to her brain failed and she looked up at me sight-
lessly.

# ELEVEN

## I

I went back into the house and found Leotta slumped in the low armchair. She was clutching her left arm with her right hand, and blood was seeping between the fingers. There was a pained look on her face.

'She got you,' I said stupidly.

'Forget about me.' She nodded across the room towards the settee. 'It's her you need to worry about.'

I turned and looked at Jill, who was lying on her side, curled into a foetal position. The second bullet from Bette Haslam's gun must have found a lucky target. Or unlucky. John was bending over her and making sympathetic noises but not doing much else. He stepped aside as he saw me. 'She's hurt,' he said. 'Hurt bad.'

I dropped on my knees beside her. Her forehead was creased with lines of pain and her eyes were closed. Both her hands were clutched to her belly. I said, 'Jill, where were you hit? In the stomach?'

Her lips moved. 'Yes.'

I didn't know what to do. To move her might be the wrong thing, but to leave her might prove equally fatal. It seemed that the best thing to do was to find out the extent of the damage. Over my shoulder I said to John, 'Get me a knife, a sharp knife.'

He went away at a hobbling run and I stood up and looked at Leotta. Her training was likely to be much more extensive than mine, but I didn't know if I could put her in the position of chief medical officer in her current condition. She returned my anxious stare with a limp smile.

'You need attention too,' I said.

'It's nothing. A flesh wound. A sticking plaster and some bandages and I'll be good to go.'

Something about the trail of blood making its way down her bare arm made me doubt whether she was going to be good for anything for a while.

John came back. 'I found a kitchen knife, sir, and a first aid box.'

I burst out laughing and, even as I laughed, I detected the hysteria at the back of my mind. What struck me as funny was that John was still calling me 'sir' in that body-strewn environment.

He looked at me uncomprehendingly and with a shade of apprehension, no doubt afraid I'd stripped my cogs. With an effort of will, I chopped off the laughter with a gasp. 'Sorry, John. I'm a bit worked up.'

'That's not surprising, sir.'

'It might be an idea to make some hot, sweet tea.' I held out my hands for the knife and the first aid kit and discovered I was still holding the gun. I laid it on the table and looked around. The quick tropic nightfall was coming fast and it would soon be dark. 'Don't turn on any lights,' I said. 'Nothing that can be seen from the mainland.'

I knelt by Jill and asked, 'How is it?'

'Hurts like crazy,' she whispered, and opened her eyes. 'That woman – what happened to her?'

'She won't be troubling us again. Leotta did a good job.'

Jill closed her eyes. 'She killed her?'

'Survival of the fittest, that's all. The woman was a psycho-path. There's no knowing how many lives Leotta might have saved.' I put my hand to Jill's brow and found her clammy with a cold sweat. 'I'd like to have a look at the wound. Can you straighten out?'

'Oh, please, no. It's bad enough like this.'

'All right, then I'll do the best I can as you are.' I took the kitchen knife, which was a modern streamlined imple-ment designed on the lines of a surgical scalpel. That seemed appropriate. 'If you can just move your hands?'

Slowly she relaxed her grip of her stomach and I saw the entry point, to the left and just under the rib cage. There seemed to be very little bleeding but I didn't know if that was a good or a bad sign. Maybe she was bleeding internally.

I turned to Leotta, who was watching my movements closely from the armchair. 'Any advice?' I asked.

'You need to get a better look at it, find where the bullet went.'

I cut a hole carefully in the light cotton dress and saw the wound, a gaping red mouth against the pallor of Jill's skin. It was quite small and only a trickle of blood came from it. I opened the first aid box and made up a pad from the medicated gauze. Holding it against the wound, I closed her hands over it. 'Keep that there.'

Leotta said, 'Where's the exit wound?'

I took the knife again and cut away the dress from around Jill's waist. I was dreading what I might find, but the skin of her back was unbroken, although there was a heavy and spreading bruise around a central lump. Tentatively I pressed the lump and Jill yelped, so I left it alone.

Jill said, 'Bill!'

I moved to where she could see me. 'Yes?'

'I think I'm going. Everything is getting dark.'

'You're not passing out,' I said. 'It's nightfall. I don't want to turn on any lights.'

She sighed with relief.

Leotta said, 'What did you find?' When I didn't answer, she said, 'Tell me. I've treated gunshot wounds in New York. You won't scare me.'

No, but I might frighten the hell out of Jill, I thought. I told Leotta what I'd found. 'I think the lump is the bullet. There's no exit wound so it must be.'

'It should have gone right through at that range,' she said.

I looked up as John came in with a tea tray. The old man worked fast. I said, 'You're the doctor, Leotta. There's some hot tea here but I don't . . .'

'No,' she said. 'Nothing to eat or drink after an abdominal wound.'

'How about a flesh wound to the arm? We should see to that next.'

'Just give me one of those gauze pads and a bandage. I'll be fine.'

I did as she instructed and she deftly administered her own first aid one-handed. I provided some minor assistance with menial tasks such as cutting the bandage to size, but the handiwork was all hers.

When she was done she said, 'We need to get Jill to a doctor. She needs proper treatment.'

'That's the next thing on the agenda,' I said, and looked over at the settee. Although Jill seemed all right on the outside, I was pessimistic about internal damage. A bullet carries a lot of energy, which must be dissipated before it stops. That bullet had stopped inside Jill, which didn't augur well. And where was I supposed to find a doctor? The only medic I knew on Campanilla was McKittrick, and he was in San Martin playing politics.

I went over to where John was hovering over Leotta. Even in the gathering darkness I could see that she looked better, and every sip of the hot, sweet liquid helped to put the pieces back together again. John said, 'I thought you might find this useful, sir.' He took a flashlamp from the tea tray and handed it to me.

'Thanks,' I said. 'I can use it.'

I went outside to the quay and looked out to the mainland. There were a couple of lights and everything appeared ordinary. One thing was certain: no one on the mainland could see me, so it was safe to move around. I climbed aboard Negrini's boat. Although the radio was smashed, I thought I might be able to put Jill aboard and take her somewhere safe, running the engines slow to keep the motion easy.

It was hopeless. Even as I ducked into the cabin I caught the acrid and dangerous stink of petrol. It was so strong that I knew any attempt to start the engines would send the boat up like a bomb. Philips had not only wrecked the radio but he'd done something to the fuel system. I doubted if he'd holed the tanks, but the fuel lines were probably ruptured. There'd be enough petrol slopping around in the bilges to blow the boat into matchwood.

I went back on the quay and looked at the other boat, the one in which the reinforcement had arrived. It was then I realised I didn't even know who I had killed – was it Steve or Terry?

The boat was small, about nine feet long, and with a four-horse pusher at the stern. To take a thing like that to sea at night carrying a badly injured woman would be an act of madness. I didn't know the waters, I didn't even know if I could negotiate the pass through the coral and, if we got outside, those long Atlantic trade wind rollers were too much to face at night in a small open boat.

I looked across at the mainland again. There was only one thing for it: to cross the lagoon and see what I could do over there. If Bette Haslam's friends were anything like Bette Haslam, that would be like a solitary Christian entering an arena full of lions. She had cooked up this mad scheme of hijacking LH713, and anyone she had persuaded to go along with her would be as crazy as she was. The plan she had developed was pretty elaborate, so it was likely there'd be a whole pack of wild beasts.

I went back into the house to check my lion-taming equipment. There were three pistols: Bette's, with seven rounds, Negrini's with four, and Steve's – or Terry's – with a full clip of eight. I laid the guns in a line and went over to Leotta. 'How are you doing?'

'Better,' she said. 'I'm sorry that Jill got caught in the crossfire.'

'Not your fault,' I said. 'You did what you had to do. Jill was just unlucky – collateral damage, as they call it in the army. Are you up to moving?'

'Where to?' she asked cautiously.

I didn't answer that one immediately because I didn't know how she'd take it. 'Have some more tea,' I said. 'And put a slug of rum in it this time.'

The shrill ringing of the telephone made everyone jump. John immediately made as if to answer it, so I said, 'Don't touch that phone.' He looked quizzically at me. 'That's got to be a call coming in from Mrs Haslam's crowd. They're in control of the exchange. If you answer it, they'll want to speak to her and they'll know something's up.'

Leotta said, 'If we don't answer it, they'll still know something's up.'

She was right, damn it, but it was the lesser of two evils. I said, 'Better that they wonder what the hell's going on over here than that they know for sure that she's run into trouble. With a bit of luck they'll leave it for a while and try phoning again before they think of coming over here to check on her.'

I turned away and took John by the elbow, leading him out of earshot. 'Are there any weapons in the house?' I asked in a low voice.

'No, sir. There's nothing to shoot on the estate.' I smiled at the irony. 'All we have is fishing gear.'

'Scuba stuff?'

'Some of that, sir.'

'Show me.'

I followed him through the house until we entered a room at the other side. I flashed the light around and saw game fishing rods racked up neatly and air bottles in a row against the wall. 'Are you looking for anything special, sir?'

'Spear guns.'

'Ah!' He stepped forward and opened a cupboard. I shone the light over the racked guns. Well, not guns, really – more like catapults for shooting spears. I took one that looked powerful and selected three spears. Shooting pistols causes loud bangs and I had an idea it would be better to be as quiet as possible on the mainland. The ability to kill silently at a distance appealed to me.

I said, 'How old are you, John?'

'Seventy-four, sir.' He paused. 'Why, sir?'

'I'm going to the mainland and I'd like someone to come with me. I don't know the ground over there and I'll be likely to stumble into trouble alone. I need someone who can direct me to the telephone exchange.'

There was a silence before he said, 'I can do that, sir.'

As soon as he spoke I regretted opening my mouth. It was a completely unfair position to put him in and I had no right to do it. It would have been a hell of a thing to ask someone half his age.

I shook my head in the darkness. 'No, forget it. I shouldn't have asked. It's too much. You stay here and look after Mrs Salton. Miss Tomsson is elected for the job.'

'Miss Tomsson? Is she well enough, sir?'

'She'll have to be,' I said unsympathetically.

'But sir – you don't know where the telephone exchange is.'

'Draw me a diagram,' I said.

## II

When we got back, Leotta was on her knees by Jill. If it hadn't been for the bandage on her arm and a few splashes of blood on her clothes, I'd have said she was fully fit and ready for action. I squatted down beside them. 'How are things, Jill?'

'Not too good,' she whispered. 'I'm okay if I don't move.'

'I'm going out to roust up a doctor. You just lie quietly.'

Leotta said, 'Where are you going?'

'Ashore. It's time the telephone exchange was opened up for outgoing calls. Come on.'

I stood up and she scrambled to her feet. As I turned away she caught my arm. '*Me?*'

I laid a comforting hand on hers, where she was clutching me, then I turned away and crossed the room. 'John, can you fire a pistol?'

'I never have done, sir. You just point and pull the trigger?'

'Take the safety catch off first.' I gave him the pistol with the full clip as Leotta arrived at my side. I said, 'It's possible that someone will come looking for Bette. You'll have to hold the fort, John.'

'I'll do my best, sir.' His voice was as quiet and tranquil as though I'd asked him to serve the midday rum punch.

'Before you shoot, make sure it's not us coming back.'

'I'll turn on the lights outside,' he said. 'There's a switch by the door.'

'That's a good idea.' I paused, wanting to bolster Leotta for what might lie ahead. 'Miss Tomsson and I will be trying to stay out of trouble over there. You might find trouble looking for you, John. Think you can handle it?'

'I can try.'

'That's all anyone can do. Come on, Leotta.' Without giving her time to think, I walked to the door. When I got to the edge of the quay she was still with me, so I said, 'Get into the boat.'

She stepped down into the small boat and I handed her the spear gun and the spears before joining her. My pockets were heavy with two pistols but I didn't want to burden her with the responsibility of carrying one. She'd made a fine job of patching herself up, but firing a gun with only one useable arm is a tough proposition. I wasn't even sure about the spear gun but I figured it would be less of a liability than a pistol. I flashed the light discreetly at the engine and found the pull cord. As I was wrapping it around the pulley, she said in a low voice, 'I must be mad.'

'Everybody's mad tonight, Leotta,' I said. 'Your only chance of coming out on top is to be madder than anyone else. That's how wars are won.'

I hauled on the pull cord and the engine started the first time. I said, 'Listen carefully. When we go across there we go quietly. The sole aim of this operation is to get to a working telephone and to be able to use it for at least five minutes – longer if possible, but five minutes will do. We don't shoot at anyone and we try not to be shot at. Okay?'

I opened up the throttle but kept the speed down so as to make as little noise as possible. As we crossed the lagoon to the shore, I heard the insistent bell of the telephone in the house behind us and prayed nobody would have a brainstorm and pick it up. After what seemed like an age, it fell silent. We neared the quay and I leaned forward and said to Leotta, 'The exchange is in the estate office, in that group of buildings there.'

John's diagram had been a relief. The exchange could have been up near the airstrip and I didn't want to go anywhere near there. As we approached the quay, I cut the engine and drifted in to bump gently against the stonework. I grabbed the edge and held on, waiting and listening, but there was nothing to be heard. My fingers encountered a mooring ring, so I half-turned and whispered, 'Give me the painter.'

When the boat was tethered, I went up on to the quay on my belly. A light shone from a building on the other side of the boathouse, where the estate office was, but that was all there was to be seen. Leotta handed up the spear gun and the spears, and I helped her ashore. I put my lips to her ear. 'Stick close to me,' I said. 'We go all the way around and avoid open spaces.'

So we went quietly, trying to behave as much like ghosts as possible, and gradually we approached the window with light streaming from it. I flattened myself against a wall and edged closer to look inside the room. The first thing I saw was a switchboard, which made me more cheerful than I'd been in hours. The second thing was something that cut my cheerfulness off at the roots: a hand coming into view to pick up a cup of what could have been coffee.

I drew back my head, counted to ten, took a deep breath and looked again. The man was sitting at the switchboard sipping from the cup and reading a comic book. He must have given up trying to telephone the house. Maybe he thought Mrs Haslam was too busy showing off her sharp-shooting skills to answer the phone – there had been plenty of shots fired, after all. As he put the cup down again and flipped a page, I glanced around the room and noted thankfully that he had his back to the door.

Again I withdrew, flapped my hand at Leotta, and ducked down to pass under the window and towards the door of the office. Gently I turned the handle and applied a slight pressure. It would be unreasonable to expect that the man had locked himself in, and I was glad to find that, in spite of the comic book evidence to the contrary, he was indeed a reasonable man. The door was open.

We slipped into a darkened hallway. A light shone under a door. I strung the spear gun, put in a spear, took a pistol from my pocket and whispered, 'Open that door when I tell you. Quietly.'

We crept up to the door and I waited until Leotta had her hand on the door knob. 'Now!'

Light flooded into the hall as the door swung open. The man had his back to me, teetering on two legs of the chair as he relished the adventures of Bugs Bunny. I stepped inside the room and said, 'Take it easy.'

The two front legs of the chair thumped to the floor and the man looked over his shoulder. He froze as he saw me – and what I held in my hands. I went around in a semi-circle until I faced him and then approached to put the spear's point to his throat. 'If I pull this trigger that spear will go through your throat and six inches out the other side. All it needs is one squeak out of you.'

He leaned back, trying to avoid the point. I said, 'Leotta, take this spear gun. Keep it where it is and if this boy makes a wrong move, pull the trigger.'

She came up and took the spear gun from me. Without using her left arm, she lodged the stock of the weapon against her torso to brace it and rested the point against the man's throat. I kept him covered with the pistol as I moved behind him because with Leotta the way she was, I needed a reserve. Come to think of it, he didn't know she was a semi-invalid and because her face was like death itself, perhaps she was the more effective. At any rate, he didn't move a muscle.

I took the magazine from the pistol, ejected the round from the breech, then slammed the gun heavily against the side of the man's head. He gasped and jerked as I hit him again and finally he collapsed. Leotta looked sick and lowered the spear gun.

I put my hand under the unconscious man's armpits and hauled him away from the switchboard. There was a big cupboard with a lot of electrical repair gear in it, which came in very handy. There were some robust cables to tie him up with and the cupboard was big enough to hold him. Before I closed the door on him, I made sure he was securely gagged. It could be that he'd choke to death but I didn't care much about that.

All this took time and when I had finished, I saw that Leotta was staring at the switchboard. I said, 'Can you work this thing?'

She shook her head. 'I wouldn't know how.'

'Okay,' I said as I sat down. 'Stand by and keep watch.' I looked at the switchboard and bit my lip. There were a lot of wires ending in jacks and a lot of corresponding sockets. The problem was which jack went into which socket to get an outside line? I didn't want to make a mistake and have bells jangling indiscriminately on the estate.

There was a group of three jacks at the top of the board, which were isolated. I pulled at one of them and it came out trailing a wire. Now the problem was where to put it. I put on the earphones, adjusted the microphone under my chin, and hesitated with my hand poised. There were three sockets at the bottom of the board so I held my breath, plugged the jack into one of them, and was rewarded by the welcome sound of the dialling tone.

Rapidly I dialled Hanna's number and while I listened to the ringing tone, I scanned the board. Some of the sockets were labelled and some weren't, but one was marked 'Butler's Pantry' and I noted that for future reference.

Someone came on the line. 'Superintendent Hanna's office.'

'I want to speak to Hanna.'

'I'm sorry, sir. I think he has just left.'

'Get him,' I said savagely. 'For Christ's sake, get him!'

'Is it an urgent matter, sir?'

I held myself in. 'Yes,' I said. 'Very urgent.'

'I'll see if he's still in the building.' The telephone at the other end clattered.

I waited for five full, fat minutes, each one containing more seconds than a respectable minute should. I looked around to see where Leotta was and saw she was at the window. 'Not there,' I said. 'You can be seen against the light. Go out into the hall and wait at the main door. Have it open a crack so you can see.' I nodded towards the spear gun. 'Do you think you can handle that thing? You might need it.'

Leotta nodded, grabbed the spear gun and went out into the hallway. I could hear her struggling to manipulate it with her one good arm.

Time crawled on.

Something graunched in my ear and a familiar voice said, 'Superintendent Hanna speaking.'

'This is Kemp. I want you . . .'

'I've been trying to get hold of you,' he said.

'Shut up!' I snarled. 'Listen but don't interrupt. There's a flight to Frankfurt tonight – LH713. It's carrying a few million dollars . . .'

He came in quickly. 'I know that, but how do you?'

'Will you, for Christ's sake, shut up and listen? If you can, stop the flight. It's going to be hijacked.'

His voice changed suddenly to a sharp crispness. 'Wait!' He was gone a couple of minutes then came back. 'Go on.'

'It'll fly out, give a Mayday call, and then vanish from the radar. You're supposed to think it's crashed. It'll be landing at El Cerco some time after that. This is what it's all been about, Hanna. This is why Salton was killed.'

'Where are you?'

'At El Cerco. We're in a tricky position. There's a gang here, number unknown. I'm ringing from the estate exchange but I don't know how long I can stick here. Get your men here fast.'

'That could be difficult. El Cerco is isolated. You'd better get out of there.'

'The gates will be guarded,' I said. 'Besides, I'm needed

here. There's been a lot of killing, Hanna. Negrini's dead and so is Mrs Haslam and another man. Jill Salton has been shot in the gut and she's in a bad way. We need a doctor.'

There was a startled silence. 'Jesus!' said Hanna uncharacteristically. 'That sounds like a massacre.'

'It'll be worse than that if you don't move fast. That plane is full of passengers.'

I gave him a brief rundown of what had happened and our present position, and ended by saying, 'We're going back to the house. I don't have the muscle to face this lot. I think I can plug in a telephone line to the house, so wait for my ring. It'll come inside an hour or not at all. Don't you ring here because I might make a mistake on the switchboard, and I don't want telephones ringing on the estate.'

'All right,' he said. 'I'll wait for your call, but I'll get things moving at this end. I've already enquired about the plane. No answer yet.'

'Okay,' I said. 'Wish me luck. And pull your finger out.'

I broke the connection and plugged in the outside line to the socket marked 'Butler's Pantry', then I picked up the pistol and went into the hall, closing the door behind me. Leotta was by the office entrance. 'Anyone out there?' I asked softly.

'I haven't seen anyone.'

I took her place and checked outside. Nothing moved, so I said, 'We're going back to the house.' She sighed heavily, as though in relief.

We slipped outside and I carefully closed the door to the office, then we flitted back the way we had come. As we approached the boathouse, I heard voices and the crunch of gravel on the road leading up to the airstrip. Before I knew what was happening, Leotta grabbed my wrist and pulled me inside the boathouse with her. We stood behind the open door and listened. My heart was beating like a trip hammer. God knows what Leotta felt like.

The voices came nearer and I could distinguish the words. A deep voice was saying, '. . . should have been back by now. Goddamn that trigger-happy bitch! She'll wreck this operation.'

'We didn't reckon on Kemp coming back by sea,' said the other, lighter voice. 'Someone had to go out there and keep a lid on things.'

'Well, they should have been back by now. Steve left an hour ago.' They stopped outside the boathouse. 'Let's get some lights on here. Where's the switch?'

'In the boathouse.'

I felt Leotta grab my arm and I instinctively put a silencing finger to my lips. With the other hand I raised my pistol.

Someone came into the boathouse and shone a torch around. 'This might be it.' There was a metallic snap and light flooded into the boathouse from the quay. The man went outside and said, 'I don't like her. She spooks me.'

I twisted round and peered through the crack in the door where the hinges were. The two men were standing out on the quay, which was now brightly lit. One was perhaps in his forties and wore a black beard, the other was younger, another beach boy type. He was saying, 'Well, she cooked up this job. If it wasn't for her, we wouldn't be here.'

'She still spooks me. I don't like the way she plays with guns. And where the hell is she?' There was frustration in his voice.

The younger man walked to the edge of the quay. 'Hey! The boat's back.'

The older one joined him. 'Is that the boat Steve took?'

'Yeah, I came down with him. We must have missed them coming down from the airfield. They'll be up there by now.'

'I guess so,' said Blackbeard. 'Let's get back.' They turned and walked up the quay towards the boathouse. I thought they were going to come inside again to turn off the lights, but they didn't. Instead they walked past the boathouse and out of sight, and I wondered if they would call in on their colleague in the telephone exchange. I hoped he was still out of action and out of sight in his electrical cupboard.

I needn't have worried: the gravel crunched again on the road up to the airstrip. The last I heard was the younger man saying, 'When's the plane due?' I'd have liked to know the answer, but Blackbeard's voice came only as an indistinguishable murmur.

Leotta's grip on my arm loosened. 'Come on,' I said in a low voice. 'We'll be back at the house in fifteen minutes or less.'

I tried to remember if the quay could be seen from the road to the airstrip. Now that it was lit up, anyone moving out there would stand out as though illuminated by a searchlight. And I didn't dare turn the lights off because I didn't know if anyone was supposed to be around to do it. I ran the reel of memory again and came to the conclusion that the quay was hidden by the swell of the hillside and could not be seen from the road. It was time to move.

'We make this fast,' I said. 'Across the quay, into the boat and away. And we do it now.'

We came out of the boathouse at a dead run, expecting at any moment to hear a shout of alarm. We tumbled into the boat and I snatched loose the painter from the mooring ring, but held on because now that we were below the level of the quay we could not be seen anyway. I didn't want to push straight out because that would bring us into the circle of illumination from the lights on the quay. The drill this time was to move parallel with the quay wall and into the darkness beyond, and only then to head for the house.

I didn't want to fire up the engine so I used a paddle I found on the bottom boards. It took us a fair while but we got to the house at last and I moored. Then I called softly, 'Kemp here. Hold your fire, John.'

'All right, sir.'

When I went into the house I found I was wringing with sweat.

## III

John showed me where the butler's pantry was and I picked up the telephone, wondering if this was going to work. I grinned when I heard the dialling tone and hastily spun out Hanna's number. His telephone rang once and was picked up; he must have had his hand poised and ready to grab. 'Hanna. That you, Kemp?'

'Here I am,' I said, almost cheerfully.

'LH713 took off,' he said. 'It's a Boeing 707 and it's still on radar. They're raising the pilot by radio, ordering him to turn back.'

'That might not work,' I said. 'Haslam and Philips are on board. They'll know something's up if the plane changes course suddenly.'

'It's a chance we have to take. How many do you estimate are in that gang at El Cerco?'

'How the hell would I know? I've spotted five and two of those are now dead. All strangers, apart from Mrs Haslam. There are sure to be guards on the gates and maybe more at the airstrip. For twelve million dollars, Bette Haslam could recruit a bloody army.'

'I've got boats out, which will come into El Cerco from the sea. I've raised a couple of helicopters to ferry men across the island to reinforce the police from North End. They'll seal off the landward side of El Cerco. But all this takes time. Is everything quiet at the house?'

I told him of Blackbeard and friend, and said, 'I think the younger one could be called Terry.'

'When Mrs Haslam turns up missing, they might come

looking for her,' he predicted. 'You'd better be ready for them.'

'I'm as ready as I'll ever be right now.'

'Listen carefully,' Hanna said. 'We're going to try to slip a boat into the lagoon very quietly. It will have a doctor on board. For God's sake, don't get mixed up and shoot at it.'

'I won't.'

'I've got things to do, so . . .' He stopped. 'Wait a minute, Kemp.' I heard a murmured conversation before he came back on the line. 'LH713 sent out a distress call and shortly after went off the radar screen. It seems you were right, Kemp.'

'Of course I was bloody well right,' I yelled.

'I only had your word for it,' he said dryly. 'But then, I've been mobilising the police force and what we have of an army and a navy, all on your word. Sit tight, Mr Kemp. I'm getting busy.' He rang off.

I went to see how Jill was. John was at the window keeping watch across the lagoon and Leotta was beside Jill on the settee, dabbing her forehead with a damp flannel. 'How is she doing?'

'She's burning up.'

I touched Jill's cheek with the back of my hand. The sweat had gone and her skin was as dry as paper and very hot. 'There's a doctor on the way,' I said.

'Thirsty,' Jill whispered. 'So thirsty.'

'I'll get you some water.'

'No!' said Leotta. 'She mustn't drink.'

'Can't she even swill her mouth out?' I said, and got up. I went into the kitchen but didn't turn on the lights. Working by feel, I filled a glass with water.

Jill accepted the drink gratefully, rolling it around her mouth and spitting it out. If a few drops went down her throat I thought it wouldn't do her any harm, and she seemed the better for it.

After that, there was nothing to do but wait.

# IV

'There's someone moving across there.'

I put down my coffee cup and joined John at the window. On the brightly lit quay on the mainland, two figures were visible. John passed me binoculars and I put them to my eyes. Blackbeard and another man I hadn't seen before sprang closer. They appeared to be having an argument. Blackbeard pointed down at the water and then waved his arm up towards the airstrip.

It must have been confusing for them. Bette Haslam and Steve were still missing, and the boat that had been there before was gone. I wondered what interpretation they'd put on that.

Blackbeard pointed straight towards me and then waved at the big work boat moored at the quay. His intention was painfully obvious: they were coming across to have a look at the house.

'Stand by to repel boarders,' I said.

Blackbeard walked towards the work boat and stooped to a mooring ring. I lowered the binoculars and took the pistol from my pocket. 'John,' I said. 'Remember to push off the safety catch before you pull the trigger.'

'Yes, sir.'

The air was suddenly torn apart by an indescribable noise. It swelled from nothing to a high pitch of intensity within a couple of seconds. Something moved above our heads and I looked up to see the Boeing 707 coming in right overhead, nose up and flared out for landing. It was so damned low that instinctively I flinched and crouched lower, as if to escape having my head knocked off. The undercarriage was down, the navigation lights flashing, and there was a row of illuminated ports along the side. I could even see the heads of some of the passengers as they looked out.

The noise of those four big jets at that range was deafening and made the windows rattle in their frames. Then the plane moved away towards the mainland and I saw the cherry-red heat of the jet pipes before it settled down over the brow of the hill to land on the runway.

I looked quickly across at the quay, putting the binoculars to my eyes. Blackbeard was looking back towards the airstrip and the line he was holding dropped from his hand. He turned and waved, and the other man climbed out of the work boat, and they both ran towards the road leading to the airstrip and vanished behind the boathouse.

I blew air explosively from my lungs, and said shakily, 'How old were you when you went grey, John?'

There was a smile in his voice. 'About sixty-five, sir. But I lived a quiet life.'

'I hear it's strongly recommended.' I put the pistol back in my pocket. 'I'm going to the other side of the house. If you want me, just shout. If anything moves across there I want to know.'

I stood up and walked across the room, pausing to flash a light at Jill, who still lay cramped in the same position. There wasn't anything I could do for her. Leotta was sitting in the armchair, her hands clasped over her ears, staring up disbelievingly at where the passenger jet had almost landed on top of us. I took hold of her hand and led her outside.

There was a sort of garden on the other side of the house with a bench facing the sea. I sat down wearily and looked out towards the coral reef. Leotta sat beside me in silence and, after a moment, leaned her head against me. I curled my arm behind her shoulders, pulling her in against my chest. The sun was long since down but the air was still stickily warm. Even though the night was dark, I could see the occasional flash of white in the distance as a heavy sea pounded against the coral to send up a fountain of foam. The distant roar was somehow comforting. It was something that had been going on for a long time before that night and would go on when the events of the night, no matter how they turned out, would be forgotten history. The sound would have sent me to sleep had I been in the mood.

Three-quarters of an hour later, the sound changed fractionally. It was interspersed with a thrumming noise that had a hint of a burble in it, and there was a blacker patch against the darkness of the lagoon. Then there was a splashing and I disentangled myself from a somnolent Leotta, stood up and walked to the low wall. I shone the flashlamp into the lagoon.

It illuminated a small boat being rowed towards the house and there was a grimly smiling face that I recognised. Hanna said, 'Put out that light, Kemp.'

I flicked it off and waited until the boat came up to the wall. The first man ashore was carrying a large bag. 'I'm Dr Baines.'

'You're needed,' I said. 'This way, doctor.'

'Hold on,' said Hanna from the boat. 'I'm coming, too.' As I helped him ashore he said, 'All quiet?'

'The Boeing arrived three-quarters of an hour ago. How did you get here so fast?'

'We had a boat coming in. The doctor and I flew by helicopter and transferred at sea. Not something I ever want to do again.' He turned around and bent over the wall. 'Captain, get your men ashore as fast as you can.'

I gathered up Leotta then led the doctor and Hanna to the other side of the house. I showed the doctor where Jill was lying and bent down beside her. 'Jill,' I said. 'The cavalry's arrived.'

When I flashed the light on her she was in the same position as when I had last seen her. 'Jill,' I said. 'We've been rescued.' She still didn't move, and I said to the doctor in a low voice, 'I think she's in shock.'

Hanna moved forwards from the door and stumbled over

something. 'What the . . . ?' I flashed my light on the body
of Steve at his feet.

'That's the one I shot.'

The doctor said, 'I must have light. I can't do anything
without light.'

'I don't want to light this place up yet,' said Hanna slowly.
'Perhaps if we find a room on the other side and screen
the windows.'

We went back and I realised that the house was filling
with men – tough young men in army uniforms carrying
automatic weapons. Hanna had a word with the captain and
a couple of his men began to screen the windows of a room,
using blankets from a bed. Presently Jill was brought in and
laid on the stripped bed and Dr Baines was at her side.

I went back and found John still at the window, looking
towards the mainland. Leotta was standing beside him,
staring into the blackness. I tapped John on the shoulder.
'All right, John.' I indicated the soldier behind me armed
with a submachine-gun. 'Let's let the professionals take over.'

'Thank you, sir,' he said gravely, and hesitated. 'I was
pretty nasty to you once, sir. I'm sorry.'

'Water under the bridge,' I said. 'Let's go and have a
drink. Oh, but you don't, do you?'

'I drink,' he said. 'I'm just careful who I drink with.'


# V


'Here's my problem,' said Hanna. 'It doesn't matter a damn
if I have the whole Campanillan police force and a division
of infantry as long as those bastards up there hold a hundred
hostages. As it is, I don't have too many men here. More are
coming but it takes time, which is something we haven't got.'

Leotta said, 'Does anyone know how much the stuff
weighs – the money, I mean, the twelve million dollars?'

Hanna shrugged. 'Can't be much less than two tons. Maybe more.'

'It's an hour since they landed,' she said. 'How long do you think it would take them to move the stuff from the Boeing to the Lear?'

'Depends on how many of them there are.'

'At least seven,' I said. 'That's by my count. Probably four who hijacked the Boeing and three here. Four, if the chap in the exchange has got loose. But Bette Haslam was talking about using the passengers as slave labour as well.'

'Let's go into what she said in a little more detail,' said Hanna. 'What's all this about crashing the Boeing into San Martin harbour?'

'That was going to be down to Philips,' I said. 'According to Bette, he's an expert parachutist. My guess is he'd set the auto-pilot on a long glide and jump over the sea. She said there'd be a boat to pick him up.'

'We can do something about that,' said Hanna. He turned to the army captain. 'See if you can get the San Martin harbour police on that radio of yours.'

The captain vanished and Hanna said, 'Did Mrs Haslam say anything about the passengers on this last flight of the Boeing?'

'No,' I said flatly. 'And that's what scares me. You'd have to be damned ruthless to consider dumping a hundred innocent passengers into the sea simply to cause a diversion.'

'Her record came in on the teletype just before I left,' said Hanna. 'She *is* ruthless. Utterly ruthless. She has a rap sheet as long as your arm and it's not pleasant reading: she escalated from petty drug offences to become one of America's most wanted criminals. You name it, she did time for it – burglary, fraud, assault, armed robbery. You won't be surprised to learn that there are several murders with her fingerprints all over them, although she was never charged.'

'So all that guff she gave me about being an air hostess . . .'

'Just that – guff.'

Leotta said, 'I don't understand. How on earth did she fetch up all the way out here, with Haslam?'

'Good question. They weren't married that long before he signed up with Salton. It seems to me that she might have targeted him specially for this job.'

I said, 'She told us she'd been planning it for two years.'

'My guess is that was a conservative estimate.' Hanna's sleepy look had returned. 'She may not have known exactly what she was going to do with him, but Haslam was on her radar a long while back. And it takes a certain kind of woman to go as far as marrying a man to achieve her nefarious ends.'

'Sounds like he's better off without her,' I said mirthlessly.

'Frankly, I think the world is. But what I need to know now is this: will that gang up there still carry out her plan in her absence?'

My stomach lurched. 'You can't let either of those planes take off.'

'How am I going to stop them?' he demanded. 'I have three armoured riot trucks coming up, which I can slam on to the runway to stop anything taking off. But they'll be another hour. That makes two hours they'll have had, and I don't think they'll need that much time.'

The captain popped his head around the door. 'I've raised the harbour police.'

'Good.' Hanna went out and Leotta and I followed more slowly. Outside the door we bumped into Dr Baines, who was wiping his hands on a towel. Leotta said, 'How is Mrs Salton?'

The doctor put the towel on a table. 'Easier, but we must get her into hospital.'

'I thought it looked bad.'

Baines blew out his cheeks. 'A bullet in the abdomen scrambles things up. I could do an emergency operation here, but I'm hoping I won't have to.'

I said, 'Where is the nearest hospital?'

'North End, about ten miles from here.'

'And how long before you . . . have to make up your mind?'

'An hour at the most,' he said. 'I'm going to start sterilising my instruments now, just in case.'

'I'll give you a hand,' said Leotta.

Dr Baines looked at her, then me. I shrugged. 'I'd take her up on that if I were you. You should see what she can do with a bandage.'

I went into the operations room Hanna had rigged up. He was just putting down the handset on the field radio. I said, 'Hanna, I've been talking to the doctor. We must get Jill to a hospital fast. She'll die if we don't.'

He shook his head irritably. 'Those thugs up at the airstrip think everything is going fine. They've got no reason to think otherwise, except that the Haslam woman and the man, Steve, are missing.'

'And nobody's answering the phone over here.'

'True,' he said. 'But my guess is that they're too busy with the money to worry overmuch about that.'

'So?'

'I've got ninety-two passengers and eight crew members on that Boeing to consider. I can't move in unless I have the strength and the ability to prevent a take-off. If they call my bluff, what the hell happens to the hostages?'

I stared at him. 'So you're prepared to let Jill Salton die? Just like that?'

He swung around and snapped at the man on the field radio. 'Get me Benning Airport.' He turned his head and his face was set in stern lines. 'What would you do in my place, Kemp? You don't have to make the decisions. I do.'

There wasn't much I could say to that. Hanna said, 'Take it easy, Kemp. I'm doing the best I can.'

'I know you are,' I said heavily. 'I know you are.'

The radio operator held up the handset. 'Benning, Superintendent.'

Hanna grabbed it. 'Any news of the Americans? Good. When?' He checked his watch. 'They know what to do? That's right. As much as possible.'

He tossed the telephone at the operator and whirled around. 'Captain, we're moving. Now. Get your men in the boats but be quiet about it. We need to get ashore in silence.' He jabbed a finger towards Dr Baines, who had just come in with Leotta close behind. 'Get your patient ready for moving, doctor. I'll let you have two men.'

Baines went away quickly and Hanna cocked an eye at me. 'Are you coming?'

'Try and stop me.'

'Great!' said Leotta. 'It's a party.'

# TWELVE

## I

No amount of arguing, cajoling or ordering was going to make Leotta change her mind. She was coming too. The doctor didn't need her as a nurse any more and, as she pointed out rather bitterly, she had as much at stake in this bloody charade as anyone – and more than most. On top of which, I could certainly vouch for her usefulness in a tight spot, even with one hand out of action.

Three boats had slipped into the lagoon and were moored where they could not be seen from the mainland. Rapidly they filled up and I estimated there were about twenty men to a boat, a strange mixture of soldiers and police, sixty in all. Baines was left behind with his patient and John, who had been keen to stay by his employer's side. Hanna said, 'I'll send a boat back for you. We'll be making contact with the main gate in about fifteen minutes, then you can have a free run to the hospital. There'll be an ambulance standing by for you.'

He jumped on board the boat and said to the captain, 'Is the public address system aboard?'

'Yes, Superintendent.'

'Then let's go.'

As we moved off he said to me, 'Well, you're off the hook, Kemp. I doubt if Conyers will worry about you now.'

I frowned. 'I don't see it.'

'This situation is made for him,' said Hanna. 'It takes the heat off. There'll be something else to fill the headlines instead of politics, and it clears up the mystery of Salton's death very neatly from his point of view. You'll be built up as the man of the hour, the hero of El Cerco.'

'Some hero,' I said. 'What about you? Do you still have Barstow in the jug?'

'Yes.' There was grim humour in his voice as he said, 'Maybe I'll be next Commissioner. Maybe I'll be fired. Who knows?'

The boat slid up to the quay and a crew member jumped ashore with a mooring line. There was no point now worrying about whether we could be seen from the airstrip: there was nothing we could do about it anyway. And even if we lost the element of surprise, sheer numbers would be on our side. Mrs Haslam's gang could not outgun this military operation.

The men debarked and the soldiers deployed, moving at a dogtrot, their weapons held ready. Hanna stood on the quay and said disparagingly, 'I command an army and I daren't use it. Sergeant, the walkie-talkie.'

The radio operator trotted by, heading for the road that led to the airstrip. He looked hump-backed under the load of the field radio. A group of men followed him carrying big trumpet-shaped loudspeakers. Behind us at the estate office, I caught a glimpse of three soldiers manhandling someone out through the doorway. He appeared to have his hands tied behind his back and he was gagged.

Hanna was saying, '. . . That's it, Inspector. When you hear the bangs, move in and occupy the further perimeter of the airfield. On no account attempt to rush them. Your job is just to pen them in.'

He snapped a switch, handed the walkie-talkie back to his sergeant, and checked his watch. 'About three minutes,' he said. 'Let's go up to the road.'

We walked fast, the three of us in a line, and Leotta said, 'What's happening in three minutes?'

'An air operation,' he said enigmatically. 'I've managed to find an air force, too.'

We stopped halfway up the hill, where a light machine-gun had been set up. The loudspeakers were now on stands and a technician was plugging them into an amplifier. The radio operator was fiddling with knobs and speaking in a low voice. The army captain said, 'All ready, Superintendent.'

'I hope this works,' said Hanna. 'I wish to God I had those riot trucks.'

All was quiet. A brightness in the air on top of the hill indicated that there were lights on the airfield, but no sound came from there. There was a warm breeze but not strong enough even to make the grass rustle. From one side came the clink of metal on stone and a muttered imprecation. The captain said in a low voice, 'Quiet, there!'

The radio man suddenly said, 'I'm on net, captain.' He held up the microphone.

And then the sky seemed to split open. There was a deafening bang followed by a banshee howl as a meteor vanished over the top of the hill. I stared at the place it had been with incredulity, my ears still ringing. It had been a fighter aircraft moving at the best part of a thousand miles an hour at sea level.

There was another bang and a light streaked across the sky as though drawn by a pen, so that it was not a moving light at all but, due to the persistence of vision, a white line. The world was all noise.

The third bang left me shattered. The nearest loudspeaker slowly began to topple over but someone caught it before it hit the ground.

Seconds went by. Nothing more happened. The captain switched on his torch and I saw that Hanna was speaking, but he sounded very distant and the words didn't make sense. Somewhere far away a man was letting loose with a rebel yell.

I rubbed my ears, which seemed to be full of cotton wool, then held my nose and swallowed hard, and my hearing snapped back to normal. There was a babble of voices coming from a speaker on the field radio, and again there was the rebel yell. I glanced at Leotta and saw that she had been just as shaken by the fighters as I had.

Hanna grabbed the microphone from the radio operator. 'Hey, you up there! US Navy!'

An American voice cut through the babble. 'Shut up, you guys! Someone's talking to me.' The confusion died and his voice came over strong and clear. 'Who is that?'

'Superintendent Hanna, Campanillan Police.'

'Hi, Superintendent. Commander Auerbacher at your service. Was that what you wanted?'

'That was just fine,' said Hanna.

'Do you want us to make another pass?'

'If you would. But make it slowly this time. You've woken them up, now we want them to see you as well as hear you.'

'Can do. One minute.'

Hanna lowered the microphone and I said, 'That's some air force. Where did you get them?'

'They're Phantoms from the US Navy base at Guantanamo. The Americans agreed to co-operate when they learned that half the passengers on that Boeing were American citizens.'

This time the fighters came in line astern and close together, all lights on, and flying at about five hundred miles an hour. They stooped in a shallow dive and I'll swear they couldn't have been more than thirty feet from the ground when they went over the airstrip. The night was filled with their noise.

Hanna said, 'Is that public address amplifier switched on?'

'Yes, sir,' said the captain.

The radio coughed. 'What now, Superintendent?'

'I'd like you to circle around for a while,' said Hanna. 'Just so you can be heard.'

'You want us to orbit that airfield?'

'That's right.'

'We can do that,' said Auerbacher. 'But not for long. We had to travel real fast to get down here in time and that uses fuel. We can stay up for maybe twenty minutes, but then we'll have to put down at Benning.'

'*Damn!*' said Hanna softly. He raised his voice. 'Can you detach a plane to land, refuel, and then come back?'

'Sorry, no can do,' said Auerbacher. 'They don't have our sort of juice at Benning.' He paused. 'Maybe I can stretch it to a half-hour, but that's the limit.'

'Thanks, Commander,' said Hanna, and handed the microphone back to the radio operator.

I said, 'If I was up there I'd have been scared witless.'

'That was the intention,' said Hanna dryly. 'But by now they'll have started to think.' He took another microphone and tapped it. The taps were hugely magnified in the loud-speaker horns. He took a deep breath and raised the microphone to his lips. 'This is Superintendent Hanna,' the horns boomed. Echoes sounded from the hill. 'You up there – Haslam, Philips – I want to talk to you.'

We listened to the echoes dying away but there was nothing else. 'You can't escape,' he said. 'The airfield is surrounded. The fighters have orders to shoot down any plane taking off from your airfield.'

Still nothing happened. Leotta said quietly, 'Is that true? About the fighters?'

'God, no!' he said. 'There'd be hell's own row if American fighters started to knock civilian planes out of the sky.' He nodded up towards the hill. 'But will they realise that?'

Possibly not, I thought. That sudden assault from the sky would have been enough to jar loose anyone's thought processes. My own brains seemed pretty loose in my head right then.

'Haslam, Philips, I want to hear from you,' the speakers blared. 'I'll give you sixty seconds.'

Hanna drew back his cuff and looked at his watch. Everyone was still and I strained my ears, listening to the darkness above. The technician operating the public address system shuffled his feet and the noise he made on the gravel drew him a curt and whispered reprimand.

'Thirty seconds,' said Hanna flatly.

There would be confusion up there, I thought. Everything had been going well, apart from the inexplicable absence of Bette Haslam and Steve, and they would have been working flat out to move the loot from the Boeing to the Lear. The sudden shattering appearance of those fighters and then the big voice in the night would be enough to make the bottom drop out of everything. I wondered if Hanna knew what he was doing. Those men would now be under intolerable stress and, if they were anything like Bette Haslam, they'd have been half off their hinges to begin with. Men under stress can act strangely and I began to worry for the passengers again.

'Fifteen seconds,' said Hanna.

'Maybe they're not going to talk,' I said.

'Hush!' Hanna raised his hand.

A thin cry came from above. 'You, down there.'

'Yes?' the loudspeaker slammed out.

'You want to talk, you send a man up halfway.'

'Two men,' said Hanna.

There was a pause. 'Okay, two men. But no more.'

'We're coming now.' Hanna handed the microphone to the technician. 'This is it. Come on, Captain.'

'No,' I said. 'I know Haslam and Philips. I've spoken to

them before. I know *something* about them, at least. What does the captain know? Or you, come to that?'

Hanna gave me a slanting look. 'You drive yourself too hard, Mr Kemp.' He shrugged. 'All right. Captain, if we're not back in five minutes, you are in command here.'

He strode off up the road and after three quick strides I caught up with him. A moment later, Leotta was at my elbow. When he noticed her, Hanna stopped abruptly.

'What do you think you're doing?' he demanded.

'I'm going to see this through one way or another,' she said. 'I've already looked into the eyes of one of David's killers. Now I want to see the rest of the filthy bunch.'

I tried to mediate. 'You heard what they said – only two people, no more.'

'No,' she said, and her eyes flashed defiantly. 'Only two men, they said. They never mentioned women.'

Hanna grunted and marched off up the hill again. One look at Leotta convinced me there was no point debating any further. We had to jog after Hanna to catch up.

'What are you going to say?' I asked him.

'Not much,' he said. 'But it will be to the point. What I really want to do is listen. I want to find out what frame of mind these people are in.'

There were jet noises in the sky. I said, 'They might think they hold some trumps. The passengers.'

'They'll have to be talked out of that.' A light flashed fifty yards up the road. 'Here we are,' he said. 'Let me do the talking.'

As we crunched up the road, two men came down to meet us. Hanna raised his light and I saw Philips and the man with the black beard. Philips shone a light on us and it settled on Leotta. 'Hey! What the hell is a woman doing here?'

Hanna said, 'We have no time for chit-chat. I'm a police officer.'

'I know who you are,' said Philips. 'And your nosey chum there.'

'There's one thing you need to know right away,' said Hanna. 'If we're not back down there in five minutes, an army officer takes command. Soldiers like direct action and I can't guarantee what he'll do or what he won't do. Am I making myself clear?'

The man with the black beard said, 'You mean he'll make an assault on the airfield?'

'He might,' said Hanna. 'Who are you?'

'You can call me Frank.'

'And you?'

'He's Philips,' I said quietly.

'All right,' said Hanna. 'I want you all to come down the hill. If you have any guns, leave them at the airfield.'

'Are you crazy?' said Frank. 'You want us to give up, just like that? You're nuts! And I'll tell you something else. If that soldier boy down there tries for the airfield, an awful lot of people are going to get hurt. Maybe dead.'

It was out in the open: the naked threat.

Hanna looked at him steadily. 'Is that all you have to say?'

'What the hell else do you want?'

'What do you have to say, Philips?'

'Nothing.' But he shuffled his feet and looked worried. 'It was you who wanted to talk.'

Frank narrowed his eyes and said suddenly, 'I think you're pulling a bluff. I don't think you have the army down there. I don't believe you have the field surrounded. You're not as strong as you say you are.'

'Don't be a damned fool,' said Hanna without heat. He cocked his eye at the sky, which moaned with jet engines. 'If I can find jet fighters, I can certainly find an army unit. The soldiers are down there. You don't have a chance.'

'Yes, we do,' said Frank. 'We have a hundred chances.'

He glanced sideways at Philips. 'That's about it, isn't it? I reckon there's about a hundred.'

'Near enough,' said Philips.

'Are you two elected to speak for the rest?' asked Hanna.

'We don't go much for elections,' said Frank. 'You can say we are.'

Hanna said, 'I'd like to talk to all of you.'

'You're not going to,' said Frank. 'We can pass on your message.'

'All right, then the message is this,' said Hanna. 'This is a game you can't win. But you can lose hard or you can lose easy. It's up to you.' He looked at his watch. 'Time's wasting. We'd better get back.'

Frank was suddenly holding a gun. 'Maybe we'd better keep a few more hostages.'

'For Christ's sake!' said Philips. 'You heard what he said about the soldiers.'

'I don't believe him.'

Hanna shrugged. 'You'll find out pretty soon.'

'Okay,' said Frank. 'Then you go back.' He waved the gun towards Leotta and me. 'But they stay.'

'All right,' said Hanna, and turned to face the two of us squarely. There was a steely look in his eye. 'I'm sorry, but you wanted to come.' To Frank he said, 'I'll lay on a demonstration to prove that the army is here. Keep your eye on the lagoon.'

He said no more but turned on his heel and walked down the road. Frank said, 'What did he mean by that?' He prodded me with the gun. 'I'm talking to you.'

'I don't know what he meant. I suggest you do as he says. Watch the lagoon.'

'Not from here,' said Philips. 'Let's get back. We could be jumped here.'

Frank prodded me with the pistol again and I felt like taking it from him and cramming it down his throat. But to try anything would have been stupid so Leotta and I meekly followed Philips up the road, with Frank guarding us from behind. At the top, where we came in sight of the airstrip, two men were waiting: the young man I had previously seen with Frank, and Haslam. He looked as if he was about to burst a vein in his neck.

He said, 'What the hell is going on?'

'I thought I told you to keep on loading,' said Frank. There was a sharp edge to his voice.

'The hell with that,' said Haslam. 'What's happening down there?' He looked at his two new hostages but said nothing.

'Just a lot of big talk,' said Frank.

There was a chattering noise from below and a stream of bright sparks arced over the lagoon as someone let rip with a machine-gun and fired a magazine load of tracer bullets. Then there was a thump in triplicate and three fountains appeared in the lagoon, red fire at their hearts.

'A machine-gun and a mortar,' I said. 'That's more than talk. That's the army.'

'I want to know what was said,' Haslam insisted. He jabbed his finger at Leotta. 'And who the hell is she?'

'Frank wanted a souvenir,' said Philips tiredly. 'This whole thing's a bust. It's gone sour.'

'The hell it has,' said Frank. 'They won't dare use those weapons up here. We can still make it out. Let's get back to the hangar and finish the loading.'

'What for?' demanded Haslam. He pointed to the sky. 'If you think I'm going to take off with those bastards up there you're crazy. What was the deal? There must be a deal.'

'Sure!' said Frank. 'They want us to walk out with our hands up, and then maybe we'll get our wrists slapped. Call that a deal?'

Haslam swung on me. 'Kemp, is that true?'

'True enough,' I said. 'You can't make a deal with the police.'

'I don't know about that,' said Frank. 'That plane load of people over there are our bargaining chips.'

'That might wash with a political hijacking,' I said. 'But no one's going to make a deal with a bunch of thieves.'

Frank pushed the gun into my kidneys. 'Shut your mouth! Now, for Christ's sake, let's get back to the hangar and stop this yapping.'

We trudged over to the brightly lit hangar in silence. The Boeing was parked on the apron and a number of men were busy trundling wheelbarrows about underneath it. Every so often, a big canvas bag would drop from the plane's cargo bay to the tarmac, then someone would heave it into a barrow and transfer it to the hangar. I did a quick count. Not including the armed man who was overseeing the operation, there were four of them in sight. That's if they were actually part of the gang: for all I knew, this was Bette Haslam's slave labour. If they were, then the odds had shortened significantly.

Inside the hangar, a man I didn't recognise was stacking the canvas bags in a pile beside the Learjet. The young man went over and began to help him. Frank turned and stared wearily at Leotta and me.

'Put these two with the others,' he said.

'I don't know what you brought them for,' Philips said. 'They're nothing but trouble. When did you figure it all out, Kemp?'

'Not long ago,' I said. 'This afternoon.'

It seemed like an age.

## II

Leotta struggled to climb the metal ladder that was leaning against the Boeing's fuselage by its rear door, but with some effort and her natural agility, she finally made it. I supervised her ascent solicitously from the ground, then followed her up. Philips watched until I was at the top of the ladder and then went away towards the hangar, shouting something I couldn't make out to the armed man below.

The passengers were jittery and I couldn't blame them. I was pounced on as soon as I went through the door and assailed by a score of voices all asking different questions. I saw a hostess elbowing her way along the aisle from the front of the plane. 'Quiet!' I yelled, and was surprised to find myself instantly obeyed. The hostess came up to me and I said, 'Where's your chief officer?'

'Captain Dehn is in the first-class accommodations,' she said in a thick German accent. 'This way, sir.'

I followed her, pushing my way along the aisle to make a path for Leotta and ignoring the questions and demands that were shot at us. Anxious hands tugged at my sleeve as I passed and a constant babble of worried voices accompanied us the length of the plane. All I would say was, 'Later! Later!' I knew this mixture of tourists and business people would be in genuine fear of their lives and could only imagine the uproar in the cabin when the hijackers had struck. Even those passengers who hadn't witnessed the actual attack would surely have worked out that something was seriously wrong when the plane banked sharply back towards Campanilla from the open ocean and then flew in low over the northern coast of the island. Unable to see the landing strip in front of them, they must have thought the aircraft was going down. That kind of helpless terror can do strange things to a person.

I wondered how long the tension in the cabin would hold before outright panic erupted on board.

The German crew were huddled together in the first-class cabin. Dehn had his jacket off; his shirt sleeve was torn and his arm was in an improvised sling.

'My name is Kemp. This is Leotta Tomsson.'

'Gerhard Dehn. Can you tell us what is happening?'

'This airfield is surrounded by police,' I said. 'I don't know their plans but I think every precaution will be taken to ensure the safety of your passengers. Do you have many casualties?'

Dehn indicated his arm. 'Only myself.'

'Snap,' said Leotta, pointing at her own injury.

The captain nodded sympathetically. 'I foolishly put up some resistance when they stormed the cockpit. And you?'

'Something similar.'

Another officer said, 'We heard firing a few minutes ago. A machine-gun.'

'And there were explosions,' said the hostess.

'A demonstration of force,' I said. 'That's all. Nothing to get worried about. Have you any idea how many men there are out there?'

'I asked Hassel to count. How many, Helmut?'

'Maybe six,' said the officer who had asked about the machine-gun. 'I don't know how many are in the hangar.'

'I think seven altogether,' said the hostess.

'What about the men shifting the bags from the plane?' I said.

Dehn shook his head. 'They picked out some of the stronger-looking passengers.'

His mention of the passengers prompted a thought. 'Somebody had better say something to those people back there,' I said. 'Tell them help is all around. And then stay with them – I'm not sure it's good for morale to have the crew separated from them like this.'

Dehn nodded. 'Helmut, you do that. Take Lise with you.'

The officer and the hostess left. I bent down to look through the window. There was a group of men just inside the open hangar doorway but they were no longer moving bags. Instead, they appeared to be having an argument. Even at that distance and not hearing a word that was said, it was easy to tell that. Men do not speak only with their mouths but with their bodies too, and the stance and postures of those men told of violent disagreement.

Dehn said, 'How many police are here?'

'I don't know. About sixty came in from the sea. I don't know how many came in from the other side.'

Someone from the arguing group walked away from the hangar and towards the Boeing. It was Haslam.

'How do you estimate our chances?' asked Dehn.

'How would I know? I've never been in a situation like this.'

'Neither have I,' said Dehn wryly.

I watched Haslam grab the ladder that was propped against the fuselage and drag it to the plane's front door, nearest to where we were talking. When he came in, he said, 'They want to talk to you, Kemp.'

'What about?'

'Just questions. But first, I have one for you.' He looked troubled. 'Do you know what happened to Bette?'

He had a pistol in his hand and that made me nervous. 'She killed a friend of mine,' I said, watching him closely. 'Then someone killed her.'

'You?'

I shook my head and made damn sure I didn't make a flicker of an eye movement in Leotta's direction. 'Someone else.'

A cloud passed across his face but I couldn't decipher its significance. He waved the gun at me, guiding me towards the door. I looked back at Leotta and she gave a determined smile. As I went through the door, she was already standing in front of the crew, taking charge.

I climbed down the ladder and Haslam followed. I could have run away into the darkness while he was coming down but that wasn't the name of the game. Not with Leotta and a plane load of hostages standing defenceless on the runway. He seemed surprised to find me waiting for him on the ground. 'I should have come down first,' he said. 'Bette wouldn't have made a mistake like that.'

We walked towards the huge open doors of the hangar and Haslam said, 'I didn't know what I'd married, Kemp. I didn't know, I swear it.'

'I can believe that. But you still did what she said.'

'It came out so slowly, a bit at a time. And she made it sound so easy. And it was twelve million dollars, Kemp. *Twelve million*.' He spoke the number like a holy incantation.

'And how much is that twelve million worth now?'

I heard raised voices from the hangar and glanced sideways at Haslam. 'What do they want to know?'

'They want you to tell them about the police down there.'

'I'll tell them,' I said.

We walked inside and the group turned to face me.

Haslam, next to me, made a sudden movement. 'For God's sake, Bruno! Put out that goddamn cigarette.'

The young man looked at Haslam in surprise, a cigarette poised halfway to his lips. Haslam said, 'You're yards away from a plane full of avgas. What do you want to do? Blow us to hell? Aren't we in enough trouble?'

Bruno shrugged, drew on the cigarette and then dropped it, putting his foot on the stub. He blew a long plume of smoke in Haslam's direction.

Frank said, 'How many police are there, Kemp?'

I took my time answering. 'I counted sixty, police and soldiers. But those came in from the sea. I don't know how many came through the gates. Maybe twice as many, maybe more. I'd say you can count on at least two hundred.'

'Jesus!' said Bruno. He looked at Frank. 'And you want us to fight them?'

Frank ignored Bruno. 'Those jets,' he said. 'Where did they come from?'

'They're American,' I said.

'That's not what I asked. Where did they come from?'

I thought of Auerbacher's remarks on his shortage of fuel and said, 'How would I know? A carrier, maybe.' I certainly wasn't going to tell the truth about that. Haslam or Philips would be smart enough to figure out the likelihood of a fuel shortage. But a carrier could be anywhere.

Frank said, 'I still say they wouldn't shoot us down. They wouldn't want that publicity.'

Terry, the one with the unlined young face, said, 'They could follow us.'

'All I get from you bastards is obstruction,' snarled Frank. 'If you want to say something, say something useful.' He cocked his head on one side and listened.

The murmur of the cruising fighter jets had changed in quality and was becoming louder. Again the Phantoms slammed low across the airfield, deadening the brain by the sheer volume of noise. It was an awesome demonstration of raw power. I knew it was also the final demonstration. Auerbacher's time was up and Hanna's bluff could be called at any moment.

The jets faded into the distance and a bellow came up the hill from a loudspeaker. 'This is Superintendent Hanna. You've got fifteen minutes to make up your minds. Then I take action. If you want to quit, then come down the road one at a time with your hands up. No guns. That's all.'

'I'm for quitting,' said Philips. 'We're not going anywhere.'

Frank slapped him down quickly. 'You'll quit when I say you can.'

'You want to know what I think?' I said.

'No,' said Frank. 'I don't give a good goddamn what you think.'

'I do,' said Bruno.

'So do I,' said Haslam, and a couple of the others made noises of agreement.

I said, 'You have two choices. You can stay here – that's

one choice. But how long for? The police have got more staying power than you have. They'll be content to wait. They can starve you out.'

'Then the people in that 707 will starve too,' said Frank. 'That's our edge and we're sticking with it.'

'All right. Suppose you fly out in this Lear. Where are you going to go?'

'You don't need to know,' said Frank. 'That's all arranged.'

'It *was* all arranged. You don't think any plans are going to stand up now, do you? If this had been a political hijacking you might have got away with it. There'd be some country that would take you in. But every government on the face of this earth will be against you. And every cheap crook in the world will be looking for you because they'll know you have money and they'll want a slice of it.'

Philips said, 'He's got a point.'

'Shut up!' said Frank. 'Can't you see what this guy's trying to do? The plan still stands.'

'With jets following you?' I let that one hang in the silence, hoping to God nobody would challenge it. 'There is something else you can do, though. You can stay here and wait for the troops. If you do, you'll be very dead, the lot of you. And you're a long time dead.'

Frank took out a gun. 'One more word and you'll be dead, buster.'

Haslam said, 'Put down that gun, Frank.' His own pistol was levelled.

Frank's eyes blazed and the two of them held their stand-off for what seemed like an eternity. At last Frank lowered his gun. 'You're crazy,' he said. 'Any minute now he'll be leading you down that goddamn hill one at a time.'

'Which is just what I suggest,' I said. 'Okay, you'll go to jail, but you'll be alive and you'll be out again one day. It may not be soon, but at least you'll be around to see it. My advice is to cut your losses.'

'I'm not going to jail,' said Bruno. There was a tremulous note in his voice.

'Listen!' said Frank sharply, and everybody looked at him.

'What is it?' said Terry.

'Just listen!'

We waited in silence. Bruno said, 'I don't hear anything.'

'That's it, you dumb son-of-a-bitch,' said Frank. 'There's nothing to hear. Those jets have gone.' He swung on Philips. 'How much have we got off the Boeing?'

'About half of it.'

'That'll have to do. We're leaving. Now.' He pointed at Haslam. 'And you are flying us out.'

Haslam stood still for a moment, then went to the door of the hangar and stuck his head out. He came back quickly. 'I think you're right. They have gone.' He nodded to Bruno. 'Bring the tractor.'

Bruno ran outside and Frank said, 'All right, everybody, start heaving those sacks.' Haslam and Philips each grabbed the nearest sack of currency and dragged them to the Lear. Terry joined in. Frank pointed his gun at me. 'And you stay quiet.'

'I'm not going to stop you leaving,' I said. I didn't care if they got away with the lot, as long as the people in the Boeing were safe.

Bruno roared in driving one of those curiously specialised vehicles you see on airports, just an engine set between wheels with a seat on top and a steering wheel. It was probably weighted with concrete so it wouldn't lift off the ground when it manoeuvred the Lear about the airstrip. He backed it up to the Lear, and Philips started fiddling with the fixings on the plane's front undercarriage strut. Haslam yelled, 'Everybody in – we're leaving now. Never mind those bags.'

Haslam was first on board and Terry followed. Bruno revved his engine and looked over his shoulder at the flight deck of the Lear, waiting for Philips to hook it up to the tractor and for Haslam to give him the signal.

Frank was about to climb into the jet when there was a faint cry from outside the hangar. 'Hey!'

Frank turned his head. 'What the hell is it, Slim?' he shouted.

The armed man who had been out by the Boeing's cargo hold appeared at the door of the hangar. 'Something's happening on the runway.'

Frank said, 'Go see what's up, Bruno.'

Bruno looked behind him, saw that the drawbar was not yet connected to the Lear, and sped the tractor out of the hangar. Philips watched it go and threw up his hands in exasperation. 'Bloody hell,' he said to no one in particular.

Then he beckoned to Frank, who joined him while keeping a wary eye on me. 'We take her out of the hangar,' said Philips. 'And as soon as we start the engines we're on our way. There'll be no preliminary run-up. If the police hear aircraft noises in here, they'll start to move. You'd better get Slim on board.'

'He can join us just before you start the engines.' He grinned tightly. 'I told you they were pulling a bluff with those fighters.'

Bruno appeared at the hangar door on foot. He came inside at a dead run, his legs pumping at the ground like pistons. He skidded to a halt and said breathlessly, 'They've blocked the runway. Looks like three trucks.'

'How far up?' asked Philips.

'About halfway.'

'Son of a bitch!' exploded Frank. 'We ought to be able to clear those. There are enough of us.'

'Not without an anti-tank gun,' I said. 'Those are armoured riot trucks.' Silently I cursed Hanna. If he hadn't done that, then this mob would have been away within minutes and the hostages would have been safe. Philips would never have gone ahead with his crazy parachute stunt now – there was no point.

Frank stared at me with wild eyes. I thought for a moment he was going to shoot me and I tightened for a quick dive. Then he yelled, 'Everybody out!'

The men assembled again in front of the Lear. Frank had pulled himself together but he was still on the edge. 'They might think they've stitched us up, but nothing's changed. We still have the Boeing, and that means we still have control. Now comes the time to separate the men from the boys. I'm staying. Who's with me?'

They looked at each other with sideways glances. Bruno said, 'What's the use? We're boxed in.'

Frank looked at his watch then said, 'You're the one who said nobody's going to put you in jail. And after two hours you're ready to give up. Jesus, what a crowd.'

Haslam said, 'Hanna gave us fifteen minutes. The time's nearly up.'

'He won't do a thing while we hold those passengers,' argued Frank. 'Especially not at night, and especially if we tell him the score. I say we hold out and see what daybreak brings. Who's with me on that, at least?'

They were badly confused but they grabbed at that one. At least it was a concrete suggestion, and Frank was probably right about calling Hanna's bluff. I said, 'I'll go down and tell Hanna.'

'You stay right where you are, buster.' Frank's pistol pointed directly at me. 'Bruno, you and Terry go down and put it straight to that cop. Tell him we have a bomb on board the Boeing and if he tries anything, we blow the goddamn thing sky high, passengers and all. That'll stop him.'

If it was true, it would indeed stop Hanna in his tracks. It was the perfect stand-off.

Frank said, 'We might as well use the time sensibly.' He pointed at Haslam and Philips. 'Get back to loading the bags onto the plane.'

The gang broke up and he glared at me. 'You I want to talk to. Come here!'

I walked past Philips and Haslam as they set to work manhandling bags, and went over to where Frank stood between the Lear and the back wall of the hangar. 'What other tricks have the cops got?'

'I don't know,' I said.

'But you knew about those armoured trucks.'

'He didn't have them when I came up here.'

Frank said, 'But you knew they were coming.'

'Hanna may have mentioned them.' I didn't like where this was going.

'And you didn't tell me,' said Frank.

'It slipped my mind,' I said. Instinctively, I backed up against the wall. My brain was working furiously, trying to find a solution to the conundrum I was confronted with: how to extricate a hundred hostages from a potentially deadly impasse. With no weapon and no leverage. On the face of it, my best shot was to hope they'd lump me in with Leotta and the hostages and let the police negotiators get on with their job.

I looked at the gun Frank was waving around and I didn't like that option much. Especially if he hadn't been lying about a bomb on board the Boeing.

'Don't get smart with me,' said Frank. 'Now, I'm asking you again. What other tricks can we expect?'

'The usual, I suppose. Tear gas, perhaps. Those riot trucks have water cannon.'

Frank thought about it and shook his head. 'They won't risk it,' he decided.

I put my hand in my pocket, trying to look more nonchalant than I felt, and my fingers closed round the pack of fat American cigarettes I'd been smoking while I was on the island. 'Mind if I smoke?' I asked casually.

'Don't be stupid, Kemp. You heard what Haslam said.

Now, think very carefully. Is there anything else that might have slipped your mind?'

I sighed. 'He has the army out there. They have at least one machine-gun and one mortar – you know that already. They have automatic rifles and submachine-guns. And they'll probably have other things that go with an army.'

'None of which they dare use,' said Frank with satisfaction. 'But I'm telling you, if they come up with some gimmick you haven't told me about, then you're dead.'

Frank took half a step towards me, brandishing his pistol, and for one mad moment I considered trying to jump him. Then something moved in my peripheral vision and I unclenched the fist I'd made in my pocket.

I'd assumed the movement I'd noticed was Slim coming in from outside. I was wrong. When I glanced over Frank's shoulder towards the hangar door, my insides lurched into my throat. The tractor was trundling, driverless, across the hangar towards us, a piece of ice-blue fabric dangling from its open petrol cap. Even at that distance, I could see that the fabric was alight.

In the open hangar doorway, I saw Leotta, stony-faced, with David Salton's inscribed cigarette lighter in her hand.

Frank must have spotted the horror in my eyes because he span round to see what I was looking at. In the instant he took his attention off me I dived. I heard his gun go off and something plucked at my shoulder. I was behind the Lear when the tractor's petrol tank exploded but Frank got the full force of it.

I rolled underneath the plane and then scrambled desperately to my feet, not caring where Haslam and Philips might be. I caught a glimpse of a great bloom of flame with Frank in the heart of it, and I felt a wave of heat propelling me towards the hangar door. As I sprinted away, the fireball enveloped the nose of the Lear, and streamers of flame ran along the starboard wing.

Then I was out of the hangar and running for the darkness. Someone shot at me but the bullet went wide and I heard Leotta shouting my name, away to my right. I veered towards the sound and finally flung myself flat on the ground beside her.

There was a dull thud as the Lear went up and I looked back. A wall of flame thundered out of the hangar door. It boiled out for perhaps a hundred feet and then licked towards the sky, and the whole airfield was lit up as though a giant photographer had set off a massive flash gun.

Haslam had been right about the dangerous properties of avgas.

Hanna found us still sitting on the ground. I was rubbing a bullet burn on my shoulder. Leotta's trouser suit was destroyed where she'd torn off a leg to create the makeshift fuse for her bomb. The runway was alive with police and troops and already the passengers were being taken from the Boeing and shepherded away. Hanna looked down at me and said, 'What happened?'

'Someone lit the blue touchpaper.'

He sighed. 'I had a navy, an army and an air force. I forgot the fire brigade.'

Beside me on the grass, Leotta shivered and I realised the night had turned cool. Hanna slipped off his uniform jacket and draped it onto her shoulders.

'How did you pull it off?' he asked.

'That's something I'd like to know too,' I said.

Leotta shrugged. 'Nothing much to it. The hardest part was getting down the ladder with this arm. I had a nasty moment when the tractor came out of the hangar, but then the driver disappeared again and his friend was too busy watching the fun and games on the runway to notice me coming up behind him.'

Hanna said, 'What did you hit him with? You made quite a dent in the back of his skull.'

'A wrench that Captain Dehn gave me on the plane. Did I kill him?'

'Oh no. I'd say he'll be ready to face the music after a bit of a hospital stay.'

I said, 'And the tractor?'

Leotta smiled. 'One of those opportunities that are too good to turn down. It was just sitting there. I improvised a fuse and used the wrench to jam the gas pedal and – *voilà!* – a mobile bomb.'

Hanna blew out a breath. 'A bit risky, wasn't it, especially with Kemp inside the hangar?'

She gave me a nervous glance. 'That was the one part of the plan I had reservations about. But I didn't have an awful lot of choice. And anyway, you'd already survived two assassination attempts. I didn't think you'd have any trouble with a third.'

I laughed.

Hanna held out his arm and helped Leotta to her feet, then did the same for me. He pointed to the still-burning hangar. 'There's an awful lot of money going up in smoke there.'

Automatically I said, 'I wonder who insured it.'

Then I began to laugh again and Hanna stared at me. 'What's so funny?'

'The Learjet,' I said, chuckling. 'A very expensive aircraft. It's insured by Western and Continental.'

I was still laughing when the doctor gave me a sedative.


# III


It was a bright London day but inside Heathrow Airport Trans-Continental Terminal Building the weather makes no difference. Rain or shine, it's always the same: a flat white glare of fluorescence. I had some time to kill so I bought *The Times* at the news stand. The information I wanted would certainly be in the old reliable *Times* and when I turned to the foreign news page there it was, a couple of paragraphs towards the bottom of the page.

The Campanillan election results made fascinating reading. The Liberal Party – 19 seats; the Conservative Party – 18 seats; the People's Party – one seat. The new Prime Minister, Dr Jacob McKittrick, was expected to make a speech later that day outlining the policy of the new government.

I smiled. I had first met Jake when he was hoeing a field of corn. He had a harder row to hoe now. Joe Hawke would see to that with the break-even vote of the People's Party. Politics on Campanilla were going to be even more interesting in the next few years.

The first passengers had started to come though Customs so I wadded up the newspaper and dropped it into a waste bin. When I saw her appear, she looked drawn and thinner. She saw me as I walked up and said, 'Hello, Bill. It's good of you to meet me.'

'Hello, Leotta,' I said. 'Are these all your bags?'

'That's right.' She paused. 'Is there anywhere we can get a coffee? The stuff they serve on the plane hardly qualifies.'

As we walked to the coffee shop, she took an envelope from her handbag. 'Mr Stern asked me to give you this.'

'Thanks. How is he?'

'He's been looking after everything,' she said. 'He saw me on to the plane.' She shook her head in wonder. 'Mrs Salton has been very good to me.'

'Did you see her?'

'No. She's left Campanilla and gone to live in the States.'

We went into the coffee shop and sat down. I ordered coffee and opened the envelope. There were two pieces of paper, one a short note:

*Dear Bill,*

*I once offered you a job if ever you needed it. I hope you will accept this in lieu. It is an inadequate reward for what you did at El Cerco and for trying to protect the reputation of my husband. It is just for you. Miss Tomsson has been taken care of, as has Mrs Ogilvie.*

*Please understand that I now want to move on with my life, so I would very much appreciate it if you did not contact me again.*

*Sincerely,*

*Jill Salton*

The cheque was for £50,000.

I was going to accept it, all right: I needed the money. I was out of a job. The noble Lord Hosmer, of course, was untouchable. He'd returned to the boardroom of Western and Continental and carried on as if nothing had happened. There's an expectation of entitlement at that level of society, and with the insulation of his seat in the House of Lords and everything which that implied, he could look forward to a long and wealthy retirement. I don't generally wish people ill, but in his case I'm prepared to make an exception.

His niece was a different matter entirely. I did understand: Jill Salton was retiring behind the barricade of her millions. Besides the traumatic experience of a life-threatening gunshot wound to the abdomen, she had seen all the elements of her privileged existence fall apart around her. Her devoted husband revealed to be a philanderer. Their shared vision for the future of their island home left in tatters by a corrupt political elite. Her own flesh and blood conspiring to destroy everything she held dear. I could see why she wanted to retreat to America.

I put the letter away and said, 'What are you going to do?'

'I've signed up for medical school,' said Leotta. 'It's all been arranged.'

'Is your arm up to it?'

'It'll have to be. Term begins in three months.' She looked down into her coffee cup. 'But the doctor did say I should rest up until then.'

'So, three months. Made any plans?'

She shook her head.

I said, 'The daffodils will just be coming out at the cottage. You're too late for the snowdrops, I'm afraid.'

When she looked up her eyes were misty.

'Why not?' I said. 'The car's pointing in the right direction anyway, down the Great West Road.' I stood up to go and she followed. She was certainly going to make an exotic addition to a Devon village.

The four-ale bar would never be the same again.

# AFTERWORD

HAY HILL
TOTNES
DEVON

POST CODE TQ9 5LH
26 March 1972

Mr Robert Knittel
Collins - Publishers
14 St James's Place
London S.W.1.

Dear Bob,

A few words about the book, BECAUSE SALTON DIED.

I have just had a bad case of 'writer's block' - in 1971 I didn't write a single productive word and four novels which I started collapsed on me. These had been what you might call 'standard Bagleys' so I decided that, if I was going to break the jinx, I had to tackle a new subject, so I decided to tackle a new subject - the classic whodunnit. This, of course, I have not done because Bagley kept breaking in. The end result is something quite different.

My method of writing is singularly ill-adapted for the writing of a whodunnit. I begin with a situation and let it develope, and the plot follows where the development leads; whereas a whodunnit should be meticulously worked out in a synopsis before a key on the typewriter is touched. My method, however, leads to a certain spontaneity. I tossed in a variety of odd circumstances, characters and situations, and let them work themselves out. Since the book is in the first person the hero was just as baffled as the writer. In fact, it was only during chapter nine that I, myself, figured out whodunnit.

The original concept was to have 12 chapters, the first 9 chapters being red herring - but interesting red herring. The denouement to come at the end of chapter 9 with all explanations complete and the last 3 chapters devoted to a slam-bang action finish. This, in essence, is what has been achieved.

However, because of my method of writing and the way I had to grope through complex thickets there is a certain amount of repetition in the red herring section which ought now to be cut down to 8 chapters, and the slam-bang ending ought to be expanded to four chapters to allow for the building up of more tension in that part.

During the writing certain concepts arose, one of which is embedded in the title. Because Salton died certain events took place which were not in any way related to why he died. The political upheavals on Campanilla, the rioting and near revolution, and the murder of Ogilvie, are all related to this aspect.

*The first page of Bagley's letter accompanying his manuscript.*

# DOMINO ISLAND: A HISTORY

There is immense gratification for a researcher when they retrieve from an archive box an item that has not been seen, or thought lost, for many years. Such was the emotion for me when, on the afternoon of Wednesday 17 May 2017, I removed a package marked 'Because Salton Died' from a box which was part of the Desmond Bagley archive, held at the Howard Gotlieb Archival Research Center in Boston, USA.

I, and others, had been aware of the existence of a typescript listed in the collection as a finished but unpublished novel written by Bagley, but no one knew the state of the novel and fate had deigned me the opportunity of actually opening the package. I found inside an original draft large post quarto typescript consisting of 243 pages, typed on a manual typewriter, together with a photocopy of the typescript. The typescript, of approximately 89,000 words, bore on its title page:

NEW NOVEL
BECAUSE SALTON DIED
(if you can think of a better, please do)

I realised that I was the first person to have opened the package since it was sent to the archive by Joan Bagley in late 1997.

Instituted in 1963 as Special Collections and renamed in 2003 to honour its founder, the Howard Gotlieb Archival Research Center is located in the Mugar Memorial Library at Boston University. It is a repository, with public access, archiving material for individuals in the fields of literature, criticism, journalism, drama, music, film, civil rights, diplomacy and national affairs. In those early days of the archive Howard Gotlieb kept a weather eye on individuals whom he might approach with a view to asking them to donate their papers to the archive in the future. Howard Gotlieb personally wrote to Desmond Bagley on 23 December 1964 requesting just that, which showed great foresight as Bagley had by then only published his first novel *The Golden Keel*.

Following the publication of the author's second novel *High Citadel*, in 1965, a Bagley novel was published every year until *The Freedom Trap* (London: Collins, 1971). Bagley was in the habit of starting novels only to abandon them if he felt they were not progressing as he wished. He often returned to some of these projects, revising and redrafting them and occasionally borrowing sections for other novels as the years progressed. Although a prolific writer he suffered from brief bouts of writer's block and 1971, as it happened, turned out to be a particularly bad year for the author.

On 22 July 1969 Bagley visited Iceland to conduct research for his novel *Running Blind*. It was Bagley's first espionage novel and the first of his published novels to be researched on location, the consequence of which is a story displaying a detailed authenticity of background. It was to become one of his most popular novels, which was later produced by BBC Scotland as a three-part television series. However following publication in 1970 it was Hollywood that had taken an interest in this novel and the author was approached by film producer Aaron Rosenburg who asked Bagley to visit Los Angeles to write a screenplay for the novel.

Bagley's visit to Hollywood during late 1970, early 1971

turned out to be quite an unpleasant experience, he later recalled:

> *This was a terrible experience that I would not wish to experience again. Everything you have read about Hollywood is true. I felt it was a great honour when I was informed that a movie would be made from the book and that I should travel to Hollywood to write the script. But my experience of the capital of cinema was a poor experience. I was there three months, and during the whole time we could not agree on a script. I sat there with a good idea in mind whilst around me sat a group of senior men who could not agree.*

Bagley and his wife returned from the USA and very soon afterwards, during January and February of 1971, went on a month-long tour crossing the Sahara desert. In responding to a personal letter before the visit, the author mentioned that he was considering writing a novel about the desert for publication in 1972.

Returning from the Sahara, Bagley attempted a first draft of a book with the working title *Sahara Novel* but abandoned it quite quickly, and was still faced with the problem of providing Collins with a book for publication in 1971. He decided to revisit *The Freedom Trap*, originally started in 1966 and abandoned, completing it in May that year for publication in June. 1971 was a troublesome year for the author, for in that year he started four books, all of which collapsed somewhere between chapters four and six. He attributed this period of writer's block mainly to his Hollywood trip, and during that year Bagley became increasingly frustrated with the movie industry, writing on 16 July:

> *One thing that frets me about the film industry is that the movie moguls are hypnotised by instancy – a book must be written now, now, now.*

In fact back in June 1968 Bagley had been asked by Robert Clark of the Associated British Picture Corporation (ABPC) to write on the specific topic of heroin smuggling with the view to a film being produced. The author duly produced the requested novel, delivering *The Spoilers* to his publishers in November of that year. Following publication of the novel ABPC was taken over by EMI and the film project was shelved. This joined a growing list of titles that had seen a similar fate: *The Golden Keel, High Citadel, Landslide*, and more recently *Running Blind*. Later that year Warner Brothers Productions Ltd, who had by then acquired films rights to *The Freedom Trap*, made a request to change the name of this novel for the publication of the hardback edition in the United States. Bagley thought that *The Freedom Trap* was a good title, and didn't want to change it without a good suggestion.

Bagley decided that he must break the jinx of 1971 and wrote to his publishers on 2 January 1972 indicating that he would be starting a new novel the next day. The drafts he started, of which there were three, centred around a former ex-long range desert group army colonel, named Fermor in two of the drafts and Col. Andrew Mathieson in the third. Other characters in the drafts bore the names of Major Andy Tozier, and John Follet, characters that had previously appeared in his novel *The Spoilers* written for ABPC.

These drafts were abandoned and on 26 March 1972, Bagley delivered a completed manuscript to his publishers with the working title *Because Salton Died*. He told his editor in an accompanying letter that in an attempt to break his writer's block he changed writing style and started to write a *'classic whodunnit'*, which in the event he didn't achieve because his familiar style kept breaking in. He noted:

*My method of writing is singularly ill-adapted for the writing of a whodunnit. I begin with a situation and let it develop, and the plot follows where the development leads; whereas*

*a whodunnit should be meticulously worked out in a synopsis
before a key on the typewriter is touched. My method, however,
leads to a certain spontaneity. I tossed in a variety of odd
circumstances, characters and situations, and let them work
themselves out.*

What resulted was a classic Bagley *tour de force* involving
murder and corruption on a Caribbean island and a protag-
onist in the form of a former army intelligence officer, now
working in London as an insurance investigator.

Collins promptly scheduled the book and began selling
rights: in less than two weeks the first translation deal
(Swedish) was completed. However on 11 April 1972 a
Collins internal memo stated that Bagley had withdrawn
the novel and there would be no novel for 1972, indicating
the author would write to the Swedish publishers to explain
the reasons for the delay.

It's probable that with Warner Bros due to commence
filming of *The Freedom Trap*, which had now been renamed
*The Mackintosh Man*, by September, Bagley's US publisher
Doubleday had managed to persuade the author to withdraw
*Because Salton Died* in favour of writing a novel similar to
the impending film, in order that the two might be marketed
together. So the typescript was returned to Bagley and was
put aside in favour of other projects.

The following month Bagley and his wife embarked on a
tour of Scandinavia, first visiting Strängnäs in Sweden to stay
with a close personal friend, Iwan Hedman *aka* Iwan Morelius.
Morelius (1931–2012), a captain in the Swedish army,
founded the Swedish crime fiction publication *DAST Magazine*
in 1967 and had started to correspond with Bagley in 1969.
On this particular visit Bagley conducted a book signing at
the local bookshop and also visited a publishing house in
Stockholm before travelling on to Drammen in Norway where
he met Mona Røkke who, then police superintendent for

Drammen, later went into local politics and became a Member of the Norwegian Parliament. Drammen was to feature in Bagley's next novel and with the bout of writer's block well and truly behind him he commenced work on his new novel, *The Tightrope Men* (London: Collins, 1973), sending the final draft of the novel to his publishers on 29 September 1972. His close friend Iwan Morelius was to later feature as a character in his 1977 novel *The Enemy*.

Following her husband's death in 1983, Joan Bagley completed and oversaw the posthumous publication of two of his novels – *Night of Error* and *Juggernaut*. In the latter months of 1997 she took up the offer made to her husband by Howard Gotlieb 33 years earlier and donated his papers to Boston University, where they now rest in an archive of unparalleled diversity and richness. Joan had been an integral part of Desmond Bagley's work from the very first novel until the last, faithfully preserving his literary legacy until her own death on 30 June 1999.

*Because Salton Died* remained set aside and was thought lost until discovered in Bagley's personal papers in May 2017. The author had indicated on his typescript that if the publishers could think of a better title they should go ahead.

Well, they did . . . *Domino Island.*

**Philip Eastwood**

# DESMOND BAGLEY

Desmond Bagley was born in 1923 in Kendal, Westmorland, and brought up in Blackpool. He began his working life, aged 14, in the printing industry and then did a variety of jobs until going into an aircraft factory at the start of the Second World War.

When the war ended, he decided to travel to southern Africa, going overland through Europe and the Sahara. He worked en route, reaching South Africa in 1951.

Bagley became a freelance journalist in Johannesburg and wrote his first published novel, *The Golden Keel*, in 1962. In 1964 he returned to England and lived in Totnes, Devon, for twelve years. He and his wife Joan then moved to Guernsey in the Channel Islands. Here he found the ideal place for combining his writing and his other interests, which included computers, mathematics, military history, and entertaining friends from all over the world.

Desmond Bagley died in April 1983, having become one of the world's top-selling authors, with his 16 books – two of them published after his death – translated into more than 30 languages. In 2018 a blue plaque commemorating Desmond and Joan Bagley was unveiled at their former home in Guernsey, coinciding with the discovery of a complete unpublished novel written in 1972, *Domino Island*, published in 2019.

# MICHAEL DAVIES

Michael Davies began his career as a newspaper journalist, going on to edit numerous publications. Since moving into fiction, his writing has appeared on stage, screen, radio, the printed page and online. His debut play, *Rasputin's Mother,* won a national playwriting competition and subsequent work includes scripts, novels, radio plays and short stories. Most recently, he wrote the book and lyrics for *Tess – The Musical,* an adaptation of Thomas Hardy's classic novel *Tess of the d'Urbervilles*. He is a lifelong Desmond Bagley fan.

# PHILIP EASTWOOD

Philip Eastwood is a literary researcher who runs the website *thebagleybrief.com*, promoting the legacy of Desmond Bagley. Since 2007 Philip has worked in remote areas of Iceland on behalf of the Icelandic environment agency, and has also mentored and led volunteer conservation teams. His interest in Iceland was originally inspired by Desmond Bagley's novel *Running Blind*, and he has become a leading authority on the author's life and work.